THE BIG NICKELODEON

Other Books by **MARITTA WOLFF**

WHISTLE STOP

NIGHT SHIFT

ABOUT LYDDY THOMAS

BACK OF TOWN

MARITTA WOLFF

THE BIG NICKELODEON

RANDOM HOUSE

FIRST PRINTING

Library of Congress Catalog Card Number: 56-8810

Grateful acknowledgment is made to the following for permission to reprint:

From the poem, "Short Master," from *Transfigured Night*, by Byron Vazakas, copyright, 1942, 1943, 1944, 1945, 1946, by Byron Vazakas. Published by The Macmillan Company.

From the song, "Rock Around the Clock," by Max C. Freedman and Jimmy De Knight. Copyright, 1953, by Myers Music, Inc.

From the song, "That Old Black Magic," by Johnny Mercer and Harold Arlen. Copyright, 1942, by Famous Music Corporation.

Designed by George Salter

Manufactured in the United States of America
By The Haddon Craftsmen, Inc., Scranton, Pa.

THE BIG NICKELODEON

one

IT WAS several hours still before dawn, and the police patrol car drove steadily up the beach, buffeted by the wind. It was a night in the fall of the year, and the wind was blowing in hard from the dark churning sea, whipping across the sand and the smooth strip of highway to the great looming shapes of the foothills, black against the sky. The moon had already set. The air was very clear, with lights twinkling miles away along the curve of the beach, and the stars sharp and bright overhead.

Traffic was light at this hour, with only a few swift and thunderous trucks, intent upon their destinations. The stretch of beach along which the police car drove was deserted, parking areas were empty and the occasional restaurant building closed and forbidding.

It was warm inside the dim small shelter of the car, and an impersonal voice spoke unhurriedly from the radio.

The man behind the wheel yawned.

"Man, that wind's sure whooping in tonight," he said. "Feel the car pull?"

The man beside him grunted.

In the beam of the headlights, thin trickling rivulets of sand raced silently across the road in front of them.

The car rounded a towering thrust of headland, and all at once the man beside the driver stiffened.

"Jesus Christ, what's that?"

In the dark sky ahead, two great piercing shafts of light leapt up suddenly like giant sword blades, spread slowly apart, and began to fan back and forth across the sky with rhythmic measured majesty.

For an instant, both men were transfixed and still. Then the man at the wheel trod down upon the accelerator and the car sprang forward.

"What is it? Where they coming from?" the other man said, his voice soft and filled with awesome wonder. "There's nothing but empty beach along here for miles!"

"Aah, there's a new roadhouse up the line, they just built it," the man at the wheel said shortly. "They must have had those things out here for the opening tonight. What in hell's somebody want to start fooling around with them this time of night for? Damn kids! Boy, the things kids will think of!"

The man beside him stared at the vast, serenely swinging beams as though he could not take his eyes away.

"Those babies are nothing to fool around with either," he said at last. "Must take a lot of juice. Anybody'd have to think twice to fool around with those things."

"Not kids, they wouldn't," the other man said succinctly.

The car sped on and neither man spoke again after that. They both watched uneasily while the immense streaming shafts of light continued to swing slowly and imperturbably across the sky.

The wind huffed at the car, and along with the even voice from the radio, there was a constant undercurrent roar from the sea.

They drew nearer and the beams became blinding bright, particled white light swirling up endlessly into the darkness.

4)

"Yeah, there's the roadhouse up ahead," the man at the wheel said finally. "That's where they are all right. Man, somebody's in for a lot of trouble, leaving those things setting around out here."

"Wonder how you turn them off?" the other man said, leaning forward tensely in the seat. "Boy, there's a lot of juice in those babies. I'd sure hate to do much fooling around with them."

They were nearly abreast of them now, and the sand and sea and highway were bathed in an eerie, blindingly unsparing, white radiance. There was the sprawling redwood building, hung with red- and blue-lettered banners, its windows dark, the empty parking lot, and on the sand beyond, the two squat machines that supported the unbearably bright swiveling giant disks.

The police car screamed to a stop and both men piled out. The wind blew hard against them, and, down below, the sea roared deafeningly, with a grating metallic undertone as churning rocks ground their pumiced surfaces together in the powerful wash of the waves.

The two men trotted forward with a trained alertness and caution.

"Jesus, just like a movie opening," the one man called, and laughed.

The other man laughed too, a short and grim sound in his throat, and stopped abruptly just at the edge, where the sand fell away in a steep slope to a rocky strip of beach below.

"Look down there," he said. "This is no opening, it's a closing!"

They scrambled down the bank of sliding sand and ran together toward the still, sprawled figure that lay close to the angry foaming edge of the sea; a figure inert and final in the unearthly illumination of the humming arc lights, and beside it, the revolver, like a small, black, final punctuation mark against the pale sand.

two

THERE IS a multitude of beginnings to any single ending, but in the simplest shape of circumstance, the beginning that led sequentially to this particular ending was the day when Stush first arrived in California, a stranger, with still no single link or tie of relationship to anyone or anything.

That was a day in the spring of that same year, months before the dark fall night when the police car hastened up the beach toward the great arc lights fanning the sky ahead. That was a day in the spring when the wind also blew in from the sea, a stiff blow that whipped the dark blue water into frothing whitecaps and drove billowing puffs of clouds scudding across a dark blue sky.

Farther back down the same beach, on the afternoon of that earlier spring day, a few fishing craft and launches were bobbing at anchor behind a breakwater, and the long windswept pier was deserted except for the screaming sea gulls wheeling above it, gliding and riding on the wind. The merry-go-round was still, the rows of gaily bedizened horses frozen in mid-gallop, legs stretched, eyes wild, and manes streaming.

Beyond the pier, and an ancient weather-beaten bathhouse beside it, was a wide, flat bathing beach. At the far edge, the sand sloped a little to meet the splashing tumult of the lazy powerful breakers; on the opposite side it ended at a cement promenade lined with nondescript, weathered little buildings, souvenir stores with abalone shell jewelry displayed behind the dirty window glass, seafood restaurants, palm readers, salt-water taffy, bathing suit shops with great rubber flippers and goggles hung from the doorways, and the innumerable, tiny, open-air stalls with popcorn machines and faded, hand-lettered signs that advertised coffee and sun oil and beer.

The wind blew hard along the promenade, rattling the signs along the shop fronts and scurrying discarded candy wrappers and wadded paper cups.

On a wooden platform built over the sand, four or five men with the long shaggy hair and the broad barrel chests of wrestlers were clustered together, naked to the chill wind except for brief trunks. They lifted weights, or merely struck elaborate poses with infinite solemn concentration in order to ripple the bulging bicipital overdevelopment of their powerful arms.

Behind them, on a slatted wooden bench that bore a placard advertising a mortuary, an old woman wrapped in a bright yellow coat huddled over a bit of newspaper folded to a crossword puzzle and wet the point of a stubby lead pencil between her colorless lips.

A few yards away, three boys in sweat shirts lay on their stomachs with their heads together over a spread blanket, the quart bottles of beer uncapped before them. They were accompanied by a large motheaten-looking parrot who walked about aimlessly on the sand, its bright green plumage ruffled by the wind, cocking its head now and then at the noisy circling sea gulls and squawking disconsolately.

And in one of the little open-air stalls along the promenade, Maggie Harrison shivered on a stool before the counter and burrowed her chin into the collar of the heavy, dark-blue woolen sweater that she wore buttoned over khaki-colored shorts. She shuffled the big, sticky, dog-eared fortune-telling cards clumsily

(7

together in her cold hands, and began to lay them out once more across the counter top.

"George, why don't you hang a dish towel over that thing?" she said accusingly. "I'm sick of looking at it."

The counter man looked over his shoulder to the wall behind him where she pointed, a faded beer advertisement with the picture of a smiling girl in a bathing suit poised on a diving board.

"Yeah, I know what you mean," he said.

Maggie read the caption out loud, her voice mocking.

" 'It's Lucky when you live in California!' Aah, nuts!"

The big, dark, theatrically handsome boy lounging on the stool beside her stirred lazily.

"Quit your bitching, Harrison," he said. "You know you really love it."

"Yeah, sure, I really love it," Maggie said. "I love everything, I love everybody. I could go out in the garden and eat worms, too."

"George-O, give the lady a wormburger," the boy said. "Make one for me, too, while you're up."

The little man behind the counter gave a brief hoarse snort of laughter.

Maggie leaned back, stretching her long bare legs, and then hunched forward again upon her elbows over the cards, her chin propped between her hands, her slim face downcast and unsmiling as though all its color and animation had drained away somehow into her bright ruddy hair pulled back severely into a long, straight pony-tail, swinging on her shoulders.

"George, your cards are no damn good," she said complainingly.

"You're not laying them right," the counter man said. "They never come out when you just fool around with them. How about some nice hot coffee?"

8   )

He filled all three of the thick white crockery cups and carried them back to the narrow counter top.

"Thanks, George."

They lifted the coffee cups in common accord, Maggie and the counter man, and solemnly linked their two bent arms together.

"Here's to that crazy big muddy river," she said reverently.

"Flow on, oh Hudson!" the boy beside her murmured.

"Ah, shut up, Dickie," she said. "It's the Mississippi we're talking about, man!"

"All right, I'll drink to it anyway," he said. "If I could just once get as far as the Mississippi, I'll bet it wouldn't take me long to make it the rest of the way."

They drank together piously, and outside the sun shone brightly for a moment between the clouds and then as suddenly was gone, flickering out like a bad electrical connection, while the wind continued to huff at the inadequate shelter of the coffee stall, rattling a loose board somewhere at the back, and swinging a metal Coca-Cola sign screeching back and forth on its hinge.

"Did you ever hear the story about the two actors who met in the train yards in Kansas City?" Dickie said mournfully. "One of them was on a train for New York and the other was on a train for the Coast. As the trains passed there in the yards, the two actors waved at each other like crazy, and they each leaned out the window and yelled, 'Go back! Go back!'"

"Very funny," Maggie said over the cards. "At least you're working, chum. What about me? What am I going to do about a job?"

"I told you, come out to the studio with me," Dickie said. "An extra's life is a great life, you'd learn to love it."

"My face and figure are not my fortune, thank you," she said.

"You'd do very well," he said. "This thing I'm on, they need a million Roman slave girls. Couldn't you be a Roman slave girl?"

(9

The little counter man cleared his throat disapprovingly.

"What you'd really ought to do is go to school and learn how to typewrite and all that stuff."

"Takes dough, George-O," Maggie said sadly. "Where do I get the dough? If I was only bright enough to build airplanes out at Douglas! Ah, the hell with it! I wonder what's keeping Bud? I'm freezing to death. Do you think it's going to snow?"

"I wouldn't care," the counter man said wistfully. "I sure would like to see just one more snowstorm sometime before I die. They always tell you any time you want to see some snow all you got to do is drive up there in them mountains, but it don't seem like it would be the same to me."

"Let's all wish," Maggie said. "Can't you just see it floating down?"

The counter man leaned closer, his voice lowering.

"Yeah, and see them crazy bastards out there," he said fiercely, motioning toward the wooden platform on the sand. "If it should snow right here on this beach, I tell you them crazy bastards would still be out there in them little pants, up to their asses in snowbanks, still standing right there in the middle of the goddamn blizzard just wiggling their muscles up and down!"

She patted his arm sympathetically.

"Take it easy, George. I'll believe you. Crazy, man, crazy!"

"Real cool," Dickie said with delicate mockery in his deep resonant voice. "I dig it the most!"

"We didn't wish hard enough," Maggie said. "No snow. Never any snow."

They huddled silently and dejectedly over the coffee cups, and outside an old man in a checkered cap passed by, pushing a bicycle along the promenade, his hairy knobby legs bare beneath dirty white shorts. Over the sound of the wind there was a brisk flurry of hard-soled shoes along the cement, and a short dark-haired man in a sharply cut sports jacket paused at the front of the stall.

"Hi, George," he said cheerfully. "Sure turned cold in a hurry, didn't it? Ruined the business for this Saturday. How you doing, Red?"

"Hi, Tony."

Maggie glanced over her shoulder and waggled her fingers in a brief and totally unenthusiastic greeting.

The man cupped a lighter between his hands, the cigarette white against his broad, tanned, merry face with the shrewd dark eyes.

"What's the matter with you characters anyway? You all look like you been to a funeral. Where's that cute little boy of yours, Red?"

"Saturday is the day Jamie spends with his father," she said, her voice expressionless. "What's with you, Tony? I thought you'd be down in Tijuana having yourself a ball?"

"I changed my mind, I'm going down next Saturday," he said. "You going to change your mind and drive down with me honey?"

"Oh, sure!" Maggie said without interest as she dealt the cards. "I wonder why it is that nobody ever offers me a ride down to Mexico City for a change?"

The man laughed good-naturedly.

"You know, honey, some day I'm liable to fool you and take you up on that. See you around."

He walked on, and inside the stall Maggie said, "I'll give that no-account brother of mine just five more minutes. Then if he doesn't show, I'll hitch a ride home with you, Dickie. I want to get cleaned up before Tom brings Jamie home."

"Whenever you're ready. Sun's gone for today anyway."

Dickie slid down from the stool and stretched lazily, lifting his arms high, flexing his big, tanned, smoothly muscled body in the blue swimming trunks and pull-over shirt.

"Another Saturday under the bridge," he said. "How you say, c'est la vie, another day, another dollar."

(11

"Yeah, me too," Maggie said dolefully. "Home again, supper time, jiggety jog! Maybe tomorrow. Maybe tomorrow you'll get the lead in *The Brothers Karamazov* and I'll swim the Catalina channel, no hands. Or maybe George'll strike oil in the left-hand coffee urn!"

"You got it bad today, ducky," Dickie said affectionately.

"Ah, I'm really bugged!"

She flung down the last card.

"There," she said with grim relish. "That's really all I needed. 'The Hanged Man'!"

"It isn't what you think," the counter man said. "It doesn't have to be a bad card."

"You tell my fortune, George," she said coaxingly. "Tell me that something wonderful is going to happen to me. Please, George. You told us yourself, you're a seventh son of a seventh son . . ."

"Born with a caul," the little man finished. "And that's nothing but the truth, too. But I can't tell fortunes no more, I'm out of practice. How about some nice hot coffee?"

"Give me a hamburger, huh?"

They had not heard him come until he spoke behind them, and they all looked quickly at once.

He was broad-shouldered and narrow-hipped with a shock of dry, pale-yellow hair above a wide-boned sunburned face. By some strange inner quality that he possessed, he seemed bigger than he was, big beyond proportion, to fill the whole tiny coffee stall to bursting. He wore dirty Army fatigue trousers and a sleazy, gaudy, flowered sports shirt obviously not his own, since it strained at each button across his wide chest. He was very young, and he smelled of sweat and liquor, and he was very drunk.

He moved forward, catching at the edge of the counter, and sat down heavily upon a stool that seemed all at once too flimsy to bear his sprawling weight.

12)

While George scraped at the grill plate, he poked with one thick finger at a few coins scattered on his big brown hand.

"Hold it," he called suddenly. "No hamburger. Give me a coffee."

He dropped the dime bouncing onto the counter top and groped for his trousers pocket to return the remaining pennies. One of them slipped out between his fingers and rolled purposefully away across the uneven floor. He watched it go with great concentration, and then grinned, dismissing it with a half wave of his hand.

He settled forward against the counter and stared at the wall in front of him for a moment, his forehead wrinkling as he brought his eyes slowly to focus.

His lips moved silently as he read, and suddenly he laughed. "That sign up there's cute," he said.

He read it aloud, slurring the words a little. "It's Lucky when you live in California!" He laughed again, uproariously.

And then he said to no one in particular, "That's all right though. California's a great place. I just got here today but it's a real great place."

His head lowered and it seemed that he might already be asleep where he was, his sprawling body suddenly relaxed and somnolent as a giant cat's.

George put down the cup of coffee in front of him, his face disapproving, and scooped up the dime to carry it away to the ancient cash register.

He roused then, pulling his body erect on the teetering stool.

"Yeah, real great place," he said.

His hand reached out to the glass jar and he poured a careless stream of sugar into the cup and followed it with a great splashing dollop of milk from a red plastic pitcher so that the cup overflowed, the muddy-colored coffee spilling down the sides to form a puddle on the counter top.

"You know, it's a funny thing," he said.

He turned his head to Maggie and to Dickie beside her, his pale eyes blank in his sunburned face as though he really did not see them at all.

"You ever happen to notice something? People always wanting to buy you a drink. Crazy to buy you a drink. All the time saying, 'Come on, Stush, let me buy you a drink!' Hardly ever say, 'Come on, Stush, let me buy you some supper!' You ever notice that?"

He laughed again, his loud free laughter, and once more he sagged forward dangerously over the leaking coffee cup.

Without lifting his head, with his eyes still closed behind his pale stubby lashes, he slowly raised his hand and snapped his fingers loudly and impatiently.

"Come on, come on, baby, give me a butt."

Maggie hesitated, and then finally shook one loose and held out the pack to him silently.

He opened his eyes and reached for it, and momentarily he smiled a wide engaging smile. He felt of his shirt pocket clumsily with his other hand and said, disarmingly, "Give me a light too, huh? Looks like I got nothing."

It was George from behind the counter who held the lighter for him, cupping the small flickering flame against the sea wind.

He puffed until the cigarette was burning, and then his head sank down again between his wide shoulders. He was still, relaxed and completely at rest, breathing slowly and deeply, the smoke curling up from his fingers.

"You ever see such a goddamn-looking mess?" he said all at once, pointing at the coffee cup.

When he turned his head, he was smiling again.

"Let me tell you a little secret," he said serenely. "I never drink coffee anyway. Old Stush don't even like coffee. How you like that!"

He laughed his easy, deep-chested laughter and stepped down

from the stool so swiftly that it fell away from him, crashing to the floor. Still laughing, he walked to the entrance of the stall without looking back, moving lithely and with a kind of superb, self-contained assurance, for all that his feet were not quite steady.

The instant after he disappeared, Maggie said, "Oh, damn! You never know what to do about characters like that! You suppose he was really hungry, should we have offered to buy him a meal or . . ."

"Aw, he was nothing but a bum," George said dourly. "I get them guys in here all the time. Busted loose from some all-day drinking party down the beach and . . ."

But Dickie was already on the move toward the entrance-way.

"Hey, there goes the jitney," he said rapidly, his voice strange and a little breathless. "I better catch it this trip, my car's parked way down the beach. 'Bye, ducks!"

"Dickie!"

Maggie's voice was sharp and urgent, so that he stopped short in the doorway, his body poised there, tensed and straining and eager to be gone. He looked back, his extravagantly handsome, boyish face mute, his dark eyes pleading.

She was still, and then she said quietly, "Be careful, baby. That character looks like he could be a real tough cookie if he wanted to be."

He went instantly, catapulting out onto the promenade and away.

They were silent in the coffee stall. George rattled dishes loudly together at the sink and the wind blew and the one loose board somewhere at the back banged disconsolately. Maggie was slumped forward, her bright head between her hands, her eyes fixed unseeingly upon the warped, stained, unpainted boards of the counter top and the big deck of greasy, dog-eared cards.

"Ah, George, it's a great life, you know it? What's it all add up to, you tell me. Give me the answer to the jackpot question and win yourself a million dollars and a free trip to Tahiti!"

"You just got the blues today, that's all," he said. "You're going to feel a whole lot better when your divorce business is all over with. You'll even feel better when your little boy gets home tonight."

"I suppose so," she said. "It's funny, I really do miss Jamie, even this one day a week that Tom has him. Little stinker!"

She folded and unfolded a bit of paper napkin endlessly in her fingers, her face remote, her eyes turned far away.

And suddenly she said, "That's funny, I just thought of it. I just remembered what it was that that character kept reminding me of all the while he was sitting here."

"What character—oh, him."

"The wheatfields back home when I was a kid," she said, her voice gentle and brooding. "George, remember the wheatfields late in the summer just baking in the sun, so yellow and dry and dusty and hot? Remember how they smelled, and then a wind would come up and the whole field would move like some big alive thing. That was the time of year the threshing rig came, oh, George, those big old-fashioned threshing machines, they don't even have them any more! I remember men that looked like him working the threshing crews too, big guys all sunburnt and sweaty and covered with dust, laughing and drinking water out of the dipper down by the pump.

"Oh, George!" Her voice was a cry.

"You're just homesick," he said, his voice soothing and crooning. "I get the same spells, everybody gets homesick, honey. You get over it."

She reached out slowly to the metal container for another paper napkin and wiped at her nose with it. She sat quietly for a little longer, shivering on the stool, her face still brooding and remote. And then without warning, she slipped down from the stool and struck the flat of her hand hard upon the counter top.

"George, by god, I'm sorry," she said. "I didn't mean to weep all over you. I'm a real square. I'm sorry, George."

"That's a girl, now you're feeling better."

His face was pleased as he walked up the counter to her, drying his hands on a towel as he came.

"Shake?"

They shook hands vigorously across the shelf, smiling both of them, Maggie's face suddenly warm and vibrant.

She pulled a little red purse out of her sweater pocket and counted coins out onto the counter top rapidly.

"Here's what I owe you, George-O," she said. "I'll pay for Dickie too. He forgot to, he went chasing out of here so fast after that big sex pot on wheels."

George separated the coins deftly, pushing part of them back toward her.

"Naw, Dickie can pay me himself next time he comes down."

"Well, now it looks like I've missed my ride home but good," Maggie said cheerfully. "Where is that kid brother of mine anyway? As if I didn't know! He's the one that would still be up there on the courts swinging a tennis racket if the snow was up to here. When he comes in, tell him I couldn't wait any longer, I had to take the bus. I don't like to be out this late on Saturday, Tom might just happen to bring Jamie home a little early or something, and I'd want to be there. See you, George-O."

three

MAGGIE need not have hurried on Jamie's account.

Inland from the beach, the skies were clear, and in the valley beyond the great brown coastal foothills, it was even hot. A bright merciless sun beat down upon the vast, flat valley bottom covered over with its thousands of newly constructed houses, street after street, mile after mile of them, all interspersed with super market shopping centers and steak house restaurants, schools and animal hospitals and antique shops and dozens of small furniture stores with all their windows crowded with the identical cheap maple furniture and brass plant containers and gingham-checked lamp shades.

Tom Harrison's house was in the middle of a medium-priced housing tract, with the one large picture window in the living room staring out sightlessly at all the other exactly similar houses that lined the straight paved street where no single tree had yet grown to a height above the expanse of one-story roof tops bristling with television antennae.

Behind the house, there was a small square of back yard enclosed by a high redwood board fence. The fence was lined with new plantings of flowers and shrubs, spaded and weeded, well-watered and perfectly pruned, so that not a leaf or twig was out of place. The small grassy area in the middle was lush and green, the house itself glistened with fresh yellow paint.

Immediately behind the house there was a little patch of cement patio with a combination barbecue and incinerator built out of brick at one end of it.

A young woman clad in white sun-shorts and halter lay face down upon the green canvas pad of the lounge on the patio, her head covered with a pink bath towel. Near her, Jamie played beneath a redwood picnic table. He was a small light-haired child with a slim bright face like Maggie's own. He wore blue jeans only, the legs tucked into the tops of shiny, red- and black-leather, miniature-heeled cowboy boots, his waist encircled by a wide, studded leather belt below his bony little back where the shoulder blades sprouted like tiny spiny wings. He crawled back and forth under the table happily, endlessly re-arranging the several odds and ends of lumber with which he played, and the two gun holsters fastened to his belt on either side dragged back and forth across the cement with him.

Tom Harrison, in an old pair of tennis shorts grown a little tight for him, leisurely pushed a lawn mower the length and breadth of his small plot of grass. Along with the peaceful whirr of the mower and the child's aimless contented chattering, there was the drowsy patter of water sprinklers from neighboring yards and a distant steady rumble of traffic from some nearby busy street.

The young woman sat up suddenly on the lounge and wiped her flushed pretty face with the bath towel.

"Gee, it's really hot today," she said lazily. "The first really hot day this spring. What you doing down there under the table, fellow?"

"You can't see me because the door's closed," the little boy said.

"Oh, I see. That's your house that you've built and you're inside and the door's closed."

"It isn't a house," Jamie said disgustedly.

"Okay, what is it then?" she said as she tugged the halter more securely into place over her full breasts. "Is it a train?"

"It's not a train either, silly," the child said. "Can't you see? It's a space ship!"

"Tom, you hear what he said?" she called out delightedly.

Tom Harrison stopped obediently and leaned upon the handle of the lawn mower.

"You talking to me?"

"Did you hear what Jimmy just said? I asked him if that was a house he's built down there under the table and he said, no, it was a space ship. Isn't that something?"

Tom smiled broadly.

"Kids nowdays pick up everything," he said in a pleased voice. "Where you going, honey?"

"I'm hot," she said. "I'm going in the house and look for something cool to drink."

"That sounds like a pretty good idea at that. How about bringing me out a cold can of beer?"

The little boy stuck his head out from under the table top.

"Junie, I want some Coca-Cola."

"Well, I don't know. You've had two bottles already," she said a little dubiously, and then, lifting her voice, "Tom? Jimmy wants another Coke, should I give it to him?"

"Why not? If he wants it, let him have it."

"He's had quite a lot already. You don't think it will make him sick or anything, do you?"

"Naw! Let him have what he wants."

She returned from the house several minutes later, nudging open the screen door with her shoulder as she maneuvered a tray ahead of her. Tom dropped the handle of the lawn mower and strolled across the grass to meet her.

"Hey, what's happened to the sun?" she said. "Don't tell me it's down back of the mountains already! What time's it getting to be, anyway?"

She carried the tray over to the picnic table, shoving aside a black cowboy hat in order to make room for it.

The little boy came up from under the table and waited expectantly while she poured fizzing Coca-Cola into a glass.

"Here you are, honey," she said. "And there's potato chips in the bowl here on the tray. Now. What does Junie get for giving you nice Coca-Cola, do I get a kiss?"

She bent down and the child came to her obediently, reaching his arms about her neck.

She straightened up, lifting him with her, holding him tight against her with her cheek resting against his.

"Uhmmm! Sweetest little guy I ever knew, could just eat him up, yes, I could!"

And then she said carefully, "Junie loves you an awful lot, Jimmy, do you know that? Do you love me?"

"Yes," he said, after considering it for a second.

"Well, then give me a big hug and a kiss."

Tom watched them with a pleased and tender look upon his face. He reached out his finger and poked it into the little boy's ribs.

"Whoever heard of a cowboy kissing the girls!" he scoffed.

"Well, I like that!" Junie said, her voice gaily belligerent. "What are cowboys supposed to do anyway, kiss horses?"

"Cowboys haven't got any time for girls and all that sissy stuff."

This time he poked his finger, cold and wet from the beer can, into her ribs, up under the edge of her sun halter.

She wriggled away, squealing.

"Ah, that daddy of yours!" she cried to the child. "Let's us show him, should we? Let's go get him, let's beat him up!"

She hurled herself upon him, carrying the child with her. There was a melee of flying arms and legs, and the patio rang with their shouts of laughter and the screams of delight from the little boy sandwiched between them, clinging with an arm about either of their necks. They came apart suddenly, with Junie tumbling over backward onto the grass, her legs sprawling, and Tom swinging the little boy high above his head and down to the ground again where he stumbled, red-faced and breathless with laughter.

"Tom, for heaven sakes!" Junie giggled, tugging the sun halter up over her breasts again.

The little boy drank thirstily from the glass of Coca-Cola while Tom ruffled his fine pale hair affectionately.

"That taste good, fellow?"

"It sure does," Jamie said, with a deep breath. "I'm starving to death, Daddy."

Tom looked up quickly to the sky overhead.

"I guess it is about your supper time at that. Where's the time go to, anyway!"

And, all of a sudden, some of the light and warmth seemed to fade from the pleasant, well-kept little back yard.

Junie got up from the ground silently, brushing fresh-cut blades of grass from her shorts, and Tom turned around to the package of cigarettes on the lounge behind him. Only the child seemed quite oblivious as he sipped happily from the glass held between both of his small grimy hands.

As Junie walked slowly past him, Tom spoke with the cigarette wobbling between his lips.

"We better get going. You want to shower first, honey?"

She answered with her face turned away. "No, I think I'll go on home now, Tom."

"Why you have to go home? You got clothes over here. It's way out of the way for me to pick you up over there when I take Jimmy."

"I didn't mean for you to pick me up over there," she said, still without looking at him.

"I don't get it," he said impatiently. "You're going to ride in with me when I take Jimmy, aren't you?"

"I guess not."

"Sure you are," he said. "After we drop Jimmy, we'll have

dinner in some seafood place over there on the beach and then we can go to a movie or something if you want to."

She picked carefully at a loose thread hanging from a seam of her shorts.

"I just don't think I should, Tom."

"You don't think you should! For god sakes, what does that mean?"

"I mean I don't think I should go with you to take Jimmy home."

"Well, you've done it plenty of times before," he said, his face baffled and irritable. "Why shouldn't you go with me?"

She reached out to open the screen door at the back of the house.

"I just don't think it looks right, that's all. Oh, lots of reasons, Tom. Besides, I think it's nice for you and Jimmy to have some time together without some—some outsider always being around."

"Junie!"

Just as the door banged shut behind her, the little boy burst into tears.

"I don't want to go home yet, Daddy! It isn't dark. Why do I have to go home so soon today, Daddy!"

He flung himself, weeping, upon his father.

"Jimmy, let go of my leg!" Tom said rapidly, and then, lifting his voice, "Junie! Wait a minute, honey. Don't go, I'm coming!"

He struggled to extricate himself from the clinging child, and finally sat down quickly upon his haunches, shaking the little boy gently by his shoulders.

"Jimmy, shut up and listen to me!" he said desperately. "How'd you like to eat your supper tonight in a drive-in? You hear me? If you'll quit crying and let loose of me right now, we'll go to a drive-in. How about that!"

The little boy stopped in mid-wail, his face lighting.

"We're going to a drive-in! We're going to a drive-in!"

(23

He flung himself down upon the patio in his ecstasy, his red boots waving delightedly in the air above him.

Tom stepped over him in one great stride and yanked open the kitchen door. He found her at the front of the house in the dim, sparsely furnished living room. She stood by the door rummaging in the bottom of a large purse for car keys and crying into a piece of Kleenex all at once.

He seized hold of her rigid shoulders and tried to pull her against him.

"Junie, what's the matter with you? I don't get this! Why are you crying, what's upset you? Is it the kid, does he get on your nerves? I thought you liked being here on Saturday and . . ."

She turned to him instantly then, her face wrinkling and distorted as she cried more loudly than ever.

"Tom, don't say that, it isn't him! You know how crazy I am about that baby, I love him like he was my own! You know that, don't you, Tom? These Saturdays with him are just wonderful, they're the happiest times we have."

"There now, honey, don't cry like that!"

He gathered her into his arms tenderly, holding her tightly against his chest, his face resting against her tousled, light brown hair.

"There now, take it easy, Junie. Tell me what's the matter then. Come on now, tell me."

She spoke between sobs, her voice muffled against him.

"I don't want to talk now, Tom. I'm all crying and upset."

"Okay, we'll talk later," he said soothingly. "You go ahead and have yourself a good cry. After we drive Jimmy in, then we'll . . ."

Her body stiffened against him.

"Didn't I say I wasn't going with you to take Jimmy home?" she wailed.

"All right, all right," he said quickly. "Look, honey, I'll tell you what then. You stay right here. I'll drive Jim in and get back just as fast as I can. You can take your time cleaning up after I'm

gone, and have a beer and watch TV or something. I'll be back before you know it. Okay?"

"All right." Her crying was quieting.

"That's a good girl."

After a moment, he said softly, "Junie, you know this is the first time I ever saw you cry? The very first time!"

She stirred and said sharply, "Well, don't you dare say I look cute! No girl looks cute blubbering and bawling."

"Can I help it if you always look cute to me, no matter what you do?" he complained.

And then he said with his voice rough and urgent, "Junie, I don't know what's wrong to make you cry like this, but until I find out, you just remember one thing. I love you. You know that, don't you?"

She raised her head, leaning away from him to see into his face.

"Do you, Tom? Do you love me?"

"Oh, honey, what do you think!"

They kissed, with caressing hands moving unsteadily, and bodies pressing together.

And in the doorway on the other side of the room, Jamie appeared suddenly, his bare feet silent without the leather boots. He stood for a time, watching their embrace with a disinterested small face and then rubbed his nose ferociously with the palm of his hand. He hopped up and down three times on one foot, his arms flailing for balance. He looked at them again and yawned with his mouth opening wide, and at last he said disgustedly, "Aw, come on, Daddy, let's go to the drive-in now."

four

AT THAT MOMENT, a mile or so from the beach, an automobile horn hooted melodiously in the quiet of Juniper Street, and in one of the small, old-fashioned stucco houses that faced upon it, Maggie Harrison ran to the window. By the time she had pulled back the heavy drape, the car was gone, its red taillights just vanishing beneath the lacy, low-hanging foliage of several large old pepper trees at the end of the block.

"Oh, balls!" she said softly.

She walked back in the direction from which she had come, carrying a clean, starched, white shirt carefully in her hands, the needle attached to it by a length of thread. She went through an archway into a shadowy, cluttered dining room and on, to an untidy kitchen at the back of the house, where she sat down again in a chair beside a red-painted wooden table and resumed her sewing.

From nearby there was a sound of running water, and over it, a masculine voice shouted, "For Pete sakes, haven't you got that button sewed on yet?"

"Keep your wig on," she called back. "Old bachelor like you, Buddy boy, you're lucky to have somebody to sew your buttons for you, so you shouldn't complain. You're late to work already, what difference is a couple more minutes going to make?"

"I am not late," he yelled back crossly. "I'm not due in till eight o'clock. I went in early for Gus last night and he's coming in for me tonight. So will you kindly get a move on?"

"No, I just heard a car out front so I went to see," she said. "It's past time for Jamie to be home, you know that?"

"He'll be here," the male voice called back. "Always fussing over that poor kid, for gosh sakes!"

"Don't say I fuss over him," Maggie said. "I don't either fuss over him."

She tugged at the needle, and then sucked her pricked finger, her face brooding.

"At least, I don't think I fuss over him, do I? I hate women that fuss."

"You talking to me?"

"Yeah, but listen, Bud," she said. "Suppose Tom didn't bring him back. You ever stop to think of that? Suppose some Saturday Tom just didn't bring him back?"

"You're crazy! Tom'll bring him back. What makes you think he doesn't want to? Besides, if he didn't, the court would make him, wouldn't they?"

"Uhmmm."

"Quit worrying, Mag, he'll be here," Bud said. "Probably Tom took him out to eat or something. Hey, how is old Tom these days anyway?"

She jabbed the shiny needle viciously into the fabric of the shirt.

"Just peachy dandy, I guess. How should I know?"

"Aw, that creep!" he called back over the splashing water. "You know, he used to play a pretty fair game of tennis too, till he started letting himself get sloppy and out of condition."

Maggie giggled.

"Man doesn't live by tennis balls alone, baby."

From the front of the house, a telephone began to ring.

"Oh, damn, now what?" she said.

She sprang up from the chair, hastily securing the needle on top of the button, and then she ran again, carrying the shirt

with her, her bare tanned feet light and swift in her flat sandals.

A tall rawboned boy erupted into the kitchen from the other direction, rubbing at his face and shoulders vigorously with a bath towel, his sandy-colored hair standing on end.

"That for me, Mag?" he yelled.

He waited but there was no answer from the other part of the house, only the soft indistinct murmuring of her voice.

"Goddamn it, where's my shirt?" he bellowed. "Quit yacking all night on that telephone and hurry up with that shirt!"

He wheeled around and disappeared again into a narrow hallway that opened from one end of the kitchen.

When Maggie returned a moment later, her face was amused. This time she remained standing beside the table, lifting her foot to the chair seat and spreading out the shirt over her knee as she searched for the needle. All at once, she laughed out loud.

"What's so goddamn funny? Who was that on the telephone anyway?"

"Ah, it's mean to laugh," she said. "But I can't help it, he kills me. It was Cliff."

"Not Clifford the creep!"

"The very same."

She snipped the thread with a pair of scissors and carried the shirt down the hallway to the open bathroom door.

"Here you are, sweetie."

"What did old Cliff have to say, anyway?"

She laughed again and shuffled her feet, bobbing in a mock curtsy.

"Why, he wanted to take me out to dinner tonight. How about that!"

"Oh, my god!" Bud said incredulously as he pulled the shirt together over his brown shoulders. "Old drippy Cliffie! I never thought he had it in him."

28)

"Me neither. Ah, he was so funny on the phone. I nearly flipped."

Bud fastened buttons hurriedly and then began to tuck his shirt tails into the top of his tan-colored trousers.

"What did you tell the poor guy?"

"I was very nice," Maggie said. "I just told him that Jamie wasn't home yet and things like that."

Bud made last adjustments to his neatly plastered hair at the mirror over the washbowl, scowling and grimacing.

"Listen, Maggie, no kidding though," he said soberly. "Naturally I don't mean Cliff, but you ought to start getting out more. Nights, I mean. It's no good for you, just goofing around this house every night, reading books and playing the radio and . . ."

Maggie leaned against the door jamb, her hands thrust into the pockets of her tight, faded blue jeans.

"I love you, Bud, when you make a noise like a big brother. Don't worry about me. Remember I was out beating around having myself a ball before you even knew which end was up. I've had it!"

"Don't give me that either," he said. "No kidding, Maggie. All day long you look after the kid and nights you sit around here all alone till you're getting stir-crazy. You come up with crazy ideas like Tom making off with Jamie and stuff. It's no good for you. It isn't as if you had to sit home. My gosh, there's a lot of guys around the beach that would be tickled to death to . . ."

"Those wolves?" Maggie said. "You're a sweetheart, Bud. Just don't worry."

He still fussed with the comb, absorbed in his own reflection in the mirror.

"I wish I was like you, Mag," he said dolefully. "You're terrific. You got a lot of trouble, your marriage busting up and everything, but nothing ever gets you down. I wish I was like that. I guess I'm just the moody one in this family."

(29

"Think so, baby?" Maggie said, her face tender and amused. "What's the matter, you have a fight with Barbara or something?"

"Aw, I don't know. Barbara doesn't hang around the beach much like she used to. Ever since she had her picture taken a couple times in a bathing suit, she's got it in her head she's a model or something. She wants a guy now with a lot of dough that can take her to fancy places where she figures people are going to see her."

Maggie was silent for a moment.

"Bud, while I think of it," she said offhandedly, "that catalogue I sent for from UCLA, you haven't even looked at it yet, sweetie."

"I will," he said quickly. "Honest, I will, Mag. First chance I get."

Maggie sighed, and then she said cheerfully, "Listen, will you get away from that mirror and quit admiring your sun tan, you goddamn beach athlete, you! Who was it yelling at me to hurry up around here?"

"Cripes, yes! I'll have to barrel."

She went back to the kitchen and he rushed off in the other direction with a flurry of footsteps through the uncarpeted hallway and a rapid clicking of light switches before he bolted out into the kitchen after her, a tan-colored jacket flung over his arm.

"See you, Mag," he said hastily, and then with a yank at the long ruddy tail of hair swinging from the back of her head, "Remember what I told you now. You got to start getting with it, baby."

"Listen to who's giving advice to who! Have fun at the parking lot. Don't bash the tail fins off any more Cadillacs tonight than you can help."

He paused at the door.

"Listen, Maggie, if Barbara or anybody should happen to call, be sure and ask her if there's any message for me, huh?"

"Don't I always?" Maggie said. "Why? Is she supposed to call tonight and leave a message?"

"Naw," he shouted back. "If she should just happen to call, that's all."

She followed after him to the back door, leaning out into the darkness where he was already climbing into the old convertible parked in the driveway close to the house.

"Bud, take it easy driving in now, I mean it. Five minutes more never matters getting some place, so . . ."

"I'll be careful, I'm always careful. So long, Mag."

The motor roared away as she closed the door, and after it was gone the house was very still. Maggie looked quickly at the big clock hanging upon the wall behind her and then determinedly gathered up a handful of dirty dishes from the shelf and carried them to the sink. She turned on one of the water faucets and picked up a green plastic sponge. But in a sudden burst of impatience, she turned off the water again and tossed the sponge into the sink on top of the dirty dishes. She went to the table instead and took a cigarette from the package lying there.

She was looking at the clock again when there was the sound of a door opening at the front of the house and she spun around to the doorway.

"Hello?"

"It's just me, Maggie."

She nearly collided with the tall, erect old man who hurried out into the kitchen, dapper in a well-pressed gray suit, his sparse white hair neatly combed over his pink scalp.

"Ah, Grandpa, you startled me!" Maggie said. "I didn't hear you come. Is something the matter, I thought you were out for a night on the town?"

"No, no, just forgot something," he said abstractedly. "Passed

Bud down at the corner, isn't he kind of late tonight? Now where's that blasted flashlight anyway?"

He pulled out drawers rapidly all around the kitchen and banged them shut again.

"Over by the stove, second drawer from the bottom. Well, he isn't due in till eight tonight, so he's not that late. Listen, Grandpa, Jamie isn't home yet. It's way past his supper time. What do you think, do you suppose . . ."

The old man paused with the flashlight in his hands, his face kindly as he looked at her.

"Now, Maggie, he's all right," he said mildly. "Tom'll be walking in here with him any minute. I wouldn't get to fussing."

"Goddamn it, why does everybody keep saying that I'm fussing!" she yelled. "Jamie's supposed to be home to have his supper at five-thirty, it's now six minutes to eight o'clock! Those batteries in there still working, Grandpa?"

He pushed the button on the side of the flashlight experimentally as he walked to the back door.

"Getting kind of weak at that. Why, I told Mildred I'd get her a little posy to wear on her dress. Seen a couple pretty ones just this morning on that big camellia bush out by the garage."

His voice trailed away as he went out the door.

"Oh, is Mrs. Stacy with you?"

Maggie hurried into the living room where a small, elderly woman was perched on the edge of the sofa. Her dark-colored cloth coat was open and beneath it she was resplendent in a sleazy organdy dress cut low at her thin wrinkled neck and the skirt of it billowing over her feet onto the floor around her, a dress the same vivid pink color as the round spots of rouge on her cheeks.

"Hello there, Maggie, how are you?" she said heartily.

"Oh, fine. I was in the kitchen and I didn't hear you come in. How've you been, Mrs. Stacy?"

"Just fine and dandy. Where's our little boy tonight? He hasn't gone to bed already?"

"No, he . . ." Maggie hesitated. "He spends Saturday afternoons with his father, you know, and he isn't home yet. It's getting pretty late for him, too."

"Well, he'll probably be here soon, I wouldn't fuss," Mrs. Stacy said soothingly. She nodded her head several times reassuringly, her glasses shining in the light.

Maggie bit hard at her lip, her eyes flaring, and then she said meekly, "You look pretty sharp tonight, Mrs. Stacy. You look real pretty."

"Aw, now, Maggie!" Her voice was pleased and she blushed beneath her bright spots of rouge. "Honest to goodness, I just wonder what the folks back home in Iowa would say if they could see me all decked out like this!"

She lowered her voice confidentially.

"You know, Maggie, for years I had a hankering for one of these long party dresses. Never owned such a thing in my life and never expected to. Then last fall I seen an ad in the paper when they was having sales at the May Company and I don't know what got into me. I says to myself, 'Mildred, you're not getting a day younger,' and I just went down there and bought me one. Never had it on, except to home once in a while to parade around in front of the looking glass and show the girls. Then when your grandpa and I decided to go down to the Rosewood Ballroom tonight, I just made up my mind I'd dress up and wear it. You see plenty other old fools down there swishing around in their long skirts, so I won't be the only one."

"Good for you, Mrs. Stacy," Maggie said, her voice warm. "You'll be the prettiest girl there tonight, and Grandpa's going to be so proud he'll pop the buttons right off his coat, wait and see."

"Aw, now, Maggie!"

She laughed, preening a little, still blushing and twiddling at the large round pearls screwed onto her ear lobes beneath the elaborate waves and curls of her white hair.

The old man hurried in from the kitchen just then, carrying a little stem with two soft, pink-colored blossoms, the dark waxen leaves around them.

"Here you are, Mildred," he said proudly. "Now didn't I tell you I had camellias blossoming?"

She jumped up from the sofa excitedly, tripping on the skirt of her dress.

"Look at that! Now aren't they just beautiful!"

"Wait," Maggie said. "Let me get you a pin for them."

She disappeared through the archway and when she returned a moment later she carried a long pin with a green pearl top and an ornate bow of shiny tinsel ribbon.

"Look what I found," she said cheerfully. "I knew I'd seen this ribbon doojigger around the house some place but I never expected I'd be able to find it. Now, give me your posy and let's see if we can make this work."

Her fingers moved carefully and delicately as she pulled the ribbon over the little dark twiggy stem.

"You better wear them on your coat till you get there, and then you can put them on your dress, okay?"

She bent down and pinned the flowers securely in place at the old lady's shoulder and then stepped back.

"Now, isn't that as pretty as any boughten corsage you ever saw!" the old lady cried delightedly, ducking her head down to look at the two soft perfect blossoms lying against her shoulder above the shining cascade of ribbon.

"They look fine, Mildred," the old man said, tipping his head critically. "That little bow on there is just the thing. I'd say you look as dressed up now as anybody going. Well, we best not linger, we got that long drive ahead of us, all the way downtown."

He took hold of her arm and they hurried toward the door

together, a tall erect old man and a short dowdy little woman with her long skirts flapping along the floor beneath her tight street-length coat, and something absurdly youthful about them both in the zest and eagerness of their haste.

Maggie tagged after them, her face amused and affectionate. From the doorstep, the old man reached back to pat her shoulder.

"Now don't you worry, Maggie. Tom'll be bringing the boy home any minute now."

And Mrs. Stacy pulled her face down for a hearty kiss.

"Thanks a lot, Maggie. And you kiss that blessed little boy for me when he gets home too."

"I will, Mrs. Stacy. You come and see him real soon. Have fun now."

As they hurried off, Mrs. Stacy turned back a last time.

"Aw, Maggie, I wish you was coming with us tonight! Don't seem right, us old folks out gallivanting around and a pretty girl like you sitting here to home on a Saturday night when you ought to be out dancing and having a good time."

"Get along with you!" Maggie said humorously. "Wait'll I get my kid raised, then I'll have time to go dancing too. Go on now, have fun and cut a rug for me."

They were finally gone with a chorus of laughter and good nights, and Maggie closed the door. Without pausing, in a continuation of the same motion, she whirled across the room, through the archway and on to the kitchen and the large round-faced clock hanging on the wall there.

She stared at the sharp black hands flung wide across the clock face at a quarter past eight.

She bolted off again, down the narrow hall this time, past the bathroom to a darkened doorway, her hand reaching in unerringly to the light switch. The stubby greenish-colored hands of the alarm clock that ticked noisily on a table between the

(35

twin beds were already closing together at past the half hour. Maggie sucked in her breath and turned off the light.

She moved back down the hall, pausing at another doorway, turning on a light once more. This room, too, was a bedroom, clean and orderly with a nondescript dresser and limp white curtains and an old rocking chair, but a child's room unmistakably, with a half-completed structure of red and white blocks standing in the center of the floor and other blocks scattered around it, a toy chest overflowing beneath a window and a miniature hat tree hung with small sweaters and a bulbous spaceman's helmet, and then the row of battered, dirty stuffed animals limply propped against the wall along the inside of the small low bed.

Maggie stood there quietly for a moment, her face infinitely tender.

She stooped finally and picked up a glassy blue marble from the floor just in front of her, leaning in to drop it carefully into a box that already contained broken crayons, minuscular plastic cars and similar treasure.

She left the lights turned on in that room.

Back in the living room once more, she switched on the radio and sat down determinedly in an old-fashioned over-stuffed chair with a bulging padded back. She spread open a magazine but after a moment her gaze wandered from the pages until she stared unwinkingly at one of the empty beige-colored, stippled stucco walls around her. She tossed the magazine away and fidgeted, tucking in the tails of her white shirt, turning up the collar high at the back of her neck, tightening the screws on the big silver hoops that she wore dangling from her ears. And at last she bounded up from the chair, frantically.

She darted to the telephone that stood in a wall niche near the door, and swiftly dialed a number. It rang for a long time as she listened, and at last a soft and tentative female voice spoke in her ear. Maggie dropped the telephone, as though it had bitten her, her face grim.

After that, she waited at the window, a large vacant pane of glass, hung on either side with heavy maroon-velvet drapes, and looking out across a small patch of grass to the sidewalk, the street beyond and the lights twinkling from the windows of houses on the other side.

The wind still blew, stirring the foliage of trees until the whole street danced with shadows, scurrying papers along the curbs, and rustling the dried fronds of a palmetto at the corner of the house.

She waited, her body stiff with anxiety, watching each car that passed beneath the low trailing limbs of the old pepper trees. She waited until the right car came at last, hurtling out of the darkness down Juniper Street and pulling in sharp to the curb in front of the house. Maggie looked only long enough to be sure, and then she turned away, catching hold of a chair back, limp and sagging with her relief.

But only for an instant, and then she bounded across the room to fling open the door.

"Goddamn it, don't you think it's about time!" she shouted into the darkness.

The child came first, running up the cement walk awkwardly in his cowboy boots, holding a teddy bear in one hand, and clutching at his big black cowboy hat with the other.

He bounced up the one low, wide step, slipped in the boots, skated perilously and regained his balance before he hurled himself against her.

"Mommy! We was in a smash-up!"

"Jamie, my god!"

"No, we weren't," Tom Harrison said quickly as he followed up the walk. "We saw a smash-up, that's all. We came over on Sepulveda and a couple cars had piled up just before you get to the tunnel. That's one reason we're so late. We sat over there bumper to bumper for a half-hour before . . ."

She was no longer listening. Kneeling, she gathered up the child into a great exultant bear hug.

"Ah, baby, baby, am I glad you're home," she murmured.

The little boy wriggled, his voice muffled against her.

"Mommy, we went to the carnival. And Daddy got me some new shoes."

Maggie stood up swiftly, drawing the child into the house with her, and Tom followed after.

"New shoes?" she said. "Well, let me see. Looks like you've got a new hat too."

"I'm sorry we're late," Tom said again. "It was partly this wreck over on Sepulveda, all the traffic was tied up and . . ."

"Mommy, see? See my new shoes?"

The little boy tugged at her demandingly and extended his foot.

"Okay, okay, Jamiekins."

She knelt again, steadying him with one hand and lifting the red and black leather boot a little higher by its heel.

"Well, what do you know! Dig these crazy shoes!"

She poked him in the ribs gently, flinging back her head to laugh, her face soft and engaging all of a sudden, with color and animation. The little boy laughed with her delightedly, rolling onto the floor with his teddy bear.

"Dig my crazy shoes, Mommy!"

Behind them, Tom was silent and unsmiling as he waited, his hand resting on the door latch.

Maggie stood up quickly.

"How about his supper?" she said impersonally. "I suppose he's eaten?"

Before Tom could answer her, Jamie shouted, "I had my supper, Mommy. At a drive-in! Mommy, Daddy took me to a drive-in."

"Coca-Cola and hot dogs," she said. "And candy and popcorn all day at the carnival."

"Hot dogs aren't going to hurt him once in a while," Tom said, his voice as stiff and controlled as hers had been. "He's crazy to go to drive-ins. He thinks it's the greatest treat there is."

She hunched her shoulders and turned back to the child.

"Okay, Jamie. Way past your bedtime and away we go. No, no arguments. No. Here, let Mommy unfasten your belt. You go on to the bathroom and wet and I'll be in. Wash your hands good with soap when you're through and wash your face, too. Come on now, off you go."

"Got a kiss for your Daddy, Jimmy?" Tom said quietly.

The child ran to him obediently, and Tom scooped him up, holding him high against his shoulder.

"Daddy, let's go to the carnival again tomorrow," he said ingenuously. "Let's go again tomorrow, you and me and Junie. Can we, Daddy?"

Maggie turned away abruptly, crossing the room to the table beside the overstuffed chair. She selected a cigarette painstakingly from the package there.

"Not tomorrow, fellow," Tom said, his voice a little forced and hearty. "But we'll go again next week though, okay?"

Maggie struck the match to her cigarette and remained with her back still turned to them, her shoulders erect and rigid.

"You be a good boy now, Jimmy. Daddy'll see you next week. We'll go to the carnival again and have a big time. Okay, cowboy?"

"Yes," he said reluctantly, and then with his voice suddenly wistful, "Daddy, you come in and read my bedtime story. I want you to read me my bedtime story."

"I can't, Jimmy. I have to go. Your Mommy'll read to you."

"But I want you to do it, Daddy. You got time. Junie said she'd wait for you."

"Aw, Jimmy! Look, fellow, I can't tonight, I . . ."

Maggie turned then and walked back to them swiftly.

"Next time, sweetie," she said gently. "See, you were awfully late getting home tonight, going to the drive-in and everything. Now your Daddy has to go. Maybe next time he can read to you and tuck you in. All right?"

"Yes," he said finally.

Tom kissed him and put him down.

Her voice was still gentle as she said, "Jamie, did you tell your Daddy thank you for all the fun you had today and the new shoes and everything?"

"Thank you, Daddy," he said with a great yawn after it.

"See you next week, cowboy," Tom said steadily. "Don't forget now and go to bed with those new boots still on."

The little boy giggled and shuffled away sleepily, still holding onto the teddy bear and clutching at his trousers that had slipped down around his knees, just below his small white underpants.

There were identical expressions of tender amusement on both their faces as they watched him go.

"Ah, what a kid!" Tom said fondly. "You know he's getting taller all the time? I can notice it every week now. Kid must have grown an inch just in the last month."

"You really think so?" Maggie said. "I haven't measured him but I think he has, too. Of course, it's harder for me to tell, being with him every day. He isn't getting much fatter though."

"Aaah, he'll fatten up later on, I don't worry about that. Remember those pictures of me when I was a little kid? I was always skinny as a rail, too."

"Yeah, and what about me, I was just the same," she said.

"You know, he's really crazy for those carnivals," Tom said. "You'd think he'd get sick of going on those same rides all the time. No, sir, he's crazy for all of them. And not scared of anything, he went on everything they had over there today!"

"Not the whip?" she said quickly.

"Aw, no, I wouldn't let him ride on that yet. They had a little roller coaster over there though, it was quite a deal. Of course it was just a little one, but a lot of the kids wouldn't go near it. Not him, he went on it all by himself and rode three times. I just about had to drag him off it. He got real sore at me too, you should have seen him. 'Daddy, why you do that?' he kept saying."

They laughed together softly and all of the stiffness and tension was gone from the room.

"Say, you know that little son of a gun can count?" Tom said proudly. "Counts all the way up to ten! And fast, nor you can't fool him into making a mistake either."

"He really counts up to twelve," Maggie said. "I meant to tell you to ask him. I push him in the swing down at the beach, you know, and we count the pushes. He gets up to twelve without a single mistake, but you ought to hear him when he gets to the twenties. 'Twenty-eight,' he says, 'twenty-nine, twenty-ten,' and he keeps right on going."

They laughed again and then they were silent, a warm and intimate communication.

At last, Tom sighed.

"Yeah, he's a great kid all right."

He stepped back and reached for the door handle.

"Well, I better get going." And then he added in a careful voice, "I've got a date with Junie tonight, he heard us talking about it. She went to the carnival with us today. She's this girl I've been going around with."

He hesitated, rattling the metal door latch.

"Far as I know, I'll still be having Saturdays off for a while. I'll pick him up about eleven next week, okay?"

"Better make it eleven-thirty," Maggie said briefly. "Then I'll give him his lunch early before he goes."

"Okay. Oh, I almost forgot."

He dug his hand into a bunchy jacket pocket and drew out a small pair of scuffed brown oxfords.

"Here's his shoes."

She reached for them silently, her face suddenly grim, and a red flush of color flamed across Tom's cheekbones.

"All right, you're sore because I got him the boots," he said, his voice shaken and angry. "I suppose you won't let him wear them now either."

"Damn right I won't," Maggie said coolly.

She twitched back her hair as she looked hastily over her shoulder in the direction in which Jamie had gone, and shoved her hands hard into the pockets of her blue jeans.

"Look, I hate kids in boots and you know it perfectly well. So what do you do? You take him right out and buy him a pair. Well, I won't have him hobbling around in the silly damn things. You can ask Dr. Blake or any other pediatrician that you want to, they're bad for their feet."

"Other kids wear them, don't they?" he said. "But of course you don't want Jimmy to be like other kids! You want to make some kind of a—a sissy out of him, or something. They don't hurt other kids' feet, do they? What about real cowboys, I suppose they've all got bum feet too!"

"Ah, don't be stupid! Cowboys wear boots to ride horses. You ever hear of anybody turning up at a track meet in a pair of boots? And I suppose you got him a gun, too, while you were at it?"

"Sure, I got him a gun," Tom said furiously. "A belt and holsters and two guns, what do you think of that? I had him leave them over home because I knew you'd raise the roof if he brought them back here. And let me tell you something else, I'll buy him fifty more guns too, if he wants them. I'm not going to sit around and let you make some kind of a sissy freak out of my kid. I suppose that's stupid, too, huh?"

"You took the words right out of my mouth! Stupid."

42)

Maggie teetered on her toes, taut and stiff-legged as a gamecock.

"And don't you tell me I'm trying to make a sissy out of Jamie! Teach him to ride, teach him to swim, teach him to box, but like Dad always said . . ."

"Don't say it!" Tom roared. "Don't you quote your old man to me, I've heard it a million times. 'Give a boy a hunting rifle when he's twelve and teach him to use it!' Christ almighty!"

Bitterness was suddenly there, like a tangible monstrous mushroom growth springing up out of the floor, a poisonous puffball alive and feeding on old hurts and old angers, huge, and swelling with every second until it threatened to burst apart the very walls around them.

"I've had enough," Maggie said in a soft deadly voice. "You come dragging in here three hours late with him, and then you're the one that's yelling and hollering and . . ."

Tom clenched his hands helplessly in front of him.

"Oh, god, you make me sick!" he said incoherently. "You're the one that never has enough, you can make a fight out of anything and you love it! I take the kid out and buy him some stuff the one stinking lousy day a week I get a chance to do it, and then you jump all over me. You're always the same, you know it all, bossy bull-headed stuck-up . . ."

"Ah, ah!" Maggie said sweetly, her blue eyes bright and venomous. "Visitation privileges but not family brawls. Besides, Junie's waiting for you, remember?"

"Jesus, I knew it!" he yelled. "I've just been waiting for you to get around to that. Well, you leave Junie out of this. She's none of your goddamn business. One thing you can always say about Junie, she's a sweet, lovable, good-natured girl you can live in peace with and . . ."

"Who said leave Junie out of this!" Her voice was dangerous.

"Daddy," came a plaintive small wail from the other part of the house. "You going to read me a bedtime story, Daddy?"

The room became abruptly and thunderously still.

Tom cleared his throat.

"I'm just leaving, Jimmy," he called. "Get to bed now like a good fellow."

"Mommy'll be there in a second, sweetie," she chimed in with him.

They were both silent after that, Tom turned half away, frowning over the metallic rattle of the door latch under his thumb.

"Sorry I was late getting the kid back here," he said finally, his voice controlled. "I said I was sorry."

She hunched her shoulders. "It's all right. I can't help but worry, that's all."

"How's Bud and Grandpa Kennedy?"

"They're fine," she said. "Bud's at work, Grandpa's out with Mrs. Stacy."

He studied the door latch as though it were some rare and specially wrought antiquity.

"I'm sorry about being so late, honest. I imagine you've got a date or something, and I hate to hold you up."

Under his covert glance, Maggie's chin lifted.

"I said it was all right so skip it. My date isn't till later on."

For an instant longer he seemed caught and fascinated by the intricacies of the worn old metal door mechanism, and then he said rapidly, "Well, eleven-thirty next Saturday then, okay?"

"Fine," she said.

He went out the door quickly, closing it behind him.

Her body slowly relaxed with the sound of his feet, hurrying off down the cement walk. She stood quietly, her face remote, and listened to the short final sequence of sounds that marked his departure: the slam of the car door, the throaty purr of the starter, and then the motor sound that changed key with the shifting of the gears as the car pulled away from the curb.

She made a small breathy sound in her throat, scornful and a little rueful, before she hurried away toward the child's bedroom.

Jamie knelt on the floor there, half into a pair of faded-blue sleepers, shivering and yawning over his blocks. Maggie went about his bedtime ritual swiftly, her voice gay and soothing as she lifted him up to fasten the snaps down the front of his sleepers and inspect the cleanliness of his face and hands. While she turned back the covers of the bed, he sleepily sorted through a stack of books on a shelf, and when he had selected one, she pulled the rocking chair around into the light and gathered him up onto her lap. Part way through the story concerned with the doings of a small but valiant train engine, his head fell back against her shoulder, his eyelids drooping. She read on more rapidly to the end, and then carried him to the bed and pulled the covers over him. She adjusted the windows and shades and then returned, bending a last time to kiss his rosy drowsy face. She tiptoed away, turning out the lights and closing the door behind her softly.

And then she stood irresolutely in the narrow hallway, for the first time that night all her haste and purpose gone.

She wandered into the bathroom and put fresh bright lipstick on her mouth before the mirror.

She drifted out into the kitchen and opened the door of the old refrigerator, lifting lids and coverings on several containers undecidedly, nibbling at a bit of cold meat from one of them, and finally pushing the door shut again. She went to the stove and turned on a low blue gas flame beneath an aluminum coffeepot that stood on one of the burners, and then helped herself to a banana from a bowl of fruit on top of the red table. She munched at it without relish and turned the gas flame higher under the coffeepot. She drifted on into the dining room.

A small cot bed was shoved against the wall behind the dining table and on a little stand at the head of the bed next to a make-shift reading lamp were piled several books in lending library jackets. She leafed pages through them idly and at last chose one of them, taking it with her back to the kitchen. There, she poured stale strong black coffee into a cup, and carried book and coffee both into the silent cheerless living room and the overstuffed chair beneath the floor lamp.

But at the last moment she hesitated. She tossed the book into the chair instead and turned on the radio, standing to sip gingerly at the hot coffee.

The radio crackled, an unctuous male voice caught in mid-sentence spoke suddenly and stopped and the monotonously gay and lively music filled the room. Maggie put down her coffee cup and turned off the radio with a definite small click.

Once again she hesitated in front of the overstuffed chair and the bright-covered book. She lifted one foot against the edge of the seat cushion and for a long time she stood with her hands in her pockets, studying her own bare brown toes as they flexed and wriggled against the thick sole of her sandal.

And suddenly she kicked at the old chair viciously.

"Junie!" she said out loud, in a soft fierce voice. "Junie, for god sakes!"

She spun around and strode to the telephone. She lifted the instrument and dialed the numbers rapidly, her finger jabbing down into the little round slots.

She waited and then she said, "Mrs. Malott? Hi, this is Maggie Harrison. Ah, we're all fine, how are you? Uhmm . . . Oh, really? Uhmm . . . Look, Mrs. Malott, I know it's terribly late to ask you, but I wonder if you could come over and sit with Jamie for me for a while tonight. You could? You sure now, because it isn't anything awfully important, I didn't have anything planned, I just thought I might . . . Oh well, swell then. No, that's all right, finish what you're watching on TV, I'm not even dressed yet or anything. See you then. 'Bye."

Her face was bright as she pressed down the bar on top of the telephone. She stood for a moment, chewing at her lip, and then released the bar and dialed again, another number out of her memory, with sure hasty fingers.

She hummed softly while she waited and then spoke again into the telephone.

"Lorraine, it's Maggie . . . Oh, nothing much is cooking over here, I just got Jamie to bed. What's cooking over at your house, how are Bill and the kids? Uhmm . . . Ah, terrific . . ."

She listened, and slowly her smile faded and her face sobered into disappointment, but when she spoke again her voice was perfectly unchanged and light and gay.

"Look, why don't I call you back tomorrow then, you better rush, you're going to be terribly late. Uhmm . . . Well, I'm dying to see you, too. Sure, let's try to make it the very first of the week. Maybe we can gang up and take all the kids to the beach or something, if it's warm enough. Swell—that's wonderful. Okay, you and Bill have fun now, I'll see you. 'Bye."

This time she put the telephone down when she was through. She stood for a moment thoughtfully and then lifted the instrument again and dialed another number more slowly. She waited for the space of eight or ten rings before she put it down. She lingered beside the telephone, riffling the pages of a little brown book filled with names and matching numbers and at last she abandoned it and shoved her hands once more into her pockets.

She walked away slowly for several steps and suddenly she laughed out loud, a wry sound, with no mirth at all in her face.

She turned back to the niche in the wall and sorted out a bit of white paper from among several others slid in under the little square of tapestry beneath the telephone. She dialed methodically, her eyes upon the paper.

"Hello," she said. "May I speak to Clifford Brunner, please?"

And then she said, "Oh, I see. No, no message. Thanks a lot."
She dialed one more time, with a weary finality.

"Mrs. Malott? Hi, it's Maggie again. Look, I feel like a jerk
to keep bothering you like this when you're right in the middle of
a good TV show, but I decided I'd better stay in tonight. No, no
really. No, honestly, Mrs. Malott, I know you're glad to do it.
No, you see, all I had in mind was going out to a movie, and
it really is terribly late and I've just been looking in the paper
and there isn't anything I specially want to see anyway. Ah,
you're real sweet! Well, I'll be calling you again soon, don't
worry. Thanks anyway, thanks a lot. Good night."

She walked away from the telephone. She looked at the overstuffed chair and the book and walked on, her feet making a
measured definite sound. In the kitchen, she turned on the light
and opened one of the cupboard doors, reaching in behind the
narrow wooden partition to lift down the bottle of whiskey
and carrying it together with a glass to the shelf beside the
sink. She poured a little liquor into the bottom of the glass and
added water from the tap. She held it to the light judiciously and
then added a little more whiskey from the bottle.

And then she lifted the glass with a little mock flourish to her
own faint reflection against the dark pane of the window.

"Well, cheers!" she said aloud into the silence of the empty
room.

five

TOM HARRISON swung back into his own driveway and stopped the car beside the house with a squeal of brakes. He turned off the lights and motor without running the car on into the garage, and stepped out hastily into the mild warm night air. From a neighboring back yard, outdoor light shone over the high dividing fence and there was a festive mixture of voices and music and laughter. His own house was dark and silent, with only a dim light somewhere at the front of it.

Tom went in through the kitchen door, his hand groping for the light switch.

"Junie?" he called. "Gee, honey, I'm sorry it took me so long. I hurried just as fast as I could. Junie?"

There was no answer from her or sound of any kind, and he walked on quickly toward the living room. The floor lamp was turned on there but the room was empty, the one chair vacant, the TV screen blank and glassy.

"Junie?" he called again, his face alarmed.

"I'm in here, Tom."

"Oh, god, you scared me to death," he said. "I thought you'd got sick of waiting and gone home."

He turned on the light as he passed the switch, his feet echoing along the hallway to the bedroom door.

"Hey, I bet you were sleeping, I bet I woke you up."

"No, I wasn't sleeping," she said, her voice thick and strained and unnatural.

She was lying on her back on one of the twin beds, the pillow wadded beneath her head. She wore her sun shorts and halter still, with a blanket pulled up over her bare legs. When Tom bent to kiss her, her lips were cool and lifeless under his, and she turned her face away as he sat down heavily upon the edge of the bed beside her.

"What a night!" he said, reaching for the cigarettes in his shirt pocket. "First we went to the drive-in. You ever try to make a little kid hurry up when they're doing something they like to do? Well, you might as well butt your head against the wall and be done with it. When we finally got away from there I went on down Ventura to Sepulveda. I had a feeling the minute I started that I should have gone over on the Freeway. Sure enough, two cars had piled up just before you get to the tunnel and I'll bet we sat there bumper to bumper for an hour before the police finally had the road clear. What a night! I knew I should have took the Freeway."

"What's the difference?" she said. "Look what happened to me last week on the Freeway, only I was caught for two hours before they had traffic moving again."

"Yeah."

He cocked his head toward the open window, the tip of his cigarette glowing in the dim light.

"Sounds like quite a party over at Jack and Betty's. Listen to Jack. You can hear him laugh a mile away when he gets started."

She made no answer and after a moment he said, humbly, "Junie, what's the matter? Why were you crying? Why are you lying here in the dark like this?"

"Can I have a cigarette?"

He gave her the one that he had just lighted and went about lighting another one for himself.

"What is it, Junie?" he said again.

When she did not speak, he leaned down over her, trying to see into her face in the dim light streaming in from the hallway.

"Don't, Tom!"

He straightened abruptly.

"Don't what? I just want to see you, that's all. Hiding away in here in the dark so that . . ."

"No, don't," she said quickly. "Don't turn on the light. Please, Tom. I don't want you to see me like this. I'm an awful mess."

"You've been crying some more, haven't you?" he said.

He was silent for a moment and then he caught hold of her arm roughly.

"Junie, I want you to quit beating around the bush with me. Whatever it is, I want to know about it right now."

"What's the use?" she said with a sob in her voice. "There's no use in talking, Tom."

He sprang to his feet and walked away blindly around the foot of the bed.

"Women!" he said. "Christ almighty! Why can't a woman just once come right out and say what's on her mind? Why they always have to beat around the bush and snipe at a guy and . . ."

"Tom, please," she wailed. "Some things are hard to talk about, that's all, some things you just can't. All right, you're so crazy to know, I'll tell you. It's us that's no use. It's not going to work. I don't want us to be together any more."

"Now you really are upset and talking crazy," he said out of the darkness. "Look, honey, let me ask you just one question, yes or no. Do you love me or don't you? You ought to be able to tell me that."

"Ah, Tom! I love you, you know I love you!"

"All right then," he said. "And I love you. I love you more than I ever loved anybody before in all my life. So where's the big problem? What's all this crazy talk about it's no good, it's no use, we shouldn't be together any more?"

"You make it sound so easy, Tom," she said forlornly. "Just two people being in love. But you're wrong, nothing is ever so easy as all that."

The room was still except for the sounds coming in through the window, the thumping raucous music and the laughter.

"Junie, I know what the trouble really is," he said quietly. "I know how hard it is on you, having to live the way we do right now. But don't you understand there's nothing I can do about it? I'd marry you tomorrow if I could, hell, I'd marry you right this minute. But we can't do that. We got to wait for my divorce to be final, it's the law, what can I do?"

She caught her breath and spoke rapidly, the words tumbling together.

"But, Tom, don't you see, if it weren't for me maybe you'd go back to your wife, maybe there wouldn't be any divorce at all!"

"Oh, no!" he said loudly. "Now wait a minute, Junie, you . . ."

"You wait!" she said, her voice anguished. "It's Jimmy I'm thinking about right now. Ah, Tom, he's such a wonderful baby. You're crazy about him and he's just crazy about you. It's not right for you to have to lose him. For his sake alone, you ought to go back with your wife and try to . . ."

"Not in a million years, not even for the kid," Tom said. "Look, Junie, this is something we better get straight right now. Our divorce was all set and decided on before I ever even met you. You had nothing to do with it, so get that out of your head.

"Here," he said. "I got the ash tray right here."

He sat down beside her again on the edge of the bed, and held out the little round glass tray for her to extinguish the burning end of her cigarette.

"You say that, Tom. Of course you'd say that."

"I don't say it, it's the way it is."

And then he said slowly, "Look, Junie, I never told you much about it. I can see now I should have, then none of this would have come up. I'll tell you what there is to tell right now."

She moved her head on the pillow.

"No, Tom, you don't have to. It's none of my business."

52)

"The hell with that! It is your business. You get these crazy ideas in your head, this is something we got to thresh out."

He bent forward over his knees and put the ash tray on the floor, just under the edge of the bed.

"God, listen to that racket next door," he said. "Just listen to Jack. You can't tell me anything is that funny. Aaah, shut up, you drunken bum!"

He pulled at his knuckles, staring at the patch of light that shone in the open doorway from the hall.

And finally he said, his voice forced and rapid, "Well, we got married just before the end of the war, see. I was in the Army and I was stationed outside her home town the last place before we shipped overseas. Aw, I've told you all of this. I met her at the USO. She, oh, I don't know, she was the liveliest kid in that whole jerk town, she was the belle of the ball around there. I don't know how she happened to pick me. I guess I looked good in my uniform."

He moved restlessly.

"Aw, I don't have to tell you all this stuff. You had one of these bum war marriages yourself so you know how easy it happened back in them days. Everybody was all charged up and . . . Well, anyway, we got married before I shipped out, just like all the rest of them."

He reached again for his cigarettes.

"I went to the Pacific, so I shipped from out here. I'd never been in California before. One look at this country and it hit me right then, and I made up my mind if I got back all right that California was where I was going to live some day. Of course when I did come back, when I first got out of the Army, I went back to my old job. We had an apartment out there."

He thought about it for a moment, frowning.

"When you come to look back, I figure both of us knew even then that it wasn't going to work out, only we didn't want to admit it. We stayed there over two years, but I still had California in my mind all the time. When I got money saved up, then we moved out here. It was all right with her, maybe she wasn't crazy to come like I was, but she was willing to come all right. So we came. I got the job at the factory, and we had an apartment at first and finally toward the last we rented a house. I liked it out here right from the start, it sure felt like coming home to me. But after a couple years, she started complaining, she didn't like it out here. I just didn't get it. It wasn't as if she was lonesome for her family, because about six months after we come, her grandfather sold out back home and moved out here too, him and her kid brother. It was her grandfather that brought her up, see, her and her brother went to live with him after her father died, so they're the only near family that she's got. Her grandfather bought this house over at the beach where she's staying now with Jimmy, and her kid brother finished school out here. Of course, when she first started in about not liking California, it was before Jimmy came, and I figured it was just one of those ideas women get sometimes when they're pregnant. But she never did get over it. I was doing good out here, you'd have thought she'd have been tickled to death. I got a better job at the factory, and a year or so later I worked up to a better job yet. All along I had it in my mind to buy a house and live out here in the Valley. Pretty soon I had the money saved up, and that's when she really blew the roof off. She wasn't going to live in the Valley. Period."

He moved again restlessly, groping along the floor for the ash tray.

"Aw, it's none of this stuff that counts, me buying the house out here in the Valley, and her not liking California and all that. We were finished long before any of that happened and we both knew it. We just never got along. It was just one of those things. You see how it is?"

He looked at Junie hopefully, and she laughed, a small mournful sound in the darkness.

"Ah, Tommy, you're funny," she said. "You haven't told me

a single thing. If you're going to tell me, tell me. What was the trouble, why didn't you get along with her? You talk and talk but you haven't told me anything."

"Huh?"

And then he said ruefully, "Yeah, I guess I see what you mean."

"What was the trouble between you? What's she really like, Maggie?"

"Maggie," he repeated.

His voice filled with quiet fury.

"She's the goddamnedest woman I ever knew, that's what she's like! She's bossy, and mouthy, and stubborn as a mule. There's nothing she likes better than to pick a fight. She'll stand up in front of you and shoot off her mouth till it's all you can do not to hit her or something. And on top of everything else, she's a screwball, she's a real honest-to-god crazy screwball. You can't live with her, nobody could live with her."

He struggled for control.

"They always claim there's two sides to every story, okay. Leave what she is out of it, and look at it, the kind of a guy that I am. You know me, Junie. I'm just a regular ordinary quiet kind of a guy. Now, you take this house. I always wanted a house of my own like this, that I could mow grass and tinker around and take care of. I like to save up and buy nice things for it, I like to see a house fixed up real nice and modern. This house right here means an awful lot to me. Oh, I wouldn't say that maybe in a few years when I'm doing better I wouldn't like to sell it and get a bigger place with a swimming pool and all that. But anyway, I'm the kind of a guy that thinks a lot of my home. That's why I never could understand about Maggie. Sometimes I even think she don't give a damn where she lives or what she's got, it's all the same to her. You know yourself how women do, they read the ads in those house magazines, they hang around the stores downtown and get ideas on things to buy to fix a place up nice. Well, she says she hates stores, and she makes fun of those magazines. She'll come home lugging some little old-fashioned trunk or something she found in some crummy second-hand store somewhere, some piece of junk I'm ashamed to have folks see setting around in our house. Do you know she'll make a bigger fuss over a piece of junk like that than she did a great big brand-new refrigerator, the latest model going, when I had it sent out to the house and set up in the kitchen?

"And that's only the beginning of it. I'm a quiet kind of a guy, like I said, I work hard all day at my job, and at night I want to come home to a nice clean house and a good meal on the table. That's the kind of a house my mother kept, and it's what I was used to. And after supper I want to read the paper, and sit around with my shoes off and watch TV for a while and go to bed. It's just the kind of a guy I am. But you can't live like that with Maggie. With her, you never know what you're going to get into, from one day to the next. So maybe she gets a streak of housekeeping, then she'll knock herself out scrubbing and waxing and shoving the furniture all around, and the kitchen full of cook-books and fancy meals ready right on the dot. But then for the next two weeks the place can look like a pigpen and you can eat beans out of a can because all she wants to do all day long is sit on her hind end and read library books and walk the floor and talk and argue with you when you get home about what she's read in them. She's the same way about clothes and everything. She can go slopping around for a week in the same dirty old pair of pants, and then all of a sudden she'll spend half a day just fixing her hair and fixing her face, and when you get home she's all dolled up and wanting to go out some place and dance. Christ almighty! But that's the way she is. She gets streaks of wanting to do things. She wants to chase way off downtown and go to burlesque shows, she wants us to take up chess or photography or some crazy thing, she wants to go to the circus, she wants to sit up all night and play phonograph records and drink beer, she wants to drive all the way down to Tijuana to the bullfights, she wants to take lessons on the flute!"

He flung out his hands helplessly.

"How can you live with somebody like that? You never know what they're going to think up next. And then she don't get along with people, nor she won't try. Now me, I always like to make friends with the neighbors. I enjoy that. You swap tools back and forth and Saturday nights you get together at each other's houses and cook steaks out on the barbecue and play cards or watch TV and maybe drink a little beer. But that's not good enough for Maggie. I bet you she never made friends with over two or three of the neighbor women, all the places we ever lived. And when I'd try to tell her, she'd take my head off. What was she going to talk to them about, she'd always say. But some old Japanese woman that had a vegetable store down on the corner, she could spend half a day down there talking to her, she knew what to talk to her about all right. But my friends were different. Of course, that was it, the only people she wanted to be friends with was screwballs, just like she was herself.

"There's one thing I always remember," he said broodingly. "It don't amount to anything when you tell it, but I guess there is always one thing like that, that you remember, the first time when it really hits you, and you know for sure that you're through. I remember this yet, just as plain as day. It was when Jimmy was just a baby, and we were still living in the apartment we had. I came home from work one night, I was bushed and it was real hot. The minute I walked in that door I felt just like running away or something. Nobody was there, and the bed wasn't made in the bedroom, diapers and newspapers littered all over and the breakfast dishes still piled up out in the kitchen with the ants crawling on them and the flies buzzing, no supper ready or anything. And while I was still standing there just inside the door, I heard her voice. It was a real crazy thing because I could see the whole apartment was empty. 'Hi, Mr. Touhy,' she says. I even remember that name to this day, he was a dry-cleaner fellow we had back then. 'Hi, Mr. Touhy,' she says. 'There's a pair of pants to go, in on the bed. Did your wife get to feeling better after that bad spell she had last week?' And then I figured out where she was. There was a great big old tree out in the court back of our apartment unit, and the top of it was just outside our living-room windows, and that's where she was. Up in that tree. I walked over to the window and then I could see her. She was way up in the tree, sitting straddle of a limb in her old pants with her hair hanging down, fiddling away with a kite string that had gotten tangled up in the tree branches. She looked around and saw me then, and I'll never forget it. 'Oh, Tom, it's you,' she said, as ordinary as could be. 'Sweetie, you must be home awful early. Hand me a knife, will you, or the scissors or something?' Just as ordinary and cool as that, like she was sitting on a chair right there in the house. And then I could see Jimmy down below in his stroller, just laughing his head off. He thought that was the funniest thing he had ever seen, his mother way up in that tree. Come to find out, when she went to the store that forenoon for groceries, the market was giving away this big kite with two boxes of soap flakes or breakfast food or something like that. And so she'd spent the whole day outdoors, romping and racing around, flying that kite. I'll never forget that as long as I live, how hot it was, and the musty dirty smell of that apartment and no supper or anything, and her out there in a tree with a kite, and her hair shining red in the sun. And right then, something kind of turned over inside of me, and I knew I'd never forgive her, I'd never feel the same, I'd had enough and I was through. I'll never forget it so long as I live!"

"Ah, Tommy, poor darling," Junie whispered.

"Well, now you see," he said wearily. "If she was the last woman on the face of the earth, we couldn't make a go of it. Maybe it all sounds kind of foolish to you, it's nothing big or terrible that I blame her for, like chasing other men or getting drunk and neglecting the baby or something like that. It's just that we can't live together, she drives me crazy. And it's not all one-sided either, I guess she's just as sick and tired of me as I am of her. Now you understand, Junie?"

"But maybe she'd change, Tom. Did you ever really talk to her and give her a chance? Maybe if you explained it all to her, she'd try to take an interest and keep house better and . . ."

Tom laughed.

"You sure don't know Maggie! You don't tell her anything, anyway I never had any luck trying. Besides, what makes you think she'd want to change, even if she could? No, the way I figure this, we're both going to be a lot better off with a divorce, and she feels the same."

"Ah, but, Tom, it seems like all these things you talked about are the kind of things that could be worked out. If two people try, if they really want to, why . . ."

"Junie, lay off, will you?" he said, his voice sharp. "What's the matter with you tonight anyway? Why you so crazy to try to talk me and Maggie back together again? Is that what you really want to see happen? Well, you might as well give up. In the first place, I wouldn't go back with her if she was the last woman on earth. And in the second place, she wouldn't have me back either. Why, you talk like this was all on my side. Maggie feels just the same. This divorce is about the only damn thing we ever solid agreed on, all the years we been married. So just cut it out!"

She rolled away instantly, with her back to him and her face hidden in the crook of her arm.

"Okay, I'm sorry I yelled at you," he said. "It just made me kind of sore to hear you keep harping on it like that. I know what you'll say, like you said before, it's Jimmy you're thinking about. Sure a divorce is tougher when there is a kid mixed up in it, you don't have to tell me that. I miss him like hell yet, and I get the blues every Saturday when it comes time to take him home. But what can you do? You said it wasn't right for me to lose him, well hell, I'm not losing him nor I don't ever intend to, he's my kid. I see him every week and later on when he's older he'll always spend vacations with me and stuff like that."

He reached out to stroke her short tousled hair.

"Look, Junie, the way I feel, you only live once and everybody's entitled to live the kind of a life they want to, but you got to have the right kind of a person to live it with you or it's no good at all. That's why I feel like my luck has changed already. I've got you now, Junie. And you're damn right there's more to it than just two people being in love. You and I get along together, honey. We got all the same ideas, we like all the same things. We're going to have a swell life together, aren't we? Well, aren't we?"

"We could except for one thing, Tom," she said, her voice straining to speak without tears. "There's just one important thing it seems like you've forgot all about."

He lifted her hand, nestling it against his cheek.

"Aw, you're a crazy," he said caressingly. "What have I forgot about?"

"I told you right away when we first started to get serious," she said. "You never can say that I didn't tell you right from the beginning, Tom."

"Tell me what, for god sakes?"

"How can you forget about that! I can't have children, Tom. I had that operation and now I'll never be able to have any children!"

"Jesus, now what's that got to do with all this?" he said wonderingly. "I haven't forgot that you told me that. Nor I haven't forgot what I told you then either, that it didn't matter to me. Sure, in a way I was sorry when you told me. I sure would have liked for us to have a little girl that looked just like you. But you can't, and it's just another one of those things. Honey, I love you for a wife, I'm not picking out a breeding rabbit or something. Maybe if I hadn't already had Jimmy I'd feel dif-

60)

ferent about it, I don't know. Anyway, that's how I feel and I told you that. What's on your mind, Junie? I don't understand what you're getting at?"

She rolled over again, her body curling against him, her hands clasping behind his head.

"Tom, listen and try to understand how I feel," she said, her voice beseeching. "If it weren't for that one single thing, I'd say sure, fine, we could start over again together, and I'd be able to make a whole swell new life for you. But this way, how can I ever do it?"

"Like hell you can't! Look, Junie . . ."

"No, listen to me, Tom. You'd always be missing Jimmy, don't try to tell me you wouldn't. I've seen you with that baby, and I know how crazy you are about him. You'd always be missing him, and I'd always be feeling rotten because I couldn't have any children for you, to sort of take his place. Can't you see?"

"All I see is, you're just borrowing trouble and talking crazy!"

His voice was muffled, with his face turned nuzzling against one of her soft bare arms.

"Look, honey, if you had sixteen kids they couldn't take Jim's place, that shows how little you know about having kids. Besides, if that's the way you feel about it, you're going to make such a fuss about having kids, we can always adopt one. We can adopt three or four of them if you want to."

"Ah, Tom, don't make fun of me! Anyway, I don't believe in adopting children. Getting some baby, you don't know nothing about what kind of people the parents were or anything. I wouldn't ever do that. There's just no way to work this out!"

"Boy, women!" he murmured affectionately. "You never know what's going on inside a woman's head. Here we are today, having a nice afternoon with the kid, and all the while you're walking around hatching up these crazy ideas. Come on, snap out of it, honey."

"Don't laugh, Tom. You don't even try to understand how I feel. Just try to look at it from my way for a minute, can't you? Don't you suppose all the time we were married, every time Jimmy came to visit, I'd always think of it, that no matter what kind of a wife she'd been to you, she was still a better wife than I could ever be, because she had children for you!"

"Junie! Boy, you're a killer! Look, honey, I'm not going to listen to any more of this crazy talk. You're just having an off day today. You and Jimmy get along just fine together, it tickles me to death. Today you got to looking at him and thinking about it, and it just happened to hit you all wrong. You'll get over it, honey."

"Will I, Tom? Oh, will I?"

"Sure you will, honey."

They kissed, their voices murmuring together, and then he pushed her over suddenly to make room and lay down beside her on the bed, their bodies close, her head upon his shoulder.

"Tom?" she said.

"Hummm?"

"Tom, I was just thinking. Maggie sounds like such a funny kind of a person. She doesn't sound like the kind of a person that would like being tied down with kids and everything. Besides, she's still young enough to marry again and have another family. So I was just thinking. Maybe after we're married she'd let Jimmy come and live with us. You think she would?"

"Maggie? Naw!" He laughed softly. "Honey, you just don't know Maggie. If there's one thing in the whole world she's really crazy about, it's that kid. She'd sooner jump in the ocean than give him up to come and live with me! Where's the god-damn button anyway?"

"Here, let me, you'll tear it! Tom? Listen, Tom. But if she's such a screwball like you say and everything, it don't seem to me that she'd take very good care of poor little Jimmy. So maybe if you was to bring all that up in court, why . . ."

62)

His hands suddenly stopped still and the room was very quiet, and even the party noise from the house next door seemed to have ceased abruptly.

"Junie, you don't understand," he said. "Maggie takes wonderful care of that kid, she always has. Maybe she hasn't got any system about anything else, but she sure has about the kid. He eats on time and he goes to bed on time and he's scrubbed and everything just right. You always got to say that for her, she's a wonderful mother. She's got a lot of screwy ideas about bringing him up maybe, but I figure I can handle that, the time he spends with me. Look, listening to me, I guess you just got the one side to the picture. Maggie's got a hell of a lot of faults, sure, but believe me, along with it, she's a really sweet terrific gal!"

"Aw, Tom, I shouldn't have said that, I'm sorry. I didn't mean anything, I just thought . . ."

He still lay motionless.

"You know, that's something I never even thought of before," he said in a bewildered voice. "I never dreamed you'd feel so strong about it, Junie. Boy, wouldn't that be something, to have Jimmy to live with us!"

"Ah, Tommy, wouldn't it be wonderful, darling?"

His hands began to move again, automatically, upon her body.

"Yeah, boy, that sure would be something!"

And in the window came a sudden burst of whooping hearty male laughter from next door.

"Listen to that crazy Jack!" she giggled.

six

THE WIND still blew.

Back in the house on Juniper Street, Maggie had finally gotten around to the stack of dirty dishes in the kitchen sink. In the uncompromising light from overhead, she scrubbed and scratched at them fiercely, blinking her reddened eyelids defiantly against tears that she refused to shed.

On the beach, the coffee stall was closed and dark, the front securely boarded against the steady onslaught of the sea wind. George, the counter man, was already sleeping in a musty, dilapidated apartment house nearby, a small still mound beside the mountainous bulk of his wife under the covers of a sagging double bed.

But Dickie was still awake.

In his own apartment, miles away, he was reclined upon a divan that he had spread into an impromptu bed, his handsome boyish face intent upon the book that he was reading. He sighed all at once and closed the book over his finger to mark the place. He reached up behind his head to the glaring floor lamp and pushed the top of it a quarter turn away on its swivel. The light was too bright for reading, and he closed his eyes, rubbing at them gently.

He put down the heavy volume of collected plays and lighted a cigarette from a package on the coffee table. Suddenly, he swung his bare legs out from under the blanket to the floor, turning to poke dubiously at a loose spring of the divan that humped up beneath the upholstery, just where he had been lying.

The living room was small and filled with the characterless hodgepodge of a cheap furnished apartment. There was a tiny immaculate kitchenette at one end of it, and, at the other, an open door into a microscopic bathroom. The whole place was tidy and very clean, with a scattering of bright-colored cushions and several prints fastened to the drab walls with Scotch tape. A great bouquet of shaggy white daisies arranged in a water pitcher stood on the coffee table. There were five or six large photographs around the room, some fastened to the walls, others standing in easel frames on table tops. Most of them were of Dickie himself, several were of other handsome smiling young men. The low bookcase against the wall held a few worn volumes and a stack of bright-jacketed paper-backed editions. The rest of the shelves and the top of it were crowded with figurines, wooden, metal, ceramic and glass, in various sizes and conceptions, stances and poses, but all of them horses.

Dickie coughed, strangling the sound in his throat, and put out the cigarette in a mottled pottery ash tray. He looked longingly at the little radio on the table, and then got up swiftly, crossing the room quietly in his bare feet. He stopped by the closed door, bending his head to listen intently. There was no sound at all from the other side of it.

He went to the window, leaning there with his arms braced against the sill. The apartment was on the third floor of the old building jutting out from the steep hillside, so he looked down over treetops to the thousands of sparkling city lights of Hollywood stretching away far below. The night was cool and clear, the lights twinkled starlike in the darkness, a crowded complex galaxy beyond the tossing black tree limbs. He looked out for a long time; then he shivered suddenly and lowered the window.

He walked on to the bathroom, turning on the lights there.

He studied his own reflection earnestly in the mirror above the washbowl, carefully arranging the careless disarray of his dark curly hair over his forehead, peering at himself full face and either profile. He became enrapt, and completely absorbed in what he was doing, trying a variety of expressions, one after another, upon his handsome mobile face, standing back on tip-toe and looking over his shoulder in the small mirror to see as much as possible of his tanned, smooth-muscled torso, naked above his white underwear shorts. And at the end finally, he sighed and leaned in close to the mirror, resting his forehead for a moment against the cool glass, the reflected face smiling sadly against the real one. And then he washed his hands briskly and methodically beneath a faucet, drying them on a towel before he turned off the lights.

Back in the living room, he walked directly to the closed door. He listened once more, and turned away. He circled slowly once around the room and returned, inexorably. This time, his hand reached out toward the doorknob and hovered there, until at last he took hold of it, turning it carefully and delicately without sound.

He pushed the door ajar a little and released the knob with the same infinite care. Through the crack of the door came now the sound of deep, rhythmic, heavy breathing from the darkness within. Inch by inch, ever so carefully, he pushed the door silently open.

The golden light slashed in around him and came to rest at a sharp geometric angle across the bed on the far side of the small inner room. Dickie stood rigid where he was in the doorway, without motion, without even seeming to breathe.

Inside, the stranger from the coffee stall lay sprawling on his back across the bed, his pale hair white in the dim light, a sheet pulled partly over him and one leg dangling off the bed side, relaxed and limp with the bare arched foot only an inch or so above the floor. He did not stir nor did the rhythm of his heavy breathing break or alter, and after a moment Dickie crept soundlessly a little nearer.

The sleeper's sunburned chest and shoulders were dark against the bed. One of his big muscular arms was doubled and flung above his head, the limp fingers curling up from the palm. Sleeping, he appeared smaller, strangely, back in proper scale, and his face, tipped away from the heavy columnar symmetry of his throat, was very young and peaceful and innocent, his mouth a little open.

He did not move, his deep steady breathing did not change, and Dickie suddenly sank noiselessly to his knees beside the bed. He crouched there for a long time, his face gentle and brooding and wistful as he looked. Finally, with the greatest caution, ever so slowly, he stretched out his hand barely to touch the shaggy pale hair delicately with the very tip of his finger.

At the same instant, he saw the sudden shine of opened eyes behind the pale stubby lashes. He jerked his hand away, his body drawing together in panic, the boards creaking under him and his knees thumping against the floor as he scrambled hastily to his feet.

"I just came in to see if you were all right," he said, his voice a dry whisper in the room.

The man on the bed did not move at all, but his eyes were open and the sound of his heavy breathing was stilled.

"After you ate, you passed out again. I thought I'd better come and see," Dickie said rapidly in the same dry desperate whisper.

The man on the bed moved one hand, scratching his flat belly leisurely, but he did not speak.

Dickie cleared his throat nervously, but, even so, when he spoke again his voice was pitched still only the barest notch above a whisper.

"Maybe you don't even remember. I was in that hamburger place on the beach when you came in. I talked to you outside and you said you hadn't any money or a place to stay so I offered you a place here with me tonight. You sort of passed out in the car coming in, but I got you awake enough to get upstairs. You ate supper and passed out again and I put you to bed in here. That was why I came in to see if you were all right, I . . ."

"Sure I remember," the man said suddenly, in a normal tone that seemed by contrast booming loud in the room.

He grinned and then stretched voluptuously, lifting both his doubled arms with the thick, tufted, pale hair at the armpits, raising his narrow hips up from the bed under the sheet and slowly lowering them again.

"Hey, that was some feed you gave me," he said, appreciatively. "I bet I drank two quarts of milk, didn't I? I sure needed that chow."

"I guess you were really hungry."

Some of the tension began to leave Dickie's body as he edged farther away from the bed cautiously, and he began to speak a little more loudly.

"My name's Dick Whitfield, and this apartment is in Hollywood in case you'd like to know."

"Hi," he said carelessly, with his easy grin. "You can call me Stush if you want to. Everybody calls me Stush."

He yawned with his mouth wide for a moment.

"Well, seeing you're all right, you'd probably like to sleep some more now," Dickie said. "I just thought I ought to look and make sure you were all right."

"Yeah, sleep's a good idea," Stush said. "Say, it's pretty nice of you, letting me stay here like this. I bet I got your bed too, huh?"

"No, that's all right," Dickie said quickly. "I've got another bed out in the other room. It's perfectly all right."

"I still say it's pretty nice of you. California sure is a great place all right."

He stretched out his arm suddenly, over the side of the bed.

"Come here," he said.

Dickie's whole body was rigid and unbreathing again in an instant.

"Come on over here. Come on!"

Dickie at last took one tentative step closer.

Stush yawned once more.

"Naw," he said impatiently. "Get down here close like you were before."

Dickie came slowly and helplessly, his face wary and wondering, fascinated and half-frightened, but he came, dropping down again stiffly and awkwardly to his knees beside the bed.

Stush stretched out his arm, his thick fingers moving along the stiffened bones of Dickie's smooth bare back.

"So you like me, huh?" he said, grinning again, his voice amused. "Well, what you so scared of, then? Relax, why don't you? Relax!"

Under his hand, Dickie's body was trembling. Stush reached out his arm further, pulling Dickie in close to him over the edge of the bed.

"What you so scared of?" he said complainingly. "You never made love with anybody before, or something?"

Dickie's voice was the merest breathless whisper.

"You mean you're . . ."

Stush laughed, his great free loud laughter that filled the room.

"Honey, I just don't let it worry me. I'm the double tread, reversible, three-speed model. I like the girls, sure. And sometimes I like the boys. What I really like is a lot."

He spread out his big hand along the side of Dickie's face and shook his head back and forth playfully.

"You're shaking like a leaf," he said. "You're scared to death. Boy, you sure must want it bad, bringing me home with you as scared as you are!"

And then he added abruptly, his voice exultant, "And that's good, baby."

His hand moved, his fingers quickly and cruelly grabbing into

(69

Dickie's thick curly hair, as he pulled his face down to his. He kissed him strong and demandingly. All in the one motion, with his mouth still pressed upon Dickie's, he slid over and pulled him effortlessly up onto the bed into his arms.

seven

A FEW BLOCKS below Dick Whitfield's apartment, toward the bottom of the steep plunging hillside, was the Strip, a broad band of glittering, pastel-colored neon light in the darkness. There was a noisy flow of automobile traffic there, between the double row of smart restaurants and night clubs, clothing, antique and decorator shops, the expensive photographic studios, and the offices of a myriad of actors' agents.

At the edge of a little parking apron beside one of the small night-club buildings, Maggie Harrison's young brother Bud shared brackish milky coffee and a sack of hamburgers with Gus, his fellow parking attendant.

Inside the club, the floor show was in progress, and for the moment they had no work to do. Gus sat on a folding camp stool, munching at a hamburger, a comic book spread open across his knees, and Bud stood in front of him, at a vantage point from which he could watch the entrance to the club.

"Somebody's coming out," he said suddenly, with no particular interest. "Hey, you know this is the first walk-out they've had on the new show?"

Gus looked over his shoulder, chewing methodically.

"Guy must be loaded. Yeah, look, he's really stewed."

"I'll take it," Bud said. "I think it's that red Jag I parked up the hill."

He handed his paper cup of coffee to Gus and trotted off toward the couple who waited in the bright lights of the entrance way. The man was noticeably unsteady, he held himself erect with one hand against the wall for balance. His youthful face was good-natured and vacuous beneath a crew haircut, and he wore a rumpled tweed jacket over gray flannels. But it was the girl who stood quietly on the steps behind him, at whom Bud was looking as he approached.

She was small, her body as thin and flat as a young boy's. She wore a short white dress with narrow shoulder straps and a wide petticoated skirt, and carried a black coat over her arm. Her face was pale with enormous eyes accentuated by slanted pencil lines, and her hair was dark, cropped close and smooth to her small, perfectly shaped head. She stood quietly with the utmost composure, her head lifted, poised and proud, above her childishly bony, bare shoulders.

Bud heard her clear unhurried voice just as he came up to them.

"Don't be silly, Bubber," she was saying. "Of course I can drive it."

"It's a red Jaguar. Hurry it up, will you?" the man said to Bud. "Yes, sir."

As Bud turned away, he heard the man saying expansively, "Honey, I don't let anybody drive it. This is one kitty that nobody knows how to stroke but me."

Bud loped along the sidewalk to the corner and turned off to his right up the narrow, dark side street. He ran easily and lightly, even up the steep hillside. It was a block and a half before he found the flamboyant sports car wedged in between other cars with its wheels to the curb beneath the tall old trees. Bud signaled to another of his cohorts stationed farther up the hill, and climbed into the low-slung leather seat. His face was pleased and admiring as the motor started readily with a powerful, throaty, humming sound. He maneuvered the car out carefully into the street, backing down a little to a driveway where there was just room to turn the car around. He gunned up the motor then with a great roar and shot off down the hill, grinning to himself.

"Nice kitty!" he said satirically. "How you like the way I pet you for a change?"

At the intersection below, he brought the car to a smooth stop and then edged out its long sleek nose, waiting for a chance to turn left against the steady traffic. He tramped on the gas pedal suddenly and shot around with seconds to spare. He repeated the maneuver in front of the club, swinging the car onto the parking apron and bringing it to a jaunty stop before the entrance way. He set the hand brake and slid out from under the wheel, leaving the car door open.

The man moved, but the girl was quicker. She came down the steps, wearing the black coat now, and slid onto the seat, her small hands reaching out competently to the steering wheel.

"Thank you," she murmured to Bud as he trotted around the back of the car to open the door on the other side. But the man followed after her to the right-hand side instead, balancing himself against the fender of the car.

"I told you, Caro," he said impatiently. "Nobody ever drives this car but me. Move over."

She looked up at him, her face tilting, the wide sleeves of her taffeta coat falling away from her thin bare arms lifted over the steering wheel.

"Listen to me, Bubber," she said softly. "You've had too many drinks. Do you want to smash up this car, too?"

"What do you mean?" he said, his voice suddenly pugnacious.

"So I had a few drinks, I'm perfectly all right and I'm not going to smash up any car. Now get over like I tell you."

He pushed at her shoulders and instantly she dropped her hands from the steering wheel. She slid across the seat and out the open door, all in one swift graceful motion, and stood up beside the car on the other side.

"Boy," she called to Bud composedly in her clear voice. "Would you get me a taxi, please?"

While Bud hesitated, the man half fell into the car.

"Come on, get in here," he said. "What in hell's the matter with you, Caro?"

She wrapped the loose coat about her, folding her thin childish arms to hold it in place. She looked back at him, turning her small proud head deliberately, her face disdainful and disgusted.

"I won't ride with you," she said. "If you're determined to smash yourself up, Bubber, go ahead. I'm going home in a cab."

"Listen, don't make a scene," the man said quickly. "If there's anything I hate, it's girls that make scenes."

He slid over, and with surprising speed and coördination he reached out of the car and caught hold of one of her wrists.

Without moving at all, except to tilt her chin a little higher, she said, "Good night, Bubber. Don't call me again. I can't think of a duller way to spend an evening than to go out with you."

His face wrinkled like an angry baby's, and he tightened his fingers cruelly over her thin wrist.

"You needn't flatter yourself," he said. "I only took you out tonight to please Helen, what do you think? Now shut your mouth and get in the car and quit acting like a stupid bitch!"

He began to pull at her and she resisted with all her strength, her small body braced and rigid.

"Boy, could you hurry with that taxi?" she said, panting, and her voice much less assured.

Bud moved then, walking closer to them slowly, with Gus drifting along a few paces behind.

(73

"I wouldn't do that, fellow," Bud said quietly. "You're going to hurt her."

"Listen, buster, you tend to your car parking and stay out of this," the man in the car said angrily.

Bud made one short, quick, chopping motion with his open hand, just the edge of it striking upon the man's forearm, and the girl jerked her wrist free.

"Bud, lay off!" Gus wailed softly. "You're going to get in trouble."

"You're in trouble all right, you son of a bitch!"

The man floundered in his attempt to scramble out of the car, and in that instant, the girl darted away to the curb, waving frantically.

A yellow cab cut in to the edge of the parking apron, its brakes squealing, the door swinging open. She climbed in swiftly without once looking back and slammed the door behind her. The next moment the cab was gone again, pulling away to merge with the steady flow of traffic in the street.

They watched it disappear, all three of them, and the man in the car said, "Aaah, the hell with it! I'll take care of you later, buster!"

He righted himself at the wheel, releasing the brake and gunning the motor. Suddenly the low red car hurtled forward, shooting out into the busy street. Brakes screamed, there was a crash of metal as a bumper gashed into one of the sleek shining red fenders, and an outraged male voice yelled over the traffic sounds, "What you think you're doing, you crazy . . ."

But the red sports car was already out of sight.

"Cripes, Bud, what's the idea anyway?" Gus said. "You trying to lose your job or something?"

"Well, what are you supposed to do, for gosh sakes," Bud said crossly. "She looked like a nice kid. I didn't blame her for not wanting to ride with that character. He was stewed to the ears, you see the way he pulled out of here just now?"

74)

"Yeah, nice kid," Gus said cynically. "You notice the slick way she beat it and left you holding the sack with her boy friend, too. She didn't even wait to say thank you. Real sweet kid!"

"There's the show break," Bud said. "Here we go."

The small entrance way was immediately clogged with people.

As they ran, Gus said, "You know, that stew bum is just the type to turn out to be a bosom pal of old Alison's, too."

"All right. All he can do is fire me, so let him," Bud said. "What's yours, sir?"

They worked steadily after that, the frantic tortuous process of bringing cars down the hillside, one after another, and through the heavy traffic of the street to the parking apron. But gradually the impatient crowd of people waiting at the club entrance dwindled. The two o'clock closing hour passed, and finally the last late stragglers toward the end of the night's work.

"You doing anything, Bud?" Gus called to him. "Want to come over to my place for a while and drink some beer with the guys?"

"Not tonight, Gus," Bud called back. "I got a date to play a guy at one o'clock tomorrow so I better get to bed. Thanks anyway."

While he was still speaking, he saw the trim little blue car pulling in from the street, and he recognized her instantly, the distinction of her smooth dark head. But for no reason that he was able to identify, he turned quickly away, pretending that he had not seen her come at all, as his fingers fumbled with the stacks of coins that he counted out on the narrow ledge for the tip pool.

There was the sound of the motor as she stopped the car behind him, and then her clear voice calling out, "Hello?"

"Hey, Bud, it's your girl friend," Gus muttered in his ear. "Driving a special job and everything! You're doing all right, kid!"

Bud turned and walked toward the car, his heartbeats thumping loudly in his ears.

The little open car was bright blue colored and scaled to her

(75

size. She sat erect upon the seat, wearing a white leather jacket and a vivid blue scarf knotted at her throat.

"Hello," she said again.

"Hi," Bud said awkwardly. "Did you get home all right?"

"Yes, thank you," she said. "You were terribly nice. Bubber's such a fool when he's drinking. He didn't make any trouble for you, did he? I mean, he didn't go telling stories about you to Kim Alison, did he?" she hurried on before Bud could answer her. "I thought I'd better come over and see about it. Because I can fix it if he did. Kim Alison's a friend of my sister's."

"No, it's all right," Bud said. "He left right after you did. He didn't do anything."

Then he said, "I think it's pretty swell of you though to come back here to find out about it."

"Don't be silly. You were terribly nice and I didn't even say thank you."

She looked up at him directly with her huge, extravagantly made-up eyes.

"I'd like to thank you. Could I buy you a cup of coffee when you're through work?"

"Go ahead, Bud," Gus muttered delightedly from just behind him. "I'll finish up here, go ahead."

"That's swell," Bud said embarrassedly. "But you don't have to do that, I mean, unless you . . ."

"Don't you want to?" she said in her grave clear voice.

"Oh, sure!" Bud said. "I just mean, No, that would be swell."

"Good," she said serenely. "I expect you've got a car so why don't we go in yours. I live just a few blocks from here so we could drop my car off at home."

"Right," Bud said. "I'll follow you then, okay? I'll get my car, it's parked down below. It won't take a minute."

"All right."

Bud ran, plunging recklessly out into the traffic in the middle of the block, fumbling for the car keys in his pocket as he went.

His old convertible was parked just below the street. The motor was cold and he coaxed it impatiently until he got it into gear. When he drove up to the intersection, she was watching for him from across the way. She waved and indicated the direction before she drove out into the street.

The traffic was lighter at this hour, so that Bud was able to execute a left turn and fall in, just one car behind hers. He edged over into the center lane, but without looking back she lifted her arm high in a right-turn signal and he pulled back again. It was several blocks, however, before she actually made the turn into a side street, with Bud swinging around the corner behind her to follow. She drove fast and competently, the gay little blue car shuttling through the dark, quiet, well-kept streets.

After a few more blocks, she dropped her arm suddenly in a stop signal and turned in sharp at a driveway. Her car glided away behind shrubbery at the side of a house, and Bud pulled in slowly to the curb in front. He looked about him curiously then, at the hushed dark street with tree limbs meeting overhead, the huge immaculately painted stucco houses set side by side with small well-tended lawns about them.

Bud looked, and hastily opened the glove compartment in front of him and pulled out a wad of rag. He scrubbed at the worn car seat with it, carefully wiping away the drops of moisture and a little sand.

She came a moment later, running lightly down the drive in her tight short black trousers, swinging a little pouch purse of the same white leather as her jacket.

"I put the car in the garage, I don't know why I was so tidy," she said as she climbed in beside him. "Then I had to hunt my purse. Was I very long?"

"No, that's all right," Bud said. He took a last dubious look at the big house, standing dark and elegant in the midst of its manicured shrubbery.

"You sure it's all right for you to come out like this?" he said hesitantly. "It's pretty late. I wouldn't want you to get in trouble or anything."

"Don't be silly," she said. "There's no one home but me. My sister's in Palm Springs this week end and she took the children. It isn't as though I had to keep hours anyway. I'm older than I look, you know. I expect I'm older than you are. What's your name?"

"Bud," he said. "Bud O'Toole. What's yours?"

"I expect Bud's a nickname, isn't it? What's your name really?"

"Michael," Bud said. "I was named after my father, so they started calling me Bud when I was little. I guess I'm so used to it, I never stop to think. But my name is really Michael."

"Michael's a nice name," she said. "I think I'd like to call you Michael. Do you think your father would mind?"

"Huh?" Bud said. "Gosh, no! Anyway, he's dead. He's been dead for years. What's your name?"

She looked at him, with the slow, deliberate, graceful gesture that she made out of the simple turning of her head.

"My name is Annise," she said.

Bud swung the car around a corner, staring through the windshield into the dim puddle of light that traveled before them.

"That's a pretty name," he said carefully. "But I guess you have a nickname, too. I heard that character keep calling you Caro tonight."

For the fraction of a second, she was still, and then she laughed, a gay tinkling burst of laughter.

"This is always happening to me," she said. "I make up the nicest names for myself and then I get found out before I have a chance to enjoy them. I expect it's childish, it's just that my real name is so dull. Caroline! Bubber's known me forever, that's why he calls me Caro like my family does."

"I think Caro is pretty," Bud said. "I think it's prettier than Annise."

"Do you, Michael?" she said.

She reached out her small hand to his arm suddenly.

"Michael, you're not thinking that I'm a liar now, are you?" she said urgently. "Just because of this silly business about telling you my name. Please don't think that I'm a liar."

"No, of course not," Bud said reassuringly, his face a little bemused. "People are always doing things like that about their names. Hardly anybody ever likes the name they've got. It doesn't mean you're a liar. Why should I think you're a liar?"

"Ah, good!"

She sank back again on the seat beside him.

"I expect it's just that I'm sensitive about it," she said pensively. "Because I used to be such a ghastly liar. I used to tell lies all the while, it was awful. But I don't do it any more, it's been two years now. Truly."

"Oh," Bud said.

"Except about my name once in a while and I think I'm going to make myself stop doing that, too. I did make myself stop lying, you know. It wasn't the psychiatrist, I really did it by myself."

"You did?" Bud said.

She nodded.

"Once I really understood about it, it was easy," she said, wisely. "Do you know why people tell lies, Michael? Because they simply cannot bear themselves, the way they are. It's terribly strange, how you have to work these things out for yourself, and once you do, they seem so easy. I've been to two, no, it's three, psychiatrists now, quite good ones. My sister dotes on psychiatrists. Anyway, you know what psychiatrists are like. Emotionally mature, emotionally mature, they say it over and over like a record that's gotten stuck. And you know, it wasn't until just lately that I think I've finally thought it out by myself, what they mean by being mature. It isn't anything so terribly witchcraft mysterious. It's simply being able to bear yourself, and everything in the world around you, just the way it all really is. Don't you think that's it, Michael?"

(79

"I don't know," Bud said. "I never thought much about it, I guess. It sounds right to me."

"Good," she said. "It sounds right to me, too. My sister says that I talk too much, so now it's your turn to talk."

Bud grinned weakly.

"Right now I can't seem to think of anything to say. You go ahead and talk some more."

"You are terribly nice," she said. "See, you can just sit quietly and be something. That's the thing I can't do. It's why I talk all the while like this, trying to prove what I am to people. Trying to prove something to myself too, I expect. I wonder. That's something I'll have to think more about."

"Seems like you do an awful lot of thinking, you know that?" Bud said, grinning again.

"That's true," she said seriously. "Anyway, tell me about you, Michael. What do you do? Do you go to school?"

"Not any more," Bud said. "Not since I finished high school in February, I mean. My family sort of wants me to go to college, my sister especially. I guess I just don't see it that way."

She pulled herself up on the seat, kneeling to face him with her legs folded under her.

"You know, you're perfectly right, Michael. I went this last year, to quite a good school in the East. I never felt sillier in my whole life! Children and idiots! I won't go back. I've decided that the only thing is to somehow do it for yourself, only there's so much of it to do. I'm trying to be terribly methodical about it. This week I've gotten up to Schopenhauer."

She laughed again, her gay chiming laughter.

"I've been reading Collette along with him. For the woman's point of view, you know. What's your very favorite book, Michael? I think mine is *The Magic Mountain*, at least for right now it is."

"I don't read books very much," Bud said. "I did when I was

in school, the stuff you have to, you know, but since then I haven't. I guess I should."

"No," she said. "If you don't, it's probably because you don't need to. What do you do, Michael? Tell me what you really do?"

"Oh, I don't know," he said slowly and self-consciously, frowning a little. "I guess what I really do the most of and what I really like the best of anything is just playing tennis."

"Wonderful!" she said. "I knew it! Do you play well?"

"I'm pretty good," he said offhandedly. "And my game is still developing, that's the important thing. I got a long way to go though, I don't know. Sometimes I don't know whether I'll ever make top tournament play or not. Anyway, it's the one thing I really like to do. That's why I'm a car-park nights, so I can play tennis every day."

"There now, you see, Michael," she said in a pleased voice. "I was right about you. I can always tell, just by looking at people, when they do something. With you, it's playing tennis. I think it's wonderful. You're very lucky, you know."

Bud laughed.

"You're sure a relief after all that 'tennis bum' stuff that people are always handing out to me!"

"Do people do that? They shouldn't. It's the most important thing in the world to find the one thing you really like to do, and then do it, regardless of everything and everybody. That's why I think you're so terribly lucky to have found the thing you like to do already. It's being much harder for me."

"Yeah, what about you?" Bud said. "What do you do? When you're not going to school or thinking or reading books?"

"That's just it," she said dismally. "I don't do anything, not really. It's terribly hard to decide. The thing that would be the easiest for me to do, is be in motion pictures, but . . ."

She looked up at him quickly with her long doe eyes.

"Ah, Michael, now you think I'm lying again, don't you? I

didn't mean that exactly the way it sounded. If you'll let me explain . . ."

"No," Bud said softly. "You don't have to explain that to me, and I don't either think you're lying. The minute I saw you standing there on those steps tonight, I knew you could be in pictures if you wanted to be. Honest."

"Michael, you're very sweet," she said. "I meant to ask you this before, you're not gay, are you? Please tell me now if you are."

"You mean a queer?" Bud's face was thunderstruck. "Well, for Pete sakes! If you're not the funniest girl I ever met in my life!"

"Don't be silly," she said. "It just happens that the only other two really attractive men I've met in the last six months were gay. That's why I asked you. Are you?"

"No, I'm not," Bud said shortly.

"Good," Caro said. "I'm not either. In case you wondered. No, what I was going to explain about being in motion pictures. You see, until he died, my father was a picture producer for a long time.

"Before taxes, too," she added with a small wry face.

"And my sister used to be married to a man who's still a producer. She knows hordes of people, which is very important. And then it just happens that I photograph quite a bit better than I am. I've even been to dramatic school for a year."

She stopped to laugh.

"That was back when I was being such a really awful liar, right at the worst of it, and my sister was at her wits' end. I expect she thought dramatic school might be a way to legalize my failing. I didn't specially mind going."

"Don't you want to be in pictures?" Bud said.

"No, I don't," she said. "I know enough about it since dramatic school to know that I'm not cut out to be an actress, not really an actress. So what would be the use of me being in pictures? I want so much to really do something. I'd like to dance or write or paint. I know that sounds childish. If I were cut out to do any of those things, I'd be doing them right now instead of talking about it. It makes it terribly difficult, because those are the things that I have the greatest respect for. And you have to do something. If you don't, you're not anything, and the days slip away, and finally you're lost."

She slid over closer on the seat.

"Anyway, I expect some day I'll find out what it is, the thing I really like to do, like playing tennis is for you. I hope I find it soon, it's very hard until you do."

"Hey, look where we are," Bud said. "It's just force of habit with me. We were talking and I kept driving and now here we are at the beach. I live out here, so I just drive to the beach automatically."

"I'm glad you did," Caro said. "It's so beautiful. Look, Michael, the moon's just setting."

"How about that coffee we were going to have? Maybe you'd rather drive back to some place in town?"

"I don't really want any coffee, do you?" she said. "I only said coffee because it sounds a little more sensible than just walking up to someone that you don't know and saying that you'd like to talk to them. Though I don't see why it should be, do you?"

"I don't want any coffee either," Bud said.

Then he added, a little tentatively, "We could park here on the beach for a while if you'd like to. It's still sort of windy, but it's pretty to look out at the ocean."

"Good, let's do that," she said readily. "I don't mind the wind, I like it. That's a very good idea, Michael."

Bud slowed the car down, drifting along past a scattering of parked cars without lights that dotted the public beach, all facing out to sea. He found an empty spot where there were no other cars close, and turned in across the rough, dusty parking area. He stopped the car at the very edge of the low bluff, with the narrow rocky beach below, and farther on, the great expanse of

(83

restless water, shining and shimmering in the light of the round waning moon.

"Ah, Michael, Michael, it's so beautiful!" Caro said. "Don't we seem silly and unimportant beside all of that? But in another way, it's like a knife that keeps jabbing into you. Because it does make us seem so insignificant and meaningless, and we're here and alive for such a very little time, we have to do something besides just eat and breathe and sleep and die! We have to be something!"

She stopped, and then she said, "Michael, why don't you kiss me? You sit there staring at me and thinking about it, and you're not hearing a word that I'm saying."

"You are a funny girl," Bud said, with a shade of anger in his voice. "Do you want me to kiss you?"

Her small proud head lifted.

"Yes, Michael. I think it might be nice."

She came to him, reaching her arms about his neck. Bud took hold of her carefully and a little awkwardly, as though she were the first girl, rather than the dozenth or so one, that he had ever kissed upon this same car seat at this same stretch of beach beneath the moon.

They kissed, with their faces clinging and lingering together. The wind blew in soft gusts, the great sea stirred, and upon the highway behind them a huge trailer-truck came thundering around a black curve of headland, shining silver in the bright moonlight, and was gone again with a final constellation of red and green lights disappearing into the darkness.

Caro moved first, turning her face away suddenly, and pushing herself apart from him with her hands upon his arms.

"See, Michael, it was very nice, wasn't it?" she said softly and a little breathlessly.

Bud gathered both her small hands gently into his large ones. Her fingers were cold and very small, delicate bone under soft skin, and tipped with tiny, pale, round, smooth, unpainted nails.

"What about that character you were out with tonight?" Bud said. "What about him?"

"Poor Bubber," she said. "He's such a fool, you know, even when he isn't drinking. Once in dog's years we go out together, because his sister and my sister are such good friends. I've known Bubber forever, ever since swimming class when we were children."

Bud closed his hands, tight and warm, over hers.

"Caro," he said wonderingly. "Caro's a really terrific name and it's just right for you. Don't ever go around trying to change it any more."

And then he said humbly, "Gosh, I don't even know what to say to you. I guess everybody's already told you a million times how beautiful you are."

She slipped her hand away and lifted it for a second to his cheek.

"Nice Michael," she said gravely, looking up with her enormous, long, dark eyes.

He reached to take her into his arms again, and she said quickly, "I expect I'd better tell you, Michael. I like kissing you but I don't want to do anything else. I mean, I don't sleep with anybody. I thought you ought to know."

Bud laughed, his cheek resting against the top of her smooth head.

"You are the funniest girl," he said tenderly. "Don't you know you don't have to go around telling a guy stuff like that? Guys like to take it the way it comes and find out things themselves. Besides, how can you really tell ahead of time what you'll want to do, or not want to do?"

"I know I won't do it, no matter what," she said. "That's why it seemed only fair to tell you. Michael, this is something else I lean over backwards about. Because there was a time for a while

(85

when I used to sleep with almost anybody, you know. I'm not like that any more. It's been quite a long time now. I'm not going to be like that ever again."

And then she said, "I expect you don't like me telling you this, Michael. Men are so terribly funny about these things. Does it make you think of me entirely differently?"

Bud held her gently, and laughed again.

"You're the funniest little thing I ever saw! You know, you better buckle down and start thinking again and getting to work some more on this story-telling business."

She leaned away from him to see into his face.

"Don't you believe me, Michael?" she said quietly.

"Uh-uh," he said. "There's some things a guy can just tell about a girl, no matter what kind of stories she tries to give him. Of course, mostly they tell stories the other way around, but still you can always tell. That's why I know you were making up what you just said."

She looked at him gravely for a moment, and then once again she lifted her hand to his cheek.

"Good sweet Michael!" she said, with a little catch in her voice.

They kissed again, gently and tenderly, for a long time.

"I've never known a girl like you before, Caro," Bud whispered. "I guess I never felt just like this before either."

She nestled close to him, her head upon his shoulder.

"Look, Michael," she said. "The moon is nearly gone. It looks almost as though the sea were taking it back again. Do you know what they say, Michael, that the moon used to be a part of the earth, the part that used to be right here where the sea is now? Do you suppose it could be true? Isn't it strange to think of it, a piece of this earth, alone and cold, flung away out there in the sky?"

"Gosh, I just don't know what to say to you," Bud murmured. "I guess nothing really like this has ever happened to me before in all my life. It's really wonderful."

"Poor moon," Caro said. "I expect we're all a little like it, looking back to where we used to be and never knowing how to return again. Ah, Michael, I do like you so much, you know."

eight

AT ELEVEN O'CLOCK the next morning, Stush and Dickie were just finishing a leisurely Sunday breakfast. The sun was bright and hot outside and through the windows, shoved open to the tops of their frames, came a noise of traffic and voices and the other busy faraway sounds of daytime activity down the hillside. But the apartment was still dim and cool and airy, and pleasant with soft symphony music coming from the little radio in the living room.

Since Stush alone crowded the tiny kitchenette, Dickie sat cross-legged on the floor at the entrance way with a coffee cup and ash tray, and watched Stush with unconcealed delight. He was sitting at the little drop leaf that served for a table, eating cornflakes and milk, shoveling the heaping dripping spoonfuls of cereal into his mouth with great speed and gusto, and complete absorption. He wore shorts of Dickie's and a dark sports shirt that he had made no attempt to fasten across his wide sunburned chest. His pale hair was still wet from the shower and shining with moisture in the electric light from overhead.

"Well, we could always go to the beach if you'd like to," Dickie said. "It's a lot hotter today, it should be perfect weather at the beach."

Stush picked up the cereal box from the table without answering him, and turned it upside down over his bowl. He shook it and thumped it with his hand, but the box was empty and only a last few flakes of cereal tumbled out.

"Here, you want some more?" Dickie said. He leaned over on one elbow and opened the door of a little cupboard that was stacked with tin cans and grocery supplies. He handed up another full unopened package of the cereal to Stush.

"Hey, looks like I'm eating up everything you got around here," Stush said.

"Don't be silly. Would you like me to cook you some more eggs, too?"

"Naw," Stush said cheerfully. "I'm just tapering off now."

He tore into the thin cardboard top of the box with large, blunt, strong fingers, ripping at the inner paper impatiently, and finally pouring out a great stream of cereal.

"I sure like cornflakes," he said contentedly, his eyes upon the bowl as it filled.

Dickie laughed.

Stush looked up, his face instantly suspicious and on guard. "What's the matter?"

"Ah, Stush, you're wonderful!" Dickie said.

"Yeah, I am for a fact," Stush said, relaxing again and reaching for the milk bottle on the table. "You really go for old Stush, don't you, baby?"

"No, I didn't mean just that," Dickie said. "Everything you do, you're wonderful. I've never seen anyone quite like you before. Everything you do, you seem to do it bigger than other people do, and you get more fun out of it. Even if it's just sitting eating cornflakes."

Stush thought about it for a moment and then went on chewing again.

"Yeah," he said. "That sounds like old Stush all right."

"And then when I think of you yesterday," Dickie went on,

his voice marveling. "There you were, really hungry and just pennies left in your pocket, and drunk and not knowing anybody or any place to go. But you didn't seem to be worried about it. Doesn't anything ever scare you or worry you, Stush?"

"Naw, I don't ever worry," Stush said cheerfully. "Why should you worry, something always turns up. So look at yesterday. You come along, and I did all right, didn't I?"

"Yes. But suppose I hadn't come along?" Dickie said.

"Then somebody else would of, that's all," Stush said serenely, with his mouth full.

"Yes, I suppose you're right."

Dickie's face sobered and he rubbed out a cigarette butt slowly and with great concentration, on the bottom of the ash tray.

"Stush," he said carefully. "Do you really like me at all? Or am I just somebody that came along at the right time to take you in and feed you and give you a place to stay? What do you really feel about me?"

"Listen, let's get something straight, huh?" Stush said, shaking a dripping milky spoon for emphasis. "You and I get along fine, baby. Just don't start in picking at me, okay?"

"All right," Dickie said. "I'm sorry, Stush. I didn't mean to pick at you."

"The thing about me is, I'm a real simple guy," Stush went on expansively, still waving the spoon. "I don't like people starting getting complicated with me, see? That's what Miss Broderick always used to say. She was my drama teacher. She was a smart woman too, I used to screw her pretty regular. She always used to say that—Stush, she'd say, you're the least complicated human being I ever knew. And that's what she meant, that I'm a real simple guy."

"Oh, no!" Dickie said incredulously, and suddenly he began to laugh.

"Yeah, that's just what she used to say," Stush said with his sudden, wide, engaging smile.

(89

He spilled a few more cornflakes into his dish and spooned them down into the milk reflectively.

"Broderick was all right though. She was smart and she was a good woman to go to bed with. But that's what she always used to say. Stush, she'd say . . ."

"Your drama teacher, oh, no!" Dickie said helplessly.

He struck his forehead several times with the palm of his hand.

"Stush, don't tell me," he said, his voice shaking with merriment. "Don't tell me that you're an actor and you've come out here to get in pictures. Don't tell me!"

Stush was suddenly completely still. His big, fluid, catlike body slowly gathered together in the chair, his smile faded out and his pale eyes narrowed in his sunburned face.

"What you laughing at?" he said softly. "I could be an actor, couldn't I? You gave me a lot of crap last night about you being an actor, didn't you?"

"Stush, it's not you I'm laughing at," Dickie said quickly. "I'm not laughing at you being an actor. Honest I'm not. I'm just laughing because it's a—a coincidence. You turn out to be an actor, and I'm an actor, too. Don't you see?"

Stush did not move or speak.

"Don't be mad, Stush," Dickie said. "I wasn't laughing at you, honestly. It's just something that always breaks me up, I can't help but laugh. People come out here all the while to try to get in pictures. They just come out here. I've worked so hard at it for so long, I've had parts in five shows on Broadway, and still I've hung on out here for two years now and practically starved off and on, trying to get a break. And then people just come out here! Stush, believe me, I wasn't laughing at you. I was laughing at myself."

Stush moved at last. He shoved away the empty cereal dish and turned with the chair creaking beneath him, to reach to the shelf for a clean washed glass that was draining there. He filled it to the brim with milk from the bottle on the table.

"Stush, please don't be mad," Dickie said penitently.

Stush snapped his fingers.

"Come on, butt me!"

Dickie hastily handed up the package of cigarettes and matches with it.

"Please, Stush?" he said humbly.

Stush drew deeply on the cigarette, his face expressionless. And then suddenly his body relaxed and he smiled his warm unexpected smile.

"Let me tell you a little secret," he said. "I'm not an actor anyway. Broderick was just the drama teacher in the high school I went to back in Detroit. She talked me into being in three or four of the plays she put on, but I think it's all a lot of bull. So don't get your pants in an uproar over it."

"Well, just as long as you didn't think I was making fun of you or something," Dickie said, his voice relieved.

He watched Stush as he drank with relish, and then refilled the glass, draining the last of the milk from the bottle.

"You know, this gives me an idea though," Dickie said. "I'd like to take you out to the studio with me. They're casting right now for a bit in the picture. I've seen some of the boys who came in, and I think you're about the type they're looking for. How about it, Stush? Why don't you stay here with me for a couple days? I'll get a call from the studio for either Tuesday or Wednesday, it's pretty sure to be Tuesday, and then you'd be here to go out with me. It wouldn't hurt to try. Even if you got it, it wouldn't amount to much, but at least you'd pick up a little money to stake you. How about it?"

Stush stretched leisurely, his big muscular arms lifted on either side of his head, his cigarette dangling out of the corner of his mouth.

"Uhhhm," he mumbled disinterestedly.

"Would you like to do that, Stush?"

Stush slid out from under the table, knocking against it so that all the dishes rattled, and the chair toppling behind him against the edge of the sink. He shuffled his feet, moving very lightly and lithely for a big man. And suddenly he crouched and began to punch into the air, easily at first, then harder, in a kind of stylized shadowboxing, with his body moving fluidly and gracefully and his face withdrawn and lost and far away.

Dickie watched him, his dark eyes nakedly moved and tender.

"Stush, will you stay? Just for a few days anyway?"

Stush jabbed smoothly with his left hand and then threw a long, fast, looping bolo, his face still dreaming.

"Please stay. Will you, Stush?"

"Okay, okay, okay!" he mumbled. He feinted and jabbed a last time and then stopped impatiently, his face coming back into focus once more.

"Listen," he said. "Didn't I tell you to quit picking at me?"

Dickie got up from the floor silently, without looking at him. Because of Stush's strange, larger-than-life quality, Dickie appeared almost small and slight beside him, although he was as tall as Stush and nearly as well-built.

"All right," Stush said. "So I'll hang around for a couple days. Okay! What's the difference, I wasn't going anywhere special anyway. Now quit picking at me!"

Dickie piled dirty dishes into the small sink without speaking.

Stush watched him for a moment, but then with one of his sudden changes of mood, his body relaxed. He rocked up and down on his toes several times, easily and smoothly, and when he spoke again, his voice was good-humored.

"I'm sick of setting around. What we going to do today?"

"What would you like to do?" Dickie said. "We can see a movie or just drive around for a while. Or go out to the beach. Or if you'd rather, we can stay right here."

"Yeah, we could go back to bed some more."

Stush weighed it.

"Naw, I tell you," he said. "Let's go out to the beach for a couple hours first, okay? I could use some sun, sun's real great for baking the booze out of you. Okay?"

"Fine," Dickie said. "You know that anything you want to do is fine with me, Stush."

Stush laughed, his great unrestrained laughter.

When he was through, he reached out his big hand to Dickie's head and shook it back and forth several times playfully.

"Boy, you sure got it bad for old Stush, haven't you, baby!" he said, his face amused.

nine

THE FOLLOWING SATURDAY, Tom Harrison brought Jamie home punctually at five, while yellow sunlight still baked the front of the small house on Juniper Street. Tom parked his shining well-kept automobile smoothly at the curb, and before the car was hardly stopped, Jamie erupted out of the door and ran for the house, his feet in blue and white sneakers pattering up the cement walk. He carried a big, bright-colored, cardboard box and the string attached to a large red balloon that wafted along in the air behind him in a stately progression of starts and jerks.

"Take it easy, cowboy," Tom called after him. "Wait a minute and I'll open the door for you."

But the little boy had managed it already for himself, holding the screen open with his shoulder as he awkwardly maneuvered his box through the doorway, and even the red balloon swam in safely and unhurriedly, just ahead of the slamming door.

(93

Tom followed slowly, his feet dragging and his smooth sun-tanned face somber. He hesitated on the doorstep, hunting cigarettes and a lighter out of the breast pocket of his gaudy red and white sports shirt. The street behind him was deserted, the double row of shabby, old-fashioned, stucco houses squatted face to face amid their lush overgrowth of trees and shrubs and vines, somnolent in the slanting sun. From here and there behind the peaceful stucco façades came the muted sounds from radio and television sets, from farther up the street somewhere there was the drowsy whirr of roller skates and the mournful hoot of a bakery truck whistle. Tom lingered, his forehead wrinkling in frowning concentration. At last he sighed a little and squared his shoulders deliberately as he reached for the handle on the screen door.

Inside, the living room was hot and dim, with the musty maroon velvet drapes closed against the afternoon sun. Grandpa Kennedy, in immaculate white shirt, sat in the old overstuffed chair with a newspaper, electric light shining down upon his neatly combed, sparse white hair. Jamie was leaned against his knees, rummaging into the contents of his cardboard box spread open upon the old man's lap.

"See, Grandpa? Here's the big engine, and these pieces are the track and they go together, like this, see? And there's a whole lot of freight cars that hook together, here's the caboose, see, Grandpa? Are you looking?"

"Well, what do you know about that!" Grandpa Kennedy said affectionately. "Hello, there, Tom. How are you?"

"And, Grandpa, look! Here's the key right here in the side of the big engine and you wind it up and then it goes on the track like a real train. I want to show my train to Juan. Is Juan over at his house? Where's my mommy?"

"It's a dandy, all right," Grandpa Kennedy said. "Why, your mother's in there in the bathroom, I just heard her turn the shower off. What's new, Tom?"

94)

Jamie scrabbled up the box and ran, streaking away through the archway into the dining room.

"I'm fine, Grandpa. Everything's fine. How've you been?"

Tom leaned against the door jamb, jingling coins in one pocket of his brown slacks.

"Fine as silk," the old man said. "Can't complain about a thing. How's everything over at the shop, Tom?"

"Pretty busy," Tom said. "They got a new model just going on production. I been putting in quite a bit of overtime."

"Good, glad to hear it," Grandpa said. "Sure was hot again today, wasn't it? Seems like it come off summer overnight this year."

"Well, it suits me fine," Tom said. "We're just beginning to get those warm balmy nights over in the Valley again. Seems real great."

Grandpa Kennedy cleared his throat in the silence.

"Won't you come on in and have a chair, Tom?"

"Oh no, no thanks," Tom said quickly. "I can't stay. I got to shove, I . . ."

He moved uneasily, stretching out his arm to brace himself in the doorway, his bright shirt hanging loose from his wide shoulders down over the top of his trousers.

"You still working at the lumber yard, Grandpa?" he said uncomfortably. "They pretty busy over there?"

"I hope to tell you we're busy over there," the old man said importantly. "Nor I don't see any letup coming either, the way building's going up out here."

"I see they're subdividing another big tract over there by Garden Grove somewhere," Tom said.

"That's what I hear," Grandpa said. "Well, I tell you, I never seen anything to equal it in my whole life, the way they keep building out here."

"That's right," Tom said, a little desperately. "Before they're

(95

through, I guess California'll be the first state in the Union. You see if it isn't."

"Oh, it's bound to be. Never seen the equal of it."

The room was still again except for the nervous jingle of coins in Tom's pocket.

"Tom, did you want to see Maggie about something?" Grandpa Kennedy asked mildly.

Tom's face pinkened instantly.

"Oh no, that's all right," he said hastily. "I mean, if she's busy or something, why, I can always . . ."

"I hear her out there in the kitchen, I'll call her," Grandpa said. And then, lifting his voice, "Maggie?"

"Yeah, Grandpa?" she called back from somewhere in the interior of the house.

"Tom's in here waiting to see you, Maggie."

After the smallest pause, she called back, "Be right there!"

A moment later she appeared in the archway, her feet noiseless in straw sandals, a blue cotton, Japanese bath kimono wrapped tightly about her and her damp hair carelessly coiled and pinned upon the top of her head. Jamie trailed after her, still lugging the train box, and plucking at her skirts as they came.

"But, Mommy, why can't I?"

"Because it's supper time, that's why," Maggie said. "Hello, Tom."

"How are you, Maggie?" he said.

"You wanted to see me about something?" she said impersonally, and then she added quickly, "No, that's all right, Grandpa. Sit still."

Grandpa Kennedy sank back in his chair again unhappily under her gaze.

"You're just a no-good mommy at all!" Jamie said darkly.

Maggie's face was scrubbed and pale without lipstick, and unsmiling as she looked at Tom expectantly.

"Why, I guess you're in a hurry to get dressed, I . . ."

96)

"But why can't I, Mommy?" Jamie howled.

"What's he yammering about anyway?" Tom said helplessly.

"He wants to go over next door and show Juan Martinez his new train," Maggie said. "I told him he'd have to wait till after supper."

Grandpa Kennedy bolted out of his chair, his face relieved, and seized the little boy by the hand.

"Now that reminds me," he said hastily. "I been meaning to speak to José about that tree out in the back. We'll just step over there for a minute."

"Okay, you guys, but don't stay now," Maggie called after them as they disappeared through the archway. "Supper's all hot on the stove.

"And, Gramp?" she added, her voice lifting, "If Margie's home, ask her if she wants to baby-sit tonight, will you?"

"Sure thing, Maggie."

They were gone with the diminishing sound of the child's eager voice, and a final bang of the back-door screen. The room was stuffy and hot, and silent except for the throaty chattering of birds outside the house and the dry rasping scrape of the palmetto against the wall.

"He's sure crazy about that little train all right," Tom said at last in a fond voice, his eyes carefully turned away. "The minute he saw it in the toy store, I couldn't even get him to look at anything else, that was it."

"Um hum," she said.

Tom glanced at her quickly out of the corners of his eyes.

"Why, I made extra sure I'd get him back here on time tonight," he said placatingly. "I always hate to hold you up, Saturday night and everything."

"Yeah, I noticed. Thanks," Maggie said briefly.

Her face was downcast, and she poked absently at a ruddy wisp of her hair that straggled over her temple.

Tom's eyes lingered upon her this time.

"You feeling all right, Mag?" he said. "You look kind of peaked. That kidney isn't acting up again, is it?"

"No, I'm fine," Maggie said.

She moved impatiently, walking farther out into the middle of the room, and suddenly she stumbled, tripping over the long skirts of her kimono. She cried out, a soft strangling sound in her throat, and then doubled over, brushing at her face frantically with both hands.

Tom bounded across the room and caught hold of her shoulders.

"Mag, what is it? You got a pain? You faint?"

Maggie sagged in his hands, her face white in the dimness of the room and her breathing fast and shallow. She pointed upward, wordlessly.

Above their heads, the big red balloon, inflated with helium, hovered innocently against the stuccoed ceiling, dangling its long length of string beneath.

"I didn't know that goddamn thing was there," Maggie said, her voice shaken and breathless. "It's so dark in here I didn't see the string. It felt just like a spider on my face."

"Well, that figures," Tom said, with faint amusement in his voice. "Scared to death of spiders! You think they're all black widows, and they're all laying for you. Hey, you're shaking. That really scared you!"

He began to draw her toward his broad chest but Maggie moved away and he stepped backward quickly, suddenly self-conscious.

She moved on swiftly across the room to the big front window.

"Dark as pitch in here," she muttered, yanking at the dusty faded velvet. "And so hot you can't breathe!"

She pulled at the heavy drapes, sliding the rings that supported them back to the ends of the wrought-iron spear that served for a curtain rod. The sunlight sprang in through the big window and paled out the puddle of electric light behind her. Maggie gave a last tug to the ancient drapes, and then sneezed and rubbed her nose in the middle of a cloud of flying dust motes that danced about her in the light.

"You wanted to talk to me about something?" she said, a self-consciousness in her voice, too.

"Oh. Well, yeah," he said. "It's nothing special. I mean, maybe you're in a hurry to get dressed. You're going out or something. Maybe we better make it some other time."

"No, it's all right. I have a dinner date at seven so I've got plenty of time. Go ahead if you want to."

She switched off the floor lamp and helped herself to a cigarette from a package on the table. Tom fumbled in the pocket of his bright shirt for his lighter, but she struck the match herself.

"Yeah," he said, frowning a little. "Okay."

Maggie sank down in the shabby overstuffed chair, stretching out her legs in front of her, and resting her head against the back. She closed her eyes.

"Ooof!" she murmured. "My heart's still pounding. I thought it was a big black spider, big as your hand. With hairy legs!" She shivered and opened her eyes.

"I'm sorry," she said. "Go ahead, Tom."

"Well, I thought there were some things we might talk over, that's all," he said reluctantly.

He lighted a cigarette of his own, and at last he said, "The thing is, all you have to do is listen. There's no sense you getting upset or mad the first thing. It's not going to cost you anything to listen, it's just some ideas I had. You don't like it, all right, that's all there is to it. So there's no use you flying off the handle the first thing."

Maggie lifted her hand, palm upward.

"Who, me?" she said, with delicate incredulity. "But this begins to sound interesting. Go ahead."

Tom's face was reluctant to the last, but he cleared his throat and came forward a step, squaring his shoulders resolutely, towering tall and erect in the middle of the floor. When he began to speak, the words came rapidly and a little too smoothly, as though he might have rehearsed them in his mind many times before.

"Well, the thing is, I guess right now you must be busy making plans for yourself, deciding what you want to do now and everything. That's why I thought this would be a pretty good time for us to get together and talk some things over. I mean, it only stands to reason you'd be making some kind of plans now, the divorce will be final in another few months and everything."

"Stands to reason," Maggie said softly.

"I guess you'll be figuring on getting some kind of a job somewhere pretty soon. Maybe you got it in mind to get out of here after a while and get a place of your own to live in, plans like that."

His voice was tentative at the end.

Maggie extended her legs in front of her and studied her own straw sandals, dangling from her bare feet by the toe thongs.

Tom cleared his throat, his forehead wrinkling.

"Of course, you may think that none of this is any of my business any longer. I guess it isn't either, when you come right down to it."

He stopped again and looked at her questioningly, but Maggie was still engrossed with her sandals, flapping them up and down off the tips of her toes.

"The thing is," he went on, still speaking rapidly and with a rehearsed fluency, "you got to realize it's only natural for me to be interested, and it's only natural for me to want to help you get started again any way I can. You know I mean that, don't you, Maggie? Well, don't you?"

"Okay, okay," she said softly from behind the drifting cigarette smoke. "So what have you got in mind?"

"Yeah. Well, it isn't that I've got anything in mind, exactly," he said. "I just had a couple ideas I thought we might talk over, that's all."

He jingled the coins in his pocket, and suddenly he turned abruptly, walking to the screen door and flipping away his half-smoked cigarette onto the concrete walk outside. He spoke again with his back to Maggie, and his voice quite altered, no longer rehearsed but direct and angry.

"Look, Mag, I just wanted to put it to you, that's all. What's the harm in that? Then all you got to do is tell me how you feel about it. That's all there is to it, that's all I got in mind. Lots of people, it wouldn't do any good, you can't figure out how they really feel about something, no matter what they say. But with you it's different, because I guess you're just about the most honest person I ever knew in my life. I guess that's one thing I'll always remember about you."

He lingered, working the catch on the screen door, and Maggie was silent in her chair. When he walked back into the center of the room, his face was a little desperate, but his voice was once more controlled and fluent and rehearsed.

"The thing is, I been doing a lot of thinking about how really tough on you it's going to be. It's sure as hell no picnic for a woman to start in all over again on her own, specially when she's tied down with a little kid. Maybe when you're alone it's not so tough, but when you're tied down with a little kid, it gets really rugged."

He paused and Maggie gently lowered her feet to the floor.

"Yeah, I been doing a lot of thinking about it. Like when you come to get a job, for instance. Right from the start you'll have to pull down a pretty good salary so you can pay somebody else for looking after the kid while you're working. Of course, my alimony payments will help out, but just the same it makes it pretty tough on you when it comes to swinging an apartment of your own and all the bills and stuff like that. But I guess you've thought of all this yourself by now. And it's not just the money end of it

(101

either. Like you'll be wanting to get out a lot now and meet people and go places and . . . Well, tied down with a kid, it just makes it pretty tough on you, that's all."

Maggie was studiously engaged in snuffing out her cigarette in the glass ash tray on the table beside her.

"Well, see, that's the kind of stuff I been thinking about," Tom went on. "It's a pretty tough proposition for you, and I guess you know it as well as I do. But, you look at it this way. I've got the house now, you've never seen it but it's a pretty nice little setup out there, two bedrooms and two baths and a nice back yard and plenty of fresh air and everything. Of course, right now I'm not exactly organized yet to have a regular home, but . . ."

"But later on you might be," Maggie said in a small quiet voice.

"Yeah, that's right," Tom said, immediately grateful. "Later on . . . Oh hell, I don't know, maybe I'd hire a housekeeper, or maybe I can talk Aunt Ellie into coming over there and keeping house for me, or . . ."

"Or maybe you might be getting married again," Maggie finished it for him in the same, small, quiet voice.

"Well, yeah, that's right, you never know."

Tom stared at her searchingly, but her face was still turned away over the ash tray, only the bright coil of her hair was visible where it had slid down precariously onto the side of her head.

Tom took a last deep breath.

"That's what I mean," he said. "You just never know how things are going to work out like that. Or you might be the one getting married, one of these deals where it wouldn't work out, you being tied down with a kid. Anyway, it's a nice little setup out there, like I say, and once I get squared away and have a regular home again, well, I figured it might help you out if . . . Hell, I mean I'd be glad to do it for you till you get yourself straightened around again . . . What I mean is, maybe you'd want to let Jimmy come to live with me."

The room was very still. The sun dipped away behind the red tile roof of a house across the street and the light faded swiftly and perceptibly and all color with it until the room was drained and gray. Tom waited, tinkling the coins in his pocket nervously. Maggie was motionless, her head bent, and once Tom leaned forward, craning his neck as he tried to look into the pale oval of her face.

"Well, what do you think?" he said at last, lamely.

"What?" Her voice was indistinct.

"I said, 'what do you think?' "

A car passed along the street outside and a small gust of wind stirred the dried palmetto fronds along the rough stucco wall.

Tom's face was wary, and puzzled.

"What do you think about it, Jimmy living with me after the divorce is final?"

"I don't think," Maggie said.

She reached out to the cigarette package on the table, but her hands were shaking so badly that she thrust them hurriedly away into the voluminous sleeves of her kimono instead.

"No," she said in a shaking disembodied voice. "Go home and tell what's her name—Junie—the answer is no!"

"Huh?"

Tom's face was thunderstruck, and the next instant, flaming guilty red.

"Now wait a minute," he said loudly. "You don't have to drag Junie into this. This has got nothing to do with Junie. You got the crazy mixed-up kind of mind that . . ."

Maggie turned then, her arms folded about her as though she were shivering with cold, and her face, when she lifted it, pinched and sick.

"Ah, Tom, don't!" she said, her voice still shaking. "We know each other, you and me. You'd never ask me to give up Jamie. There has to be somebody else mixed up in this."

"All right," Tom said angrily. "So I talked it over with Junie. I don't mind admitting that. Hell, why wouldn't I talk it over with her, it's only natural, isn't it? It's her life too, how she feels about having a kid around and everything. Sure, I talked it over with her, but it wasn't her idea. What's so funny about a guy wanting his own kid to come and live with him?"

Maggie was shivering in the chair, her face lifted to him mutely.

"Quit looking at me like that!" Tom yelled. "I didn't kidnap the kid, I just asked you how you felt about it, that's all. You're acting like I was some kind of a freak or a criminal or something, for even talking about it. Christ, this whole setup stinks if you want to know, and the goddamn divorce laws in this country back women up in it all the way down the line. Guy's a regular heel if he just happens to speak up once and mention that he loves his own kid and might happen to want his own kid come and stay with him sometime. Ah, you make me sick!"

"Tom, listen to me." Maggie was struggling for control. "I'm sorry. I'm sorry but what do you expect me to do? Jamie's all I've got, he's it. We can't split him down the middle, can we? Like you say, the law is all on my side. But you've known that right from the beginning, it's part of what a divorce means. So why are you bringing this up now? That's what I'm getting at. You never mentioned this before, not once when we were talking about a divorce, or when we came to court, or with the lawyers. Not ever. Why are you bringing it up now?"

"All right, all right!" he said desperately. "So I didn't think so much about it till I met Junie and we started planning on getting married. What's wrong with that? Before that I didn't have a regular home, I didn't have any way to take care of a kid the way you should. But once Junie and I are married, I'll have a home again, and Junie loves that kid as though he were her own. Jesus, I should think you'd be glad she feels that way about him, some women would be mean and jealous of him and . . ."

Maggie rose slowly to her feet.

"I should be glad?" she repeated, wonderingly. "I should be glad this—this Junie wants to take my baby away from me?"

"Kee—rist!"

Tom struck his palm to his forehead, his face agonized.

"What are you talking about, are you crazy or something? Who ever said Junie wanted to take your baby away from you? In the first place, 'your baby' happens to be my kid, too, though you don't seem to remember that any more. Nobody said a word about Junie taking him away from you, you twist everything around, you're really crazy, you . . ."

"Well, what else am I supposed to think?" Maggie said softly. "Look, Tom. I know you. I know you inside out. You never made up your mind all by yourself to ask me to give up Jamie."

Tom opened his mouth and then closed it tight, his big hands clenched at his sides.

"All right," he said at last with simple dignity, his voice controlled and firm. "All right. I told you right at the start, all I wanted to do was mention it to you and find out how you'd feel about it. Well, now I sure as hell know how you feel, don't I? So there's nothing more to talk about. I can't see any sense in you taking it like this. I tried to explain it to you the best I could, but you don't listen, you twist everything around to suit yourself. Why are you so bound that this has to be somebody else's idea? Don't you think I care about that kid just the same as you do? I told you I talked it over with Junie to see how she'd feel about it, and that's all Junie's got to do with it. Sure, it happens that Junie loves that kid like he was her own, but . . ."

"You know, I'm getting tired of hearing you say that," Maggie said quietly. "What in hell do you mean, she loves Jamie like he was her own? She's spent a few Saturday afternoons with him, so just what do you mean by that anyway?"

"Okay," Tom said patiently, "she doesn't love him like he was her own then. Have it any way you want it. You don't know a thing about Junie. She's a sweet terrific girl and she really does love that kid. She's crazy about kids anyway and she knows how to get along with them. Jim's crazy about her already."

Maggie's eyes flared. She came up onto her toes very slowly, and then teetered there, poised and stiff-legged.

"You know, I'm getting kind of sick of good old Junie, too," she said.

Tom lifted his arm in a hopeless gesture and turned away toward the door.

"Now you're beginning to fly off the handle," he said. "Well, there's nothing more to talk about anyway. Just drop it, that's all."

Maggie tossed back a streaming hank of her hair and bounded after him.

"Why shouldn't I fly off the handle? Goddamn it, if there's one thing I hate, it's a liar and a hypocrite! Why couldn't you come in here and talk this over with me like a reasonable human being? No, you had to stand up there in the middle of the floor and make a mealy-mouthed two-faced kind of speech about how you'd been worrying about me and you wanted to help me. You wanted to help me, balls! You weren't even thinking about me once, you were thinking about yourself and her, so why didn't you say so? Junie! Ah, she's a dear sweet girl, she is! Well, if she's so goddamn crazy about kids, what's to prevent the two of you having a dozen of them? She doesn't have to have mine, does she?"

Tom stopped short with his hand on the door handle and turned back again, his face red and angry.

"You've got no business making dirty cracks like that," he blurted. "You don't even know what you're talking about. It's fine for you to stand up there loud and smart and say let Junie have a dozen. Sure, just because it's as easy for you to have babies as—as some goddamn rabbit or something. It just happens that Junie isn't able to have children, so don't you go around saying . . ."

"Ah, so that's it! So now it all adds up!"

Maggie stretched out her arm triumphantly, draped with the

long festooning length of kimono sleeve. All her hair was down and flying, and the skirt gapped open over her long bare, suntanned legs, as she came after him.

"And don't you talk to me as if having babies was some dirty habit of mine! I suppose because of her, now you think that ladies don't have babies. No, ladies don't have babies, they just try to snatch other people's! Poor Junie, my heart bleeds! Well, if she can't have them, then let her adopt children or let her go without. What's she to me, that you'd walk in here and try to con me into giving up Jamie because poor Junie's crazy about children and can't have any of her own. Are you so crazy in love with her that you don't even know what you're doing? I think you're really out of your mind!"

Tom lifted his clenched hands helplessly.

"One of these times," he said softly and prayerfully. "By Jesus, one of these times. I don't care if they put me in jail or what they do to me, one of these times . . ."

"Oh, shut up and go home," Maggie said rudely.

She spun around and flashed across the dim shadowed room toward the archway. And then several things happened all at once. Once again she collided head-on with the dangling balloon string, and once again she jumped back, screeching softly and clawing at her face.

"Watch out," Tom said spitefully. "Spiders'll git you!"

Maggie caught her breath. She leapt forward and hauled at the string, batting viciously at the big bobbing balloon with all her strength. And in the same motion, she seized up a squat, blue and yellow pottery bowl from a table top and hurled it at Tom's head. He ducked, and the bowl struck the door jamb with a soggy thud, falling to the floor in a hundred tinkling shards of pottery. The balloon broke then with a deafening explosion in the small hot room, and Maggie burst into tears.

"My god, my god!" Tom said incoherently.

He bolted out of the door and down the step, colliding blindly with Bud in shorts and tennis sweater as he ambled up the cement walk, whistling cheerfully.

"Hi yuh, Tom," Bud said happily. "How you been, boy?"

But Tom hurtled on desperately toward his car, without even answering him.

ten

WHILE Tom was still clattering out the front door, Maggie fled through the archway toward the bathroom, her sole place of refuge in a house where she had no private corner of her own. She slammed the door behind her and leaned against it, and for a moment or two she wept bitterly and silently, her face stretched into a tight distorted grimace.

"Mag? Where are you, Mag?" Bud was calling from the kitchen. "Anybody home? Hey, Mag, a vase got busted in the living room."

Maggie did not answer him.

A moment later, there were voices outside the window, as Grandpa Kennedy and Jamie cut across the back yard to the kitchen door.

Maggie stopped crying. She tugged at her kimono under the belt, lapping it tightly about her again, and wiped her nose on a piece of Kleenex. She gathered up her loose flowing hair in both hands, skinning it back savagely from her face to tie it at the back of her head with a scrap of soiled white ribbon she found lying on the top of the toilet tank. Last of all, she leaned in close to the mirror for an instant, hurriedly wiping at the tear marks around her eyes with the tips of her fingers. Then she straightened her shoulders and marched out the door, her chin tilting.

In the kitchen, Bud was sprawled on a chair at the table, eating a banana out of one hand and balancing a thick book open in front of him with the other. Jamie crouched on the floor beside his train box, busily fitting together sections of the metal track.

"Quit munching, you'll spoil your supper," Maggie said. "It's all ready on the stove."

"Not for me," Bud said cheerfully, his eyes upon his book. "I ate some junk a while ago. This'll hold me."

"Don't be silly. It's all ready, and you've got plenty of time."

"Uh uh, I'm not hungry, honest," Bud said. He crammed the last segment of banana into his mouth and washed it down with a great draught of milk from a glass in front of him on the table. "Besides, I have to go in to work early tonight and I still got to shower."

Maggie rattled pot lids at the stove.

"You, too, sweetie," she said to the child. "You get your hands washed now and come to the table, okay?"

"Bud and me don't want any supper," Jamie said. "We're not hungry."

"Sure you are," she said cajolingly. "I made that good beef stew that you like, and a big glass of cold milk. How about that!"

"Why's it always have to be milk," he complained. "My daddy and Junie give me Coca-Cola to drink."

Maggie closed the refrigerator door with a slam.

"You tell your daddy and Junie, I said Coca-Cola makes holes in your teeth."

"Hey, what was eating old Tom today, anyway?" Bud said, frowning over his book. "Boy, he come charging out the door and almost knocked me over. He never even stopped to say hello."

Maggie did not answer him, and after a moment he said dreamily, "Gee, this is a terrific book, you know that? Caro loaned it to me, it's her favorite book. *The Magic Mountain.* You ever read it, Mag?"

"Yes, I've read it," Maggie said. "When you finish it, you be sure and tell me what you think of it. This Caro of yours sounds like quite a girl."

"She is," Bud said seriously. "She's the most terrific girl I ever met in my life. She's really wonderful. I want you to meet her, Mag, you're going to be crazy about her. Hey, Mag, you coming to this beach brawl tomorrow, up at Cliff and Bob's?"

Maggie set plates and silverware swiftly around the table.

"I guess so. What's it supposed to be? Mostly the volleyball bunch, isn't it?"

"Yeah. On account of Bob and Dora getting married, I guess. Cliff call you?"

"Yes." Maggie paused. "I'm going out to dinner with him tonight."

Bud looked up from his book abruptly, but Maggie was already whisking away through the doorway into the hall. For an instant his face was dumbfounded, and then he began to laugh.

"Funny, funny girl!" he said. "You fracture me!"

He guffawed with laughter, his sandy head flung back and his long, solid, bare legs thrust out beneath the table.

Maggie came silently back into the kitchen with a wet washcloth in her hand.

"Here we go, sweetie," she murmured to the child as she knelt on the floor beside him. She wiped his small face, still bent down stubbornly over his train track, and tried to catch and rub his busy chubby hands streaked with dirt and the tiny soft nails rimmed in black.

"Old Cliffie, the creep!" Bud chortled delightedly. "Mag, you kill me! How'd you stall him this time? Why don't you just tell him you're allergic to yogurt?"

"It just happens I'm not joking," Maggie said tersely. "I'm

going to dinner with him. You like to shut up now and mind your own business?

"There we are," she finished to Jamie, her voice gentling. She lifted him to his feet and for a moment held him tightly, her face hidden against his soft neck.

"Did you have a good time today, my sweetie?" she said. "Did you go to the carnival?"

"Yes," Jamie said. "Mommy, I like to go to the carnival. Why don't you and me go to the carnival instead of always going to the silly old beach?"

The tears were bright in Maggie's eyes again suddenly, as she knelt before him, straightening back his fine fair hair.

"Well, for one thing, darling, it's pretty hard to get to the carnival on a bus. You just about have to have a car to go to the carnival, you know that?"

"Then why don't you get a car so we can go?" he said crossly. "My daddy's got a car. Junie's got a car too."

"Has she?" Maggie said. "That's nice. Well, some day we'll have one. Come on, darling. Come have your supper now."

Jamie struggled away, his arms and legs flying.

"Mommy!" he wailed. "I want to play with my train."

Maggie rose, turning her tear-marked face quickly away from Bud's gaze. She went to the stove and began to ladle savory brown stew out of a kettle onto a yellow pottery dinner plate.

Bud's ingenuous boyish face was penitent as he watched.

"Mag, I shouldn't have kidded around like that about you going out with Cliff," he said awkwardly. "Cliff's a good guy, he's . . ." His voice trailed out but he rallied gallantly. ". . . He's . . . the best volleyball player they got, out of that whole crowd down there. Listen, wasn't I the one that was just telling you how you ought to start getting out a little? I think it's a swell idea, honest."

Maggie carried the plate of stew over to the table.

"Here you go, baby," she said impersonally. "Move your book, huh?"

(111

"No, none for me," he said. "I have to barrel. Besides, I'm really full, I couldn't eat a thing."

His open face suddenly lightened and was happy again.

"I had tea with Caro this afternoon," he said in a burst of confidence. "She likes to have tea. You know, she's the only person I ever knew in my life that really did that. Caro has tea every single afternoon, even if she's all by herself." His voice was dreamily ecstatic.

Maggie moved away silently and put down the plate at another place at the table.

"Grandpa?" she called as she turned back toward the stove. "Where are you? Supper's ready."

He answered her from the front of the house.

"Why, I'm just leaving now, Maggie. I forget to tell you, I thought I'd wait tonight and have a little bite somewhere with Mildred."

"I'm not going to have any either," Jamie yelled. "I'm not going to be the only one in this whole house that has to eat my supper!"

Two pot holders and a large metal spoon fell out of Maggie's hands to the floor, and she slumped back suddenly against the white stove front.

"Goddamn it," she said. "Doesn't anybody want my bloody, stinking old stew!"

At the sight of her face, Bud sprang up from his chair, his knees rattling against the edge of the table.

"Aw, Maggie," he said contritely. "Something's the matter. Something's happened to make you feel bad!"

And just at that moment, Grandpa Kennedy sashayed out into the kitchen, with his springy, eager, youthful step, a white straw hat set at a rakish angle on his head, and his gray suit-coat folded neatly over his arm.

"Must be getting along over there to pick up Mildred now," he said brightly. "Why, Maggie, I forgot to tell you. Margie Martinez said she'd be over here to sit for you at seven o'clock."

He patted Maggie's shoulder affectionately.

"Have a good time tonight, honey."

And then unobtrusively he slipped the little wad of several folded bills into her hand.

Maggie flung out her arm in a sharp gesture of final despair, her fingers spreading wide apart and the money balanced on her palm. She lifted her other hand aimlessly, her knuckles pressing hard against her cheekbone, her agonized face goaded and driven, her silence as piercing as a scream in the room.

And then she leapt after him and caught him at the kitchen door.

"Grandpa!" Her voice was thin. "I don't want you giving me money like this. I've told you that before. Now take it back right now."

Bud's face was embarrassed and he melted away, his feet padding down the hallway toward the bathroom.

"Now, now, Maggie," the old man murmured soothingly.

She held out the bills to him, her chin high, but he did not take them.

"No call for you to be touchy about it, honey," he said mildly. "You earn every penny of it and more besides. You do for us, you wash and cook and keep the house and . . ."

"You do for Jamie and me too, don't you?" Maggie said. "A roof over our heads, and three meals a day?"

"Now, Maggie, what makes you talk like that," the old man said embarrassedly. "You pay your own way here, you know that. You insisted on my taking the money every week right from the beginning."

"That's out of Tom's money for Jamie," Maggie said steadily. "I try to pay my way with the damn little housekeeping I ever do around here. That makes us even-steven, and you don't owe me anything, Grandpa. I still owe you and Bud more than I can ever pay you for taking us in like this when we needed it."

"Now, Maggie!"

"Go on and take it, Grandpa," she said. "You work hard over there at that lumber yard in the broiling hot weather and I'm not going to take your money. It seems to me that all my life practically, you've had to take care of me. Well, it's about time it stopped. You'd think at least by now I'd be in a position to take care of myself, wouldn't you, and maybe do something for you for a change."

The quick tears appeared in the old man's eyes, and he reached out, closing his fingers tightly several times upon her shoulder.

"Now you listen to me a minute, honey," he said quietly. "I may not be as young as I once was, but I still provide for my family and I don't allow for any such kind of talk as this. As long as I live and have a roof over my head, there'll be a home here for you and the boy if you want it. And no women folks of mine have ever gone without a little spending money in their pocketbooks nor they never will. Now put your money away, we're not going to talk no more about it."

"Ah, Grandpa!"

Maggie flung her arms about his neck, and for a moment he held her close, patting her back tenderly.

"There, now," he said. "Times are just kind of hard for you right now, Maggie. There's ups and downs in everybody's life, I never seen anybody yet that didn't have them. You got a nice little boy and the best years of your life are still ahead of you. You're going to be all right."

He released her and fumbled at his pocket, shaking out the neatly folded square of spotless white handkerchief. He blew his nose loudly.

"Well, say, I better be getting on along," he said. "Mildred will jaw if I'm late." He reached down to ruffle the little boy's hair. "Now you're my helper, so you look after everything good while I'm gone, all right?"

"Have a good time, Grandpa," Maggie called after him as he hurried out the door with his jaunty step.

"I sure will. You, too, Maggie. Good night."

The door slammed behind him over the muffled sound of splashing water from the bathroom.

Maggie wadded up the money in her hand and wiped her nose fiercely on the sleeve of her kimono.

Jamie pattered across the floor to her and wrapped his arms about her legs.

"Mommy," he said softly, tipping up his solemn face. "Mommy, I'll eat some of your stinky stew, if you want me to."

"Ah, my baby!" Maggie said with a catch in her voice as she swung him up into her arms.

eleven

SEVERAL HOURS later, that same evening, Maggie and Clifford Brunner came out through the glass doors of a large brightly lighted cafeteria onto the sidewalk. The night was unusually mild, the sidewalk was crowded and the street was noisy with cars.

"Why, uh, what would you like to do now?" he said awkwardly. "I don't know what's playing at the movies."

"I think there's a good Italian film at the State," Maggie offered. "Or maybe you don't like foreign films?"

"That sounds nice," he said. "I tell you, I don't go to the movies much myself. I think it's bad on the eyes."

"Well, we don't have to go if you don't want to," Maggie said. "What would you like to do?"

"Oh, no," he said quickly. "If you like to go to the movies, I think it would be nice. Why, uh, would you mind if we walked around for a little first, though? It's kind of a habit I have, I always like to take a little walk after I eat. I seem to digest my food better that way."

"Fine, let's," she said. "It's a wonderful night just to be out, anyway."

They moved over to the curb at the corner, and when the traffic light turned green ahead of them, they stepped down together. Clifford placed his hand carefully beneath her elbow and they crossed the broad, well-lighted street unhurriedly. Maggie was very dressed up in a slim black dress, hose and heeled pumps, and a black woolen shrug sweater pulled about her shoulders. Clifford towered above her, his big athlete's body confined in a neat business suit, brown hair bristling in a crew cut over deep-set plaintive eyes and indeterminate bony features.

On the other side, there was a narrow strip of park running parallel to the street along the edge of the palisade above the sea. They strolled down one of the dimly lighted cement walks there, between beds of stiff canna lilies and squat luxuriant date palms. The benches in the shadows at either side were occupied, old women in print dresses, white shoes and knitted shawls, old men in checked caps and loud sports jackets. And everywhere there were couples like themselves, murmuring together and strolling hand in hand in the mild night.

"It must be the santana wind blowing from the desert," Maggie said. "Feel how hot the air is. The sea's beautiful tonight, isn't it?"

She paused, and for a moment they looked down over the railing at the sea far below. It was very calm, the tide going out; long shallow waves folded gently against the dark wet sand; the great expanse of water shimmered silver in the light of a large rising moon, and was dotted at one side with placid golden pools of reflected light along the pier.

"Why, uh, like I was saying back at the restaurant." Cliff cleared his throat and they walked on slowly. "I hope you will decide to come to one of the meetings with me. It's something you'll never regret, I promise you that. I'd just like for you to hear The Kalammah talk just once."

He stopped short suddenly.

"What did I do with that pamphlet I brought for you? I must have left it on the table when I was reading to you there at the restaurant."

"No, I've got it," Maggie said. "You gave it to me just as we left and it's right here in my purse."

"You got the other one too, the one on dietary principles?" he said anxiously. "I think that one's very important for you to read too. It really goes into this whole thing about commercial processed foods and the bodily requirements. I think it's very important you should learn about the health foods when you've got a growing child to consider."

"It looks very interesting," Maggie murmured.

She stopped again, fishing into the top of her purse for a cigarette and matches.

Cliff hastily took the folder out of her hand and struck the match, cupping the flame carefully as she bent over it.

"Why, uh, I got another book at home I'd like you to read sometime, too," he said. "I'll bet you'd find it pretty interesting. It really goes into it, the effects of nicotine on the human body, and caffeine and alcohol and things like that."

"Is that so!" Maggie said politely as they strolled on.

Across the street just ahead of them, there was a large hotel, a low, sprawling stucco building surrounded by lush well-kept vegetation. The parking lot behind it was crowded and humming with activity, there was a sound of dance music from within and a stream of couples climbed a short flight of steps to an entrance way at the side. As Maggie watched, a man in a dark suit pulled the door open wide with a mock flourish for a laughing girl in a full gauzy skirt, and for an instant there was a silhouette of dancers against the soft yellow light within.

" 'Mr. Sandman, bring me a dream . . .' " Maggie chanted the words softly to the burst of lively music from across the way.

And then she said, "Tell me about your work, Cliff. You're in the engineering department out at one of the aircraft factories, aren't you?"

"That's right." And then he said doggedly, "Why, uh, I think you'd find Kalammah pretty interesting all right. For one thing, it gives you a whole positive way of life. I couldn't begin to tell you all I've got out of it and I'm still just a beginner, comparatively speaking. I'm still at the First Escarpment, as we say in Kalammah, but I tell you, it's changed my whole life completely already."

"I don't think I'm much of a mystic, Cliff," Maggie said.

"Oh, you are!" Cliff said solemnly. "You got a very spiritual face. I noticed that right away, the first time I ever saw you down on the beach. You just don't realize your own potentialities. A lot of people are like that today. They're searching for spiritual values; you might say they're starved for the things of the spirit, but lots of them don't even know it themselves."

They walked slowly on along the cement path, with the sound of Maggie's sharp heels echoing away into the darkness.

"There's just nothing else you can compare it to," Cliff said, warming to his subject. "I know you hear a lot about some pretty crackpot stuff, but I tell you frankly, I'm too intelligent for that, and I think you are too. You got to realize right from the start that Kalammah is something completely different from all that. I've made quite a study of these things, Far Eastern philosophies and religions and so on."

He paused under a street lamp, lifting his wrist and pulling back his sleeve.

"We still got plenty of time," he said enthusiastically. "I always like to get to bed between ten and eleven, how about you? Anyway, seeing we've got the time and everything, I'd really like to tell you about this because I think you're very intelligent and I think you'd find it very interesting."

"Cliff," Maggie said. "I'm terribly sorry. I think I'd better go home now, if you don't mind."

"You think you should?" he said reluctantly. "Of course, if you're tired. I guess you do have to get up pretty early in the morning to look after your little boy. But it's still pretty early yet. I tell you, there's an empty bench over there where we could sit down if you are tired. I think this is something you'd really enjoy hearing about."

"I'm sorry, Cliff. Not tonight."

He was silent for a moment, and then he said, his voice brightening, "Well, maybe you're right, at that. You probably wouldn't get so much out of it if you're feeling tired and sleepy. It is getting kind of late. I guess I was enjoying myself so much talking with you that I lost all track of time. It certainly has been an enjoyable evening."

They wheeled around and began to retrace their steps along the winding cement walk.

"I tell you," Cliff said. "I make it a rule never to go out during the week when I'm working. I was thinking about next Saturday night though. If I pick you up around six instead of seven, that would give us that extra hour to eat, and then . . ."

The sound of Maggie's footsteps ceased abruptly.

"Cliff," she said miserably, reaching out her hand to his arm. "Oh, look. I'm terribly sorry, it's all my fault. It's my own stupid fault for coming out tonight with you in the first place. It was a mistake and I shouldn't have done it. I can't go out with you again."

"Oh?" Cliff said, his voice puzzled. "I suppose you mean on account of your husband and everything. I understand that your divorce isn't final yet and all that, but people tend to be a lot more liberal about such things than they used to be. After all, you are separated from him and you are getting a divorce, so . . ."

"Well, that isn't exactly what I meant," she said uncomfortably. "Anyway, it's all my fault, I hadn't any business starting it. I shouldn't have come tonight. I was terribly lonely and . . ."

"I know," Cliff said hollowly. "The terrible loneliness of the human spirit. You might say we're all starving for the Companion, for the Oneness of the Twoness, as we say in Kalammah. I'm a terribly lonely person. I guess that's why I hate to hear you say it was all a mistake after we've had such an enjoyable evening and everything. It means an awful lot to me to find an intelligent girl like you and I was really looking forward to us . . ."

"Well, don't," Maggie said a little desperately. "I—I'm still a married woman. You have to consider the spiritual implications of the marriage tie, I . . ."

"Yeah, but what about the barbecue tomorrow?" Cliff said. "I already told the fellows at my house that I was bringing you and everything. I realize your position, but . . ."

"All right," Maggie said. "I did promise you I'd come tomorrow, so I will. But I don't want to go out with you any more after that. I'm sorry, Cliff. We're still friends, aren't we? I'll still be seeing you around the volleyball court and everything the same as always."

"Yes, I suppose so," he said reluctantly. "I tell you though, this is something I'd really like to go into with you. It isn't that I don't respect your point of view, but I don't think you're seeing all the facts in the proper perspective maybe. There—there are certain implications to this situation that you might say we haven't had time to even begin to explore yet . . .

"On the spiritual plane, that is . . ." he ended hastily.

He took hold of her hands suddenly in both his large, rather damp ones.

"Look," Maggie said rapidly. "I'm terribly sorry, really. It was a nice evening, thank you for the dinner, I'll read your pamphlets, I'll come to the barbecue tomorrow. Don't bother to take me home. I'd like to walk if you don't mind. It's a—a habit of mine. All right?"

She was already edging away from him, back down the shadowy walk.

"Well, sure, I guess so," Cliff said, his voice totally bewildered. "I don't like to just leave you out alone on the streets at night this way though. If you'd rather walk home, I could leave my car here and . . ."

"No, I wouldn't want to put you out, it's perfectly all right," Maggie called back over her shoulder. "I'm—out alone on the streets all the while. Thanks a lot, see you tomorrow. Good night!"

"Why, uh, good night!"

She was already in flight, her purse hugged tightly under her arm and her heels clattering along the walk. Cliff stood irresolutely under the street lamp and watched her go, blinking his plaintive doglike eyes, his face wistful in the light.

"Maggie?" he called out suddenly. "You just took the wrong turn. That's the ramp going down to the beach."

"I know." Her voice floated back to him. "I like to walk down there. The ocean helps me meditate."

The steep sloping ramp was deserted, and once Maggie was out of his sight, she ran fleetly on her toes, her hair flying behind her. She came to a skidding stop at the bottom, on the cracked uneven sidewalk that ran along beneath the pier. The great spans and underpilings of the pier loomed over her in the darkness, in front of her there was a stretch of empty sand down to the flimsy wooden backsides of the small buildings that lined the promenade. Maggie was breathing quickly. She kicked off her high-heeled pumps impatiently, stooping down to pick them up, and then she plowed off across the sand on a long diagonal in the direction of a gap between the buildings where the lights of the promenade showed through.

By the time she reached the promenade itself, she was completely breathless. Part of the buildings there were already closed and darkened, although a remnant of the daylight beach crowd still surged leisurely back and forth along the wide cement walk. Maggie hurried on until she saw the light still shining out of the open front of the coffee stall, and then she slowed, walking lightly in her stockinged feet, catching her breath again.

The stall, when she reached it, was empty except for the little counter man who was mounted on a stool at the back, swabbing out one of the tall coffee urns.

"Hi, George-O!"

The little man started, the stool rocking perilously beneath him, as he jerked around.

"Maggie! Honest to god, you like to scared me right out of my britches! What you doing down here this time of night? Another two minutes, I'd of been closed up and gone."

He came down from the stool, staring at her curiously as he wiped his hands on a towel.

She was still breathing quickly, her eyes very large and dark, and tendrils of her bright hair escaping over her forehead. She walked over to the counter slowly, swinging her purse in her hand.

"What's the matter, honey? You look kind of beat."

She sat down on one of the stools, depositing her shoes and purse on the counter top beside her.

"Ah, George-O!"

She smoothed at her hair, her hands lingering for a moment on either side of her face.

Suddenly she began to laugh—softly at first and then louder, with the clear unstudied peals of pure hilarity. She laughed, clinging to the counter edge, her head flung back, her whole body shaking with mirth.

George leaned across his folded arms, grinning at her sympathetically.

"Boy, whatever it was, something sure must have struck you funny!"

She was able to stop finally, her face flushed and shining with merriment.

"Ah, George," she gasped. "I guess I'm getting old!"

She rummaged a handkerchief out of her purse and wiped her eyes with it, and then groped again for cigarettes.

"Let's you and me have a cup of coffee," the counter man said cozily. "I been keeping a little dipper of it hot for when I finished with the cleaning up. How about a nice cup of hot coffee, okay?"

"George, he was so funny," she said. "I nearly flipped, I couldn't help it. That poor gone character! Ah, I shouldn't laugh at him. I'm not, really. I'm laughing at myself."

She paused to light the cigarette.

"Harrison," she said, "good old Harrison! Out for a big night on the town. First night out to celebrate being free and single and over twenty-one!"

She bit at her lip, her eyes shining. The little man put down the steaming, thick white mugs upon the counter top and stuck out his chin pugnaciously.

"Listen, some bum hasn't been giving you any trouble, has he? Who was this character anyway?"

"Nobody you know, George," Maggie said. "Just one of the beach athletes from over at the volleyball court. And no trouble, the shortest, driest first night out on record. George-O, you got any idea what caffeine can do to your bodily requirements?"

"Aaah, them beach bums!" the little man said with his scornful hoot of laughter.

"Well, here's to it, George."

Maggie extended her coffee cup to him and they solemnly linked their doubled arms across the counter.

"Here's to that big, beautiful, muddy old river," she said, sighing a little.

"Yes, sir!" George chimed in wistfully.

There was a familiar brisk sound of footsteps along the cement outside, as they drank, and the short dark-haired man appeared suddenly in the open entrance to the stall.

"Well, what do you know!" he said humorously. "If here isn't my favorite redhead. You know, I thought I saw you sitting over here, from way over there on the pier. I couldn't believe my eyes, so I had to come over and take a closer look. Hi yuh, George?"

Maggie gave him her languid flip of the hand.

"Hi, Tony. What's new?"

"You," he said. "What you doing out after dark like this? I thought you always went to bed with the chickens."

"I do," Maggie said briefly. "Us chickens are out late tonight, that's all."

He leaned upon the counter and studied her appreciatively.

"Hey, Red," he said. "You know I never seen you in a dress before? You're all right. Look, it's Saturday night, so what do you say? Let's us go to town and find us a good mambo band."

He lifted one arm and circled slowly, shuffling his feet as he hummed the rhythm, grunting on the fourth beat.

"Uh uh," Maggie said good-naturedly. "I don't know how to mambo, Tony."

"I'll teach you," he said. "How about it, I mean it. Perez Prado's playing at the Crescendo on the Strip. Come on, Red, what do you say? Let's us have ourselves a ball, okay?"

"Thanks anyway, Tony," Maggie said. "It's really way past bedtime for us chickens right now."

"Don't be like that!"

"No, thanks, Tony."

"Okay," the dark man said, shrugging. "Have it your way. You're sure one persistent female all right. Why can't you come out and have a little fun for a change? You're acting like some kid, what's the matter, you think I'm planning to rape you?"

"Why, Tony!" Maggie said mockingly. "Pretty fellow like you,

you wouldn't have to! Maybe sometime, Tony. Not tonight. I just don't feel like it. See you around. All right?"

"Yeah, sure," he said. "Okay, I'll take a rain check. You ought to watch it though, Red. You keep on hanging out with the chickens like this, your springs are liable to get rusty, don't you know that?"

"I'll take my chances," she said. "See you, Tony."

Maggie looked after him, the diminishing sound of his footfalls away down the promenade.

"George," she said. "What does Tony do anyway? You always see him around down here."

The little counter man snorted. "Aah, he's a no-good bum! You keep away from him."

"He's nice-looking," Maggie said lamely. "He makes an awful noise like a wolf, but . . ."

"You got the right idea so keep on staying away from him," George said sharply. "Boy, I sure wish you'd meet a nice steady fellow some place."

"Old George Cupid!" Maggie said affectionately. "Didn't you know, a good man is hard to find?"

She cupped her chin between her hands, her shoulders slumping, her face turning away toward the glittering white breakers where they folded endlessly against the sand.

After a while the little counter man yawned prodigiously and reached around over his shoulder to the dipper of coffee on the electric plate.

"Crowd's thinned out," he said softly. "It's about all over for another day."

"I should go home," Maggie said, her eyes still fixed upon the ruffling water's edge.

"What's your hurry?" George said. "Have some more coffee. I'm not in no rush, now the crowd's gone. My wife's gone to some church business anyway."

He filled the thick white cups again, and hitched himself

(125

around more comfortably, with one foot braced against the edge of the metal sink behind the counter.

And suddenly, Maggie laughed.

"Oh, George," she said. "Honestly! You get to a point where you might just as well laugh as cry! How do you get out of bed some morning and start a whole new life for yourself, where do you begin? Make plans, get a job, buy a car, meet some people . . ."

"It takes a while for anybody to get started," George said. "You're going to do all those things. It takes a little time."

"But, George, I don't understand it. What's happened to me? While I was married it seemed like there were a million things I was aching to do all the while. I used to feel so bottled up, I couldn't wait for the divorce and to be free and to start doing the things I wanted to do. I felt like I had so much wasted time to make up for. I felt so strong and so full of all these millions of things I couldn't wait to be doing."

Maggie laughed again.

"And look at me now! Just take a good look at me! George, I hate cowards and whiners and wishy-washy people. I hate myself the way I am these days, drifting along, complaining all the while about my goddamn stupid little troubles, talking about getting a job while I go right on living off my grandfather, and . . . George, I am in trouble and I'm scared. You want to know the truth? I don't think I can depend on myself any more. Maybe I was married so long I've just forgotten how. I don't know what it is. But I don't feel strong any more, I don't feel anything. I'm not even a person any longer. I'm just something like Jamie's old Mrs. Duck, with all the stuffing lost out of her. There isn't anything left inside of me any more either, just a great big empty hole. What's going to become of me, George?"

"Now, listen, I've known plenty cases," George said fiercely. "Like I'm telling you, a divorce makes a big change in your life, that's all. So you figure on a divorce and you want it real bad.

Just the same, when it first happens, it knocks the wind right out of you. It takes a while to get back on your feet. It takes a while to get moving again. You hadn't ought to crowd yourself like this. Give yourself a break and give yourself some time."

"Time?" she said. "George, that's all I have got! But it's going to take more than time. What's there for me to depend on if I can't depend on myself any more? I always thought that I could, and now in the clutch when I need everything that I've got, it turns out I haven't got anything. Just a big empty nothing inside of me, like Jamie's Mrs. Duck."

"You got no business laying it in to yourself this way," he said. "The trouble with you is, you can't take it easy, you want things to happen all to once. You're going to get over all this, it's like having the measles or something. Boy, I really know, I been through all this myself. It's all just part of getting a divorce."

"Is it?" Maggie said. "Do you honestly believe that, George? But why! I haven't been in love with Tom for years, and I wanted this divorce more than anything in the world. Oh god, and I thought a divorce was such an easy simple thing, just sign a couple papers and pack up your suitcases and walk away to a whole brand-new happy life!"

"Sure," George said. "And you want to know something, a couple years from now, you're going to look back, and that's the way it's going to seem like it was to you, too."

"Do you promise?" she said. "Okay, George, hope springs eternal! Break out the fortune-telling cards, here I go again!"

twelve

EARLY the next afternoon, Bud O'Toole drove his battered old convertible into the curb beneath the well-pruned trees that lined the quiet street. He shut off the motor, and then for a moment he hesitated, smoothing surreptitiously his sandy hair, his eyes warily fixed upon the imposing white façade of the big house. As he looked there was a sudden stir of motion behind the draperies of a second-floor window and he caught a glimpse of Caro's small, sleek, dark head there, and her hand waving to him.

Bud waved back, his face instantly relieved, and settled himself behind the wheel to wait, whistling very softly to himself.

Inside the house, Caro turned away from the window and walked unhurriedly along a dim wide corridor. She was wearing tight white trousers and a long, bulky, black and white striped pull-over, and she carried a coat slung over her arm. She passed a half-opened door and heard the sound of a voice there. She hesitated and then walked back again, her feet in flat black sandals silent upon the thick carpeting. She paused in the doorway.

It was a luxurious cheerful room with sunlight streaming in at the windows past elaborate white draperies patterned with a blue flower and green leaf design. The same fabric was repeated upon the small tufted chairs, in the slip cover of a chaise longue, and in the ruffled valance of the dark-green spread that covered the huge outsized bed in the alcove. A small dark-haired woman in a pale-blue satin robe sat before a powder table, with a white telephone lifted to her face.

When she caught sight of Caro in the wide-sectioned mirror in front of her, she waved, beckoning her into the room.

"Darling, I know," she said into the telephone, her voice sympathetic.

She listened again, turning in her chair to the breakfast tray on the rack beside her. She poured coffee into a china cup and then lifted the cup and saucer onto the powder table in front of her, making room for it amid the confusion of crystal jars and bottles there.

"Darling, believe me," she said into the telephone. "I couldn't agree with you more, I'm simply saying . . ."

Once more she listened, and when her eyes caught Caro's in the mirror in front of her she indicated the coffeepot on the tray beside her invitingly.

Caro shook her head. She dropped her fleecy white woolen coat upon a chair, however, and folded her hands in front of her, standing quietly with her thin back very straight.

"My poor sweetie!" the woman murmured sympathetically into the telephone. Cradling the phone with her shoulder, she groped for a cigarette from the box and then held a matching alabaster lighter to it, her red fingernails bright and perfectly rounded and polished against the veined white stone. She was very like Caro. She had the same clearly defined small features and cropped, well-groomed dark hair, but she was older, her body more rounded and mature, and her face not at all cool and remote but instead tremendously and vitally alert and alive.

Suddenly she shook her head vigorously behind the telephone, smoke spurting away from her small, sharply cut nostrils.

"Darling, don't be silly," she said rapidly. "Of course I agree with you, I'm in exactly the same position myself, after all. I'm only telling you exactly what I told Janna just last week, and Lucy Mantz not three months ago. Of course it isn't fair, of course he's had a fabulous year, of course you're entitled to an increased amount for support. You'd be stupid if you didn't get your lawyers working on it right today. But you can't afford to take him into court, that's all I'm saying. Sweetie, judges are men too, and they all stick together, you ought to know that."

She was silent again, her face exasperated finally, and as she listened she absently turned a sapphire brooch set in a cluster of small diamonds, the light refracting endlessly from the smooth tiny facets of the stones.

"Sweetie, you're not thinking straight. We've both seen it happen time after time. The moment you force them into court, instead of giving you an increase, they try to cut you down. Before you know it, you've got a fight on your hands, and you're lucky to get out with your skin. . . . Well, darling, I wasn't being personal, I don't think any of us can afford it, god knows I couldn't. You know what lawyers are like as well as I do. They drag out everything, every dressmaker's bill, every charge account that you have, every week end you've ever spent in Las Vegas, every trip to Honolulu. And they don't stop with those things either. . . . All right, but look at Mary Goetler, she's a terribly good example of what could happen to any of us, her own maid, for god sakes! Jim Goetler's lawyers got onto that maid somehow, and for a few filthy dollars that perfect bitch stood up there in court and talked her head off and it simply ruined Mary. She ended up with a custody fight on her hands and her support cut to the bone. Really, she was lucky to come out of it with the children at all."

Behind her, Caro still waited quietly, her hands childishly clasped in front of her and her face completely detached and very far away.

The woman at the telephone stretched voluptuously, her back arching, her head flung back and the telephone instrument moving with it.

"No, darling," she said patiently. "I'm simply saying there are other and better ways. Sweetie, call me back, will you? . . . Well, I'll see you at Janna's this afternoon anyway, won't I? No, of course I want to talk this over with you. Just don't do anything until we've had a chance to talk again. See you at Janna's then, 'bye."

She dropped the telephone with a thud and swung around in the chair.

"Now really!" she said. "Henny Morrison! I hate stupid women. I can't think why I take the trouble. Anything that happens to her, she really deserves it. Why, darling, what I wanted to know, are you coming in for dinner?"

"I don't think so," Caro said. "Should I?"

"Well, the only reason, Eddie Stutz is coming over here after. I'm having dinner at Margaret's but I'm meeting him here around nine-thirty. It's a business thing, about an investment deal he's putting together. I thought you might like to sit in on it."

"Helen, don't be silly," Caro said in her clear unhurried voice. She turned away, picking up her coat from the chair.

Helen poured coffee briskly into her cup, her face keen and exhilarated, with her look of great and complete alertness.

"Actually, darling, it happens that I'm only considering this as an investment for myself this time. I simply thought you might enjoy sitting in. Eddie's so marvelous at this sort of thing. He has the most absolutely clever, lucid mind. Bring your boy, if you like, and try to get back, will you?"

"Michael works at night," Caro said from the doorway. "Anyway, I expect he wouldn't really be very interested."

Helen shrugged, snapping the top on the alabaster lighter.

"All right," she said mildly, "but try to get back yourself then, sweetie. I think you'd be fascinated. After all, these are things you have to learn sometime, darling."

"Must I really?" Caro said, her voice very grave.

Helen's face was vastly amused.

"Of course you do. Women have to be able to look out for

(*131*

themselves these days. I'm not going to let you be a stupid one like poor silly Henny Morrison. Try to be back by ten o'clock. All right, darling?"

"I'll try."

Caro moved off swiftly along the corridor to the top of the wide curving stairway. She descended rapidly, her feet pattering down the shallow, thick-carpeted steps. She crossed the entry way below in two bounds and pulled open the heavy front door. She paused in the burst of sunlight at the top of the steps outside and waved to Bud, still waiting patiently in the car at the curb, and then she came on again, running lightly along the curved cement walk out to the street.

"Michael, have I kept you waiting terribly long?" she said breathlessly. "I'm sorry, truly."

She flung her fleecy white coat into the back of the car and then climbed in, sliding under his arm as he leaned across the seat to hold the door for her.

"I didn't mind," Bud said humbly. "I guess I was early anyway."

"You weren't, you were exactly on time," she said. "I particularly noticed it because I'm very punctual myself and I like other people to be. And I was ready, truly. I had to wait to speak to my sister before I left and she was talking to someone on the telephone, and that's what made me late. My sister's absolutely fantastic about the telephone, she talks forever. I am sorry, Michael."

"Gosh, that's all right," Bud said. "I really didn't mind waiting. We got plenty of time."

He seemed quite unable to stop looking at her face, his own face bemused, his hand groping along the dashboard for the ignition key.

"Gee, you look wonderful," he said softly. "I think about you all the while, how beautiful you are and everything. And then each time I see you again, I guess I still don't believe it."

"Sweet Michael!"

She touched her hand briefly to his cheek, but her face was abstracted and thoughtful. She turned on the seat, pulling her legs up beneath her as he drove the car out into the street.

"Michael, what do you think about money?" she said seriously. "What do you really think of it?"

"Huh?" Bud said. "Gosh, I don't know. I never had much of it to think about and I guess I never will. Why, I guess it's pretty nice when you have it. You don't have to work and you can do everything you want to. Yeah, I guess money's something that's pretty nice to have."

"I wonder," she said. "Anyway, I expect that's the very sensible and practical way to look at it. It's something that's very difficult for me to make up my mind about. In theory, I know exactly what I think. If you were to ask me, I'd say that money is one of the very least important things that there is. But just the same I realize that all my life I've had quite a bit of it and every day I use quite a bit of it, without ever really thinking very much about it at all. So I don't expect that I'm really being quite honest, do you, Michael, when I say that it's something that isn't important."

"I don't know," Bud said. "I've seen people that had money, and they were real snobby about it and looking down their noses at everybody. But you're not a bit like that. You stop to think about it, maybe it's just as right for you to say money isn't important when you've got it, as it is for me to say that it is important when I've never had any. I don't know how you'd figure it."

"I expect that isn't quite the same thing though," she said. "It's something I'll have to think about. It really is very difficult. I know that my sister feels quite differently about it, she . . ."

Caro stopped suddenly, and then she said, "Let's not talk about it any more, shall we, Michael? What a heavenly day it really is! I'm very glad we're going to the beach. Tell me more about this party that we're going to, Michael, what are the people like?"

(*133*

"Gosh, I don't know much about it," Bud said. "It's liable to be a pretty dull party. If it is, we don't have to stay. The main reason I wanted us to go, my sister's going to be there and I been wanting you to meet her. You and Maggie have got a lot in common, I think you're going to like Maggie a lot."

"Good," Caro said. "I'd like very much to meet your sister. Does your sister play well? What was it that you told me that it was? I'm very silly about sports, Michael."

"Volleyball," Bud said, grinning at her fondly. "No, Maggie doesn't play at all, she just knows most of the people. You know how it is at the beach, when Maggie first started going down, she went with me when I went to play volleyball, and people sort of get used to a certain place and they always go back there. There's a whole bunch of people that know each other from around the volleyball court, and there isn't half of them that ever play. I guess you don't know about the beach though. You hardly ever come down there, do you?"

"Not in a very long time," Caro said. "Our nana used to take me to play in the sand when I was quite small and then my sister belongs to a beach club and later on I used to go to dances there sometimes in the summer. Most summers since then I've been away. But I think it sounds very nice, people always coming back to the same spot on the shore each time and getting acquainted with each other. Do they very often have parties like this?"

"Not this crowd," he said. "They see each other at the beach and mostly that's enough. They're a bunch of people that got hardly anything in common except they happen to like to play volleyball. This party is something special, on account of Bob and Dora getting married. They're having it at the house where Bob used to live, farther up the beach toward Malibu, but I guess they invited all the volleyball crowd because Bob and Dora first met at the volleyball court last summer."

"I think that's very nice," Caro said. "I think people are entitled to be sentimental about such things if they want to be, don't you? Are you very sentimental, Michael? I expect somehow that you are."

"Oh, I don't know," Bud said, squinting his eyes against the bright sun as he maneuvered the car through the traffic. "Yeah, I guess I am. I guess I always been a pretty sentimental sort of guy. How about you?"

They were driving now upon one of the main highways leading to the beach and the traffic was heavy, with a constant blare of motor sounds and brakes and horns, and the stench from many exhaust pipes. The sun shone hot, and hotter still where it shimmered up from the smooth hard surface of the roadway and the shining metal sides of automobiles.

Caro hitched closer to him on the seat and lifted her voice above the traffic noise.

"I think men dislike being told so, but they really are much more sentimental than most women," she said. "No, Michael, I'm not a sentimental person at all. I used to be, it was ghastly, I absolutely wallowed in it. But it's another thing I didn't like and decided to change about myself. I'm glad that I did because I like being the way I am now, a completely unsentimental person. Poor Michael, I'll never remember what day it was when you and I first met! Are you very shocked at me, Michael?"

"Uh uh," he said with his wide and cheerful grin. "You're really cute, you know that? You're all full of these crazy ideas you got about yourself and only about ten percent of them are true. You really think you're some kind of a hardboiled character, or something?"

"Not that, necessarily," she said gravely. "But I'm not a sentimentalist any longer. Look at it this way, Michael, it's simply a matter of clutter. I expect I have a thing about clutter. I hate drawers crammed full of old dance programs and menus with autographs and snapshots and used cocktail napkins. When I open a book, I don't like pressed rosebuds from old corsages

(135

tumbling out. It would be silly not to at least try to keep my mind as carefully as I keep the place I live in, don't you think, Michael? I know perfectly well that we are only the total of the things that have happened to us, but at least we can try to select out of all our experience. I think we should carry just the very least along with us that we are able to, only the very most valuable and most beautiful. I expect that's what I really want the most, to be all of one piece, inside and out, every single thing about me carefully selected and put together like a room in a Japanese house, all sparse and lean and beautiful and no clutter anywhere. Can you understand that, Michael? I'm not really explaining it very well, I know."

"Sure, I understand you," Bud said with his fond grin. "It just happens that I don't believe a word of it, that's all. You may think that you don't care about anything or remember anything, but you're not a bit like that. I know you, I can tell. Listen, not to change the subject or anything, but it's really getting hot and this stinking traffic. We got plenty of time, why don't we stop off some place and have a Coke or something? Would you like to?"

"Good. Let's," Caro said absently.

Bud was occupied with his driving for a moment, maneuvering the car over, and finally shooting out into a gap that appeared briefly in the traffic in the right-hand turn lane.

And then he said, "Hey, what's the matter? You're real quiet all of a sudden. You mad at me or something because I wouldn't believe all this stuff about you being this free, uncluttered-up, hardboiled character?"

"No, I was thinking," she said quite seriously, with the complete and lovely gesture that she made out of the slow turning of her head. "Sometimes you frighten me. Truly, Michael. Do you know that? Sometimes I think the very first instant that you ever saw me, right then you made a complete picture of me in your mind— the kind of person that you wanted me to be. And not once since then have you ever really looked at me, or tried to see me for

136)

the kind of person that I am. I tell you things about myself quite honestly, and if they're things you don't like to hear about me, you simply won't believe them. Didn't you know, Michael, that it isn't fair to make your own image of a person? And it's a very dangerous thing to do. Because, sooner or later, you know, the two won't match, this picture you have of me, and the kind of person that I really am. You will be very disappointed in me, Michael."

"Yeah?" he said. "Okay, I'll take my chances. You ever stop to think you got a picture of yourself in your own mind, too, and maybe that doesn't match up so good either? Oh, hey, how about Ned's? You remember, the place we went to that time you came out to the tennis courts? Want to stop off there? They got a good juke box, maybe we could dance or something."

thirteen

IN THE LIVING ROOM of Dick Whitfield's apartment on the hillside high above the Strip, Stush lay prone upon the divan while Dickie washed dishes at the sink in the tiny kitchenette near by. The radio droned soft dance music, and the Venetian blinds stirred and rattled against the window sill, bright sun creeping through the slats into the warm and stuffy room. Stush's pale hair was damp with perspiration and his broad sunburned shoulders were too wide for the narrow divan cushions. He squirmed uncomfortably, burrowing his face into his doubled arm, and then lay motionless once more, his heavy body instantly sprawling and relaxed as though it had been flung down there from some enormous lofty pinnacle.

(*137*

Dickie stacked the dishes to drain in a rubber rack beside the sink and wiped off shelf and table tops neatly. Last of all, he removed the towel that he wore tucked into the waist band of his blue beach trunks, folding it precisely to hang upon the rod with several others. He moved quietly into the living room, picking up the package of cigarettes lying on the coffee table.

"Stush, are you sleeping?" he said very softly.

"Let me alone," Stush mumbled. "You want to go some god-damn party, go ahead and go."

"I just thought you might like to," Dickie said.

The room was close and airless. Dickie's hair too was damp, falling in black curls over his forehead. His handsome youthful face looked somehow thinner and a little tired.

"It's going to be a terribly hot day in town, Stush," he said, his voice coaxing. "This apartment is like an oven already. At least the beach would be cooler. Bob and Dora are sweet kids, they're all nice kids. We wouldn't have to stay if you didn't want to."

"Listen," Stush said, his voice louder but his face still hidden. "The top of my head's blowing off. Will you shut up now and let me alone!"

Dickie moved away, walking restlessly the length of the room to the window. He picked up a book from a table top and put it down again. The room was becoming undeniably hotter, and he mopped at his face.

"Shall I get you some more aspirin?" he said.

Stush did not answer him.

Dickie drifted back to the coffee table. There were heavy stalks of pungent-smelling white stock in the flower bowl, and Dickie rearranged them, his hands gentle and loving as he pinched away several wilted flowerlets.

Suddenly he spoke again, his voice strange and strained and not quite steady.

"Well, wherever you went last night, you certainly must have had a lot to drink anyway!"

For an instant, Stush's body gathered together and was very still, and then with one of his sudden catlike motions, he rolled over and sat up.

"Pick, pick, pick!" he mumbled. "Jesus, you're worse than some goddamn old lady. Sure I had a lot to drink last night. You think I lay around and chew aspirin tablets for fun?"

Dickie moved off quickly toward the window again.

Stush held his head between his big hands, moving it back and forth cautiously and experimentally.

"Boy, I had a hell of a time last night if you want to know," he said. "This sure is a real great town all right."

He flexed and limbered his great bare shoulders next, and then reached out for the cigarettes on the table.

"Come on, give me a light," he said impatiently.

Dickie hesitated for only the fraction of a second, and then he turned wearily, his face somber, and came with the match folder in his hands.

"Listen, you so goddamn crazy to go this party, let's go," Stush mumbled, the cigarette bobbing in his mouth as Dickie held the flame for it. "You got some dark glasses I could wear in the car going out there? I'll go in the water and cool off and then lay around in the sun for two or three hours and bake the booze out of me. Come on, let's get a move on, what do you say?"

"All right," Dickie said. "Fine. Lovely."

Stush doubled his arms and lifted them slowly above his head, muscles rippling smoothly under his dark sunburned skin.

"Jesus," he said through the smoke, his face suddenly amused, "I think maybe I'm going to live at that! Listen, where you got your car parked? I don't feel like walking around any goddamn hills hunting for the car. Why don't you go get it first and drive it up front here, okay?"

(139

There was a sound of running water from the bathroom, but Dickie did not answer him.

Stush sprawled back against the divan comfortably, his legs wide apart, his arms dangling, the cigarette still hanging from his mouth.

"Hey, you got any tomato juice in the icebox?" he called. "I could sure use about a gallon of it if it's cold. Is there any in there?"

"I think there's a big can that hasn't been opened yet," Dickie said, his voice flat. "Help yourself."

"Come on, don't be like that, baby," Stush said teasingly. "You get it and fix it up nice for old Stush, you know, like you did that other time, with the raw eggs in it, and that black bug juice stuff out of that bottle you got. What the hell is it you call that bug juice?"

"Worcestershire sauce," Dickie said, but his voice was not amused and neither was his face, as he came out into the living room.

"Yeah, that's it, Wooster-bug juice," Stush said pathetically. "I sure could use a slug of that Wooster-bug juice right now. My head's splitting wide open. Come on, honey, you're the one that knows how to take care of old Stush and make him feel good! You sore at me about last night, you want to let me die on purpose, or something?"

"Stush, honestly!" Dickie said.

But he went. And over the sound of hastily banged cupboard doors in the kitchenette, his voice bubbled back, exasperated and chiding, but happy once more and somehow relieved.

"Stush, you're crazy, you're such a character! My god, don't you realize you left me sitting here last night waiting to meet you at six-thirty, you're gone all night long, you never even telephone, I nearly go out of my mind worrying that something has happened to you, you roll in here this morning roaring drunk, and I do mean roaring. God knows where you've been or who you've been with or what you were doing. And then you sit there and moan about your hang-over and I'm supposed to fall all over myself to take care of you and doctor you up with pick-me-ups and aspirin tablets and—Stush, you're crazy, you're really mad!"

"Yeah, sure," Stush said. "Hurry up with that stuff, huh? This crummy apartment is getting hotter than the hinges. Let's get the hell out of here and get down to the beach."

"Keep your shirt on, will you?" Dickie called back contentedly from the kitchenette. "There wasn't any tomato juice on ice, I'm pouring it over ice cubes to chill it for you. Stush, you can't imagine what a night I spent last night, worrying about you. And then you walk in here this morning and expect me to act as if nothing had happened at all. You're a character. I just never knew anybody like you, you're fabulous!"

Behind him, Stush smiled his sudden, warm, engaging smile.

"Yeah," he said serenely. "That sounds like old Stush all right."

And then he said, "What's the matter, baby? Was you scared I was gone for good?"

fourteen

WHEN MAGGIE arrived at the beach party that Sunday, a crowd had already collected, overflowing the terrace of the house and spreading out across the unkempt stretch of sand. Cliff excused himself immediately and hurried away to purchase the additional beer and hamburger buns that it seemed certain they were soon to need.

(*141*

Maggie pushed through the crowd slowly, holding tightly to Jamie's small sweaty hand and lugging a big, bulging, green-canvas beach bag in the other. She stopped to greet several people, and suddenly someone called: "Maggie! Hello, Maggie!"

It was Dick Whitfield who plunged through the crowd toward her, his dark hair hanging in wet ringlets on his forehead, and a white bath towel draped over his neck.

"Hello," he said again. "I've been watching for you guys. Look at this mob, will you, it's turning out to be quite a party. Hi, Jamiekins. My lord, what have you got on your head?"

It was a little inverted metal saucer with a large red and yellow plastic knob on top of it, all held firmly in place by a wide, soft plastic chin strap.

Jamie jumped up and down delightedly.

"Dickie, look at me! Look at me, Dickie!"

"Righto. Looking right at you."

The little boy stuck the rubber tube that dangled from his strange headgear into his mouth, puffing out his cheeks to blow. Immediately, a jet of shining soap bubbles streamed out out of the knob on top of his head.

"Heavens to Betsy," Dickie said with mock astonishment. "Never saw anything like that in my life!"

"He would wear it," Maggie said. "He'll have sunstroke with that tin on his head, but what can you do? Dickie, I haven't seen you in ages, how are you? My god, everybody turned out today, it must be the weather."

"Mommy, I want to take off my shoes," Jamie said, pulling at her black shorts excitedly.

"Just a second, darling. Let's get out of this crowd first."

"Come down where we're sitting," Dickie offered. "We're down the beach a way. Stush is sleeping."

As he spoke he lifted the little boy up from the melee of trampling feet, swinging him onto his shoulders astride his

142)

neck. He secured him there with one hand upon the child's ankle and reached for Maggie's bag.

"Wonderful," she said. "I'll get Jamie organized and then I'll come back up here and look for Dora."

They walked together across the sand, out beyond the edges of the crowd to where Stush lay sprawled in the middle of a little oasis of spread towels. He lay relaxed and motionless upon his belly, his face hidden in the crook of his arm, his magnificent sunburned body mahogany red in the bright sunlight and his hair albino pale. He did not stir as they approached.

Maggie spread a towel of her own, kneeling upon one end of it and anchoring the other end with her bag against the wind. Dickie lowered Jamie to her and she stripped off his T-shirt and removed his canvas sneakers. She rubbed his bony little back and chest with thick white lotion from a bottle and, last of all, at his insistence, carefully adjusted the bubble hat back in place upon his head. She presented him with a large bent metal spoon then from the depths of the commodious bag.

"There now, off you go."

He darted away immediately, running toward a cluster of children near by who were engrossed in the communal digging of a great hole in the sliding sand.

Maggie sank back comfortably and cupped her hands over a match for a cigarette.

"What a wonderful wonderful day," she said, her eyes upon the vast, shining, blue water. "Perfect beach weather. I'm going to sit a minute and then I'll go back up to the house. Maybe I can help at the barbecue or something."

"I'll go with you when you go," Dickie said.

He was silent then, lounging upon his elbow, and Maggie studied him covertly, her eyes sliding away to Stush, who still lay motionless beside them.

At last she said carefully in a soft voice, "You seem pretty quiet today, chum. Nothing's the matter, is it?"

"Oh, no," Dickie said quickly. "It's perfect. Nothing could possibly be better. Honestly, Maggie."

"Well, good for you," she said, her face not quite convinced.

Jamie ran back to them suddenly, carrying a tin beer can.

"Mommy, I found this and I want to take it home. Put it in the bag."

"All right," she said good-naturedly. "Let's be sure it's empty though."

She shook it several times before she crammed it down into one side of the canvas bag.

Jamie lingered.

"Who's that?" he asked, pointing his finger.

"Haven't you met Stush?" Dickie said. "No, I guess you haven't. He's a friend of mine and his name is Stush."

"Why's he want to sleep at the beach?" Jamie said skeptically.

He circled Stush curiously, coming around to his other side and stooping to peer into his face. He stared intently for a moment, and suddenly he yelled at the top of his lungs and blew on his bubble tube, twisting up his face at the same time into a fierce, small, bubble-headed gargoyle.

Stush rolled over and sat up all in one swift motion.

"Mother of god!" he said softly, his face blank.

Dick and Maggie laughed together.

"I'm awfully sorry," Maggie said. "Jamie, that really wasn't nice at all, you know."

Stush stared unbelievingly for another instant and then threw back his head and laughed uproariously.

Jamie waved his arms and gyrated in a transport of delight, frenzied streams of little bubbles pouring out of the top of his head to whip away in the sea wind.

"Stush, meet Jamie," Dickie said amusedly.

"Listen, bub," Stush said, quite serious all at once. "Stand still a minute, will you? Let's see how that bubble thing works."

"I'll show you," Jamie said, instantly pleased.

144)

He loosened the chin strap and they bent over it together, their two fair heads close.

"You put the bubble juice in here, see?" Jamie explained. "You know. Bubble juice from the store. And then you screw the top on and when you blow, bubbles come out of your head."

"Well, how do you like that!" Stush marveled, his face intent and engrossed. "Let me try it once, huh?"

"All right," Jamie said generously. "I'll help you put it on."

He adjusted the tin hat on the top of Stush's head, and then stepped back a little.

Stush puffed on the tube, screwing up his face into the most frightful grimace of them all.

Jamie shrieked with laugher and threw himself upon the sand, his feet waving in the air.

After a moment, Stush loosened the chin strap.

"Okay, bub," he said gravely. "Now it's your turn again."

And then he added to Dick and Maggie, "Hey, this hat sure is something, no kidding!"

He laughed just as uproariously and spontaneously at Jamie's second performance with it. They traded it back and forth several times, with continuing mutual delight. Finally, at the end of one of his turns with it, Stush put the hat down upon the bath towel and raised himself effortlessly to his feet.

"Okay, what do you say, bub?" he said to Jamie. "Let's us go get wet and cool off a little. You want to?"

"Okay," Jamie said worshipfully, reaching out for his hand.

"Don't worry, I'll hang on to him careful," Stush called back to Maggie over his shoulder.

They ran down the sloping sand together, hand in hand, the large man and the small boy. At the water's edge, Stush scooped the child up easily under one arm, and splashed out into the running surf.

Maggie watched them go, her face puzzled and half-frowning.

"Well, what do you know!" she said. "And Jamie's the shy type! I never knew him to make up with anyone that quick before, in all his life."

Dickie, too, looked after them.

"Well, I suppose it's because Jamie can tell that they have so much in common," he said, laughing softly. "Stush is—ah, Maggie, isn't he really fabulous? He can be so exactly like a child."

His eyes lingered upon Stush's great shoulders shining in the sunlight above the restless water.

"You know, it's funny, he's always reminding me of that, the wonderful times you have when you're a child and everything is new and exciting to you. He makes me remember when I was a little boy and lived with my aunt, the lovely rainy Saturdays when we went to matinées, how terribly exciting it was, splashing through the streets in a taxi and the crowds outside the theatres, and the ice cream sodas we had after, the way you'd sit there trying to make it last forever. Stush is—I guess I'm sort of going on about him, aren't I? I know that you don't like him very much."

Maggie's eyes were intent upon an endless figure eight that she drew with her finger in the hot sand at the edge of the beach towel.

"I'm sorry, Dickie," she said. "For some reason, I just don't trust him. I don't want you getting hurt, sweetie, that's all."

"Don't worry," Dickie said simply. "And even if I did, it would be worth it."

"Where's your sun oil?" Maggie said. "Your back's getting all red, stupid. Here, turn around."

He turned obediently and she squeezed the tube, rubbing the lotion briskly across his shoulder blades.

Over the booming tumult of sea sound, there came a humming motor from the clear blue sky where a small plane flew slowly up the beach. It trailed a great banner after it, like an insect crawling half-emerged from a chrysalis, a great diaphanous streamer swelling gently across the deep sky with gigantic red block letters that proclaimed, "Jesus Saves."

Stush came out of the water and ran back up the sand, carrying Jamie slung upon his hip. Maggie shook out a towel in readiness and he dropped the little boy into her lap.

"Hi, my sweetie," she said. "Did you have a good swim?"

"Yes," he said breathlessly while she rubbed at him vigorously with the bath towel. When he was dried, his fair hair standing on end, he caught up the bent spoon and ran to Stush, who stood with his legs thrust apart, shaking water from his ear.

"Come on, Stush," he said. "Let's us make a big hole in the sand, should we?"

"Look," Maggie said quickly. "Stush has been real nice to play with you. Now he wants to sit in the sun and dry off. You run play with the other children for a while, why don't you?"

"Yeah, you go ahead, bub," Stush said. "We'll play some more later. Okay?"

"Okay," Jamie said, moving off reluctantly.

Stush dropped down upon the spread beach towels.

"Boy, it feels real good," he said contentedly. "That water freezes you, and then the sun is hot. I sure like the beach."

For a moment he lay sprawled and motionless like a drowned man, rivulets of water running on his body and his face, his hair plastered to his skull, and even his pale eyes glistening with water.

He rolled over onto his belly and lifted his head to look at Maggie, his gaze at once intimate and personal.

"You got a real cute kid," he said.

He reached out deliberately, his big blunt fingers closing warm over Maggie's bare foot.

"I guess he takes after his mother, huh?"

"That water must be quite cold yet," Maggie said shortly. "Have you done much surf swimming?"

"I said your kid gets his cuteness from you, right?"

Maggie moved her foot then, but his fingers tightened around it.

"Uh uh," she said.

"What you mean, 'uh uh'?" Stush said, the beginnings of amusement on his face.

"Just what you think I mean," Maggie said, her eyes flaring. "Dickie, shall we go up to the house and get a drink or something?"

"Fine," Dickie said. "Want to come, Stush?"

Stush's face was vastly amused.

"Naw," he said. "You guys go ahead. I need another drink today like I need a hole in the head, no kidding. I'll lay here some more and bake the booze out of me."

He rolled slowly over onto his back, lifting his arms and stretching voluptuously. He turned up his eyes to look at her out of a strange-planed, upside-down satyr's face.

"What's the matter, Red?" he said softly. "You afraid in another minute I'll get you going?"

"Let's go, Dickie," Maggie said tersely. "I can keep an eye on Jamie just as well from the terrace."

fifteen

BY THE TIME Bud and Caro arrived, the party was in full swing. There were cars parked solidly along either side of the highway, a collection ranging from dusty jalopies to sleek sports cars and including one polished ornate motorcycle with a silver-studded saddlebag. Bud drove by slowly, pulling off the road at the first empty spot.

There was a steady roar of traffic along the broad highway. On one side of it loomed the great coastal foothills, on the other side the sand sloped away down to the water's edge. The house was on the sea side, set on the sand, with its nondescript frame back turned to the road.

It was a completely ramshackle old place, weather-beaten and without paint, enclosed by a high board fence with a low tumble-down garage beside it. It was a house so weather-beaten and indigenous to the stretch of empty rocky beach upon which it stood that it might have been possible to pass by it many times without once particularly noticing its presence there at all.

Bud and Caro hovered at the side of the highway, and then suddenly darted across, running fleetly hand in hand before another onrushing wave of automobiles. The sun was dazzling bright and hot, and there was no sight or sound of life anywhere about the house, only the roaring traffic sound mingling with the constant thunderous booming of the sea.

"It's very quiet for a party, isn't it?" Caro said. "I expect this couldn't be the wrong house, could it, Michael?"

"No, this is it," Bud said.

He pulled open a sagging wooden gate in the fence and they stepped through into the deep shade of a sheltered patio along the side of the house. There was no sun there, and the stones were damp and mildewed underfoot, and drifted here and there with sand.

"There's a terrace down back on the beach side. I guess everybody must be down there."

A gliding sea gull screamed high overhead and Caro shivered.

"Michael, I don't like this house," she said. "It's dank and dark and still and shut away. Michael, do you ever get feelings like this about places, just by stepping into them? Do you think there really could be places that give off some sort of psychic emanations? I don't like the feeling that I get from this house."

"Naw," Bud said reassuringly, reaching his arm about her thin shoulders. "It's just walking into a dark place like this out of the sunshine, it makes you come out in goose bumps. This is a terrific house. I been up here a couple times with Bob and Cliff. I wouldn't mind living up here myself, not one little bit!"

Caro moved forward with him reluctantly, the drifted sand grating beneath her feet.

"We could go back, Michael," she said, her eyes very large. "If we went right now very quickly, no one would see us or ever know we'd been here."

Bud laughed.

"You'll be all right once you're back in the sun. There's a door here some place that goes to the steps down to the terrace. Oh yeah, here we are."

The door was set flush in the fence and was nearly indistinguishable from the other similar weathered boards. Bud pulled it open and instantly the sun leapt in, and with it the vista of pale sand and sparkling blue water down below and the faint indefinable party sound of music and mingling voices. The rocky beach was dotted with people, a lively group in bathing suits who pummeled a ball back and forth among them, huddles of supine sunbathers, the children who raced with pails and shovels at the water's edge, and the strollers who drifted aimlessly from one group to another, carrying glasses and beer mugs in their hands.

There was a short flight of railed wooden steps leading down to a kind of landing built out from the side of the house, and then a longer steeper flight continuing on below it. A suntanned young man in swim trunks was racing up the lower flight of steps, with a bucket in his hand.

"Hey, Bob!" Bud called down to him. "What do you say, boy!"

He lifted his pleasant tanned face to look.

150)

"Bud! Glad you could make it, kid. Come on down, every-body's out back here on the terrace."

"This is Bob," Bud said. "Bob, this is Caro. Hey, it looks like quite a party. Where's Dora?"

"Glad you could come, Caro," Bob said. "Dora's taking a turn at the barbecue. Go on down and say hello to her. I have to get some more ice from the kitchen, I'll be right back."

He disappeared into the house through a doorway that opened onto the small, railed wooden platform of the stair landing.

As they descended, the sounds from below increased into a pandemonium, with an enthusiastic chorus of singing voices and the twang of a guitar audible above all the rest. By the time they reached the lower steps, the terrace came into view. It was a broad unroofed sort of porch with a low wide wall running all the way across the back of the house and supported over the sand by immense wooden pilings. There was a large brick fireplace area at the far end with a charcoal fire smudging beneath a grill grating, and a long table in front of it loaded with baskets of buns, stacks of paper plates, huge wooden bowls of salad and all the paraphernalia of bottles, glasses and ice buckets. The whole terrace swarmed with people and spilled over down the several broad concrete steps to the sand.

The guitar player, a slim boy in tight blue jeans, was perched on the low wall near the barbecue so that the knot of singers that surrounded him was a constant impediment to all the activity centering around the food and drink area. The rest of the terrace space was taken up by groups of people in all varieties of informal beach attire, packed together as they talked and munched at hamburgers, lighted cigarettes and drank from mugs and glasses.

"Boy, what a rat race," Bud said appreciatively. "Looks like everybody came all right and brought their uncles along be-sides. I don't see Maggie anywhere. Why don't you stay here

(*151*

and I'll go and look for her. You like a drink? I'm going to see if they've got any cold Coke."

"No, thank you, Michael," Caro said. "I'll wait for you here."

Bud plunged away into the crowd, and Caro turned to the person standing nearest her, a thickset woman in tennis shoes and a mismatched skirt and blouse, her grizzled gray hair a wild untidy mop above her darkly suntanned face.

"How do you do?" Caro said composedly. "It's a very nice party, isn't it? Do you play volleyball?"

"Christ, no," the woman said cheerfully. "I'm just one of the neighbors. I live a half mile down the beach, back that way, on the sand the same as Jere is here."

"I expect the beach is a marvelous place to live," Caro said. "Do you like living out here very much?"

"Well, I don't know why anybody'd ever live anywhere else," the woman said heartily.

She caught hold of Caro's shoulder all at once.

"Honey, look down there. See those big rocks where the tide's going out? Don't you tell a soul I said so, but I bet you that's as good a piece of moonstone beach as you'll find anywhere on this whole coast. Wonderful rock beach all along here, no good for shells but I never cared beans about shells anyway. Rocks and driftwood! Honey, you ever take a good look at the big piece of driftwood Jere's got over there in his place? That's one of my pieces, found it right here on this beach, did all the work on it myself and gave it to Jere for Christmas last year. What do you think of that?"

"I'm sorry, but I've never seen it," Caro said. "I've never been at this house until today. Who is Jere?"

"Oh, I guess you must be a friend of some of the boys," the woman said. "Didn't you meet Jere yet?"

She looked around quickly over her shoulder.

"Well, I don't see him now. He was right over there just a

minute ago. Jere owns this house and rents out the rooms to the boys. He's a writer, he's a real nice fellow."

"You know, that's very curious," Caro said. "What's his name, really, I mean? Because years ago I used to know a man called Jere and he was a writer too, a screen writer."

"Tidings," the woman said. "Jere Tidings. Light-haired tall fellow. He the one?"

Caro was silent for an instant, her face expressionless.

And then she said, quietly, "How very odd! Yes, of course. He used to be a friend of my sister's. I haven't seen him for ages."

"Well, I guess it's just like they always say, it's a small world," the woman said cheerfully.

"It is, isn't it?" Caro said. "You know, I think I'd like to have a drink now. Does one just ask over at that table, or what?"

At that moment, Maggie was standing amid a group of people congregated off the end of the terrace.

"Whoops," she said suddenly. "I think that's Jamie crying, I'd better see."

She handed her glass to someone quickly, and ran off across the sand.

"Jamiekins, here I am," she called soothingly. "What's the trouble, darling?"

She knelt, holding out her arms for him, and just as he flung himself upon her, she caught sight of the bright red rivulets of blood running over his wrist.

Maggie caught her breath and held him back away from her.

"Darling, let me see your hand," she said, her voice suddenly sharp and urgent. "Let me look at it. Jamie, don't, darling, I have to see it!"

The little boy threshed and struggled, howling more loudly than before. Maggie caught his tightly doubled fist in both of her hands, her teeth set as she worked desperately at prying open his small resisting fingers, already red and slippery with blood.

Several other children clustered around to watch, their faces solemn. A chubby little girl with pale braids and a blue bathing suit said, "We didn't do nothing to him, honest. We were just picking up stones in the water and all at once he started hollering like that. What's the matter with him? His hand is bleeding something awful, isn't it?"

"Oh, damn!" Maggie said softly.

She took one brief despairing look at the inside of his hand, covered and shining with blood, and then bundled him up into her arms, rising swiftly to her feet.

"He's cut himself, I can't tell anything until I get his hand washed off. I'll have to take him up to the house."

She set off as rapidly as she was able in the soft sand, her head bent as she murmured soothingly to Jamie, and the small procession of children tagging after her.

A tall light-haired man in faded blue denim trousers and a white pull-over detached himself suddenly from a group of people and fell into step beside her.

"Someone have an accident?" he said sympathetically. "Can I help?"

"He's cut his hand," Maggie said, her voice a little rapid and distracted, her face pale with her blue eyes bright and distended and a long smear of blood drying across one of her cheeks. "Ah, darling, don't cry like that! I can't tell how bad it is until I get it washed off. Do you know where there's a bathroom?"

The light-haired man, meanwhile, had been examining Jamie's tightly clenched, bloody, sandy fist.

"The one in my place will be quickest," he said. "Come on, fellow, we'll have you fixed up in a minute."

As he spoke, he lifted Jamie out of Maggie's arms and gathered him against his shoulder.

"He's all right, you fellows go back and play now," he said

to the flock of wide-eyed children as he set off rapidly with his long, sure-footed stride.

"We go in over this way," he said to Maggie briefly as she hurried after him. "Don't worry, I think it looks much worse than it is."

He passed swiftly along the length of the terrace and around the end of it to where a few uneven wooden timbers nearly buried in the sand served as steps leading up the slope to the glass-enclosed front of a wing attached to that side of the old house.

He shoved open one of the glass panels, and carried Jamie in ahead. Maggie had a brief and confused impression of a cavernous, dimly lighted room as she quickly followed after.

The man passed through another doorway at the back, snapping an electric switch on the wall inside the door. It was a large white tiled bathroom with a glassed shower at one end of it. By the time Maggie was through the doorway, he had Jamie seated on the tile shelf beside the washbowl and was holding his small hand firmly beneath a running stream of water from one of the faucets.

"We'll have you fixed up in a minute so that you can go back to play," he was saying to the child conversationally. "What's your name, do you know you haven't told me? Look, if you'll sit still just a bit longer, there's something in my desk drawer that you may have. It's a surprise. Do you like surprises?"

He lifted Jamie's hand from the stream of water and studied it calmly.

"Here we are," he said to Maggie as she crowded forward anxiously to see.

"It's a cut across the tip of his forefinger," he said, indicating the little gapping slit where dark red drops of blood already gathered again.

"It looks like he might have gotten hold of a piece of glass.

It's not too deep though, and it's clean. We'll put something on it and he'll be good as new, won't you, fellow?"

"Oof!" Maggie said, a small soft sound of her relief. "I'm always terrified when I see him bleeding like that! You never know with these little characters."

The man glanced at her quickly.

"What you need is a drink," he said sympathetically. "I'll make you one in a minute."

She reached out gently to the child, pushing back the tumbled fair hair from his forehead.

"There now, my sweetie, it's all right," she said softly. "It's just a little cut on your finger. You'll be all better in a minute."

Jamie's weeping quieted into small breathy gulps and he watched the ministrations to his finger fascinatedly, his face red and streaked with tears.

"I can take over now," Maggie said. "You've been very kind."

"Won't take another minute," the man said. "I think there are cloths in that cupboard over there if you'd like to wash his face."

He rummaged among bottles lining the shallow shelves of the mirrored cabinet over the washbowl.

"You know, this will sting a little," he said to Jamie. "I tell you what, do you know how to count? Because if you can count, I'll guarantee you that by the time you've counted up to six, it isn't going to hurt any more. Now, are you ready? Here we go. One, quick now, what comes after one?"

"Two," Jamie said unwillingly, and then, his face suddenly screwing up again, "Ow! You're hurting me!"

"Poor sweetie," Maggie said sympathetically, wiping at his face with a wet doubled washcloth. "We have to fix your finger, darling. You're getting to be a big fellow now, you have to be brave."

"Look here, would you like to see a rabbit?" the man said quickly. "If you'll watch, I'll show you a rabbit, but you must sit very quietly and not cry or you'll frighten him away. Now, are you watching?"

He unrolled a length of narrow sterile gauze, manipulating it swiftly in his fingers.

Jamie giggled.

"That isn't a rabbit," he said scornfully. "It has to have ears up tall to be a rabbit!"

"Do you mean to tell me that you've never seen a lop-eared rabbit before?" the man said sternly. "This is a lop-eared rabbit, and this is how he looks when he's eating a carrot."

He manipulated the gauze again, and the little boy shouted with laughter.

Maggie watched, smiling.

The man was tall and thin and quick, with a hard, resilient, muscular-looking body, his arms and face deeply suntanned. There was a faint odor of alcohol about him, and his hands, as he deftly wrapped a fresh length of sterile bandage about Jamie's finger, were not quite steady.

"There you go," he said, snipping at the bandaging a last time with a pair of manicure scissors.

He swung the little boy down to the floor.

"Now," he said, "you go out to my desk and open the long drawer that's right in the middle, and in the front of it you'll find a Hershey bar. That's for you, that's the surprise."

He laughed as Jamie sped away, and began to return the bottle and bandaging to the cabinet.

"Would you like to wash up?" he said to Maggie. "I'll be out of your way in a second."

"Thanks," Maggie said. "And thanks very much for the first aid. You're awfully good, you know that? Do you have six children of your own, or does this just come naturally?"

The man laughed again, his contagious light-hearted laughter.

"It's an acquired talent," he said, "developed mainly, I'm afraid, from doctoring dogs and horses. Now then, towels over there, and here's combs, powder and things if you'd like to use them. I'll see how our patient is doing."

He closed the bathroom door after him.

Maggie slowly lathered her hands with soap at the washbowl, her eyes thoughtfully fixed upon the several shiny tubes of lipstick and the hairpins on the shelf.

When she came out into the big room again, a single bright shaft of sunlight was streaming in where a white muslin curtain had been pulled back from a section of the glass. In that light, Jamie hovered over a small table with a checkered black-and-white tile top, arranging and rearranging the ornately carved ivory chess pieces.

"Jamie! Oh, hey!" Maggie said quickly.

"It's all right," the man said, walking swiftly to meet her. "It was my idea. Now how about that drink? Jamie and I introduced ourselves while you were in the johnny. I'm Jere Tidings."

"I'm Maggie Harrison," she said. "Hello."

"What would you like, there's vodka, scotch, bourbon . . ." he said from the little bar cabinet in the corner.

"No, really," Maggie began, and then she said, "You know, I think you're right, I do need a drink after that. Scotch and soda, but very light. Please."

"Right you are."

While he mixed drinks in the corner, Maggie looked about the room. It was very large, with a high-beamed ceiling and a floor of some dark polished stone. The front wall toward the sea was glass, the glass continuing around the corner for a section of the side wall, all of it curtained with plain white muslin against the sun. A commodious, deep-cushioned window seat was built into the corner. The rest of the side wall was shelved to the ceiling and lined with books and phonograph albums. There was a long desk shoved against the shelves, the top of it littered with papers and untidy stacks of books.

The opposite wall was constructed almost entirely of stone,

with a great fireplace raised on a low platform from the floor, and a divan and several chairs arranged before it. All of the furniture was old. It was a comfortable disorderly room, with music sheets and wooden recorders in several sizes strewn carelessly upon the divan cushions, a bundle of rolled charts and maps spilled on the floor beneath a large telescope mounted on a tripod, and everywhere objects of weathered stone and wood and metal, as strange to Maggie's eyes as the big colorful abstract painting hung upon one wall.

"What a really wonderful room," she said. "If this were mine, I'd never leave home again."

The man laughed merrily.

"Only trouble is, the other part of the house is a shack," he said. "I've thought of burning it down for the insurance, naturally, but do you think I could depend on the Malibu fire department to save this wing for me?"

"I'd never risk it," Maggie said, laughing with him. "How long have you lived here?"

"Here we are," he said, walking briskly back across the room with the glasses in his hands. "Tell me if this isn't right, I took you at your word when you said light."

He led the way to the cushioned window seat in the corner, behind a low, round, wooden coffee table. Once they were seated, with the glasses lifted, he said lightly, "Well, here's to a successful operation. The patient seems wholly recovered and happy as larks."

"Yes, doesn't he?" Maggie said, her face tender as she looked away to Jamie's bent head where he leaned over the table, blissfully gnawing at a square of chocolate as he arranged the chess pieces endlessly in some intricate fantasy of his own.

"Poor baby! Thank you again. Really. I'm not very good in these minor emergencies. I stumble through if I have to, but I'm always weak in the knees when it's over."

(159

"Very good sign," Jere said cheerfully. "Be damn unfeeling of you if you weren't."

He studied her for a moment unabashedly as she leaned forward to put her glass on the table top that was filmed with dust and ashes and strewn with tobacco tins and pipes and twisted cleaners.

"Tell me," he said. "You don't quite look a friend of the bride's somehow, nor a female volleyball player either. Are you a broken-hearted former girl friend of the groom's then?"

"None of those things," Maggie said. "Does that mean that I'm here under false pretenses? After all, Cliff did invite me."

At the instant brief surprise and then amusement in his face, Maggie reached for her glass again, her chin lifting.

"My brother's the ball player in our family and quite often I come down to the beach with him. We know Cliff from around the volleyball court."

"My god, I'm relieved to hear it," Jere said. "I was afraid that you were going to turn out to be a Joyous Meditation girl from the outskirts of the great Kalammah. You're not, are you?"

"No, cross my heart," Maggie said with her wide smile. "Cliff loaned me a book, but I'm afraid I'd never get to first base, let alone the First Escarpment."

"You know, it's very odd about Cliff and the great Kalammah and all the rest of it," Jere said. "Cigarette? When you first meet him you never peg him for what he is, a first-rate mathematician and a very sound man in his own field. He plays championship chess, you know, which, just between you and me, is the reason I rented him the room here in the first place."

"That seems like a good reason. Do you always rent out rooms with such ulterior motives?"

"Absolutely," he said. "With Cliff, I got much more than I'd bargained for, too. He's turned out to be a wizard at working out everyone's share of the phone bill on the slide rule."

"It sounds as though you have a well-planned household,"

Maggie said. "I suppose you rented the room to Bob in order to get your traffic tickets fixed."

"Well, there are certain legal advantages to having a policeman in the house," Jere said amusedly. "But did you know that by hobby, Bob is a damn good mechanic? We're going to miss him now he's leaving us. He kept all our cars tuned up, just for the fun of it."

"Very well-planned household," she said. "What's your contribution, besides the first aid department?"

Jere laughed delightedly.

"Didn't you know? I am highly regarded for my leaky sailboat and the three horses that I have stabled up in the hills. Are you ready for another drink?"

"No, thanks."

It occurred to Maggie for the first time that he was a very handsome man, with his lean, strangely sculped face and his odd, green-hazel eyes.

"Let me freshen it up anyway," he said as he rose to his feet.

"No, really," Maggie said. "Small fry. Clear head for future emergencies, you know."

He was laughing again as he went swiftly down the room to the bar in the corner.

Maggie pulled her legs up onto the seat and leaned against the cushions comfortably, the drowsy warmth of the sun upon her back. With the curtains closed over the glass, the whole corner of the room swam in a soft light, diffused and strangely submarine, and there was the constant, thunderously booming crash of the sea just outside the windows.

"You know, I was just remembering," she said to Jere when he returned with a fresh drink in his hand. "There was one whole summer when I was a little girl back in Indiana that I spent sitting in the top of a big tree out in the orchard pretending that I was the keeper of a lighthouse off some rock-bound coast. I could pretend that a whole lot easier sitting right here."

"I spent a night once, years ago, in a lighthouse off the rock-bound New England coast," he said as he sat down. "It was a bit like trying to sleep in a hotel off Times Square. There was a wind gauge instrument rattling and whining somewhere just over my head all night long, and the light flickered on and off like an oversized neon sign outside the window. Keeping lighthouse in an apple tree would be a good deal more satisfactory than the real thing, I should think."

"Well . . ." Maggie said dubiously. "Anyway, it was a cherry tree. And it was full of walking sticks, green ones, big as my hand."

She shivered.

"Did you ever see a live stick? My brother cut one in two once and do you know what happened? The two pieces just went walking off like so, in opposite directions. Awful!"

He laughed again and put down his glass, turning toward her on the cushions, his head rested on his hand.

"So that's what brought you to California. Where do you keep lighthouse, anyway?"

"I don't," Maggie said. "Actually, I haven't seriously considered it since that summer when I was nine. As I remember, I gave up the whole idea in the fall and decided to run away with the gypsies instead. No, these days I do my lighthouse keeping in a Moorish period stucco in the middle of a funny little backwash neighborhood a mile away from any beach. Well, that's life."

"Every time. Who do you lighthousekeep for?"

"Well, you've met one third of my household already. Besides Jamie, there's my brother and my grandfather. It's very light housekeeping too. I make a stinking bad housewife."

"Another fairly good sign," Jere said. "How old is your grandfather?"

"Over seventy. He's very nice. The idea was, he came to California to retire. But then the first thing we knew, he'd blossomed out with a part-time job at a lumber yard, and lessons at Arthur Murray's. Now he works full time and has a string of lady friends and goes dancing every Wednesday and Saturday nights."

"Good for him."

"He really is wonderful." Maggie was silent for a moment, turning the warm empty glass between her hands. "Though sometimes, between Grandpa and my brother—Bud's eighteen—I feel a little like a housemother at a dorm."

His eyes upon her were suddenly warm.

"What a goose," he said. "Any resemblance between you and any housemother, living or dead, is purely imaginative. Tell me more."

Maggie looked up at him quickly, his lean alert face, his sinewy, bare brown arm with the delicate veining at the wrist.

She hesitated and suddenly she said abruptly, pointing over his shoulder, "What's that beautiful thingamabob up there on the wall?"

Without turning his head, he said, "It's African. Do you like it? It's a sort of mask they use in funeral ceremonials."

"It's beautiful," she said. "But very sinister. Come to think of it, it reminds me a lot of someone that I know. The friend of a friend of mine."

"That sounds like another story," Jere said. "Tell me about it."

But Maggie turned away, putting down her glass upon the table top with a small and final sound.

"Thanks for the drink," she said. "I really have to go now."

"Go where?"

Maggie rose to her feet.

"Home," she said. "Dull of me, isn't it?"

"Then why must you?" he said. "This party hasn't even gotten off the ground yet."

"Small fry," Maggie said. "Look at him, he's yawning his poor head off. He's had it for one day. He wants supper and bed."

"You could feed him and then bed him down in here," Jere offered.

"No, not really," she said. "He'd never give up and go to sleep. I'd better take him home."

"Come back after you've gotten him in bed?"

Maggie shook her head.

Jere made a small gesture of resignation and got up swiftly.

"All right, if you must. The responsibilities of parenthood, but, ah, the privileges! Wait a second, will you?"

"Jamie, hasn't this been a nice party, sweetie?" Maggie said as she turned away. "Now it's way past supper time and we have to go home, you know that?"

While Jamie protested over her coaxing, Jere rummaged hurriedly in a desk drawer across the room. He found several odd chess pieces and dumped out a foil-wrapped typewriter ribbon in order to drop them into the round tin box. He added three tiny wooden monkey figures, carved in the postures against evil, and a cellophane-wrapped candy before he closed the lid. And then he hastened back down the room to join them at the door.

"Surprise," he said, offering the box. "But you're not to open it until you're home, all right?"

For a moment he lifted the child's soft round chin gently in his lean hand.

"I'm sorry you hurt your finger the first time you came to visit at my house," he said gravely. "Will you come again, Jamie?"

"Yes," Jamie said, his eyes straying away down to the little tin box as he turned it curiously in his hands.

"Now then," Jere said briskly to Maggie. "Do you have a car, or shall I drive you?"

For an instant, her face was openly and nakedly regretful.

"Thanks anyway," she said. "But Cliff did bring us, you know. He was off getting more buns or something, but he must be back by now. I don't think he'd like it much if someone else took me home, do you?"

"Look here, you're not really going to let Cliff come between us, are you?" Jere said humorously. "You mean to say that you'll worry over what Cliff's going to think about it, when I telephone you tomorrow?"

Maggie began to smile, at first her eyes and then her whole face lighting.

"I claim constitutional rights," she said. "I decline to testify under the Fifth Amendment."

"Sustained," Jere said. "I'll talk to you tomorrow. Look out for those steps, they begin to get damp and slippery this time of day."

An hour later, the limpid cloudless sky flamed red and gold in the west, and the sun swiftly dropped out of sight behind the dark horizon line of the sea. In the brief waning twilight, last children were hurriedly rounded up from the beach and bundled into sweaters, good-byes were said, and the flight of steps up from the terrace was suddenly clogged with people, a boisterous exodus mingling there with a trickle of equally boisterous late arrivals. The party hangers-on donned coats and shirts against the sudden evening cold. An impromptu bonfire was built on the sand down the slope from the terrace and one segment of the late-stayers congregated there together with the indefatigable guitar player, while the rest of them crowded together in the warmth from the barbecue fireplace on the terrace itself. A portable phonograph was produced and a few couples began to dance. Lights came on within the house, shining out of the windows with a mellow golden warmth into the swift-gathering darkness.

In the last of the dim light, Bud and Caro picked their way around rocks on the deserted sand, returning toward the house from a walk far up the beach. The air was chill and bracing, the wind freshening, and Caro held her fleecy white coat wrapped about her, the collar pulled up like a cowl to cover her head, her other small hand warmly enfolded in Bud's large one.

"You warm enough?" he shouted down to her, his voice almost lost in the sea sound.

"Yes, it's wonderful," she shouted back, her pale uptilted face ecstatic and excited. "Michael, I love this! It's so marvelous, the darkness coming and the wind and the sea!"

"Yeah," he said. "But it gets freezing cold in a hurry this time of year, once the sun's out of sight."

She stretched up from her toes close in front of him, holding the great hooded collar of her coat tightly against the wind.

"Poor Michael! You should have worn your jacket. Are you very cold?"

"Naw, that's all right," he said. "We're back now anyway. What shall we do? Do you want to stay at the party a while longer, or shall we leave?"

"Let's not stay, Michael. This is all so marvelously much!" Her gesture encompassed beach and sea and sky. "After all this, I can't sit down somewhere where there are lights and make party small talk to anybody. Do you mind, Michael?"

"No, it's fine with me," Bud said, smiling indulgently. "We'll shove off right away then."

"I expect we must," she said reluctantly.

She whirled away from him, clutching her coat against the wind, turning back to the sea for a last moment where a long dark roller broke over in a frothing tumult of water just beyond an unmoved placid assemblage of sea gulls, standing together, stolid and ducklike, upon the wet sand.

"But we really must," she said, turning to take hold of his arm penitently in both her hands. "Michael, you're shivering! It's bad of me to keep you waiting, but I do love this so! We'll go quickly, right this minute."

And then she said as they began to climb the slope of sand on a long diagonal toward the lighted terrace, "Michael, before we really leave, I expect I'd better find a girls' room. Do you know where there's a bathroom?"

"Well, let's see," Bud said. "Oh, hey, there's somebody going into the house right now. Let's ask him, should we?

"Hi!" Bud called out, and they scrambled up the timbered steps together after him.

The man was a tall thin silhouette in the darkness as he paused to wait for them.

"Lady wants to powder her nose," Bud said. "Do you know where there's . . ."

"Yes, in this way," the man said, sliding open the glass panel. "It's the door back there, where the light's on. If you'll wait a second, I'll get some other light for you."

"Thank you, I can manage quite well," Caro said.

"I'll wait for you up on the terrace," Bud called after her as she disappeared wraithlike into the dimness, enveloped in the hooded white coat.

"All right, Michael. I shan't be long."

When she opened the bathroom door again quietly, there were soft shaded lights turned on all around the large room, and Jere Tidings knelt on the edge of the raised hearth, his back toward her as he bent over the small flickering flames as the wood fire began to kindle there.

Caro came down the room silently in her flat sandals, her coat collar flung back over her shoulders, and her cropped dark head once more combed and smooth.

"Do you mind?" she said as she came up beside him, holding out her hands toward the fire. "This sea wind gets into your bones, doesn't it?"

He looked up quickly, and suddenly they were both quite still, only the spit and crackle of the fire, and the rosy light from it dancing over both their faces.

"My god!" he said softly. "I don't believe my eyes! It is Caroline Bellamy, isn't it?"

"Yes, of course," she said. "I didn't think you'd remember, it's been such ages."

"Caro Bellamy," he said wonderingly as he rose to his feet. "Do they still call you Caro? My god, how long has it really been anyway? Four years—five? Let me get a good look at you."

He took hold of her shoulders, turning her around into the light.

"Caro, of course," he said as he looked down into her face. "But very grown up all at once."

And suddenly he laughed.

"You know, I've written this script at least fifteen times to my certain knowledge, and now I'm not able to use it. You weren't fat when I saw you last, and you didn't have braces on your teeth. You were nearly as lovely then as you are right now."

"Thank you," she said serenely. "But you needn't scrap the whole script, I expect. Isn't there always a part about the foul-tempered horrid brat she used to be?"

He laughed again.

"Ah, that you were," he said. "But several other things besides, all of them interesting. How is Helen?"

"Helen," Caro said. "Helen is exactly, exactly the same. Truly. Only the children have grown up a bit. The only difference."

"All the children have grown up," he said. "You know, in a minute this will hit me and I'm going to feel very ancient. This is really incredible, I can't believe it yet."

He turned away to kick judiciously at a top log on the fire, and then he said briskly, "I think this certainly calls for a drink, don't you? We have a lot to catch up on, I want to hear everything you've been doing. Could we keep your young man waiting?"

"Only for five minutes," Caro said. "Because he has a job he must get to, he works at night. And only a very small drink for old times. Something to make me warm."

"You know," he said as he went off down the room with his

quick nervous stride. "I remember very well the last time that I saw you. Do you remember when it was?"

"Of course," she said, following slowly after him. "I expect you're afraid that I might be sensitive about being reminded of it, but I'm not at all. You were there that night when there was that last really fearful row, when Helen went absolutely to pieces and was walking up and down and screaming about sending me to a convent."

She stopped and laughed, and he laughed with her.

"That was the time," he said. "You know, I think Helen really might have packed you off to a nunnery that very night too. Except her current pet psychiatrist finally arrived on the scene, all fat and breathless, remember, and talked her into sending you to boarding school instead. Somewhere in the East to study, what was it, dramatics?"

"Dramatics, but yes," Caro said. "They really did ship me off the next day, you know. Of course you were there that night. I remember perfectly well because you were rather nice to me, you were the only one who was. Everyone else was shouting and being quite venomous. Wasn't it a ghastly row? Helen was absolutely raving."

He grinned at her fleetingly over his shoulder as he bent over the liquor cabinet.

"You might admit that Helen had some provocation. Weren't you being a little difficult and loving every minute of it?"

"You didn't really think that I was enjoying it, did you?" she said seriously. "If I believed you really thought that of me, I'd be very disappointed in you, Jeremy. I always felt somehow that you understood me quite well in those days and that you were the only person who really did."

He laughed delightedly.

"My own Caro! The only living human who has ever called me Jeremy! Well then, perhaps you weren't enjoying yourself, that night. Funny, but I have a faint impression somehow that you were."

"I wasn't at all," Caro said. "I was dying inside of myself all the while those days. I used to think quite seriously of killing myself, you know. It was awful!"

"And you didn't enjoy even that notion just a little bit?" he said gently. "Well, it doesn't matter anyway, it was a long time ago. I'm glad you don't mind remembering it."

"I don't mind at all," she said. "I expect the reason I don't is because I'm quite a different person these days. I am, truly, though you've only my word for it, of course."

She paused, and then she said, "As a matter of fact, I've gone quite the opposite. I don't sleep around at all any more, Jeremy. It's been years now."

"Now you alarm me even more than you did then," he said gayly. "Don't tell me that you've given up sex altogether!"

"Yes, I have," Caro said. "But only for the time being, naturally."

He was laughing again as he gave her the small liqueur glass and put his arm about her, leading her back toward the fire that flamed high now upon the hearth.

"You're not to laugh at me," she said accusingly. "I thought it all out rather carefully. I didn't want to do it at all for a long time and I was able to stop quite easily once I'd made up my mind. I won't ever do it again now until it's something that's very meaningful to me. I never want to be untidy and cluttered in that way again. When I have sex again I want it to be because it's something I want to do more than anything else in the world with some one person more than anybody else in the world. Do you think that's being terribly young and naïve about it, Jeremy?"

"No," Jere said. "On the whole, I think that's rather a good attitude for you to have about it. As the headshrinkers say, it's being laudably mature. So long as you don't overdo it, that is. But hadn't you ought to have found a meaningful prospect by now? What about this young character waiting out there on the terrace?"

"Michael's very sweet and good," she said. "I'm very fond of Michael. I don't somehow think he'll ever be that meaningful to me."

She rolled the little glass thoughtfully between her hands, her head bent to the aroma, her eyes fixed upon the leaping fire.

"There was a boy lying on the beach here this afternoon," she said dreamily. "He had the most enormous shoulders and the palest hair. He was like a great cat lying in the sun. Who was he, do you think?"

Jere laughed delightedly.

"Now I needn't worry about you any longer! You know, I told Helen a hundred or more times back in those days that if she were only able to leave you alone, you'd manage to grow up into a marvelously charming female creature, and now it seems that I was right."

"I expect Helen hated you for saying that," Caro said in a very quiet voice.

"Of course not," Jere said. "Why should she have?"

There was a sound from the darkness outside the glass door suddenly, and Bud's muffled anxious voice.

"Caro? You all right?"

"I'm coming, Michael."

She gave the little glass to Jere quickly and pulled her coat together about her.

With her small grave face lifted and framed by the deep-piled white fabric of her collar, she said, "May I come to see you, Jeremy? I'd like it very much."

He reached out, cupping her face for an instant in his hand, a swift and tender gesture.

"Would you come really?" he said with a matching gravity. "I'd like you to very much. I'm in the Malibu phone book, by the way."

"I know," she said serenely. "For years I've looked in all the directories until I finally found you there. I even memorized the number. Good-bye."

She went swiftly and gracefully, letting herself out through the glass panel and sliding it closed again quietly behind her.

Jere watched her go and turned back to the fire, lifting one foot onto the hearth, his body leaned forward and supported with his arms spread wide, his hands flat against the rough warm stone of the wall. The fire crackled and the big room was filled with the sound of the sea.

After a long time, he said softly, " 'Helen, thy beauty is to me . . .' "

And then he shrugged and laughed, and turned away.

sixteen

WHEN Bud O'Toole awakened the next day, the bedroom was warm and stuffy, and he felt the first faint and queasy pangs of what was for him a rare headache. From the other side of the thin wall, there was the sound of cheerful splashing water in the bathtub, Jamie's giggles, and Maggie's voice lifted merrily in a spirited rendition of "Old MacDonald Had a Farm" with complete sound effects.

> *Here an oink, there an oink,*
> *Everywhere an oink, oink . . .*

Bud rolled out of bed and scooped up a shoe from the floor, throwing it all in the same motion.

"Goddamn it!" he yelled, as the shoe bounced hard off the wall.

"How you expect me to sleep around this madhouse anyway? Will you kindly pipe down in there?"

"It's after twelve o'clock, you know that?" Maggie called back imperturbably. "You never sleep this late, it's time you were up."

Bud pulled on his underwear shorts and bounded barefoot down the hallway to the open bathroom door.

"Listen, you going to stay in here all day?" he said. "I have to take a shower."

"Keep your wig on, can't you?" Maggie said, where she knelt upon the floor beside the bathtub. "Why don't you have breakfast first and then take your shower? I'll have Jamie down for his nap in a flash, then I'll come get your breakfast, all right?"

Bud disappeared, muttering. Back in the bedroom, he ransacked in the shallow overcrowded clothes closet until he found a white terry-cloth robe. He donned it, knotting the belt about his waist, and glaring down at the hem of it that had shrunk up to his knees. Then he set off, barefoot, down the hallway again.

After a moment, came a bellow of utter outrage.

"The newspaper's all cut to pieces! What's going on around this madhouse. The paper's cut to pieces!"

"Oh, it is not!" she yelled. "Jamie cut some pictures out of the ads, that's all. He never touched the sports section and that's all you ever read anyway. Look on the kitchen table."

With a few last bangs and scrapes and thumps, the noise in the kitchen subsided. When Maggie arrived there five minutes later, Bud was hunched over the paper at the kitchen table, glumly sipping at the last of his orange juice.

"Howdy doody," she said gayly, reaching out to ruffle his hair as she swept by him. "How are things in Glocca Morra?"

"Cut it out," he said crossly.

"Mercy, you did get out of bed on the wrong side, didn't you? How you want your eggs, baby?"

"Huh? Oh, sunnyside," he said, his eyes upon the outspread

newspaper. "What's the matter with the crazy weather, smoggy or something?"

Maggie glanced out the open kitchen door into the hazy sunshine.

"Little bit, not bad," she said. "We shouldn't complain. Imagine what it's like downtown, if we're getting it out here. It's cooler today anyway."

The kitchen was in a state of complete confusion, with dirty dishes piled high in the sink, and the stove top covered with still more of them, but Maggie flitted back and forth cheerfully amid the chaos, and in a moment the room was filled with the pleasant cooking aromas of coffee and toast and bacon.

" 'Mr. Sandman, won't you send me a dream . . .' " Maggie sang happily, and the refrigerator door swung shut behind her with a resounding thud.

Bud winced and clapped his hand to his head.

"Listen, would you kindly pipe down? I got a headache."

"You are grouchy," Maggie said. "Why don't you take an aspirin and fly right?"

"I am not grouchy," Bud said belligerently. "What's got into you all of a sudden anyway, that's what I'd like to know. What you got to feel so extra good about, you're busting out all over?"

"Me?" Maggie said mockingly. "You talking about little old Pollyanna Merry Sunshine me? Why, honey, you know I always feel good!"

"Well, I don't," Bud said shortly.

Maggie dropped a pot lid with a clatter, and then suddenly stopped still, her head cocking.

"Was that the telephone?" she said quickly.

"I didn't hear anything," Bud said.

"No, I guess not," Maggie said cheerfully. "Well, how was the job last night? Parking many three-wheeled cars lately, any drunks pitching waiters out of that high-class joint you got down there, tell me news."

"Naw," Bud said drearily. "Nothing ever happens around that place. Oh yeah, Liz Taylor was there. Drove up in a big blue Caddy, custom job."

"What's she like?" Maggie said interestedly. "She's so beautiful in her pictures. What was she wearing?"

"Aw, I don't know," Bud said, rustling the sheets of the paper. "Some kind of blue dress with a full skirt. She's really terrific though, she's not like most of those movie girls, you see them out on the street and never look at them twice. She's really beautiful, but she looks kind of hippy."

"Maybe it was the dress," Maggie said. "I always had a feeling she must be really gorgeous. Why do girls in this town always want to bleach their hair anyway, tell me that? Pick up your paper, huh?"

She put down the plates in front of him swiftly and deftly and made a last trip back to the stove for coffee, pulling out the chair across the table from him finally and sitting down there with a steaming cup of her own.

"Listen, tell me about yesterday," Bud said impatiently. "I been waiting for you to tell me what you think."

Maggie slicked back hair from her flushed face briskly, and reached for the package of cigarettes.

"It was a very good party," she said. "I honestly couldn't have been more surprised, how about you? It really was a lot of fun, maybe the beach crowd should get together for parties more often."

"Not the party, you jerk," Bud said disgustedly. "Caro. What did you think of Caro?"

"Oh, Caro," Maggie said. She puffed hard on the cigarette, lighting it.

"Oh, Caro!" Bud mimicked her. "Cripes sakes!"

"Well," Maggie said, choosing words slowly and carefully. "She's really beautiful. She's perfectly lovely. It's terribly interesting to see a girl like her, she's wonderful to watch. It isn't just

(175

her face that's beautiful, I guess it really never is anyway. It's the way she moves and—well, just everything about her. I guess that's it, everything about her matches so, she's all so small and perfect and . . ."

Bud gave her a withering look across the table.

"I know all that, for gosh sakes," he said with his mouth full of food. "I told you she was beautiful, didn't I? Tell me what you think of her."

"Well," Maggie said again. "She's terribly interesting. She's completely different than most girls, she . . ."

"Look, I don't get this," Bud interrupted her, the beginnings of anger in his voice. "Naturally, she's completely different than other girls, I know that. Is that all you got to say about her?"

"Bud, look, sweetie," Maggie said gently. "What do you want me to say, for god sakes? I just met the girl for a few minutes, I didn't have a chance to get to really know her. You guys came late, I just talked to her for a few minutes, that's all. What can I tell you? What is it you want to hear me say?"

Bud suddenly shoved the plate of partly eaten food away from him, and when he reached for his cup and saucer, his hands were jerking so that the coffee slopped over onto the table top.

"Mag, sometimes I don't get you at all," he said, his voice low and shaken and angry. "I just don't get it. You've never said much about the girls I've gone around with, and I've never asked you because I could tell what you thought anyway. And that's okay because you were right. Most of them were nothing but birdbrains and chiselers and beach bums and pigs. Okay. But this is something altogether different with me. For once in my life I been lucky enough to meet a really wonderful girl. Sure she's beautiful, she's out of this world like some goddamn princess or something, I know that. But she's a whole lot more than just beautiful. She's all the time reading books like you do, she's thinking about things all the while in her head, the goddamnedest things, she . . . Well, I just never knew a person like her, ever in my life. Ever since I been going with her, I've been crazy for you to meet her. So you finally do, and look what happens! You ask me what I want to hear you say about her, I just wanted you to say you liked her, for cripes sake! But you don't, do you? I don't know, I don't get it, that's all, it don't make sense. Why don't you like her, just tell me that? Just tell me why . . ."

"Bud, listen to me!" Maggie made herself heard only by out-shouting him. "You're the one that said that, I didn't. You're making this whole thing up as you go along. I never said I didn't like her!"

"You don't have to say it, you think I'm stupid or something?" Bud shouted furiously. "You don't like Caro and I could tell it the minute you started talking about her. Okay, just tell me one thing you don't like about her. Go on and tell me."

Maggie sprang from her chair and dove for the door that opened into the hallway, closing it quickly and softly against the sound of his loud voice. When she turned around, she was laughing.

"Bud, aw, hey!" she said. "What's the matter with you today? Man, you're really bugged! You're trying to make a fight where there's nothing to fight about. I do like Caro. I never said I didn't. I like her very much."

"Oh, quit it, will you?" he yelled. "You think I'm Jamie or something, you can feed me a lot of double talk just to soothe me down? Don't you think I can tell how you feel by the way you act? Caro's beautiful, she's very interesting, she's different, yeah! All right, go ahead and tell me what you don't like about her. Go on, I'm listening."

"Bud, honestly," Maggie said, smiling at him helplessly. "Right now you are carrying on just like Jamie, you know it? You simmer down and quit screaming at me right now!"

"Goddamn it, I'll scream all I want to," Bud roared. "I asked you a question, didn't I? I'm still waiting for you to answer it."

"Listen, will you shut up a minute," Maggie said. "Was that the telephone?"

"No, it was not the telephone," Bud yelled. "You must have

telephone bells on the brain. Go on, tell me what's wrong with Caro, you're so goddamn smart!"

"Bud, I'm getting sick of this," Maggie said, with anger in her own voice. "What's got into you? You're acting worse than any baby, yelling and raving at me over nothing? I said I liked that girl, and that's the truth. I said I thought she was beautiful and interesting and different than most girls her age, and that's the truth too. It's none of my business anyway, is it? If I've got any single thing in the back of my mind at all, like you seem to think I have, maybe it's just that I wish you didn't take her quite as seriously as you do. And that's all."

The kitchen was suddenly and ominously quiet.

"Now just what do you mean by that crack?" Bud said softly.

"No crack," Maggie said. "You asked me, I told you. I could be wrong, couldn't I? It was just my impression, I think you take her a lot more seriously than she's taking you."

"I suppose what you really mean is, I'm not good enough for her," Bud said, white-lipped.

"No," Maggie said quietly. "That's not what I meant at all. I don't happen to believe that that is something you can say about people. But if I did, in this case it would be just the other way around. I'd say I thought that she wasn't good enough for you."

Bud erupted out of his chair, incoherent in his fury.

"What do you mean she . . . What you trying to say? Why, Caro's . . ."

"Oh, shut up and stop bawling at me like a lovesick calf!" Maggie said rudely. "If you're so crazy for the absolute truth, I think your girl's a little bit of a phony. Right now I think she thinks you're the one that's terribly different and interesting and that's what she likes. And the next thing you know, she'll have moved on to some other little playmate."

"Don't you say Caro's a phony!" Bud yelled. "Don't you ever say that. Caro's the most sincere person I ever met in my whole

178)

life. There's nothing she thinks or feels about anything, she doesn't come right out and tell you. It's not her fault if I . . . She's never tried to tell me she was in love with me, not ever once, she . . ."

"For god sakes, shut up a minute, will you?" Maggie said desperately, cocking her head toward the doorway into the dining room.

"Goddamn it, that is not the telephone!" Bud bellowed. "What's the matter with you? A doorbell rings a block and a half away and you start wetting your pants, it's the telephone. What is this big telephone kick anyway? Who you waiting for to call you that's so goddamn . . ."

"Bud, I want you to stop this right now," Maggie said. "You're going to wake up Jamie. Now I want you to listen to me for a minute. You're mad anyway, so you might just as well listen to what I'm going to say. Where do you get the idea that this girl is so out of this world better than you are? How do you know yet what you are, or what you can do? Bud, sweetie, when are you going to stop trying to run away from yourself galloping around tennis courts all day long, and begin to grow up? Do you feel that you're just killing time till you go in the Army or what? Couldn't you at least begin to think about going to school or getting started in some line of work that you like? What is it, Bud? Is it living in California where everything's measured by swimming pools and Cadillac cars, so that you're afraid to even try to compete? Or do all kids your age feel this way wherever they live? I know it's an uneasy kind of world to have to grow up in, is that it, you can't have confidence in anything, not even yourself and your own future?"

Bud was thin-lipped with rage.

"Don't you start in that tennis bum stuff again! I play tennis because I like to play tennis. It's the one thing I do real good. It's the most important thing in the world to find the one thing you really like to do and then . . ."

"Bud," Maggie said. "You play a good average game of tennis. Can you make a whole life out of being the bigshot best player at some little dinky public court off in a dinky little park some place? Ah, sweetie, I'm sorry, I . . ."

And then the telephone did ring, unmistakably, and Maggie ran.

Bud's face was stretched and stiff with rage. He walked blindly, kicking furiously at the sheets of newspaper on the floor with the shrunken, stained terry-cloth robe bobbing ridiculously about his ungainly, youthful, rawboned knees.

An old tennis racket stood carelessly leaned in a corner of the kitchen and he caught it up suddenly and stood still with it, getting the feel and balance of it right in his hand. And then he rocked on his feet, his face pathetic in its utter desperation, flailing smoothly and viciously so that the racket whistled through the air, hitting the endless imaginary balls sizzling away over some stretched imaginary net.

In the living room, Maggie grabbed up the telephone as she skidded to a stop before the wall niche, her hair flying. She paused for just a moment, holding it in both her hands, her face deliberately relaxing before she lifted it.

"Hello?"

"Maggie? Maggie Harrison?" the male voice said into her ear.

"This is Maggie Harrison."

"Look here, my girl," he said humorously. "Why didn't you tell me yesterday that your grandfather's name wasn't Harrison? And do you have any idea how many Harrisons there really are in the phone book?"

Maggie laughed, her face shining.

"You didn't ask me. We are a variegated household, Grandpa's Kennedy, and my brother's the O'Toole. How did you find me anyway?"

"The obvious, I'm afraid," he said. "I phoned up Cliff at his office and twisted his arm until he gave me your telephone number."

"And what did Cliff have to say about it?"

"Oh, he was a bit on the gloomy but resigned side," Jere said cheerfully. "He also warned me that I was wasting my time because you have a husband. Do you?"

"Only very technically," Maggie said. "The divorce will be final in five more months."

"Now the cat's out of the bag," Jere said. "So that's the gimmick you used to stall off poor old Cliff. Pity. Now you'll have to think up another one to use on me, in case you want to."

"I never repeat myself," Maggie said. "I'd think up a new and special one for you, in any case."

"I appreciate that. How is Jamie and the injured digit?"

"Oh, thriving," she said. "Dressings are down to a Band Aid today and he's forgotten all about it. He liked your surprise. He gathered up all the thingamabobs and put them back in the box and took it to bed with him when he went for his nap this afternoon."

"Good."

"The party was fun," she said. "Did it go on till all hours and have you dug your way out of the debris yet?"

"All cleared away as of an hour ago," he said. "Including a last couple bodies from the terrace. I'm sorry you didn't come back."

"Oh. Well," Maggie said. "There's always the baby sitter thing, you know. You can't always materialize one out of the air just when you want one."

"Could you with a day's notice?" Jere said. "Do you think you could have one materialized by tomorrow night?"

Maggie took a deep silent breath.

"I might," she said. "Why?"

"There's an old film playing in the village, a revival. Have you seen it? I thought we might make it dinner. I'll spare you my culinary efforts this time, how about Hanson's up the beach, and then the movie after?"

"It sounds nice," she said.

"Would you like to?" he said, his voice very direct.

"Yes," Maggie said. "I think I would."

"Good. Six-thirtyish all right for you?"

"Six-thirtyish is fine."

"Very good," he said. "Then we needn't hurry over dinner. Where the hell is your Moorish stucco lighthouse anyway?"

"Juniper Street," she said. "Bet you a nickel you don't know where that is."

"Bet," he said. "What number there?"

He repeated it after her and then he said, "Tomorrow night then. Tell Jamie I said hello."

"Yes, I will," Maggie said. "Tomorrow night then, six-thirtyish."

"Right," Jere said. "Phone me if you run into baby sitter trouble and we'll think of something. In an emergency couldn't we ask Cliff?"

Maggie giggled.

"No, I really don't think we could. Good-bye."

She put down the phone and spun all the way around on her toes delightedly for several times. And then she crossed the room very sedately and sat down in the old overstuffed chair. She relaxed against the cushions, stretching out her legs voluptuously, picking up her hair in both hands and coiling it absently on the top of her head, her face remote and soft and glowing.

seventeen

IT WAS seven o'clock and nearly dark when Tom Harrison drove up in front of the house on Juniper Street that following Saturday. The street, he discovered, was unwontedly parked with cars, they were lined solidly along the curb on either side so that he was forced to drive on slowly, looking for an empty space.

From the rear of the car, Jamie said sleepily, "Where we going now, Daddy?"

"I'm just looking for a place to park," Tom said. "The street's filled up tonight, what's happening around here anyway?"

But Jamie only yawned and leaned sleepily against the back of the front seat, his head drooping over the big bright-colored beachball that he hugged in his arms.

There was no parking space left at all, and at the end of the block, Tom made a U-turn and doubled back, running the car finally into the driveway beside the house. Before the motor was turned off even, the noise was plainly audible. Lively music, voices and laughter were loud in the accustomed peaceful quiet of Juniper Street.

"What's happening around here, anyway!" Jamie said excitedly, his attention caught at last, and his face instantly alert and wide awake.

He piled out of the car, lugging his ball, the minute Tom had the front door opened.

A man and woman with several children, all of them combed

and scrubbed and very dressed up, were just hurrying up the walk toward the house next door. The front door there stood invitingly open, the lighted rooms within were filled with hurrying figures, a great plume of pungent good-smelling barbecue smoke was rising from the yard behind the house, and through the foliage there was a glimpse of gleaming, bright-colored paper lanterns hanging from wires strung between the trees.

"It's a party at Juan's house!" Jamie shouted delightedly. "I want to see!"

He dropped his new ball and bolted off, with Tom bounding after him.

"Hey, no you don't!" Tom said, as he caught tight hold of the little boy's small warm hand. "You come on here in the house now. Your mother'll be looking for you."

"I'll ask my mommy," Jamie said threateningly. "My mommy'll let me go to Juan's house."

"Yeah, you do that," Tom said.

He released his hold upon Jamie's hand and the little boy ran up the walk ahead of him. Tom followed after, glancing once guiltily at his wrist watch in the dwindling daylight, and then fixing his eyes warily upon the front door as though he expected an angry Maggie to erupt there at any moment. But there was no sign of her, and he lengthened his stride to pull open the screen door for Jamie, the bright beachball bundled under his arm.

The living room was dim and stuffy, and empty except for the loud sound of cheerful voices and music from next door. Adding to the pandemonium, from somewhere at the back of the house came Maggie's voice, singing lustily and light-heartedly, something about being in love, in love with a wonderful guy.

"Hey, Jim," Tom called after the little boy as he darted through the archway into the dining room. "Ask your mother to come in here a minute, will you?"

He put the beachball down on a chair seat and waited, jingling

184)

coins in his trousers pocket, his smooth face wrinkling with faint distaste as he looked about the shabby, none-too-well kept small room.

"I'm in love, I'm in love, I'm in love, I'm in love . . ." Maggie caroled idiotically, and then her song broke off abruptly, interrupted by Jamie's shrill, excited, piping voice.

A moment later she swept in through the archway, her skirts flying about her slim tanned legs, a hairbrush still carried in her hand.

"Yes?" she said impatiently, her voice as inquiringly impersonal as though Tom were some stranger who had knocked in passing.

Tom held out a white envelope, and over the loud slamming of a door at the back of the house, he said, with his voice as impersonal as hers had been, "Something came up. I was late getting your check mailed, so I brought the money over with me to save time."

"Thank you."

Maggie took the envelope without really looking at it, or at him, and whirled around, heading back toward the archway. She was very dressed up in a full voluminous skirt of some heavy material mottled in vivid shades of blue and green, and a sleeveless jersey top with a low scooped neck and back in the same, dark, vivid green color. Her hair was loose over her shoulders, newly washed, and brushed until it was shining red and satiny smooth and crinkling with electricity.

"Aren't you going to count it?" Tom said a little spitefully to her disappearing back.

"That won't be necessary," she said tersely.

The back door banged again, there was a sound of rapid footsteps in the kitchen, and just then the telephone began to ring.

"Who is it?" Maggie called out, spinning back toward the telephone in its wall niche near the door.

"It's me, Mrs. Harrison," a young and female voice shouted

from the kitchen. "My mother wants some of those things you're keeping for her in the icebox. Okay?"

"Oh sure, help yourself, Margie," Maggie called back as she scooped up the phone.

"Hello?" she said a little frantically, clapping her hand over her other ear to shut out some of the noise and music that filled the house.

"Oh, hello, Mrs. Yamasaki! You did get my message then, I was just going to call you again. . . . Oh, you can? Oh, wonderful! I didn't know what I was going to do for a baby sitter tonight. Well, you know Margie Martinez usually sits for me, but with the party at her house tonight she couldn't. And Mrs. Malott from across the street couldn't sit either. . . . Well, I think it's terribly nice of you. . . . No, no hurry at all. Jamie's over at Martinez', he'll probably eat over there if he isn't too excited. No, that's perfectly all right, you get your family fed and the baby into bed first. And if we're not here when you get here we'll be over at the Martinez'. I'm not going out till later on. Thanks ever so much, Mrs. Yamasaki. Yes, it is quite a party, can you hear it down at your house too? Look, I can't tell you how much I appreciate this, Mrs. Yamasaki. I'll see you then."

Maggie dropped the telephone.

"Ooof, that's a relief!" she said softly. "Neighbors are a great institution."

Poised for flight back to the kitchen, she suddenly became aware of Tom again, still planted stolidly in front of the door, and she said shortly, "Well, what's with you? There something else you wanted, or you planning on standing around here all night?"

Tom flushed.

"I'm waiting to say good-bye to Jimmy the same as I always do, that's all. Where is he?"

"He's already gone over to Mrs. Martinez'," she said. "I guess he was so excited about the party that he forgot all about saying good-bye to you this time."

"Sounds like kind of a rowdy party, doesn't it?" Tom said flatly. "You intend to let him hang around over there by himself half the night?"

Maggie's chin lifted.

"It's just a barbecue and dance to celebrate a christening today. Everybody brings their children along. Juan Martinez is Jamie's best friend, they play together all the time. Juan's made a dozen trips over here to see if Jamie was home yet, he'd be heartbroken if Jamie didn't come to the party."

The back-door screen banged again loudly.

"It's me, Mrs. Harrison, Epifanio," a boy's excited voice called from the kitchen. "My *padrino* says to get ice cubes at your house. You coming over pretty soon, Mrs. Harrison? There's lots of people dancing already."

"Help yourself to ice cubes, Epi. I'll be over in a minute."

Maggie rose on her toes, poised and ready to run, and then turned back again exasperatedly to Tom who still stood stolidly before the door.

"And another thing," he said. "If you can spare some of your valuable time! What's all this stuff Jim was giving me about the other night? Some shooting around here and the street full of police cars and everything? He making it up or what?"

Maggie's eyes were flaring now.

"I don't know what he told you so how should I know. There were a couple police cars around here the other night, yes. There's an old man who lives by himself up around the corner. I guess he came home pretty tanked up and he got out a revolver and started shooting holes in the wall. The neighbors called the police and they came out and took the gun away from him. That's all there was to it, why?"

The noise from next door swelled into a cacophony of sound, shouts and applause and laughter, and then the music rose again, louder and faster.

Tom lifted his voice over it.

"Jesus Christ, why don't you get out of this crummy neighborhood," he said helplessly. "This is a crummy old house and a crummy neighborhood. Why don't you get the hell out of here and get a decent place for Jim to live in?"

Maggie caught her breath and came a quick step nearer, her voice soft and angry.

"You know, you make me sick at my stomach," she said. "What a snobby bastard you really are! I suppose your idea of a decent place to live is some smug, snobby, stinking, middle-class little neighborhood out there in your goddamn Valley. Well, so help me god, I'll never expose Jamie to places like that so long as I live! There's nothing wrong with this neighborhood. This neighborhood happens to suit me just fine if you want to know."

"Yeah, I'll bet it does at that," Tom said nastily.

Maggie's eyes blinked and for an instant she was very still, and then she said rapidly, "Look here, let's you and me get something straight right now, should we? I've been doing a lot of thinking since you were over here last week making your fancy speeches, and now tonight you've really wrapped it up with blue ribbons! I'm all done with you, you know that? I'm never going to fight with you again. As a matter of fact, I haven't got one single thing left to say to you any more about anything. I don't like you. Maybe there are such things as friendly divorces but this isn't one of them, not any more it isn't and you may as well know it. I don't like one single thing about you, and if I had my way Jamie'd never go near you again, and that goes double for your precious little Junie. You understand?"

The animosity was there at last, like the sudden spring of a striped lithe tiger, fierce and naked and deadly in the little room full of music and laughter.

"Damn right I understand," Tom said. "Because that's just the way I happen to feel about you. You act pretty damn smart these days, you've got Jimmy and you've got everything all your own way, haven't you? But let me tell you just one thing. You better watch your step, where you live and the way you live

188)

and the chasing around you do, because if I ever find out that you're not taking care of Jim just exactly the way you ought to, Junie and I will have that kid so fast it'll make your head swim. You understand that?"

"Why, you son of a bitch!" Maggie said in a clear voice. "Are you trying to threaten me? Then let me tell you something! I'll do just exactly as I please, and I'll do it where I please and when I please. And now you get the hell out of here."

"Now that's what I like, a girl with spirit, how about you?" Jere Tidings said pleasantly from the doorstep. "I'm sorry, I don't think you heard me knock. Would you like me to take a walk around the block?"

They were both abruptly still, and then suddenly Maggie laughed.

"You know, this must be my night," she said. "Come in, Jere, don't be silly. Welcome to the Harrison Laundromat. Don't trip over the dirty linen on the way in."

Before Tom was able to move, Jere pulled open the screen.

"Mr. Harrison, I presume," he said humorously. "My name's Tidings. Sounds like the makings of a good party next door, doesn't it?"

Tom turned away brusquely from Jere Tiding's extended hand, his face brick-red, but just as he pushed at the screen door to open it, it was pushed hard from the other direction. A short, plump, dark-haired woman was on the doorstep, pressing against the screen to see into the dim interior of the room.

"Maggie!" she shouted, breathless with excitement. "Maggie, come to our house quick! Your grandpa's on the television. It's the waltz contest at the dance hall on the pier. Your grandpa's dancing with his lady friend right now on the television. Quick, Mijita!"

"Oh my god, this I have to see!"

Maggie's face was shining.

"I'm coming, Mrs. Martinez! Want to come along?"

"Wouldn't miss it," Jere said.

"Come on then!"

She caught hold of Jere's hand and plunged for the door. For a moment, Tom stumbled, caught in the middle of it with the door partway open, and then they surged by him and away, Maggie running fleetly across the lawn. Jere Tidings laughed as he matched his easy long stride to hers. The little plump woman was still calling out excitedly as she trotted hard at their heels.

Tom strode off into the darkness toward his car, his face fairly purple with his fury.

eighteen

THE BEACH CROWD dispersed slowly that night, since the weather was warm, but at last the lights began to blink out along the promenade, one after another. The coffee stall was still open, and George was hunched over a newspaper spread out on the counter there. He perused the sports page gloomily, stealing continual, worried, surreptitious looks at Dick Whitfield, who was seated solitary on one of the stools in front of him.

Dickie was silent, his shoulders slumped, his hands burrowed into the pockets of his thick white sweat shirt, and his head drooping miserably over a half-filled cup of cold coffee.

George cleared his throat finally, and Dickie looked up.

"Want to close up, George-O?" he said. "Go ahead, don't mind me. I'll leave whenever you do."

"Well, I guess I better," George said reluctantly. "Sure don't look like your friend's going to show up."

"Oh, I suppose it's just one of those stupid things," Dickie said, his voice totally unconvincing. "He just misunderstood about where he was to meet me, or I was the one that got it mixed up. I'll phone the apartment one last time before we leave. Go ahead, George-O, get your cleaning-up done."

"Well, I guess I better," George said again reluctantly.

But just as he turned away toward the tiny grill plate behind him, Maggie appeared suddenly in the entrance way, the sound of her coming lost in the roar of the surf.

"Hi, George-O!" she called.

Her face was vivid and glowing, her hair windblown, and she wore a bright blue stole over her bare shoulders, the fringed ends of it whipping about her in the wind.

Dickie's face lighted instantly.

"Maggie! You look wonderful! Ah, Harrison, am I glad to see you!"

But some of the enthusiasm evaporated from his voice as he caught sight of Jere behind her, immaculate in pressed gray slacks and sports jacket and polished black moccasins, his thin mobile face smiling and alert.

"Dickie! What on earth you doing down here on a Saturday night?" Maggie cried delightedly. "We just ducked in to say hello to George, I never expected to find you here. Wonderful!"

George leaned silently against the counter, his sad, lost, cocker spaniel eyes studying Jere suspiciously.

Maggie caught hold of Jere's arm.

"Here is someone I want you to meet," she said. "Jere Tidings. Jere, meet brother beach rat, Dick Whitfield."

Dickie slid from his stool.

"Glad to have you aboard, sir," he said, with delicate mockery in his voice.

"And this is George Rocco," Maggie stretched her hand affectionately across the counter, "who brews the best coffee, urn for urn, from here to Venice Pier."

Jere turned and held out his hand again, with one of his swift nervous gestures.

"George!" he said. "I'm honored. Coming from this red-headed coffee fiend, that's a tribute."

"Hey, this is wonderful," Maggie said happily, climbing onto the stool beside Dickie's. "Imagine just happening to find you both here like this!"

"How about a nice cup of hot coffee?" George said, his voice a little restrained as he continued to eye Jere dubiously.

"No, George-O," Maggie said firmly. "We just stopped in to say hello. It's past your closing time, you go on and clean up now."

Jere swung onto the stool next to hers and leaned comfortably upon his elbow.

"Tell you what," he said. "Let's live it up. Let me buy a beer for the house."

"Deal?" Maggie turned to Dickie.

"Deal," Dickie said promptly. "Set 'em up, Daddy-O."

While George reached into the little cooler for the wet frosty cans, Maggie reached out suddenly for Dickie's hand, her eyes troubled.

"Man, what's happenin'?" she said. "Your face looks thin or something. Is everything all right?"

"Cool, real cool," Dickie said very gayly. "The greatest! How's things with you, Harrison?"

"Oh, crazy, man! Really nervous!"

Jere watched them both amusedly.

"You work in pictures, Dickie?" he asked.

"Oh, you mean because Dickie's so pretty," Maggie said merrily, but her eyes still anxious and concerned upon his face. "Isn't he beautiful? Isn't he just gorgeous? Isn't he the handsomest thing you ever saw?"

"Oh, go, girl, go!" Dickie said with mock ecstasy.

"He digs that the most," she explained lovingly.

Jere turned on his stool and said soberly to the counter man, "George, care to join me in some two-handed pinochle?"

"Aaaah, they're nothing but a couple of crazy nuts," George said, his hoarse voice tender, as he put out the beer cans and glasses on the counter.

Dickie leaned over his folded arms to look at Jere.

"I don't think we've met before, have we, but your name sounds familiar. Do you work in pictures?"

"I'm a writer," Jere said cheerfully, and then he laughed. "Now there's a statement that covers a lot of territory and a host of sins! Yes, I've done quite a bit of screen writing. Don't quote me, but right now I'm trying my hand at television. I have a batch of TV scripts over at my agent's right now, I'm still waiting to hear."

"Oh, well now I don't see why you should have to wait to hear . . ." Maggie said elaborately, catching Dickie's eye.

". . . When all you have to do is ask George," Dickie chimed in. "George can tell you right now. George is the seventh son of a seventh son . . ."

"Born with a caul," Maggie finished.

"You know, that's nothing but the truth," George said, his face pleased in spite of himself. And then he added gloomily, "Except I'm way out of practice now. I haven't worked at it for a long time, see? Oh, I get flashes once in a while, but it isn't the same . . ."

Jere laughed delightedly, the flame dancing over his pipe.

"By god, I had a feeling you were a man of natural talent, George," he said through the smoke. "What are you doing here, wasting your time counter-hopping? Why don't you set up shop and give Madame Vere DeVere, the seeress on the pier, a little competition?"

"Competition!"

(193

George snorted as he gathered up cups and scrubbed at the counter top fiercely with a wad of dirty rag.

"That's just the trouble out here. Man hasn't even got a decent chance. Everybody's in the business out here, every time you turn around. It isn't like it was back home."

"Were you in the fortune-telling business back home?" Jere asked interestedly.

"Aw, I wasn't exactly in the business," George mumbled, rattling dishes together noisily in the sink. "I never did have a license or a fancy place with a sign out or nothing like that."

He paused, darting a quick and suspicious look at Jere's face.

"Naw," he said abruptly. "He wouldn't care nothing about hearing all that stuff."

In the sudden silence, Dickie slid down from his stool.

"I'm terribly sorry, I have to dash," he said. "Stush is probably waiting for me at home. Glad to have met you, Jere. See you around. And, George-O, if Stush should just happen to turn up here before you leave, tell him I've gone home, will you? I'll talk to you, Maggie."

"Dickie, call me tomorrow," Maggie called after him, her voice urgent. "Promise me. And call from outside somewhere so we can really talk."

"Promise," he called back. "See you."

A moment or two later, Jere and Maggie also came out onto the darkened promenade. They paused, while Maggie wrapped her stole about her shoulders.

"Now, then, what would you like to do?" Jere said. "There's a party where we could drop in for a while. Come to think of it, there are two parties. Or we can drive into town if you feel like bright lights and a night of it. Your night out, so what do you say?"

"You choose," Maggie said. "So far tonight, I've been dragging you to my places. Now it's your turn."

"Fair enough," he said as he turned away from the wind for a moment, puffing at his pipe to get it drawing.

"Let's try the party up near my place, it's apt to be less brawl and nicer people. I think you'll like it. People giving it are neighbors of mine, they're nice kids. He's a sculptor and she's quite a good painter. They have a little girl about Jamie's age. Shall we try it?"

"Sounds wonderful," Maggie said.

He set off briskly, drawing Maggie along with him.

"Of course, you realize that any party is going to seem fairly flat after that wonderful one at your neighbor's tonight?"

"Wasn't it fun?" Maggie said. "The Martinez' are very nice. They've been very good to Jamie and me. That's why I had to go to their party for at least a little while. Did you mind?"

"Mind!" Jere said. "I felt very lucky to be there, it was certainly the best party I've been to in years. Thank you very much for taking me. Besides, I like seeing the people and the places that you talk about, didn't you know?"

"The small world of Maggie Harrison?" she said a little ruefully.

"Where did you learn this habit of always underselling yourself? It's a very large and real world."

"You mean it's for real?" Maggie was laughing.

"The absolute real thing," he said. "And as that character you so like to quote is always saying, 'You know that kind is getting harder to get all the while!' "

"Well, if you wanted a look at my world, tonight you hit the jackpot. You even saw Grandpa by television!"

Jere laughed.

"And your lowering former husband very much in the flesh."

"Don't go reminding me of that," Maggie said. "By the pricking of my thumbs, I knew he'd hang around until he met you on the doorstep, and he did. No, what I'm really sorry about is that seeing George and Dickie just now didn't come off better."

"It came off," he said. "I like George and Dickie."

"No," Maggie said. "I suppose I tried a little hard, jumping us all through our pet hoops for you. It just didn't quite come off."

"Never does, you know," Jere said cheerfully. "Silly goose you, for trying. It's perfectly obvious that you and George and Dickie are a closed corporation. They didn't much like you turning up there with a man in tow, or didn't you notice?"

"I suppose they really didn't," Maggie said honestly. "But only because it's a kind of threat to a common bond we have. We were all flying on one wing, that's what made us friends in the first place. The three of us have gotten whistling in the dark down to an art, we do it now in close harmony."

Jere laughed.

"The Muscle Beach amen corner? Well, George has a very forlorn look about him, undeniably. I take it that he's a frustrated soothsayer. What are Dickie's difficulties, besides the fairly obvious one?"

Maggie looked at him quickly.

"You mean that he's homosexual? Oh, I don't think that is particularly a difficulty to Dickie. I mean, it is of course but not particularly."

She thought about it for a moment.

"No, it isn't. Dickie's really a very simple, cheerful, realistic kind of person. I think he simply accepts that, just as he does any other thing about himself, the color of his eyes or the shape of his face. Or the weather, for that matter. No, Dickie's difficulties are mostly just wanting to get ahead in pictures or theatre or some place. He wants that so much. I keep hoping for him. He deserves it. He's a good actor and he's one of the kindest sweetest people I've ever known."

She climbed into the car, and Jere slammed the door after her and walked swiftly around to the other side.

As he turned the car out into the street, he said lightly, "And what of you, Maggie darling? How do you really fit in with these frustrated lame ducks of yours?"

"Oh, my troubles aren't nearly so interesting," she said. "Mine are just the common garden variety. The usual divorce doldrums. You know, there's more to getting a divorce than I thought there'd be. There's more kickback to it. You feel very unsettled and lonely and terribly at loose ends. You know? Have you ever been divorced, Jere?"

"Is that window back there on your side down a bit?" he said. "I seem to feel a wild night wind playing across the back of my neck. Sure you'll be warm enough in that shawl?"

Maggie turned to look at the closed rear window, briefly and obediently.

"You don't like to talk about yourself, do you?" she said.

"You can't be talking to me!" Jere said. "Why, once you've gotten me started on Tidings, I'll keep you up all night! In my time, I have been known to stop strangers on the street and pour out the sad stories of my life. My favorite topic of conversation, for god sakes!"

"Go on!" Maggie said. "You never once talked about yourself. And if I try to pin you down as I did just now by asking you a question, you just don't hear me."

"For the very simple reason that I probably didn't hear you," he said cheerfully. "What did you ask me, anyway?"

"We were talking about divorces, remember? I asked you if you'd ever been divorced."

"Of course, who hasn't been?" he said, his voice matter-of-fact. "Except that my situation was a bit different, and I seem to have avoided most of these usual doldrums you were talking about. My wife and I had been separated for a long time. By the time she got around to actually getting the divorce, it only seemed the driest sort of legal paper work, with about the emotional recoil of going in to buy a dog license, as I remember."

"Do you have children?" Maggie asked.

(197

He was frowning in the dim light of the dashboard.

"No, no children. How's your night vision, darling? We are now looking for a small frame house with a very large red gate, over here on the sea side of the highway. It should be about here, do you see it?"

nineteen

THE NIGHT wore on, and back in his little hillside apartment high above the Strip, Dickie was still waiting for Stush. He showered finally and then bolted out expectantly into the living room again, belting a blue and white seersucker robe about him as he came, his hair forgotten and curling for once in a genuine disarray of damp dark ringlets over his forehead. But the apartment was still empty, bright with electric light and very quiet, only the distant, muffled, disembodied sounds of life throughout the building, the snatches of music, the gurgle and wheeze of plumbing pipes, the faint faraway boom of a slamming door.

Dickie sighed and looked at the watch on his wrist. He lighted a cigarette and reached out automatically to turn on the table radio in the silence. The room was already clean and tidy and perfectly ordered, but Dickie busied himself determinedly, plumping cushions briskly, emptying ash trays, wiping away fancied films of dust from table tops, carrying a pitcher of fresh water for the sprawling bouquet of white daisies on the coffee table, and rearranging his little collection of horse figurines lovingly on the bookshelves.

He moved on to the tiny kitchenette and invented similar tasks there, scrubbing the microscopic shelf tops desperately, opening cupboard doors to stack away dishes that had drained dry in the sink, until, finally, there was nothing more that he could find to do.

The loud and merry music poured out of the radio, and he looked at his watch.

He turned to the refrigerator, pulling open the door to stare blindly for a moment at the odds and ends of food within. The door swung slowly away from his hand and settled shut with a heavy thud.

Dickie started a little, and looked at his watch again.

Suddenly, and without warning, his face crumpled in silent anguish. He buried his head upon his arms against the top of the refrigerator, his body sagging forward forlornly against the upright, cold-white porcelain box.

Voices cackled out of the radio, and then the music blared again through the warm static air. Dickie fled into the living room and grabbed at the knob on the front of the radio. The music stopped, startlingly cut off in the middle of a beat.

He lighted a cigarette unsteadily, he walked, and the next time he put his hand quickly over the dial of his watch, squeezing his fingers tightly together to hide it before he had a chance to look.

He went to the window, leaning forward to peer out through the blind into the darkness where far below the great pattern of unconcerned twinkling lights stretched away to the dark horizon.

"Please!" he said, his voice the merest whisper, frightened and pleading. "Oh, please, please!"

He began to shiver there by the window sill, and he lifted his hands nervously, testing the temperature of his dry hot cheeks and forehead. He pulled the cord on the blind and closed the narrow slats rattling together against the night.

He walked, and once more he stopped, wringing his hands

together in a frantic desperate gesture. He stood quietly for a long time, gnawing at his thumb, his face tensed and strained, and when he moved again at last it was with a sudden purpose and decision. He worked swiftly and absorbedly, pulling a chair around beneath a floor lamp, turning on the radio again but softly this time, collecting all the necessary props, the drink, the book, the cigarettes and ash tray. He arranged them together carefully like a stage set, backing off down the room toward the entrance door of the apartment to verify the proper angle and effect.

He walked back rapidly and changed the position of the chair an inch or two before he sat down there in the mellow light of the floor lamp. He went about it all quite methodically, first his body relaxing into an easy comfortable posture in the chair, his legs carelessly crossed, a placid stream of smoke rising from the burning cigarette in the ash tray, the book spread open across his knees. And last of all, his face altered with abrupt uncanny transition, the tension suddenly relaxed into an expression of lazy tranquillity.

He lifted the book and read, and for a moment the picture of ease and quiet solitary pleasure was complete. He sipped from the glass and put it down, he turned a page. And then all of a sudden he turned his head quickly to look toward the silent, closed entrance door.

"Oh, Stush?" he said, his voice perfectly controlled, casual and unhurried in the empty room. "Is that you?"

He lowered the book onto his knees, and with the timing slow and exactly right, he lifted his arms, stretching luxuriously.

"Guess what, I had the most wonderful time tonight," he said, with his voice carefully brightening and quickening. "Wait till I tell you! I went to a party, and I met the most wonderful man!"

Dickie was still for an instant after that, and then his whole body collapsed bonelessly. He pitched forward over his knees, his face burying in his hands, his back bowed despairingly.

But he pulled himself upright again almost immediately, with a slow and agonizing effort of will.

And then he did it all over again: the relaxed posture in the chair, the peaceful expression of his face, the lifted book.

Once again he turned his head quickly, looking down the empty room to the closed, enigmatic, gray-painted door.

"Oh, Stush? Is that you?"

His deep resonant voice projected effortlessly, a perfectly controlled instrument, slow and lazy, with the faintest touch of amusement.

It was no more than ten minutes after that, when Stush actually did let himself into the apartment through that same, gray-painted, wooden door.

There was his light even tread first, sounding briefly along the chipped, dingy, black-and-white tiles of the outer corridor. And then the brass-colored doorknob rattled noisily and the door swung open. Stush came in rapidly, whistling softly between his teeth. He pivoted with smooth economic grace and closed and latched the door behind him.

He was wearing baggy beige-colored slacks, and a rumpled white shirt with the sleeves carelessly rolled. He carried a jacket over his arm, and when he turned, his tie was hanging askew, his pale hair was noticeably disheveled and there were bright red smears of lipstick over his chin.

He had been drinking but he was not drunk, his face was good-humored and stimulated. And once again, by some trick of his odd vitality, merely by walking in the door he seemed immediately to fill the whole apartment, dwindling and dwarfing the room to some proportion solely of his own projection.

"Hi, baby," he said genially.

Dickie was mute, sitting taut and rigid in his chair, his pathetic stage-prop book tilted before him at some insane and unreadable angle, and quite forgotten. His face was twisted and utterly tragic, his eyelids reddening from a sudden and humiliating deluge of unshed tears crowding behind them.

(201

"Where have you been?" he cried out suddenly, his voice unrecognizably hoarse and choked and shaken. "Where you think you've been, anyway!"

Stush only grinned at him with an amused and friendly tolerance.

"Listen, there anything to eat around here?" he said easily. "I haven't had nothing to eat all night."

"I said, 'Where've you been?' "

Dickie's anguished cry was like a discordant, raucous bird screech in the quiet little room.

"Oh, quit it, will you?" Stush said.

He lifted his hand in a good-humored gesture of dismissal as he turned away toward the kitchenette.

He pulled the chain on the light there, the little metallic cord swinging and tinkling against the glass of the fixture. He banged cupboard doors and rattled dishes, whistling again softly to himself. The refrigerator door swung shut time after time with shuddering thumps, a glass struck and broke and splintered in the sink.

Dickie rocked back and forth in his chair, crumpled together in a final misery, his hands stretching over his face as he tried to cover both his eyes and ears at once.

Stush whistled merrily.

Dickie caught his breath. He sprang up from his chair all of a sudden and across the room, knocking hard against the flimsy, gray-painted wood partition as he burst out into the kitchenette.

Stush was cozily ensconced at the little drop-leaf table there, a yellow mixing bowl in front of him, and two quart bottles of milk together with the inevitable large carton of corn flakes. Around him, the whole tiny kitchenette was a shambles of pulled-out drawers, opened cupboard doors, broken glass and spilled and spattered food.

"Where've you been half the night? I want you to tell me right now!"

"Listen, why you keep harping on it?" Stush complained with his mouth full of cereal. "You know goddamn well you don't really want to know where I've been. Why you keep asking me?"

Dickie clasped his hands tightly together in front of him.

"Stush, I'm all through," he said rapidly. "I'm not going to take any more of this. I can't, because I can't stand it any more. It's getting so you're gone every single night. I can't ever depend on you to be anywhere any more when you say you're going to be. You were supposed to be home for supper last night, weren't you? I broke my neck to shop before the market closed, and I cooked, and then I waited and I waited. And now the same thing all over again today! The minute you were done at the studio you were going to ride straight out to the beach with Joey and meet me there. That was your own idea this morning, it wasn't mine. But it was just the same old story, wasn't it? I waited for you, and I waited, and made myself look like a fool in front of people that I know. Well, now I'm simply all through. I can't take any more of this, Stush. I just can't!"

He stopped, his tremulous voice breaking, and at the table, Stush spooned corn flakes rapidly into his mouth, relaxed and unperturbed.

"Well, don't just sit there!" Dickie cried. "Haven't you got anything to say to me at all?"

"You know, it's a funny thing about you, baby," Stush said conversationally while he chewed, waving his dripping spoon for emphasis. "You're the kind of person that's always got to do just so much yelling and hollering to get anything out of your system. Some guys have to get drunk to do it, or sex it up, and some guys have to pick fights, but you always got to yell and carry on before you feel good again. So what I say is go ahead and get it over with. Okay?"

Dickie turned away blindly and then spun back again.

"And another thing," he yelled wildly, "why do you have to

(203

come home here with that stupid lipstick all over your face? Why do you do that!"

Stush grinned.

The lipstick stains on his chin were beaded now with drops of milk, and he swiped at them both carelessly with the flat of his big hand.

"Girls are sure killers with that stuff," he said humorously. "I bet girls eat a ton of that junk themselves in a year's time, not counting what they smear all over guys. And I do mean all over! Boy, some of the places I've had to scrub lipstick off myself in the shower!"

Dickie stared at him, mute and trembling, with his arms hugged tightly together across his chest.

"Stush, why do you do it?" he said at last softly. "Do you do and say things on purpose because you like to make me feel bad? Or don't you even care enough about me to pay attention to the way you make me feel? If I could just understand that one thing about you! Stush, if I could just be sure of that one thing! Because we can't go on like this any longer. Don't you understand?"

He leaned upon the table urgently, and Stush grabbed to steady his teetering glass of milk.

"Listen, why don't you go on in the bathroom and have a good cry or something?" Stush said peevishly. "I sure wish you'd quiet down around here so I could hit the sack. This girl I was shacked up with this afternoon was a real crazy one, and I'm really beat."

Dickie stood transfixed and then he backed off slowly, his eyes closed, his head swinging back and forth helplessly, cords appearing suddenly like slender tensile ropes beneath the smooth tanned skin along the sides of his neck.

All of a sudden, he said in a flat voice, his eyes still closed, "You pack up your things now and get out of here!"

Stush leaned back over the table and drained the last of the milk from his glass leisurely without even looking at him.

"You hear me?" Dickie's voice rose. "I want you to pack up and get out of here right now. Don't you hear me!"

Stush did look at him then, his pale eyes rolled upward in his face, steady and unwinking. After a moment, he leaned far back in his chair slowly, fumbling at his shirt pocket for the pack of cigarettes, his big body beginning to tense and gather together.

"You know, baby," he said softly, "I've had just about enough yacking out of you for one night. You know that?"

Dickie's voice rose still a little higher.

"You've had enough!" he cried. "Oh, that's very funny. You've had enough! Oh, you're really fantastic, I can't believe it. Haven't you heard a word I've been saying, I'm the one that's had enough! My god, what do you think I am? You make me so sick I want to throw up. I thought you made love with me because you liked me at least a little. What did you think? But now I know you better. You'll make love with anything, any size or shape or thing you can pick up off the streets or out of some bar somewhere—it's all the same to you. You're worse than any cruiser I've ever known. I don't know what you are! You're worse than any animal, I think you're some kind of a monster. Now get out of here! I'll send your things tomorrow. Just get out of here!"

Stush rose up from his chair.

"Baby, what did I tell you right from the start, huh?" he said, his voice emotionless and unhurried. "Didn't I tell you that you and me'd get along fine as long as you didn't start to pick at me? Didn't I tell you that?"

"Can't you understand plain English?" Dickie screamed. "I said get out of my apartment. Get out!"

He grabbed hold of Stush's shoulder and began to push and pummel him ineptly, his eyes wide and dark and wild in his pale face. For a moment they grappled together, out through the entrance way into the living room.

"Boy, you sure gone off your rocker tonight," Stush said

(205

judiciously. "You really flipped your wig for old Stush! You don't even know what you're doing."

With a sudden swift motion he drew back his arm and slapped Dickie hard across the face, and again, and then gave him a contemptuous heaving push away from him.

Dickie toppled backwards, catching at the top of the bookshelves to regain his balance. But the flimsy shelves pitched forward beneath him, the little figurines flying, all the cherished small horses of glass and metal and pottery and wood crashing down around him as he sprawled heavily upon the floor.

For a moment out of time, there was no further sound or motion in the hot bright room.

" 'That old black magic that you weave so well . . .' " An intense husky voice sang out of the radio on the table.

Very slowly, little by little, with his body limp and loose and defeated, Dickie pulled himself up until he was sitting on the floor amid the splintered shelves and broken figurines. There was a small cut at the edge of his mouth and he wiped at the trickle of blood with his fingers.

Stush carefully straightened the bent cigarette he was still holding, and rolled the tip of it deliberately along his lip to moisten it before he struck the match.

"What did I ever do to you, Stush?" Dickie said, his voice soft and broken. "When did I ever hurt you? All I did was love you and try to help you and take care of you."

"I didn't bust up your stuff," Stush said shortly. "You did it yourself."

He came in one long lithe stride, bending and stretching out his hand.

"Come on, upsy daisy," he said impersonally.

Dickie shrank away.

"Don't!" he said, the word not quite distinct with the swelling of his lip. "I've been gay all my life, but I always felt clean and decent. You make me feel like a faggot."

206)

He began to cry silently, turning his face away.

Stush wheeled, picking up his jacket from the back of a chair as he walked toward the door.

"No, Stush, don't!" Dickie cried. "Please, please, Stush! Not like this, in the middle of the night, when you haven't any money or any place to go. Wait! Wait till morning when I can cash a check, and then if you want to, go then. Please, Stush, I'll be quiet, I promise. I won't bother you any more."

Stush opened the door.

"You want me to crawl for you, Stush?" Dickie cried frantically. "Is that what you want?"

He scrabbled over clumsily onto his hands and knees.

"See, Stush, I'll crawl for you! You want me to tell you how much I love you? You want me to come begging to you on my knees? You want to hear me say it, that I'll put up with anything if you just won't leave me? I'm saying it, Stush. See, on my knees, Stush!"

Stush stood in the open doorway, his back rigid, his hand still upon the knob.

Dickie wrapped his arms about Stush's leg, his cheek pressed hard against his thigh.

"No, Stush, no," he said, his voice gentle and pleading. "It's so late tonight, where would you go? Stay. Stay and sleep in your own bed."

He rose quickly to his feet and since Stush did not resist him, he pulled him back a step, taking the knob from his hand to close the door.

"No, no," he said, his voice crooning. "You don't want to go. It's so late and you're tired. No, Stush, no."

Dickie slipped his arms about Stush's waist, leaning against him to look humbly into his rigid enigmatic face.

"I'll never do that to you again, Stush. I'll never draw away from you like that again!"

Stush's shoulders slowly relaxed. He lifted his hand, burying his fingers in Dickie's hair, shaking Dickie's head back and forth once, in his casual gesture of affection.

"You better not, baby," he said softly. "Because next time old Stush'll walk out of this dump for good."

And then he said, "Look, you better go fix up your lip. You're bleeding all over."

Dickie hurried off to the bathroom obediently. After he was gone, Stush straightened the bent cigarette one more time and struck a match to its blackened end.

"Listen, it wasn't me that busted up your little toy horses," he called accusingly.

Dickie did not answer him. In the small brief privacy of the bathroom he was slumped against the wall, weeping again silently and fiercely and without hope.

twenty

IN THE HOUSE on the beach, Maggie and Jere Tidings still sat together on the low, deep-cushioned divan before the fire. The big cavernous room was shadowed, warm pools of light here and there, and filled with the loud and liquid roar of the sea from just outside the curtained windows.

Jere was slouched back comfortably against the cushions, his long legs stretched out before him to the hearth and his pipe in his hand.

Maggie, beside him, sat with her legs pulled up beneath her bright-colored skirt, her glass forgotten as she talked.

"So you see, it really is a very dull story," she was saying. "It wasn't anything that Tom did, I guess it just came down to the kind of person that he is. I was certainly just as wrong for him as he was for me. I think there's hardly one thing in this whole world that Tom and I see eye to eye on. I didn't really mind living in California since he wanted to so much. It wasn't until he wanted to buy this house in the Valley that I thought it was a good time for us to throw in the towel and each of us have the kind of life we wanted, since we couldn't seem to work out any kind of life together that made either one of us very happy. Oh well, it's all very dull when I come to tell it. I suppose it's one of the few divorces on the grounds of incompatibility that really is just that. There wasn't anything else, we just aren't compatible people."

Jere sat up, his pipe in his teeth, burrowing leisurely for matches in his jacket pocket.

"Probably the most valid reason of all for getting a divorce," he said mildly. "It takes a fairly enormous thing between people to hold them together if they really aren't compatible at any other point. Obviously you hadn't that, or you wouldn't be divorcing under quite these circumstances."

Maggie stared down into her glass.

"No, we hadn't," she said. "We did in the beginning. I suppose it's the only thing we really ever did have. I don't know just how or where it got lost along the line. I sometimes wonder about it."

"Well, that's not exactly uncommon," Jere said. "There's nothing in the nature of that particular thing, you know, that guarantees it's going to last at fever pitch forever. Generally by the time it's gone, people have discovered enough other things between them, bonds of affection and their children, and interests that they share."

"I suppose that's true," Maggie said thoughtfully. "Except, in our case, once the—the thing between us was gone, we didn't seem to have anything else left at all."

"That isn't uncommon enough to worry about either," he said

cheerfully. "Witness our busy divorce courts. Apparently we're all forever marrying the people we'd do far better to sleep with a few times and let it go at that."

Maggie looked up, and then back down to the glass in her hands, quickly.

After a moment, she said, "Well, I don't think I specially agree with that notion. If you don't marry for that particular thing, what do you marry for, if you're honest?"

His face was affectionate and faintly amused as he watched her.

"Right you are," he said lightly. "Very chancy and complicated business, isn't it? At any rate, you're at the beginning of a new chapter. There's Tom with his dream house in the Valley, and here are you, off to—what? All sorts of interesting things, I suspect. Incidentally, darling, weren't you being fairly generous about that house in the Valley project when it came down to divorce settlements and all that?"

"What? Oh, you mean this business about community property," she said. "But that's silly, I wasn't being generous, I was just trying to be fair. Tom worked terribly hard for a long time to save the money to buy a house, that money belonged to him. Besides, things mean a great deal to Tom, and they don't to me, the refrigerator and the stove and the gadgets, and . . . That's what I tried to explain to my lawyer. It just wouldn't have been honest. I took the few books and records that I had and my two suitcases of clothes. That's all I wanted, that's all I felt entitled to. Of course, there's the money every month for Jamie, but that seemed fair enough."

"Yes, I think that's extremely fair enough," Jere said affectionately. "Darling, what a refreshing breath of clean sweet air you must have brought into the murk and grime of that law office! I expect your lawyer hasn't recovered from the shock of it yet."

"Don't be silly."

Maggie was silent then, her eyes still fixed upon the warm glass that she slowly turned between her hands. Jere turned his head again to look at her inquiringly.

"There's more you'd like to talk about," he said. "What is it?"

"No, not really," she said. "Just what I was saying in the car tonight, I guess, about the usual divorce doldrums. I keep wondering if they are usual, or whether there's something wrong with me. Getting a divorce seems to involve a whole lot more than I thought it would. It seems so easy in the beginning, you're not happy, you're not in love with someone any more, and the laws make it quite simple, and there seem to be dozens of people getting divorces every day . . ."

Her voice trailed out, and he waited.

"It's just that you feel so terribly let down and unsettled somehow," she said lamely. "God knows I don't want to go back to Tom. It's just that I don't feel like myself. It's terribly hard to begin again on your own, to start making plans and doing things and . . ."

He reached out quickly, resting his hand for a moment upon her bright hair.

"I shouldn't worry about it a moment longer," he said. "You sound disgustingly normal to me. That's why most people prefer to drift along and endure those ills they have, and never actually off with the old love until they are safely on with a new. You're doing it the hard way, darling, and then it's a bit like walking off the end of the dock. You'll get over it."

"Goddamn it, don't you tell me, too, that it's just like having the measles," Maggie said.

Jere laughed, and she lifted her head.

"Oh, hey," she said. "I've talked about myself long enough. How'd I get so long-winded, anyway, as if I didn't know. It's having such a good audience. Now it's your turn."

Jere gave up the struggle with his pipe, and stood up from the divan suddenly, leaning over the hearth to shake the dottle into the fire. He reached for his glass from the table and drained the last of the drink from the bottom of it.

"You look fairly downcast, darling," he said. "We can't have that. What do you say, want to make a night of it? Want to go over and take a look at how they're doing at that other party?"

Maggie laughed.

"Jere!" she said protestingly. "Do you know what time it happens to be?"

"Exactly the right time for this party," he said. "By now, this party will be just beginning to stew up into a fine broth. Shall we go have a look?"

Maggie's upturned face was affectionate.

"How do you really do it, anyway?" she said, in mock complaint. "Is it something ordinary like benzedrine, or were you just born with a few extra cylinders?"

"Are you tired?"

Maggie put down her glass and stretched a little.

"Not really," she said. "Just bogged down. It's so damn comfortable here, with the fire and the sound of the sea."

"You know, you're right," Jere said. "It's much nicer right here. This party is one you can depend on to be the same old standard classic. I can see it now! Arnie Lutz will be at the piano by this time, singing the same dirty songs he's been singing at parties now for the last four years to my certain knowledge. The first wave will have just gone down to the pool to swim in the nude and found that it's too cold, and Jack Arnold will be warming up to slug some bloke who's made a pass at Moira, and . . ."

Maggie's laughter gurgled.

"Oh, Christ, what a dull party!" she said. "Do you think we should leave?"

"I think we should have a drink," Jere said positively. "What have you done with your glass?"

"No, not for me," she said. "Look, I have to go home."

"Why do you?" he said lightly. "Mrs. Yamasaki's at the helm and she looked very capable to me."

"Well, I expect Grandpa's in by now anyway," Maggie said reluctantly. "All right, make me a little thin one then, just for the road."

Jere walked off swiftly down the long room, with the glasses in his hands.

Maggie stretched her legs for a moment, and then rose from the divan to stand in front of the fire.

"What's that?" she called out, pointing.

In the shadowy corner by the bar, Jere looked over his shoulder. "It's a glass on a tripod, a telescope."

"For sighting ships at sea?"

"Sometimes," he said. "And sometimes whales if I'm lucky. And quite often the moon."

"The moon!" she said, her voice amused.

"Why not?" he called back. "I often look at the moon. I'd like to go there, wouldn't you?"

Maggie thought about it, spreading out her skirts to the comfortable warmth of the fire.

"No," she said finally. "It always looks so cold. All of the stars do. The earth's for me. There are so many places on this earth I'd die to get to. Africa! And Spain! And Budapest! Wonderful! I'd love to go up the Amazon, wouldn't you? And down the Mississippi. Ah, they're all such a long way from Juniper Street. Anyway, right now I'd just settle for anywhere the other side of the Mississippi, any place at all!"

"What heresy is this?" Jere said gayly, as he joined her beside the hearth, holding out her glass. "Renegade! Us Californians don't allow for that kind of talk, girl!"

Maggie held her glass in both her hands, her face rebellious.

"Green country," she muttered through her teeth. "And cornfields and woods and mud puddles and rivers that have water in them, for god sakes!"

Jere laughed delightedly. "Maggie, darling, you're wonderful. You make me very happy."

"Do I?" she said after a moment, her eyes suddenly direct and the faintest challenge in her voice.

"And you know it!"

He reached out, cupping her face affectionately in his hand for a moment. He bent, kissing her lightly on the mouth, lightly at first and then lingering as her lips clung to his. Maggie gasped and moved forward, pressing her body hard against him.

A little of the liquid slopped out of the glass tilted in her hand, and suddenly she jerked away.

Her cheeks were flaming and she ducked down her head, scrubbing at the small wet stain upon the side of her skirt.

"I'm sorry!" she said, her voice an anguished whisper.

Jere's hands tightened on her shoulders, and for an instant his face was surprised and moved and full of some emotion.

He took the glass out of her hand swiftly, putting it on the table as he sat down on the divan, drawing her down beside him. At first she was stiff and resisting and then she came into his arms. He held her very tightly, his cheek against her smooth bright hair.

"Now what a very silly thing to say," he said gently. "I've wanted to do that for a long time, and I hoped you'd like it when I did. I hoped like hell."

Maggie was trembling and when he tried to lift her face she only burrowed it harder against his chest.

"Look here," he said. "You're not really crying, are you?"

"No," Maggie gulped. "Well, maybe I am! Goddamn it, I'm ashamed! I shouldn't be so . . ."

"Oh, what a goose!" Jere marveled. "Where did you ever get a notion like that, anyway? My god, I think you're trying to apologize for something. You know, if I thought you really felt that way about it, I'd beat you."

He did lift her head then, by a handful of her hair.

214)

"Maggie! Goose!" he said urgently, and half-laughing. "You're not to apologize for that. Not ever, never in all your life. You hear me?"

And suddenly Maggie was laughing too, her eyes still bright with tears.

They kissed again for a long time, while the fire crackled lower on the grate, and the sea thundered against the sand outside the windows.

Maggie was the one who drew away, at first ever so slowly and then up from the divan in one lithe bound, standing before the fire again with her legs braced wide apart, tucking at her blouse inside the waistband of her skirt, scrubbing at the tear stains on her cheeks.

"Ah, what a snively mess I am," she said, her voice rich and the words tumbling together. "Hey, what happened to my nice old drink? I have to go home."

"Now what in hell kind of an idea is that?" Jere said. "Here, here's your drink if you really want it. Now come back here."

"No, sir!" Maggie said. "No, I have to go, Jere, truly. Look, it must be almost morning."

She took a long thirsty drink from the glass and then she said wickedly, "And even if I didn't really have to, I still would. Goddamnit, it's me pride! No matter what you say, I won't have you thinking I'm a pushover."

"Oh, no!" Jere said tragically. "Is this really the way they bring up girls out in Indiana?"

Maggie put down her glass determinedly, and scooped up her purse and shawl from the table.

"Must you?"

She nodded her head quickly without speaking.

Jere drained his glass as he got up from the divan.

"Well, at least I can go on record, I'm against it," he said.

He paused to draw the screen in front of the fire, and then he followed her, feeling for the car keys in his pocket.

Just outside the door in the dim light he stopped for a moment, turning her to face him and wrapping the shawl together more tightly about her.

"Maggie, darling," he said very gently, his voice almost lost in the sea noise. "Don't you really know how hard to get you are? You must be the last one like you left in the whole world!"

twenty-one

AT NOON ON SUNDAY, while Stush still slept in the bedroom, Dickie let himself quietly out of the apartment. His face was tired and haggard as he trudged dispiritedly down the worn stair steps, the two flights to the street below.

The day outside was gray and overcast with a chill dampness in the air. Once Dickie reached his car where it was parked along the street with its wheels turned into the curb, he pulled a blue woolen sweater out of the glove compartment and donned it over his short-sleeved sports shirt. He coasted off down the steep winding street, and when he reached Sunset at the bottom, he turned toward the beach.

He stopped at a telephone booth along the way and spoke to Maggie briefly, and then drove on to the house on Juniper Street. He arrived there just in time to wave at Bud who was departing with his tennis rackets, and Maggie met him at the door. They went immediately to the kitchen which was littered with dirty dishes, but cozily bright and warm and filled with the good aroma of the hot coffee on the stove. Maggie closed doors at either side of the room so that their voices would not

216   )

disturb Jamie who had just gone to bed for his nap and Grandpa Kennedy who dozed peacefully on the divan in the living room beneath a section of the Sunday paper.

They sat down over coffee cups at the red painted kitchen table, and under the barrage of Maggie's anxious questioning Dickie began to talk, haltingly at first and then faster, in an outpouring of desperate release. Maggie listened intently, her bright mercurial face shifting between warm sympathy and helpless anger, listened until his voice quieted and slowed once more, and finally dwindled out wretchedly, leaving him spent and silent in his chair.

Maggie leapt up then, whirling off to the stove to bring the coffee pot.

"Oh, damn it, damn it!" she said softly. "Dickie, I'm so sorry. I've been worrying about you, I could tell this wasn't turning out right, just the way you looked the last couple times I've seen you. But I never dreamed it was this bad, and I know you're not telling me half of it either. Dickie, listen to me, the first thing is to get him out of your apartment. You have to!"

Dickie looked up at her helplessly, his dark eyes haunted and pathetic.

"I can't," he said. "I just can't. Maggie, he's got no place to go. I couldn't just turn him out into the street, not even if . . ."

"Well, of course you couldn't," Maggie said quickly. "But if you could just get him a room then, a place of his own. Look, he must have some money, you got him this job as an extra out at the studio, didn't you?"

"Yes, but they aren't finished shooting with him, he hasn't got his check yet. He hasn't any money at all."

"Well, then, couldn't you rent him a room some place till he could pay you back?" Maggie insisted.

Dickie shook his head miserably.

"I owe my own rent right now. Besides, that hasn't anything to do with it. I don't want him to leave. I couldn't bear it."

"But I'm not saying break off with him," Maggie pleaded. "If he just had a place of his own where he could come and go without upsetting you. You've got to get some rest. Couldn't you manage the money for a room some way?"

"I couldn't do it, even if I had the money."

Dickie looked away from her, his face tragic and ashamed.

"Maggie, don't you see, once he has any other place to go, then I've lost him for good. I guess I haven't any pride left about it any more, I know I've got nothing else to hold him with, just a place to stay. It's going to happen anyway, that's what's driving me crazy. I know the minute that he gets that check, he's just going to walk out and I'll probably never even see him again. I can't bear it!"

"Oh, Dickie!" Maggie wailed. "Sweetie, listen to me! You're all mixed up. Let him go, for god sakes. What's in it for you, tell me that? Look at you right this minute, are you happy, are you . . ."

"I know," Dickie said. "You don't have to tell me. I know it's stupid, but it's the way I feel, and I can't help myself. I can't stand it the way things are, but I can't stand it to think of him leaving me either. That's what's killing me, I can't eat or sleep or anything."

Maggie dropped her head upon her hands and sighed.

"All right, then look at it this way," she began again patiently. "Like you say, you're on the kind of spot where you can't stay where you are, nor you can't move off in any direction. Well, sweetie, something has to give! Nobody can live like that. Don't you see, it comes right down to the basic thing of self-preservation. Just look at yourself right now. You're half-sick, you're worried practically out of your mind. Suppose a job came up, an important one, how could you even work, how could you . . ."

"I know," Dickie said miserably. "There's a script over at my agent's right now, I was supposed to pick it up yesterday afternoon. I'm up to read for a part the first of the week, but I don't

see how I can ever make it. Besides, the way I look and everything, I might just as well forget it."

"Well, there you are, that's exactly what I mean," Maggie said
quickly. "Ah, Dickie, believe me, it isn't worth it. Even a month
from now you're going to look back and wonder how this ever
could have happened to you. Look, if I thought there was any
chance that he'd change, if there was any chance on earth for
this to work out, but there isn't. You know it yourself. Don't wait
for him to leave, get him out of your apartment right now. You
don't have to worry about him, he'll do all right. He's the kind
that will always do all right. Look how he latched onto you and
promoted himself a home and a job. Let him do it again."

"What's the use of talking about it, I can't do it," Dickie said
wretchedly. "I just can't. I'm sorry."

"Oh, Dickie!"

And then the telephone rang in the front of the house, and she
ran fleetly.

When she returned to the kitchen, Dickie was standing at the
door, staring out through the glass drearily into the gray misty
back yard where the leaves and flowers shivered in the wind.

"Well, guess who!" Maggie said lightly. "That Tony character
that hangs out down at the pier. What I'd like to know is where
he got hold of my telephone number. Not George-O, you can
bet on that."

Dickie turned.

"I'd better go," he said. "My agent will be really furious with
me if I don't get over there and pick up that script. You were
terribly sweet to let me talk to you like this, Maggie, listen to
all this stupid mess."

"Oh, hey!" Maggie said. "I just wish there was something I
could do to help, that's all."

"I'll go out this way," Dickie said. "My car's in the driveway."

Maggie followed him to the door.

"Dickie," she said. "Listen. I've got twelve bucks that Grandpa gave me. Take it and get a room somewhere for Stush. Please?"

"Ah, Harrison!"

The tears glistened in Dickie's eyes and he kissed her quickly.

"Thanks," he said. "Thanks awfully. But I really can't. I know it's going to happen anyway pretty soon, and when it does happen, well, it just happens. He'll leave and I suppose I'll live through it someway, I guess you always do. But I can't be the one to make it happen. Don't you see?"

"All right," Maggie said reluctantly. "I guess none of us can do any more than we're able to. Look, phone me now, I'll be worrying. And any time you feel like talking or anything, you come. Try to get some rest so you can read for this part, okay?"

"Thanks, Maggie. I'll see you."

When his car started up, Maggie closed the door quickly against the draught of damp chill wind, and shivered.

"Goddamn it!" she said softly and fiercely.

She sloshed a little more coffee into her cup impatiently, and carried the pot back to the stove. She stood there for a time then, her hands jammed into the pockets of her jeans, her face intent with thought.

All at once, she caught her lip between her teeth, her face beginning to clear. She let herself out the door quietly and hurried toward the telephone in the living room.

In the beach house, Jere sat behind the littered coffee table in the windows, a slim casting rod braced between his knees as he worked absorbedly at some adjustment to the reel. On the seat beside him, Caro sat cross-legged and erect, slim in dark trousers and a heavy black woolen shirt. She talked with her eyes turned away outside the window where the gray sky merged with the dappled gray water not far beyond the slow swelling rollers breaking on the sand.

"Oh, I think that's a bit unfair," Jere was saying absently. "Marriage is a very practical institution. It also happens to be a very pleasant way to live."

"I expect it's really that I'm afraid of failing at it," Caro said. "Because deep down inside of myself I'm still such a ghastly coward. I'd be terrified of failing at it. It's ever so much easier to live with other people's failures than to have to face up to one of your own, isn't it?"

"Theoretically, yes, of course," Jere said, frowning as he spun the little handle on the side of the rod. "Though living well with other people's failures requires a rather special talent too, you know."

Caro thought about it gravely.

"I expect that's true, although I'd never thought of it in exactly that way. Then it's double the risk, isn't it? I expect what really terrifies me most of all is that it must be so terribly easy to make the failure into a virtue and live by it forever."

She paused and then she said, "Jeremy, would you mind very much if I talked about Helen?"

He looked up quickly, and laughed.

"Of course not, lamb," he said affectionately. "What made you think that I would?"

"That's something I'd like to talk about another time," she said serenely. "Anyway, it wasn't Helen in particular that I wanted to talk of now, it was Helen in general rather, and the women that she knows."

"You mean the ex-wife colony?" Jere said, his voice amused.

"Do you really think they're funny, Jeremy?" Caro said. "Perhaps they are, if one has perspective. I haven't, you see, because I've lived with them most of my life."

"No, they're really not funny at all," Jere said gently. "Not by any perspective. Tell me what it's like to be a little girl growing up among them, a ewe lamb among the lionesses."

"Lioness?" Caro said. "Why do you choose that word for them, Jeremy?"

(*221*

"Well, aren't they, rather?" he said lightly. "Beautiful and sleek, hunters unequaled, and . . ."

The telephone began to ring at the other end of the big room.

"Oh, damn," he said cheerfully as he got to his feet. "Here, hold this for me, will you?"

He went off swiftly down the room, carrying his glass with him, a little liquid and melted ice in the bottom of it. He leaned down over the corner of his desk to pick up the telephone.

"Hello?" he said, and then speaking softly, "Maggie, how nice! I wanted to call you but I thought you might have gone off to nap with Jamie."

"Not me," Maggie said. "It's an old Gipsy curse, I've never been able to close my eyes in the daylight since I was six months old. What about you, were you working?"

"Not really," Jere said. "I was ready to take a break anyway. I'm very glad you called."

"Oh damn, I was afraid I'd disturb you," she said. "But something came up and I couldn't wait to ask you, have you rented Bob's old room at your house?"

Jere crossed his legs and leaned back comfortably against the edge of the desk, lifting the phone onto his knee.

"Now don't tell me that you called just to ask me that! I can think of several reason that you might have called me and all of them much nicer."

Maggie giggled.

"So can I," she said. "Believe me! Jere, have you rented the room?"

"What a passion for real estate," he said. "No, I haven't rented it, not officially. I have a tentative prospect for next month. Why, have you found a tenant for me?"

"Well, yes and no and not exactly," Maggie said. "It's just an idea I was kicking around and . . . Come to think of it, it's a lousy idea."

"Tell me about it and we'll kick it around together," he said. "Very antisocial, kicking ideas all by yourself."

"Well, it's complicated," Maggie said. "Besides, it wouldn't work. Dickie was here, Dick Whitfield. He's in an awful stew, and when he left I was trying to think of something that would help. That's when I thought about the empty room at your house and I came roaring straight to the telephone to ask you. If I'd stopped to think a minute, I'd have known right then it was a lousy idea."

"Why is it?" Jere said. "If Dickie's in a jam and needs a room?"

"Dickie doesn't need a room, Dickie has a perfectly good apartment in Hollywood. Oh, all right. But I warned you it was complicated. It's also a long story. A few weeks ago, Dickie picked up a dubious character, male naturally, and took him home with him. The character must have made the proper passes, at least at the beginning, I don't understand that part, anyway Dickie's fallen head over heels for him. The character was stony-broke naturally, and being dubious, he just moved in on poor Dickie. Dickie even lugged him out to the studio and got him an extra bit or something on a picture."

"Up till now, this all sounds rather cozy for Dickie," Jere said. "How dubious is this character anyway?"

"Good and dubious," Maggie said. "A bastard. He's one of these big sex pots on wheels. Dickie sort of skimmed over it, but he's taken to chasing in all directions, girls, I gather, which is probably the unkindest cut, and he's very inconsiderate, that's Dickie's word, you can substitute mean. Dickie showed up today with a swollen lip. Anyway, it's all gotten pretty murky, and Dickie's falling apart. I feel so sorry because Dickie's such a nice guy."

"I suppose Dickie might try locking him out one night," Jere said mildly.

"Ah ha, you might think so. Didn't I warn you this was complicated? In the first place, this character hasn't any place to go and no money until the studio check comes through, and Dickie's too soft-hearted for that. In the second place, Dickie's got himself worked up into one of these emotional whing-dings where he knows damn well he can't go on living with the character, but he thinks he can't live without him either. I mean, Dickie's already faced up to it, that once this character gets the studio check, the character will simply walk out and leave him flat. It's just that I don't see how, what with the state he's in, poor Dickie's going to be able to last until the character gets the check. And along with everything else, Dickie has to read for a part this week and he needs the job."

"Ah, now I see," Jere said. "So you were thinking it might be wise to hasten the eventual therapeutic process by getting the character moved out and over to my house right away."

"Jere, I'm terribly sorry," Maggie said contritely. "I told you I didn't stop to think about it twice. This is a character I wouldn't wish onto any fellow human, regardless, and you least of all. Besides, he'd only stick you for the room rent."

"Don't be silly," Jere said. "I thrive on dubious bastards. This one sounds fascinating. There's one snag that occurs to me though. I take it we can't count on any coöperation from Dickie in this scheme?"

"Oh, lord, no," Maggie said. "I was even hoping there might be a way to work it so that Dickie wouldn't have to find out that I had a hand in it."

"Well, then, there is a snag," Jere said. "This character has stepped into a very good thing and he's undoubtedly shrewd enough to know it. He already has a room at this point, right in the middle of the Hollywood happy-hunting grounds, and he has three meals a day and Dickie, to boot, literally, from what you say. Now how are we to persuade this bastard, all on his own, to trade all of that for a draughty solitary room way out here in my beach shack?"

"Well, there you are," Maggie said. "I said it wouldn't work, didn't I?"

"Don't be so defeatist," Jere said cheerfully, pausing to drain his glass. "Of course it will work, if we put our minds to it. It's only a matter of baiting the trap. And as I see it according to the

224)

facts you've given me, our only problem there is deciding whose seductive body we use for bait, yours or mine."

Maggie laughed.

"Oh, god, according to the stew Dickie's in, I'm afraid it might have to be mine. No, thank you. End of plot!"

"Oh, come on, Machiavelli!" Jere said delightedly. "You can't give up this easily. Besides you've dragged me into it and you ought to know that I'll never rest now until I lay, eyes of course, on this dubious double-gaited bastard of yours. Tell me more about him, what's he look like? I wonder if he's anyone I know."

"I think he's an out-of-town bastard," Maggie said. "You entertained him at your party the other Sunday, but I imagine you didn't meet him, since you didn't meet Dickie that day in all the mob. You might have noticed him though. This character is the type you'd definitely look at twice, I have to admit that. That's what got poor Dickie into trouble in the first place. I suppose he's handsome—anyway, you look at him. He's big, he has beautiful shoulders, he's very dark from the sun, he has very light hair and . . ."

"Oh, no!" Jere was chortling. "I might have known it! Maggie, darling, I think your scheme just came in like Flynn!"

"You know, there's something I'm not getting here," Maggie said accusingly. "Give out, master mind. What's the color of his hair got to do with it?"

"Everything, as it happens," Jere said softly. "How do you like this for a coincidence, I have a friend who saw your fascinating D.B. out here the day of the party and has been yearning to meet him ever since. And there's all the bait we need."

"Well, if it's really a friend, you'd better think this over," Maggie warned. "This is not a pleasant character, honestly."

"Well, you have a point there," Jere said, considering, his eyes turned away down the room to where Caro teetered gracefully over the back of the window seat, straddle-legged in her tight

(225

dark trousers, her small, infinitely poised, smooth head lifted as she looked out to the sea.

And then he laughed.

"Well, granted I don't know your bastard, but then you don't know my bait either. This bait of mine has had to deal with bastards since she left the cradle, and bastards to a degree I doubt that you could even dream of, darling. She knows all about them, and I can't think of anyone more calculated to confuse the hell out of a dubious bastard than she is. Matter of fact, I'd bet you right now, hands down, that your D.B. is in for a very very bad time of it."

"I'm delighted," Maggie said. "I do so hope you're right."

"Now then," Jere said briskly. "The victim hangs out at Dickie's apartment in Hollywood, right? Give me the street number there, and telephone."

He jotted the numbers down hastily upon an envelope from the desk.

"Suppose I do a little spade work and call you back in a bit," he said. "I'll give you a progress report. All right?"

A moment later he put down the phone and walked swiftly back up the long room again.

"Hi ho," he said gayly. "You're the patient one, waiting for me all this time. Sorry to have been so long, friend with a problem."

"I didn't mind," Caro said. "I looked at the sea. I expect I'm absolutely conditioned to waiting through phone calls anyway, I never notice it."

"Ah, yes, Helen and her telephone," Jere said as he picked up the fishing rod again. "Which reminds me, we were speaking of Helen, weren't we?"

"Not really," Caro said. "We were speaking of marriage. In the academic sense, I mean. But let's not any more, let's talk about something else. Jeremy, do you think it could be that I have an emotional block against marriage? I shouldn't like to think I had, but just the same I'm quite sure that I'll never marry."

Jere carefully squeezed an infinitesimal drop of golden oil into the handle mechanism of the reel.

"That's an often made prediction on the theoretic level. What about that young man of yours, by the way, the one who brought you to the party that time?"

"Oh, Michael," she said. "Poor Michael!"

"That doesn't sound very promising. Are you bored with him?"

Caro sat down on the window seat again, clasping her hands around her lifted knees.

"Poor sweet Michael!" she said sadly. "I expect it's horrid of me, isn't it? Do you know, Jeremy, it's the most maddening thing, he simply won't pay attention to me! He has this fantastic picture of me in his mind, the sort of person that he must have wanted me to be. He simply doesn't care about finding out the sort of person that I really am."

"An ancient and fatal human error, alas, poor Michael," Jere said cheerfully. "Are you in the mood for new fun and games then?"

Caro turned her head.

"Jeremy, what is it? You've been looking at me in the smuggest sort of way, ever since you came away from the telephone."

"I think I've a present for you on a dull and dreary Sunday. Do you remember a man you saw on the beach the day you came to the party here?"

"Jeremy!" Her voice was pleased. "You've found out who he is! How very nice of you. I asked you about him that day but you didn't know. I asked Michael and he didn't know him either. But of course I remember him. He was lying in the sun like a huge sort of cat. He had the most enormous shoulders and the very palest hair. What's his name, Jeremy?"

"Hell's bells, I forgot to ask," Jere said ruefully. "I know where he's staying though."

"Good," she said. "I'd like to meet him very much. What's he do, Jeremy?"

"I don't know much about him," Jere said. "I think he's a movie extra at the moment. He'll likely turn out to be a very dull boy, you know. You're not to blame me for that."

"Jeremy, how very silly," Caro said dreamily. "Whatever he is, he'll be extraordinarily much so and it most certainly will not be dull. You can tell that easily, just by looking at him."

"Oh, go on," Jere said mildly. "My friend says he's just another sex pot around town."

Caro's chin lifted.

"I expect he might be that, too. But he will be other things."

She slid off the window seat lightly onto her feet.

"Could I just telephone him, do you think? Do you have the number, Jeremy?"

"Now you're going altogether too fast," he said. "There are strings to this, lamb. In the first place, a favor for a friend. I'll spare you a long story, but it seems that your fair-haired charmer is broke and he's moved in on a friend of my friend's down in Hollywood. Now he's making something of a nuisance of himself, what with his girl-chasing and one thing and another. Do you think you could bedazzle him sufficiently and just long enough to sell him the notion of moving out here to my beach shack, without particularly letting on to him that you know anything about his unfortunate home situation in Hollywood? Tell him he needn't worry about the rent for the time being. Tell him how marvelous life is at the beach and hint at tête-à-têtes out here with him, or whatever. Do you think you could do that?"

"I should think I might," she said. "What else, Jeremy?"

"Now we come to the real string to it," Jere said. "There's a promise you must make me, or it's all off. Since I don't know this character myself, bedazzle away and have your fun, but even if you were to take a liking to him, no rendezvousing in remote places or anything like it until I've had a chance to get a look at him. Promise me?"

"But of course," she said seriously. "Jeremy, how very conscientious of you! Do you have the number, please? May I use your phone, Jeremy?"

"Help yourself," Jere said as he gathered up the tools and oil tin from the table. "Number's there on that envelope beside the telephone. Would you like me to leave the room?"

She paused to look at him gravely with her huge elongated eyes.

"Jeremy, I think it's very unfair of you to laugh at me. You've never seen this boy, he really isn't ordinary at all. Do give me credit for some taste."

She walked on toward the desk, her flat black slippers pattering across the polished stone floor.

"Look here," Jere said. "You really will be careful with this joker, won't you, lamb?"

"Jeremy, how nice you are. I gave you my promise, didn't I? Besides, I've looked after myself a very long time, you know. I'm quite good at it."

"I know you are," he said. "Otherwise I wouldn't be giving you this phone number, certainly. I can fill you in on some of the details later. Did you happen to meet a girl named Maggie Harrison, incidentally, at the party here that day?"

"Of course," Caro said, her hand upon the telephone. "She's Michael's sister, you know. What's she got to do with it?"

Jere stopped short.

"My god, you mean to say your Michael is her Bud O'Toole?"

Caro was studying the numbers on the back of the envelope as she lifted the phone.

"Bud's a sort of nickname," she said absently. "I think Michael is a much nicer name, don't you, Jeremy? Do you dial for Hollywood or do you ask the operator?"

"Dial for operator," Jere said automatically. "Well, a fine witch's brew this is boiling into!"

She read the numbers from the envelope unhurriedly into

the telephone, and then she called, "What were you saying, Jeremy?"

"Never mind."

She waited, standing small and erect at the end of the desk, with the telephone lifted before her face.

"Hello," she said suddenly, her voice composed. "I expect you'll think this is very silly because I don't even know your name, nor if you really are the person that I want. Were you at a beach party near Malibu on Sunday three weeks ago, and would you mind very much telling me how tall you are and the color of your hair?"

twenty-two

JUST AFTER FOUR that afternoon, Caro drove her car along the winding street up the steep misty hillside toward Dickie's apartment building. She drove slowly, reading numbers from houses as she passed until she reached the one for which she searched. She turned her car into a driveway then and backed, swinging around in order to double-park directly in front of the weather-beaten white stucco façade.

There was no sign of life around the building. She craned her neck to look into the empty arched entrance way, and glanced at the tiny pearl-encrusted watch on her wrist. She waited with the car motor running softly, sitting quietly and very straight behind the wheel, wrapped in a fleecy white coat, her small dark head turned toward the front of the apartment building.

Several moments later, the heavy glass door swung open and

Stush strode out onto the cement step. He looked toward the street immediately, but both Caro and her small car were partially hidden from view behind a larger vehicle parked at the curb. He paused to light a cigarette, standing easily with his legs braced apart. He wore the same baggy beige-colored slacks and a brown sports jacket, and his startlingly pale hair stirred in the wind.

Caro released the brake and allowed her car to coast several feet forward.

"Hello," she called out, waving to him.

He looked up quickly, his face instantly curious and appraising.

"Hi," he called back. He came down from the step and across the sidewalk, his eyes upon her. But by the time he stepped down from the curb, his attention had shifted to her small, shining blue sports car.

"Hey, this sure is some car you got," he said, appreciatively. He stopped still to survey it admiringly, from one end to the other. "What did you say it was, a Porsche? Special job, huh? You got it souped up?"

"I'm terribly sorry," Caro said. "I didn't hear what you were saying. I expect I'm staring at you, do you mind? I was wondering if you'd look the same as I remembered you."

Stush opened the door and began to fold his large frame into the small seating space beside her.

"Yeah," he said. "Well, do I?"

His pale eyes between the stubby pale lashes were very direct.

"Yes, you do," Caro said composedly, serene beneath his scrutiny. "Exactly, exactly the same. You know, it's a terribly strange thing, have you ever noticed how . . ."

"Hey," Stush said, breaking in upon her. "You know you're pretty cute at that. You match up with this car real good. I never saw you at that party though. You know who I had you figured for after you called up? There was a blonde kid out there that day that kept giving me the eye. She had a white bathing suit on. Boy, you ought to have seen the knockers that babe had!"

"What's knockers?" Caro said, her voice a shade reserved, while the little car glided forward around a sharp curve along the precipitous hillside.

"Huh?" Stush said, his voice surprised. "Knockers. You know, boobies, tits."

Caro laughed, her lovely tinkling laughter, and Stush looked at her quickly, his face instantly suspicious and on guard.

"I think that's a terribly funny thing to call them," she said. "I've never heard anyone call them that before."

"Yeah, I bet you never did at that," Stush said unpleasantly. "Listen, what gives with you? You in the habit of calling up strange guys on the telephone, or what is this anyway?"

Caro's small chin lifted.

"Don't be silly," she said in her clear unhurried voice. "I saw you at that party that day and I simply thought you looked like someone I'd like to know. If I'd found someone right then who knew you and could have introduced us, I expect you'd have thought it was all very ordinary. Because I had to do it this way for myself, why should you feel any differently about it? I don't think that's really being fair, do you?"

"Yeah," Stush said. "And how did you find out where to call me up, anyway?"

"You know, you're really a terribly funny boy," Caro said. "What difference does that make?"

"Listen," he said. "You're a cute kid and all that. You come down off your high horse, maybe you and me'd get along. I asked you a question. You going to answer?"

For a moment the air between them was electric with animosity.

"I don't see what difference it makes at all," she said finally. "If you really have to know, I know someone who knows somebody else who knows you. A girl named Maggie Harrison."

Stush thought about it for a second, his face puzzling.

"Oh, yeah. Redhead that hangs out down at the beach. She's

got a real cute little boy. Okay, so you found out my telephone number from her. What was it you said your name was?"

"Annise," Caro said gravely, looking at him out of the corners of her huge dark eyes. "My name is Annise."

"Yeah," Stush said dubiously.

He was silent then, staring straight ahead of him, his eyes squinted against the smoke from the cigarette in his mouth, his hands shoved into his pockets.

Caro gave all her attention to her driving, her face remote and faintly displeased.

"Well, shall we have tea then?" she said at last, her voice very distant now.

"It's your party," Stush said shortly. "What's this tea kick you keep talking about, anyway? You mean drink tea, or smoke it, or what?"

"You needn't have tea if you don't want to. I expect you'd rather have a drink."

"Drug store up here on the corner makes pretty good milk shakes," he said. "Why don't you just drop me off there, anyway. Okay?"

She was silent and a moment later she braked the car abruptly, signaling a stop to cars behind her.

"Good, there's a parking space," she said. "I expect I could get tea at this drug store, don't you think?"

"Suit yourself," he said.

She maneuvered the car into the small parking space, her chin high while Stush leaned out to eye the curb and the car behind, pointedly.

When she stopped the motor, he opened the door quickly and slid over, unfolding his big body lightly onto his feet.

He turned and held out his hand to her, not very graciously, as she slid across the blue leather seat to follow him.

"Thank you," she murmured, and for just a moment they stood close together, eyeing each other warily. And then he dropped her hand and turned away abruptly, setting off down the side-walk with his long smooth stride so that Caro was almost running to keep up with him.

They came around the corner to the wide-open entrance way into the drug store. The big room within was hung with bright advertising pennants, noisy with voices and cluttered with high counters of stacked merchandise. All the stools along the soda fountain counter at the back were filled, and they sat down at one of the little round tables crowded together in a tiny cleared area of floor space next to the counter.

A sharp-faced waitress in a soiled green uniform gathered up the dirty ice cream dishes noisily, and switched her wadded dirty rag carelessly across the table top.

"What's yours?"

"Double milk shake," Stush said. "Lady's having tea."

His voice upon the words was delicately sarcastic.

He lighted another cigarette impatiently, and across the table Caro sat erect in the little metal-backed chair, her hands folded quietly in her lap, her eyes musing and very far away.

She sighed suddenly, and looked up.

"It's really terribly strange," she said. "We seem to have gotten off all on the wrong foot, I wonder why? Do you suppose we could just start all over again, as if we were just meeting for the very first time right now?"

"What did you say?" Stush yelled at her crossly through all the pandemonium of voices.

Caro's eyes flared, and for an instant she was poised and ready for flight. And then she leaned across the table toward him, her voice lifting. "I said we seem to have gotten off to a terribly bad start. I wondered if we should try again."

"Well, do you want to?" Stush said, leaning forward over his folded arms, the smoke drifting before his face.

"Yes, I want to," she said. "What's your name?"

"Stush," he said. "That's what everybody always calls me."

"What a very odd name," Caro said. "Stush. I expect it's some sort of nickname, isn't it? What is your name, really, I mean?"

"Boy, you're a character, that's what you are," he said. "I already told you what my name was. You don't like it, you don't have to. This was your own idea we should start over being friendly, wasn't it?"

Their eyes locked across the dirty untidy table top.

"You know, you're really the strangest person that I've ever met in my whole life," Caro said rapidly, her voice bristling with exasperation. "Talking is the one thing I do most easily in this world. All my life, my sister's told me that I talk too much. And now with you I don't seem to be able to talk at all about any-thing."

"Then why don't you just relax and keep your mouth shut and listen to somebody else for a change?" Stush said practically. "It might be good for what ails you, you ever stop to think of that?"

The waitress returned to the table, putting down her chipped, brown plastic tray heavily as she began to unload the teacup and the tall thick glass of foaming milk shake.

"Listen, Annie, that's some car you got, no kidding," Stush said over the clatter. "You ever had it out for road trials, anything like that?"

Caro shook her head.

"No, I only drive it around town, I expect it is a waste," she yelled back. "I liked what you said about the car matching me, or me matching it. That's why I chose it, you know, because I liked the look of it."

"Boy, I'd sure like to get it out on an open road sometime," Stush said. "Man!"

He picked up the little inky square of paper that was the check and flipped it toward her carelessly across the table top.

"Listen, I'm busted. I hope you got some dough on you, Annie."

Caro put down the little round metal teapot with a bang.

(235

"Look here," she said furiously. "Why do you keep calling me Annie? I hate that name!"

"Well for Christ's sake," Stush said. "If you aren't one hard female to get along with! What in hell am I supposed to call you? That's what you said your name was, didn't you, Annie, something or other?"

Caro's chin was very high.

"Well, if you'd really like to know, I was lying when I told you that. My name happens to be Caroline Bellamy. Most people call me Caro."

And suddenly, for the first time, Stush was smiling, his disarming, wide, engaging grin. He reached out across the table and squeezed her small hand in his large one.

"Now we're beginning to get some place," he said. "Let me tell you a little secret, hon. I think maybe you and me are going to make it yet."

"I give up," Caro said. "Truly, I give up. Where do you come from? You're not really from California, are you?"

"I'm not from anywhere any more," Stush said. "I just been bumming around for a couple of years now, ever since I got out of the Army. I been all kinds of places. Then a couple of months ago I hit Las Vegas. Boy, that sure is one town where you can spend money fast. First thing I knew, I was really out on my ass. Then I got this chance to ride to California. I'd never been to California so I figured I might as well give it a whirl. I sure didn't have nothing to lose. I been out here about a month now. California's a real great place, I like it fine. You from out here?"

Caro nodded.

"I expect I'm what they call a native daughter. I was born here, I've been here nearly all my life. What do you do, Stush?"

Stush laughed, his loud and easy laughter.

"I don't do nothing. Like I told you, I just been bumming around ever since I got out of the Army. I just been having myself a time. What do you do, hon?"

"I don't do anything either," Caro said quietly. "But not in the way that you mean that. I don't do anything. I expect I've just been waiting now for a long long time for something to happen to me."

"Yeah?" Stush said softly, his eyes direct and intimate. "You think maybe this could be it, huh? What do you think, hon?"

"I think it just might be," Caro said, her eyes upon him. "Tell me about you, Stush. Because I want to know you, I want to know every single thing about you. Tell me quickly, so we won't waste time."

Stush hunched his shoulders and spooned into the syrupy thick froth at the bottom of his glass.

"What's to tell?" he said. "I'm just a guy. I like to screw, I like to drink, I like to see different places. I like to tear around and have a big time. Boy, they sure make good milk shakes in this joint. Tell me something. You really like tea? Why you drink that stuff for, anyway?"

Caro's eyes were shining.

"Do you know?" she said. "I don't specially like tea at all. I don't know why I go on drinking it. I've never had a milk shake in my life, not ever since I can remember, anyway. Would you mind ordering one for me, please?"

"Hey, hey!" Stush said, his voice soft and exulting. "Now we're really beginning to get some place!"

He reached across the table top again and took her hand.

"Tell me about you," he said. "You're a real cute little kid. You got the biggest dark eyes I about ever saw in my life. Why you look so sad anyway? You're a cute kid, you got dough, plenty of dough, I can tell the way you act, the way you're dressed. You got a honey of a car setting out there in the street. You act like you're your own boss. What you got to be sad about, anyway?"

"Teach me, Stush," she said, her voice very soft. "Teach me how to have a wonderful time just drinking a milk shake. Teach me how to have fun just breathing air and being alive."

Stush closed his hand hard over her small soft fingers.

"Damn right," he said, his voice gentle. "You stick with old Stush, hon. I'll teach you a whole lot of things."

At six o'clock they were still talking, their heads close, holding hands amid all the littered debris on the table top, oblivious to the noise, the tread of feet, the ringing cash registers, the restless influx and outflow of the crowd around them.

The sharp-faced waitress surveyed them disgustedly, her hands upon her thin hips. "Listen, you two lovebirds planning to sit here all night?" she said. "I'm going off duty in a minute and I've got to clean up these tables, for Christ's sake!"

They went laughing, hand in hand, walking swiftly out into the gray misting air.

At seven o'clock they were in the back of a shadowy down-at-the-heel bar on a side street off Hollywood Boulevard. Caro's coat was carelessly tossed over the top of the back booth, and she stood beside the big lighted juke box, slim in a narrow, vivid, blue-colored dress with thin straps over her small, bare, childishly bony shoulders. Stush's jacket was discarded, his shirtsleeves rolled, his tie askew, and his shirt unbuttoned down his broad, dark, tanned chest.

"Now you're getting it, hon," he said exultantly. "See, all you got to do is let yourself go and get with the beat. Come on, let's do it some more."

He drained the beer from his glass thirstily, and with the foam shining on his mouth, pushed another coin into the slot.

The inner mechanism clanked and rattled, the gaudy lighted box shuddered. There was a loud tattoo of drum beats, and Stush moved lightly, catching the rhythm with his whole body.

He clapped his hands sharp on the beat, and sang the words:

> "One and two and three o'clock,
> Four o'clock, rock!
> Five and six and seven o'clock,
> Eight o'clock, rock . . ."

Caro flung back her head, laughing in delight, dancing backwards out the length of his arm and spinning there before he pulled her in again, her body absurdly small close to his large one.

A man hunched on a stool in the dim light from behind the bar leaned his head upon his hand, his eyes dreamily fixed upon Caro's small bottom, with the thin fabric of her tight dress pulling across it as she danced.

At eight o'clock they were in the car just as the early darkness fell, with an open highway twisting away before them. Stush drove, holding the wheel gently and easily, swinging in and out among the light traffic, the little car leaping forward and pulling back smoothly, as though it were only an extension of his big well-coördinated body.

Then suddenly, the road stretched away straight and empty before them. Stush laughed, and the little car hurtled forward, roaring. Caro crouched at his shoulder, the big collar of her white coat caught about her face.

"Wonderful, wonderful!" she was crying, the words torn away and lost in the great rush of wind.

At ten o'clock, they lay together, spent and quiet in the darkness, on a hard and lumpy motel-room bed.

Caro's face was wet with tears, her voice the softest murmuring whisper, "Stush, it's so right, it's so perfect! It's never been like this for me before in all my life."

His hands were very gentle.

"Hon, you're wonderful," he said. "You're such a little bit of a thing, how did you learn to make love like a great big woman? You're so little, but you fit to me. Your head goes here, and your butt right here, see, you fit just right."

Suddenly she clung to him tightly and a little desperately.

"Stush, we're not to spoil this, do you hear me! I want this to last for us, forever and forever!"

"Hon, how could we spoil this! This is for real!"

At eleven o'clock, very combed and proper, they sat together in a softly lighted nook in the corner of a quiet hotel dining room, with the lush planting and the great twisting tree limbs just outside the glass. They held hands tenderly over the heavy, immaculately white table cloth.

Stush smoothed at her small childish fingers, and said wonderingly, "Jesus, it's such a funny thing! You and me, we're just alike, hon, you know it? We're the tough kind of people. Nine-tenths of persons that you meet, they're soft, you know what I mean?"

"I know," Caro said. "I expect we're tough because we've had to be. Because right from the beginning nobody ever really cared about us, don't you see? Your family was too big, and too busy being poor, and mine was too small and too busy making money. I think it's what makes it so terribly perfect, don't you, that we are exactly, exactly alike in so very many ways."

Stush's face was remote and dreaming, and suddenly his hand closed convulsively upon hers.

"It's good to be alike, sure," he said, "but maybe it can be real bad, too. You ever think of that? Oh, Christ, let's try not to mess this all up. Let's really try!"

"Silly you!" she said fondly, cupping her other hand for a moment against his chin. "Do you want to know what I think? I think we couldn't possibly mess this up, not even if we were to go out and try very hard to do it!"

At midnight, they were the last ones left at the shooting gallery in a bleak and cheerless penny arcade. Stush cradled the rifle expertly against his chin, squeezing the trigger slowly and rhythmically, knocking down, one after another, a row of aloof, smoothly sailing metal ducks.

"What difference does it make, anyway?" he said amusedly. "This picture-acting stuff is nothing but a lot of crap."

Caro sat on the counter, her white coat, streaked with dust, folded together about her lifted knees.

"But don't you see," she said over the crisp staccato explosions

240)

from the gun. "If one does anything at all in this world, one ought to do it properly. Stush, it's perfectly ridiculous for you to be doing extra bits. I know, because the motion-picture business is the only business that I know the least thing about at all. My sister knows hordes of people, and that's half. The other half is some strange extra sort of thing, one either has it or one hasn't. And you have more of it than anyone that I've ever known. It will be quite easy. Wait and see."

At one o'clock they sat together over drinks in a hushed small room on the Strip, where a pianist and a horn player and a bassist performed intricate and muted cacophonies of sound for a silent, intensely listening audience mainly composed of serious-faced young men in glasses and subduedly restless pretty girls.

When the musicians stopped finally, there was a moment of continued silence and then a fierce burst of applause.

Caro clapped her hands enthusiastically, turning to Stush who sat slouched and easy in the chair beside her.

"Now," she said triumphantly. "Now tell me what you think!"

Stush's face was vastly amused.

"Cool," he said. "Just cool stuff. Look, hon, this crap's not for you! Let me take you to this joint over on Beverly where I was last night. I just want you to hear these guys, that's all. Was you ever down in New Orleans, that's one hell of a town. Boy, I sure'd like to show you that town some day. They got a street down there they call Bourbon Street . . ."

At three o'clock they were back on the Strip, sitting at a wooden table in the chill night air, with hamburgers and tall glasses of milk, their eyes clinging together.

At four they were in bed again, holding each other silently and fiercely.

At five they drove once more, their bodies close, with Stush at the wheel and the little car shooting like a comet along a winding drive at the edge of a canyon, the city lights lost in the mist below. They no longer talked at all.

At six, they walked shivering on the beach, their arms intertwined. The tide was out, and in the gray light the sea was smooth and still. The limpid sky was rosy pink in the east and just over their heads a large yellow moon waned, a last remnant of golden moon track still faintly glittering upon the gray water. They walked slowly, leaving the twin sets of dark footprints behind them along the smooth damp sand.

"I don't want this night to end," Caro said fiercely. "Why must it end, Stush?"

"Nothing ends," he said. "We sleep awhile, that's all. The beach is a real great place to sleep. You listen to the noise the ocean makes. Nothing's going to end."

"You promise me?"

"I promise."

She stopped then, turning to face him, standing on very tiptoe to reach up to his shoulders.

"Well, then, I'd better go wake Jeremy," she said reluctantly. "I expect I'd better do this by myself."

"You're going to stay with me," Stush said. "Aren't you?"

She nodded.

"That's why I'd better go in first by myself. Because of having to tell him that I'm staying, too. You won't mind waiting?"

"Uh uh," he said, groping for the last cigarette from the crumpled pack. "You hurry up though. Okay?"

She lingered.

"Nothing's going to change," she said. "Tell me, Stush. Promise."

"Nothing's going to change," he said. "I promise, hon."

She went quickly then, running toward the uneven flight of steps half buried in the sand. When she reached the glass door at the top, she stopped with her hand poised to knock and tried it instead. It moved easily at her touch, and she turned to look another time at Stush where he stood down below, his back to the wind, his pale head bent over the match cupped between his hands.

She slid inside, where the big room was dim and filled with shadows and the pungent smell of burned-out wood and ashes from the fireplace. She hurried down the length of the room, her slippers pattering over the stone, and at the closed bedroom door at the far end, she began to knock softly and insistently.

There was a murmur of sound from within after a moment, and she called out softly, "Jeremy. Wake up, please, Jeremy."

Another moment later, the door swung open, and Jere, wrapped in a dark woolen bathrobe, appeared in the doorway.

"Good morning, Jeremy," she said in a grave small voice.

Jere ruffled his light hair in his fingers and rubbed at his face.

"Good morning indeed!" he said crossly. "Why don't you go home to bed where you belong?"

"Jeremy, wait," she said rapidly. "You wanted to rent your room, didn't you? Well, then. Your tenant's waiting."

"Well, bully for you," Jere said without enthusiasm. "I don't suppose you possibly could have contrived this any time before the grim dawn though, could you?"

"Where are you going?" she said.

"To get bed linen for the unexpected guest, of course," Jere said. "It seems I underestimated you, lamb. I should have made up the stupid bed before I went to sleep last night."

"Jeremy," she said. "I'm staying with him. I expect you'd want to know that."

"Oh you are, are you?" Jere called back sourly. "As simple as that! Now look here, my girl! I'll play Pandarus to your Cressida, only to a point. Helen would have me strung up by my thumbs for this, and you very well know it. Besides, I thought you promised me."

"Jeremy, you're being stuffy," she said, her voice strained. "It really doesn't suit you. You hadn't any right to ask promises

(243

of me in the first place. We have been to two motels already tonight, so I think you're making quite a ridiculous thing of this, don't you?"

Jere appeared in the doorway again, the smooth folded sheets and slips over his arm.

"Well, I'll be damned," he said softly. "The worst of it is, I have an ominous feeling that I will be, too, and very thoroughly, before this is done. You're a bad girl, and I'm sure you know it. You're also putting me in a most uncomfortable spot. Why can't you just go away and find another nice motel some place then, if you must. I thought you told me that you'd given up sex anyway, you ghastly little storyteller!"

She slapped him hard, directly in the face.

"I have," she said fiercely. "This is something quite different, the one time in all my life! I won't have you talking like this about it."

"Oh god!" Jere closed his eyes. "I'm positively looking forward to meeting this marvel. But some other time. One thing I'll have you know right now, my heart goes out to him, poor chap! Here's your sheets. It's much too early in the morning for platitudes and certainly for blessings. I'm going back to bed. You do whatever you please."

He turned on his heel, and slammed the bedroom door.

twenty-three

IT WAS NOON that day before the sun came out at the beach. By midday the light fog had burned away, and suddenly the sun was shining hot over the sand and the blue dappling water.

Jere, clad in faded blue denims, sneakers, and a white T-shirt, came down the steps from his wing of the house carrying a fishing rod and bait pail, and whistling softly to himself.

At the bottom of the steps, he put down the pail and felt through his pockets for pipe and tobacco. He found neither, so he bounded back up the steps again to the glass door. He picked up a pipe from the coffee table inside, but the several tobacco tins that he tried were empty. He came outside again and walked around the house, mounting the steps along the far side that led up to the highway at the back. In the garage, he rummaged out a tin of tobacco from the stuffed glove compartment of his car. He noticed while he was there that Caro's small blue car was gone from the parking space close to the back of the house.

Jere returned down the steps, his feet silent in the sneakers. He collected the fishing rod and bait from the sand below and walked on to a large tumble of rocks that were nearly submerged now by the tide. He climbed up easily onto the top of them, finding first a secure resting place for the bait pail, and then seating himself upon a dry flat stone. He attached to the hook the bit of fish that he used for bait and stood up again, bracing his feet upon the slippery uneven surfaces before he cast smoothly far out beyond the running surf.

He sat down again, leaning his back comfortably against a rock and holding the rod against his knee while he went about filling his pipe. The sun was pleasantly hot upon his shoulders and his head, and he was enveloped in the timeless crashing tumult of sound from the surf.

A little later, there was the sound of a door slamming, coming faintly from the direction of the house. Jere looked around, idly. Stush was standing on the terrace, leisurely rubbing at his fair hair and brown shoulders with a bath towel. When Jere turned, Stush waved to him and dropped the towel, vaulting over the low wall to drop lightly onto his feet on the sand below. He was barefoot and naked from the waist, the legs of his beige-colored slacks rolled. He trotted easily along the sand toward the pile of rocks.

Jere shoved the rod into a crack between the stones and climbed down to meet him.

"Hello," he called. "You must be my new tenant. My name's Tidings, Jere Tidings. Not Jeremy, in spite of any propaganda you may have been getting."

"Hi," Stush said, taking his offered hand. "Everybody calls me Stush. Is it good fishing off here?"

"It isn't bad, you'd be surprised," Jere said. "It's better a little earlier in the morning. I was too damn lazy to get out here today."

He sucked at his pipe and then struck a match for it, his eyes appraising from behind his fingers.

Stush, oblivious, was looking away out to sea, his pale hair still glistening with water from the shower, his big brown body very easy and relaxed.

"Boy, that sun feels good," he said contentedly. "I sure like the beach. This is some place you got out here. You really got this whole piece of beach all to yourself. It's terrific."

"I like it," Jere said.

Stush looked at him directly all of a sudden.

"Listen, I'm broke. I guess maybe Caro told you already. I won't be able to pay for the room till I get a check I'm waiting for. Okay?"

"Why not?" Jere said. "Think nothing of it. The room was standing empty anyway. Glad to have you, if you'd like to stay."

"I'd sure like to stay all right," Stush said. "I really like the beach."

"Good, then it's a deal," Jere said. "It's pretty quiet out here though."

Stush's pale eyes met his again directly.

"I know. You feel like you're a million miles away from everywhere out here. That's what I like about this place. Hey, your line's out!"

246)

Before Jere had barely time to turn his head, Stush was clambering lithely up onto the rocks. He grabbed up the rod, the reel whistling in his fingers as he fed out line.

"Naw, it's gone," he said after a moment. "Boy, that line was really traveling there for a minute, did you see it? Better bait up again, huh?"

"Go ahead," Jere said, his face amused. "You like to fish?"

"No, you go on," Stush said. "You was fishing, I didn't mean to horn in. I never did any cast fishing before till I was up in Idaho way early this spring. Those streams up there are really something, you ever been up there? They catch steelheads up there, before trout season begins."

Jere took the rod again, and Stush leapt down onto the sand.

"Listen, you got a telephone here?" he called over the crash of the surf. "Is it all right if I use it? I been working out to the studio, see. That's the check I'm waiting for. They went on location. They're supposed to get back in sometime this week, and then I have to go out for one more day. Is it all right if I give them this number to call me here?"

"Of course, help yourself," Jere called back as he reeled in the line. "How do you like the motion-picture business?"

"Aw, it's a lot of crap," Stush yelled back, the sliding water frothing about his bare legs. "It's some kind of Roman picture they're making. All I did was stand around out there with a little short kind of white dress on. It stinks. Hey, you ever do any spear fishing?"

Jere shook his head.

"Never tried it. There's a whole crowd of skin divers that hang out a couple of miles up the beach from here though. Maybe you can have a try at it while you're out here."

"Yeah," Stush said. "I'd like to try that once."

"How about sailing?" Jere called back. "I've got a boat you can use."

"I don't know nothing about boats. That's something else I'd like to try though."

"Nothing to it, one the size I've got," Jere said. "I'll take you out for an hour some day and you'll be set."

"Hey," Stush said. "I'm going to like it out here just fine. Listen, you got some trunks I could borrow? I haven't got any clothes or nothing moved in yet."

"Of course," Jere said. "There's a stack of them around here, all sizes. Let me get you a pair."

He came down from the rocks, and they set off toward the house together.

"Look here," Jere said suddenly. "I just thought of it. I was going to say have a drink with me, but you haven't had breakfast yet, have you? There's eggs and cereal and things in the kitchen, why don't you rustle up something for yourself?"

"Good deal," Stush said. "I'm pretty hungry at that. Caro went home to change her clothes and then she's going to pick me up to go somewhere and eat lunch. You know how long it takes a girl to change her dress, it's liable to be supper time before she ever gets back out here."

Jere's face was amused again.

"Tell me something," he said. "What does Caro call you, anyway? Stush or Stanley?"

Stush stopped abruptly still and looked at Jere searchingly, his face on guard.

And then suddenly he flung back his head and began to laugh. He slapped Jere enthusiastically upon the back.

"Hey, you're all right, Dad," he said delightedly. "You know what, I like you!"

"Good," Jere said. "Well? Which does she call you?"

"She calls me Stush same as everybody else," he said. "Goddamn right she does!"

"Good boy!" Jere said, grinning back at him.

twenty-four

LATE THAT AFTERNOON, Dickie telephoned Maggie at the house on Juniper Street.

"Dickie! How you feeling, sweetie?" she said anxiously into the telephone.

Dickie's voice was strained and shaking with emotion.

"How do you really suppose I'm feeling? He's gone. How could you do it, Maggie? You know how I felt about this."

"Oh, hey!" Maggie said helplessly. "Do what?"

"As soon as he told me that he was moving out to the Tidings' place at the beach, I knew," Dickie said. "I know there's some girl mixed up in this, too, I don't know who she is or anything about it and I don't want to know. But Jere Tidings is a friend of yours, Stush didn't even know him. As soon as he said he was moving out there, I knew you must have fixed it somehow. Why did you do it, Maggie?"

"Dickie, honestly . . ." Maggie was floundering. "I don't see how you think I could have . . ."

"Well, it doesn't matter now," Dickie said wearily. "I know you thought you were doing what was best for me. I just wanted to tell you how wrong you were. I feel worse right this minute than I ever have before in my life!"

"Dickie . . ." Maggie began. "Dickie?"

But he had already put down the telephone.

Maggie dropped her own phone as though it had bitten her. She wiped at her forehead, and then stood motionless for a time, chewing at her lip, while the hot afternoon sun poured through the window glass into the dingy, cluttered living room. Outside, a spiny palmetto frond rasped against the stucco of the house. Like the sound of grasshoppers in the summertime back home, Maggie thought suddenly, and the tears came to her eyes instantly, for no reason.

She picked up the telephone and quickly dialed Dickie's number. She waited, her face anxious, and listened to it ring time after time, but he did not answer it.

While she was still standing there futilely, Bud swooped into the room.

"Listen, you going to hang on that telephone all night?" he said. "I'd like to make a call sometime, if you don't mind."

Maggie handed him the phone.

"Here, have it then," she said.

She walked back to the kitchen slowly.

"Okay, little one," she said to Jamie. "Let's finish your story now, all right? Where were we, anyway?"

"That puppy dog didn't have any house to live in," Jamie said sadly, holding out the book.

"No, sir, that poor puppy dog!" Maggie said. "Never mind, I bet he'll find a little boy some place who'll love him. Let's read the rest and see."

She sat down again beside the kitchen table and lifted Jamie onto her lap. For a second, she held his small, warm, wriggling body very close, resting her cheek against his stubby hair.

She had just begun to read again, when Bud clattered out into the kitchen.

"I just don't get it," he said. "Something must be the matter. We've been planning this date tonight for a week now. I just don't get it!"

Maggie stopped, closing the book over her finger.

"You're bellowing so we can't hear ourselves think," she said, a little warily. "Is something the matter?"

250)

"I don't know what's the matter," Bud said, wild-eyed. "All I know is, something must be wrong. Look, I was supposed to have tea with Caro yesterday. I waited for her up at the courts same as always and she never showed up. Finally I called her house but she wasn't there, and I called again before I went to work and she still wasn't there. All day today she never called me or anything. I kept calling her house and all I got was some stupid maid or somebody, saying that she wasn't there and they didn't know when she'd be back. And now I call again just now, and there's a message for me, she's sorry, she can't make it tonight. I just don't get it. Something must be wrong."

"Bud, I'm sorry," Maggie said wretchedly, not quite meeting his eyes. "I wouldn't worry, maybe something just came up. After all . . ."

"I can't help but worry," Bud said desperately. "Something's wrong, I can tell. You just don't know Caro. Any time she ever says she's going to some place, she's there. I just don't get it!"

He walked off quickly to the back door, staring out unseeingly through the screen.

Maggie sighed, fumbling at one of Jamie's shoelaces.

"Come on, let's read about the puppy dog," Jamie said impatiently.

"Bud?" Maggie said, her voice humble. "Do you want me to get some supper for you, sweetie? I mean, if you're not going out like you planned, why . . ."

"Never mind," he said. "I don't feel like eating, anyway. Look, I'm going out and get some air or something. If Caro should call or anything, tell her I'll keep calling her house. All right?"

"All right," Maggie said reluctantly.

Bud burst out the door and an instant later there was the sound of his car starting up.

"Mommy, come on!" Jamie said disgustedly. "Read the story!"

"All right, darling," Maggie said.

When the story was finished, Jamie slid down from her knees, trotting off toward his room on some new tangent of his own, and Maggie hurried back to the telephone.

She tried Dickie's number once again, and still there was no answer. Maggie broke the connection and dialed for the operator, giving her the number of the house on the beach.

"Maggie!" Jere's voice spoke cheerfully into her ear. "You sound positively forlorn. What is it?"

"Fine pair of conspirators we turned out to be!" she said bitterly. "Guess what? Dickie phoned me a half-hour ago. He sounded absolutely ghastly. And! He wanted to know why I did it."

"Look here . . ." Jere began.

"Uh uh," Maggie said. "Stush must have gone back there for his things and happened to mention that he was moving out to your place. Dickie put two and two together and came up with forty-four, bingo! He smelled me out quick as a bunny. He wouldn't even talk to me, nor answer his phone when I tried to call him back. He'll probably never forgive me for this."

"Don't be silly," Jere said. "He'll have gotten over this in a week or two. Just remember that your original premise is as valid as it ever was. Dickie's better off, isn't he?"

"I suppose," Maggie said dolefully. "That isn't all. Bud had a date with Caroline Bellamy tonight. She broke it naturally, and he was in an awful stew. I sat here feeling like a completely dirty dog."

"Well, it isn't your fault, you know," Jere said cheerfully. "If it's anyone's, it's mine. Comedy of errors, actually. I did neglect to tell you who my bait was, but then I had no particular reason to make the connection between Caro's Michael and your Bud, either. Buck up, Machiavelli."

"No sir, never again!" Maggie said. "I've always been a great tinkerer in other people's affairs. I hope this teaches me a lesson. Right now I feel like an interfering bitch, and that's what I am, too."

252)

"You do sound in the dumps," Jere said. "You've also lost your sense of proportion. At the rate young Caroline and Stush seem to be combusting around here, I'd say this had all the inevitability of a hurricane or any other natural cataclysm. And even if left on their own, they had managed to miss each other in the small local orbit, I still doubt if there was much future in it for either Dickie or Bud, don't you?"

"Doctor Tidings!" Maggie said. "Tell me more."

"Of course," Jere said. "You're a goose to worry over it. Look here, what are you doing tonight? Moldering and moping around the house, I assume. Why don't you and Jamie come up here and have dinner with me?"

Maggie's face brightened.

"I'd love it. You're right, I have the mopes tonight. Look, why don't I get Jamie into bed here and then . . ."

Jamie had just appeared in the living room, lugging his box of tracks and train cars. At her words, he dropped them with a crash and came running to her, roaring his disapproval.

She gathered him in soothingly with one arm.

"Sweetie, don't yell, I can't hear when I'm on the telephone. You didn't understand. I didn't mean you had to go to bed right now, silly. Now take it easy, and let me finish."

And then she said into the phone, "Sorry. That yowl you heard was because Jamie thought I meant to put him to bed right this minute, and without his supper too."

"Poor chap," Jere said sympathetically. "Why don't you bring him then?"

"Oh, that wasn't why he was yelling," Maggie said quickly. "He just heard me say something about putting him to bed and thought I meant to do it right now in the broad daylight. He doesn't really mind."

"All the same, it's a dog's life being small fry and always left out of things," Jere said gayly. "If he gets sleepy he can always conk out on my bed. How about it?"

(253

For an instant Maggie's face was frankly disappointed.

"All right," she said, riffling Jamie's fair hair affectionately. "You're nice to invite him. No wonder you're aces high in Jamie's books. What time would you like us?"

twenty-five

IN THE WEEKS that followed, Caro's little blue car was constantly on the move, shuttling restlessly back and forth over streets and highways, by day and by night. It sometimes paused in the parking lots of smart clubs and restaurants, but more often in less accustomed places, the dingy side streets near fight arenas and shabby bars, at bowling alleys, roller rinks and race tracks, and outside the cottages of many motels. Once Stush's stint was finished at the studio, they disappeared on longer jaunts; the blue car flashing off down the beach toward Mexico, across the desert to Las Vegas, and north along the mountains to San Francisco.

In the time between, Stush settled in at the beach. He dozed for hours, prone on the hot sand when the sun was overhead. He swam, he fished, he learned to ride the rollers effortlessly on a surfboard, and with a little tutelage from Jere, he sailed the small boat expertly. He rode the horses in the hills, and, once his studio check arrived, he bought himself skin-diving gear. He also paid Jere meticulously for a month's room rent.

And during all these days, it seemed, if anything, that he and Caro only became more engrossed in each other.

Bud O'Toole still telephoned Caro doggedly, but less frequently, as the days passed. He was seldom at home at the house on Juniper Street, and when he was, he was silent and moody. He spent longer and longer hours each day on the tennis courts in the park, playing with a tireless desperation until he had worn out most of his partners.

He was on the courts late one afternoon when a fog suddenly blew in from the sea, shrouding the park in an instant. There was an immediate flurry of departures through the playground. Babies were hastily collected from sandboxes, last small boys hurtled off on bicycles in the gloom, car motors roared in the parking area.

Bud, the last one left on the tennis courts, pulled on a sweater and picked up his rackets and gear. He trudged up the steep grassy slope toward the parking area, enveloped in the heavy wet mist that subtly altered every contour of the hills, shrubs and buildings so that he made his way slowly through a gray and alien landscape.

Because of the fog, he came upon the outdoor telephone booth unexpectedly, and without stopping to think about it, he stepped inside and dialed Caro's number.

She answered the telephone herself immediately and caught Bud by surprise, so that for a moment he stood miserably and embarrassedly silent.

"Hi," he said finally. "How are you?"

"Michael," she said gravely. "I'm very well, thank you. How are you?"

"Oh, I'm fine," Bud said. "Are you all right? I mean, is everything all right?"

"Yes, of course," she said. "Have you been playing tennis today, Michael?"

"Yeah," he said. "I've been playing all afternoon. I'm just leaving the courts now. I just thought I'd call you and see if you were all right and everything."

"That's very nice of you, Michael."

For a moment the line was silent between them.

Then Caro said, "Michael, I haven't really been very fair about this, have I? I'm terribly sorry."

"That's all right," Bud said wretchedly. "I guess nobody can help things like this. You don't have to be sorry."

"All the same, I am," she said. "Michael, it's only four-thirty, would you have time to meet me for tea, do you think, before you go to work?"

"Sure, I'd have time," he said with an instant shade of eagerness in his voice. "But you don't have to do that. I mean, if you don't want to, you don't have to feel that . . ."

"Don't be silly, Michael," she said. "Of course, I want to. It's been horrid of me not to have seen you before this and explained things to you. Shall we meet halfway, at the place we used to go?"

"Swell," Bud said. "I'll see you there, then. I can make it in a half-hour, is that all right?"

"Perfect," she said. "I won't stop to change. I'll see you then, Michael. Good-bye."

And then she telephoned the house on the beach.

It was Jere's cheerful voice that answered her.

"Jeremy, may I speak to Stush, please?" she said gravely.

"But of course," Jere said. "He's right here. Hold on, lamb."

He put down the phone, nodding his head to Stush, who stood beside the blazing fire with a drink in his hand. Stush came with his catlike stride, carrying the drink with him. He wore tight blue jeans and white T-shirt, and his pale hair was windblown and damp and disheveled.

"Hi, hon, what you doing?" he said into the telephone. "I been riding, I just got in. I was having a drink and thawing out a little. Hey, we're fogged in out here. When you come out, you better bundle up."

He listened for a moment, tilting the glass, and then he said,

"Sure, go ahead. Blow the poor guy off easy, huh? I got to shower and stuff anyway, take your time."

He laughed, suddenly.

"Why should I mind? You crazy or something! Give the jerk a break."

He listened again, the amusement slowly fading from his face.

"No kidding, it's nothing but a lot of crap, why you want to . . . Okay, you got it all set up, so I'll go out there tomorrow. I sure haven't got anything to lose, have I? Okay. Listen, take it easy when you drive out here, it's really fogged in. I'll see you, hon. Be a good girl now."

He dropped the phone and walked back to the fireplace where Jere stood lazily in the warmth with one foot propped against the hearth and a drink of his own.

"Boy, women!" Stush said. "When a girl gets an idea in her head, you might as well give up."

"You are so right," Jere said lightly.

Stush leaned on his hand against the stone and stared broodingly into the blazing fire.

"She's got some kind of deal set up out to a studio. She wants me to go out there tomorrow. I told her a million times already, this movie stuff's a lot of crap."

"She can do you quite a bit of good, you know," Jere said. "Or her sister can. I imagine she's gotten her sister to go to bat for you. Don't you want to be a moom pitcher star?"

"I don't want to be picked at, that's all," Stush said softly. "I sure as hell won't stand for nobody picking at me, no matter what!"

Jere looked at him quickly, his face alert and curious with interest.

But Stush did not speak again. He continued to stare into the fire with his face remote and dreaming. At last he hunched his shoulders briefly and downed the last of his drink.

"I better go shower," he said. "Listen, you better take a look at that Smokey horse's foot tomorrow, see what you think. It's the left hind one."

"I'll take a look," Jere said. "Want another for the road?"

"I'll shower first," Stush said. "I'll come back when I get cleaned up. You going out?"

"Later on," Jere said. "Have to get cleaned up myself. Come on back when you're ready."

Stush slid open the glass door and stopped for a moment under the light outside, his hands slid into his back trousers pockets.

"Man, just look at that fog roll in!" he said, his voice deeply content. "You can't even see the ocean from the steps here. This is some night!"

He stared out into the mist that swirled at the edges of the little golden puddle of light, listening to the muted restless rumble of the sea and the distant, melancholy bleat of a fog-horn.

"See you in a while."

He slid the door shut behind him and stepped out of the light into the fog.

Jere kicked at a log on top of the fire absently. The room was cheerful with light, warm and snug with the curtains drawn against the weather. He sipped contentedly from his glass.

Across the room, the telephone began to ring, an insistent tinkle of sound, and he went unhurriedly to answer it.

"Hello?"

"Jere!"

It was a feminine voice, warm and vibrantly alive on the one word.

For an instant Jere's face was indescribably weary.

And then he said gayly, "Helen! However are you, darling?"

"I'm wonderful, Jere," she said. "The point is, how are you? Nobody, but nobody has seen you in ages! Now I hear you're out on the beach some place. What on earth you doing out there, sweetie?"

Jere laughed.

"You'd never believe it if I told you. What can I do for you, Helen?"

"Well, I'm here having a drink with some people I know in Pacific Palisades. I'd like to talk to you, Jere. I'd like to talk to you very much. You're not far from here, are you? Are you doing anything right now? May I come over?"

"I'm not far at all," he said. "Come along. Do you have the number?"

"It's here in the phone book," she said. "Jere, you don't mind, do you?"

"Of course I don't mind," Jere said. "I'll have a candle in the window for you. Seriously, I'll put the car lights on, it's fairly soupy for reading house numbers. I'm on the sea side of the highway. I'll wait by the car and guide you in."

"That's very sweet of you," she said. "You sure you weren't going out or anything?"

"No, it's all right," he said. "The highway's fogged in, darling, and it's getting dark, so take it easy, will you?"

"Of course," she said. "I'm leaving here instantly, I practically have my coat on. I'll be there in five minutes."

Jere put down the phone.

He stood still for a moment, and then he walked off to the bathroom with his quick nervous stride, and snapped on the light there. He smoothed at his hair with his fingers and glanced down at his jeans and flannel shirt. Just as he began to unbutton the shirt, he smiled wryly all at once, and turned on his heel. He went out to the little bar in the corner instead, and poured himself another drink. He drank it down in two gulps and walked on to the bedroom. When he came out again, he carried a raincoat and a flashlight. He put on the coat, belted it, and shoved the flashlight into the pocket. He paused by the fireplace on his way out, studying the fire judiciously for a second and then adding another log. He turned up his coat collar and slid open the glass door.

Outside, it was nearly dark and the fog was wet and cold.

(259

There were lights turned on across the back of the house, but the heavy mist blotted up their illumination, and Jere turned on the flashlight to see his way along the sand below the terrace. He climbed the steep flight of steps, passing through the dark little fenced patio, to come out through the wooden gate onto the shoulder of the highway.

The traffic was light and moving cautiously, yellow headlights appearing suddenly out of the fog, and as suddenly gone again.

Jere backed his car out of the garage and around into the parking space close to the ramshackle rear of the house. He left the motor running and the parking lights turned on. He felt for his pipe and changed his mind. Instead, he rummaged in the compartment on the dashboard for an old pack with several dried and shredding cigarettes left in it.

He lighted one of the cigarettes quickly, and got out of the car. He waited with his hands thrust into his coat pockets, looking up the highway, smoking in rapid nervous puffs.

The moments passed, and one pair of yellow headlights after another. Then one pair came slowly, and suddenly veered off onto the shoulder on the opposite side of the road. Jere reached in the open car window and snapped off the lights and turned the ignition key. He strode across the highway just as she was getting out of the long heavy convertible on the other side.

Over the slamming of the door, she called out, "Jere, is that you, darling? My god, this is beyond civilization!"

She held out both her small white-gloved hands to him. In the fog and darkness, she was only a small dark shape beside the great bulk of the car, her face only a pale blur, but there was the sound of her laughter and the sweet fragrance of her perfume.

Jere bent and kissed her lightly.

"Well, we aren't always fogged in like this, you know. We're much more civilized out here in the sunlight."

"I should hope so!" she said amusedly.

He slipped his arm about her small fur-clad shoulders, waiting for a passing car to be swallowed up in the fog again, before he led her across the highway.

"How very clever of you to have had the car lights for me," she was saying. "Otherwise, I'd have certainly missed this place completely. I'm absolutely lost in this fog, I don't know which side of the Colony I'm on, or where. Is this the house, darling? How do you get into it?"

Jere swung open the creaking weather-beaten wooden gate.

"Through here," he said. "It looks formidable but I have a flashlight."

"My god!" she said. "Really beyond civilization!"

At the top of the steps, he said, "We go down this way. Be careful, these steps are wet and slippery. I think I'd better go first, don't you?"

She was laughing again as she descended behind him, her hand upon his shoulder.

"Jere, this is so fantastic, it's exactly like a very bad movie! Here we are after all these absolutely years, meeting again for the first time at night in a wilderness lost in a fog. Darling, I hear the ocean pounding right under our feet. Are you on a pier? Don't you get swept away in the tides? What on earth's that godforsaken beeping noise? Can it be sea lions?"

Jere laughed delightedly.

"What a marvelously town sort of girl you really are," he said. "The sea's down there a way although you can't see it in the mist. The beeping's only a foghorn down the beach."

He stepped off the bottom step onto the sand, and then paused, looking down dubiously.

"Oh, no!" she said. "Now where?"

He turned the flashlight beam onto her small, elegantly shod feet, delicate pumps fashioned out of clear plastic with absurdly thin, tall silver heels set with rhinestones.

(261

"Those aren't exactly meant for sand, are they?" Jere said cheerfully. "I think I'll have to pack you in, darling."

He turned off the flashlight and returned it to his pocket, and then he lifted her easily in his arms and set off into the darkness.

She was burbling with laughter, her hair smooth against his chin and the sweet scent of her perfume strong.

"Jere, how elemental, I love this!" she said. "But what a mad sort of house this must be! We've passed two or three doors already, where do they lead to?"

"Not mad, but complex," Jere said. "The former owner must have decided to get rid of this ramshackle old horror at his leisure, so he started building over on the far side. He got as far as one wing before he was sidetracked or died or something. Perhaps one day I'll finish it up. Meanwhile, I live in the new wing and let this part out to lodgers. There now, it's only up these steps, and we are there."

He put her down at the top of them, and slid open the glass door for her to walk ahead of him into the room.

Jere closed the door swiftly against the chill and fog and for an instant he hesitated before he turned around.

"Now then," he said matter-of-factly. "Let me take your coat and get you a drink."

She was standing close behind him when he turned, and she lifted her white-gloved hands to his arms.

"Jere, wait, let me look at you," she said. "I haven't really seen you yet at all."

They stood silently together, with both their faces curiously searching and intent. For a moment, all sound and motion was gone from the room uncannily, a single frame of film abruptly halted in a projector.

And then Helen breathed and moved again, taking a quick step away as she began to peel off her thin kid gloves.

"But you look wonderful!" she said. "You're so marvelously tanned. Darling, you look so outdoorsy!"

"You're looking very wonderful yourself, Helen," Jere said.

She smiled, her small, sleek, dark head tipped up to him, the diamonds twinkling at her ears. She was very small, like Caro, with the same delicately articulated features, but unlike Caro, her face was warm and intensely vital and brimming with life.

He lifted the heavy dark mink coat from her shoulders, the fur soft in his hands and damp from the fog. Beneath it she wore a simple, smartly cut black dress with more diamonds glittering at her wrists.

"Well, tell me everything," Jere said. "How are Laura and Patty?"

"Laura!" Helen said. "Jere, this you will not believe. She towers over me already. She's built exactly like Harry, you know. She's going to be absolutely enormous. And that's the only thing on earth I really know about her since I'm only her mother. She's being desperately adolescent these days."

Jere laughed. He dropped her furs upon the divan in front of the fire and moved off swiftly down the room toward the bar, unbelting his raincoat as he went.

"Patty's still my very own baby. She's so sweet, and still so solemn, like a little old woman, remember? Jere, you really wouldn't believe it, how the two of them have grown since you've seen them."

"I understand it's a habit children have," Jere called back. "What are you drinking, darling?"

"What? Oh," she said. "Well, it better be Scotch, that's what I've been having. Jere, this is really a very nice place, once you've gotten into it."

She looked about the room casually, and then sat down on the divan, crossing her legs and reaching out to the pocket in her furs for a cigarette case.

"And Harry, how is Harry?" Jere called back.

"Well, Harry!" she said. "How is Harry ever? Working like

a demon and his ulcer raising hell. Have you seen his last picture? It's supposed to be grossing something phenomenal. I understand he's having a gruesome time of it with this little trollop he's married to now, but he never talks much about it to me. I'll never know what he was really thinking of when he married her, poor Harry! Anyone in town could have told him."

Jere laughed.

"Well, Jere, it's true and you know it," Helen said. "I'm not being catty. My god, why should I be catty about any other wife Harry ever happens to have. Everyone knew what this one was like, they should have. She's slept with everyone in the industry at least once. And that goes for you too, darling, and don't try to pretend that you didn't."

"Wouldn't think of trying," Jere said gayly. "In many ways, I've always admired Harry's taste. You know that."

"Ah, ha!" Helen said with an engaging smile. "Thank you very much!"

Jere came with the glasses, giving the one to her and putting the other down on the edge of the hearth to strike a match for her cigarette.

She bent her smooth head over his hand.

"Jere, how's Lucy?"

He straightened to stand opposite her with his back to the fire.

"Lucy's well enough, I think. Actually, I see very little of her these days, her own idea. She got the divorce finally, and I understand she's living somewhere fairly depressing like North Hollywood now."

"I'll never understand Lucy," Helen said. "A little, weeping, damp storm cloud with a cold, sharp New England nose. Darling, in spite of everything, you were always far more charitable about Lucy than she deserved. Does she still go around in those ghastly Indian squaw skirts, I wonder, raising herbs and eating wheat germ? I never understood about the wheat germ either, it's only supposed to make you sexy, isn't it? What's she really doing, anyway?"

Jere's face was amused.

"Last report, she'd joined forces with a rather dreadful horse-faced female named Stiles and they were running an antique shop together, of all things."

"Oh, no!" Helen said, wide-eyed. "My god, how really depressing! Are they lovers, do you think?"

"I doubt it," Jere said cheerfully. "Be a little jollier for both of them though if they were, I should imagine."

They both fell silent then, and Helen sipped from her glass meditatively, her eyes fixed upon the fire. She looked up at him suddenly, and caught his eyes upon her.

"Jere," she said. "Darling, it's so terribly good to see you. I can't begin to tell you."

For another moment, time seemed stopped in the room, and the air charged and electric between them. This time it was Jere who moved, raising his glass, his face suddenly merely amused.

"Good to see you too, darling," he said. "Now what was it that you wanted to talk to me about, anyway?"

Helen was very still an instant longer, and then she sighed.

"Yes. Well, I'm sorry that you reminded me of it. Jere, you know perfectly well what it is. I understand you've been seeing Caroline lately."

"Depends on exactly what you mean by that," Jere said lightly. "Yes, I've seen quite a bit of Caro lately. She walked in here at my place on a party one Sunday, and since then she's been out a number of times. Don't tell me that you mind, Helen?"

"Jere, how could you!" Helen said. "That would make me feel very badly if I thought you really meant that. Of course I don't mind, and you know it. Tell me what you think of her."

Jere shrugged.

"I think she's fine. I'm very fond of her, as I've always been. I used to predict that she'd grow up into a wonderfully fetching female creature and she seems to have done it."

"You really think so," Helen said. "My god! But then you always take her part, Jere. You know you do."

"Oh, look here," he said.

"But it's true," Helen said. "You never really try to see my point of view in it. Caro may seem terribly amusing to you, but I'm the one that's responsible for her, for god sakes. I've had her to bring up since she was a baby and I've always had it to do absolutely alone. Harry's never the slightest bit of help with her, even the years we were married he never had time for his own children let alone for her. I've always had it to do alone, and she's been absolutely nothing but difficult since the very beginning, and she doesn't get the least bit easier either. You have to admit that much, darling."

"Well, late years, I'm a little out of touch, you know," he said dryly.

Helen turned away to the ash tray on the table beside her.

"I think the really worst of it is, she has phases. After all, you can get used to anything, but just as you're beginning to with her, she goes on to something else. You certainly must remember that grisly one years ago when she was sleeping with absolutely everybody, and I was at my wits' end. Thank god, that's one she did get over. Right after that she got terribly serious-minded all of a sudden. She had a theatre phase, and then a ballet one that was even grimmer. The last couple years, she's gotten dreadfully intellectual and completely fascinated with herself, and I think this is really the most gruesome stage of all. Don't laugh, I've had to live with this, Jere! Thick books, and looking down her nose, at me, mainly, through horn-rimmed glasses, and doing over her room in middle period Japanese or whatever it is, all straw mats and no chairs! And the most awful men! Jere, darling, you were always very clever about her, so

266)

that's one thing I wish you'd explain to me because I'll never understand it. Why is it that the more intellectual she affects to be, the more muscular the men are? Does that make any kind of sense to you? Last fall she came home with a broken-down wrestler, I'm not making this up! Thank god, she doesn't seem to be sleeping with them anyway, she only talks them to death these days. Jere, don't laugh at me!"

"Darling, be a little tolerant," Jere said. "We must each work out our own salvation in our own way. She's only very young, she's in search for her immortal soul. At least grant her this much, she is sincerely searching for it."

"Jere, that is so classically exactly what I would expect from you," Helen said. "Her immortal soul! Well, never mind. You always took her side instead of mine, darling, and I suppose you always will. What I want to know anyway is, what's this latest man of hers really like? How awful, actually, is he? Is she really sleeping with this one finally, or what?"

"You mean you haven't seen him?" Jere said amusedly.

"Of course I haven't seen him," Helen said. "I've barely seen her in weeks. And then suddenly, out of the blue, she descends on me. She has absolute tantrums. I'm to call everyone, I'm to make all these fantastic arrangements. I mean, a screen test, a screen test after all. But no! It must be Siggy on the camera, and Horner. And Harry, poor Harry's to drop everything, Harry's to direct this test if you please! Isn't it fantastic? I called Harry, I had to, she was all over me. Then I called him later to stand by until I had a chance to check this out. Jere, what on earth's she thinking of?"

Jere drained his glass.

"Well, there's an outside chance she may know what she's about," he said mildly. "You ever think of that, darling?"

Helen's eyes were incredulous.

"Oh no! Jere, I think you'd back her up in anything."

"Not true," Jere said lightly. "But do give her credit, Helen.

She has some idea about the industry, after all, she's lived with it all her life, and she isn't stupid. She may very possibly be wrong in this case, but so have wiser heads than hers been in their time. Have another drink and take a look at him for yourself, why don't you? She must also have told you that he's living out here. Isn't that really the reason that you came?"

"Ah, ha!" Helen said, with her direct and very charming smile. "Well, of course I'd want to have a look at him, wouldn't I? I can't think why she's been so secretive with this one, anyway. She certainly can't think that I'm going to stick my neck out with poor Harry or anyone else at the studio until I've had a look at him at least. What's he like, Jere? I suppose he's some sort of conniver who's using her. Is he attractive at all, darling?"

"See for yourself," Jere said gayly. "Perhaps her taste's improved, since the days of the broken-down wrestler."

"I doubt that very much," Helen said. "You should have seen the one before this. A clumsy awful boy, well, actually rather sweet, but nothing, really. I understood he played tennis and parked cars over at Kim Alison's place at night. Of course I have to admit, she didn't come screaming at me for a screen test for that one, either. Jere, you should have seen her, cold as ice and absolutely determined. And all these fantastic arrangements! So ridiculous."

"Ridiculous," Jere said, smiling at her affectionately as he reached for her glass.

"Jere," she said. "Now you are reminding me of you. You're really not hearing a word that I'm saying, are you?"

"No," he said. "But I do love very much to hear you talk, darling. Let me freshen this."

He walked away toward the bar, and she got up from the divan lithely and followed after, her jeweled heels twinkling.

"Jere," she said. "Regardless of why I really came over here tonight, I've missed you dreadfully. I've been longing to see you now for a very long time. Darling, what's all this about anyway?

What are you doing? Why are you hiding away out here at the beach? Why aren't you working?"

"Ah, but I am working," he said. "I've several things going. I regret having to use dirty words in front of a favorite lady, but I'm even trying my hand at some television scripts."

"Jere, how fantastic!"

"Why is it?" he said lightly. "If one's to sell his soul anyway, it might be less painful to do it in smaller bits and pieces, don't you think?"

"Now really!" she said. "What's all this talk of souls all of a sudden, and from you of all people? No, I'm sorry, Jere. None of this makes any sense at all, and you know it."

"Doesn't it?" Jere said. "After all, my stock wasn't exactly high when I left the studio, as you very well know. Would you rather have me in Beverly Hills selling vacuum cleaners then?"

"Darling," she said. "It can happen to anyone. I don't have to tell you that. You simply had a run of bad luck, the way it's happened to everyone at least once or twice. So don't you really think you've sulked in your tent now long enough?"

"Helen," he said gently. "This will seem fairly incomprehensible to you, so why don't you just take my word for it? I've put together a, for want of a better word, new, life for myself out here. It suits me and I'm quite happy. Let's just leave it at that, shall we?"

"All right, let's do," she said. "Actually, I don't believe a word of it, darling, and neither do you. But we certainly don't have to talk about it now. Jere, there is something I want very much to say to you. Or I did want to, but you're being very strange, you're not like yourself at all. You're making it terribly difficult for me, darling."

Jere looked up suddenly, over the top of her head.

At the other end of the room, Stush was coming in through the glass door, the fog shimmering behind him.

"Jesus, what a night!" he called out. "Hey, I didn't know you had company. I interrupting something?"

"Not at all, come in, Stush," Jere called back. "Someone who wants to meet you anyway. Sit down, I'll fix you a drink while I'm up."

Stush walked over to the fireplace with his long easy stride. He was very dressed up in a rather too sharply cut dark suit, with a white rolled-collar shirt and a knit tie. While he waited, he picked up Helen's jeweled cigarette case from the divan and examined it appreciatively, turning it in his fingers. And then he helped himself to a cigarette and closed it with a snap, tossing it down carelessly onto the cushions again and beginning to feel through his pockets for a match. His hair was shining pale in the soft light, and as always with his strange effortless vitality, merely by standing still with a cigarette dangling from his mouth he projected a sharp awareness of himself throughout the room.

"Well!" Helen said to Jere softly. "I certainly understand now why Caroline's been keeping this one hid away!"

"Helen," Jere said, his voice delicately mimicking. "Now you are positively reminding me of you, my darling!"

She laughed.

"Ah, ha!" she said. "That's pot calling kettle black, if I ever heard it. Hurry up, I want to meet him."

They came back up the room together, with Helen's small hand tucked into the crook of Jere's elbow, and her eyes fixed upon Stush.

"Darling . . ." Jere began.

"Hey," Stush said, his eyes upon her. "I bet you're Helen, huh?"

"Yes, I am," she said. "I've heard quite a bit about you, too. You must certainly be . . ."

"Stush," he said. "Everybody always calls me Stush. Hi!"

Her eyes slid away from his face over his wide shoulders.

"Hello," she said softly.

They took stock of each other unembarrassedly, with rather identical expressions of pleased interest on both their faces. Jere watched, his face amused.

"So, I hear that you're an actor," Helen said finally, as Stush held the match to her cigarette.

"Hell, no, I'm no actor," he said cheerfully. "I guess you been getting a lot of crap about that from Caro, huh? All about fixing up some test or something out to some studio?"

"I certainly have, you've no idea," she said. "But here all along, I was thinking it must be your idea. Isn't it?"

"Uh uh," he said. "She thought that one up all by herself. Boy, when a girl gets an idea in her head, you might just as well give up. I been telling her it's a lot of crap. Why don't you try telling her? No sense her bothering you with this stuff?"

"You know," Helen said, "sometimes I don't have the least bit of luck trying to tell Caro things, either. I really don't think that there is much I can do about this."

"No kidding," Stush said. "So?"

"So." Helen shrugged. "It makes for quite a problem for us, doesn't it? Do you know what I really think? I think we may simply have to relax and enjoy it, darling."

"Yeah?" he said, his eyes intimate. "So that's what you think? Well, relax is always easy, enjoying depends."

They looked at each other, with both their faces very stimulated and amused.

Helen laughed.

"Is that right!" she said. "Well, I can see that you and I have several things to talk over, haven't we?"

Jere looked at his watch deftly.

"Darling, I'm really sorry," he said. "I'm due somewhere in a bit, and I have to change. Would you mind?"

"Jere, I'm sorry," she said instantly. "I've kept you, haven't I? But I have to go, too."

"Of course not," Jere said lightly. "Why must you? Stush can entertain you while I'm showering."

"No, but I really must," she said, putting down her glass.

"I tell you what," Stush said easily. "Why don't you go ahead and get cleaned up, Dad? I'll take her up to the car, I'm not doing nothing anyway."

"Stush, that's very sweet of you," Helen said. "Do you think we'll ever find our way in this unearthly fog and all those fantastic steps?"

"Sure," he said, grinning. "Leave it to old Stush."

He put down his own untasted drink and picked up her furs from the divan.

She collected her cigarette case hurriedly and her small white gloves. She walked to Jere and stood on tiptoe, lifting her face for his kiss.

"Darling, it's been wonderful," she said. "I'd like to see you again very soon."

And then she said in a quiet voice, "But next time, I'd like to really see you again, Jere, do you mind?"

"That's much harder than you think, Helen," he said steadily. "Take it easy, darling, won't you?"

She hesitated for a moment longer, looking up into his face searchingly, and then suddenly turned away.

Stush was waiting for her at the door.

"Boy, that's sure one silly pair of shoes you got on," he said. "How you walk in sand in them things, hon? Want me to carry you?"

"Aren't they awful?" Helen said. "Would you mind? Or shall I take them off?"

"Naw," Stush said cheerfully. "You'd just get runners in your stockings. Upsy daisy."

He strode down the steps with her into the fog, and Jere closed the glass door silently upon the sound of her light and joyous laughter.

Jere showered after that, and while he was dressing in the bedroom, he heard suddenly the louder rumble of the sea as the glass door opened once again.

"Hello?" he called out.

"Hello." It was Caro's voice that answered him. "Jeremy, isn't Stush here? I thought that he would be by now."

"Come in, lamb. I expect he'll be over in a minute. He's probably still in the shower or something."

"But I'm really dreadfully late," she said. "I thought that he'd be waiting and simply furious with me. You know how very much he hates having to wait for anyone."

"Lucky you, then," Jere said cheerfully. "He'll turn up. I'm dressing. Make yourself cozy, will you?"

"Thank you, Jeremy."

She dropped her dark coat on the divan, and carried a cushion over to the floor beside the hearth. She was wearing a black skirt with a severe white top, and flat slippers of soft black kid. She sat down cross-legged, leaning upon her knees to stare pensively into the blazing fire.

After a moment, Jere called out from the bedroom, "You're very silent tonight, darling. What is it, fog in your bones?"

"It is a dreadful night, isn't it?" she said. "No, I was just thinking. I've been having tea with Michael. I do feel very sorry about Michael, Jeremy."

"Good," Jere said. "I'd be fairly shocked if you didn't have some conscience in these matters, at your tender age. Don't mind too much. He'll survive, you know."

"That isn't exactly what I was thinking of," she said. "I was thinking how really senseless it is, the way people just begin to feel a certain way about other people without even once waiting to learn whether it's at all reasonable for them to, or whether it will lead to happiness for them, or anything. You've only to see someone sometimes, as Michael saw me, or as I saw Stush for the very first time, and there it is. It's very strange, and really very untidy, isn't it?"

"But rather wonderful, don't you think?" he said. "After all, if you really want explanations for it, the head shrinkers can give you dozens of them, these days. Personally, I'd rather do without. Where's the fun in trying to make something logical and prosaic out of a phenomenon that's as really mysterious and exciting as that?"

"I expect you're right," she said. "All the same, it would be much tidier if people began together and stopped together, wouldn't it?"

Jere laughed.

"Caro, tell me something," he said after a moment. "Whose clever idea is it anyway, to pack Stush off to the studio? Is it yours, or is it something that Stush thought of by himself?"

"Jeremy, has he been talking of it to you?" she said quickly.

"He mentioned it," Jere said. "I wondered whose idea, anyway."

She hugged her knees, the firelight dancing upon her small remote face.

"It's mine, of course," she said serenely. "You must have guessed that, Jeremy."

"Are you really sure of that, lamb? Or is some of it Stush's own idea, too, by his own curious brand of indirection?"

"Jeremy, how silly! But of course I'm sure! You can't think of the trouble I've had with him over this, he won't even discuss it with me."

"Uhmm."

There was the sound of a drawer closing in the bedroom.

"All right, granted," he said gently. "Since you're apparently convinced this is entirely your own idea, and, god knows, you may even be right about that, are you so sure that it's such a very good idea then?"

"Well, isn't it?" she said. "You must know much better than I do, Jeremy. You've only to look at Stush, really. I know he doesn't know about acting, though I think he might have a feeling for it. What he's really got is that terribly extra sort of thing about him. He's got more of that than anyone I've ever known. You must have seen that for yourself, Jeremy. It's that

274)

extra thing that people have about them sometimes, that makes them seem very alive on film. It's quite rare, really."

"I think you may be perfectly right about that," Jere said. "I wasn't questioning your judgment on that side of it."

"Then what side of it, Jeremy?"

"Oh, I don't know. Would you really want him to be a movie star so much, darling?"

"Jeremy, that's supposing such a very great deal! It may not work out for him at all. Of course I'm prepared for that. He doesn't really know about acting, after all. But at least he must have the best possible chance to try."

"Why must he?" Jere said.

"Jeremy, how very strange of you," she said. "Why mustn't he? We must all be something in this world to be really happy. I think that Stush only pretends, he can't really be so very different about that than any of the rest of us, do you think? I have the strongest sort of feeling that this will be something that he can do terribly well, just as he is, that it will be quite natural for him. I'd like him to have that, to do one thing easily and naturally, and terribly much better than most other people."

"Ah!" Jere said. "Your ambition, Stush's life."

"Jeremy, how very unfair!"

"Now don't go feminine evasive on me," he said. "Regardless of whose ambitions are involved here, I don't think Stush much likes being pushed, that's the thing."

"I know that," she said. "Of course, I understand that, Jeremy. It's a sort of risk for me that goes with it. Because I think that if it does come out for him, he'll like it well enough so that he won't really mind the things that made it happen."

"You have made a tidy parcel out of this, haven't you?" Jere said ruefully.

"Jeremy," she said. "What really can be keeping Stush? Do you think he may have fallen asleep? I expect I'd better go and have a look, don't you?"

(275

"Wait a second and I'll go," Jere said casually. "It's awfully dark and wet out there."

In the bedroom, he selected a necktie judiciously, from a rack of them on the inside of a closet door.

"Darling," he said. "May I ask you something rather personal? You've quite a bit of money of your own these days, haven't you? I mean, you've come of age or something under your father's will, and you've at least a certain amount of money now to do with as you please."

Beside the fire, Caro lifted her head, her attention caught.

"Yes, I expect so, though I've never really thought of it in that way. Why do you ask me, Jeremy?"

"Then let me ask you something else, since I seem to be full of personal questions tonight. How much do you really care about Stush? Do you really care about him, not just for fun and games?"

"Jeremy, I don't understand!" she said in her clear grave voice. "You ask the sort of questions that you know the answers to quite well before you even ask. I care terribly about Stush. Stush is the very very most important thing that's ever happened to me in my life."

"Well, then," Jere said. "Let's put it this way. I'm much too old to give advice, particularly when no one has asked me for any. So let's just put it this way. Pretend that I am you. And if I were you, right this minute, do you know what I would do?"

"Jeremy, you're being very funny!" Her voice was amused. "Imagine you being me! What would you do if you were me?"

"I'll tell you what I would do," he said. "Tomorrow morning early, I'd buy plane tickets, two plane tickets. I wouldn't wait for any tests at studios or anything else. I would take Stush and I would go. To the Mediterranean, I think, or at least that far. You get very good nights for love along the Mediterranean, this time of year anyway. And when the weather began to change the slightest bit, I'd move on very rapidly to—Africa. Yes, I think Africa, definitely. I always rather fancy Stush in the Serengeti

276)

plain, it's a landscape that should suit him particularly well. After that, you might always try Singapore. Well, then, that's what I would do if I were you."

For a moment, the outer room was completely still, and then there came the sound of her gay tinkling laughter.

"Jeremy, how very silly!" she said.

"Well, there you are," he said cheerfully. "Prophet without honor. That's what always comes of giving advice. I did let myself in for it, didn't I?"

"Jeremy, you're not being serious about this," she said. "Because, if you are, I simply don't understand you. Places for themselves aren't really important to Stush. So long as he can always be moving and doing things, the place isn't the least bit important to him."

"My point exactly," Jere said a little crossly. "He could be moving and doing in Africa then, couldn't he, just as well as here?"

"What you're really saying then, is for us to run away," Caro said wonderingly. "Is that truly what you mean, Jeremy? What's the good of running away, ever?"

"Who taught you that particular bromide?" he said. "Quite often the most completely sensible thing you can do in this life is run like hell!"

"Run from what, Jeremy?" she said very quietly.

"Darling, don't you really know?"

Caro got up swiftly from the cushion.

"I expect you're trying to say that one day Stush will be bored with me. Is that it, Jeremy?"

"Look here!"

Jere came out from the bedroom quickly, buttoning a gray tweed jacket as he came.

"Now see what deeps I've gotten into," he said gayly. "Darling, did I honestly imply that in any way?"

Caro stood quietly, her hands childishly clasped against her black skirt.

"Of course I know that it could happen, Jeremy," she said. "I expect with Stush more easily than with many other people. It's a risk too, isn't it, but the one that everyone must take when they fall in love. If it's going to happen, Jeremy, it can happen in Africa too, just as easily, can't it?"

He came to her swiftly and put his arm about her shoulders.

"Of course it can," he said. "I'm sorry. It's only that I have a great mistrust of our complicated and madly competitive local environment after a peck or two of sad experiences of my own. The world is so much with us here. If I'd found my true love, I really would take it and run like hell, darling."

She looked up at him, her eyes very grave and steady.

"Jeremy," she said. "I don't really think that's silly sort of advice, you know. It's just that I can't much help myself. I know the particular risks you have in mind as well as you do, but I do want this chance for Stush at the studio, I want it very very much."

Jere cupped her face affectionately in his hand.

"Well, there's my answer," he said. "But it might come right down to which you value most, you know."

And then he said gayly, "Cheer up, lamb! All these risks we've talked of, they're not completely on your side, after all. One day, you may be bored with Stush too, right up to your pretty teeth! No, don't say it, I only said it could happen, for god sakes."

"I really can't think what's keeping him," she said. "Do you know what I think, Jeremy? I think he did get furious with me when I was so late, and now he's simply gone off somewhere."

"That could be," Jere said lightly. "Come to think of it, I believe he did get dressed early. I shouldn't worry, darling. He's probably only hitched himself a ride to the nearest bar."

"Anyway, I won't keep you, Jeremy," she said. "I expect you have to get some place. I'll wait here for Stush a half-hour longer, if you don't mind."

278)

"Of course I don't mind," he said. "I'm sorry I have to go. I'll stop by Stush's room on my way out if you like, make sure he isn't sleeping."

At the door he turned, looking back for a moment to her small erect figure beside the fire, her grave face in the soft flickering light, the proud distinction of her small poised head.

"Look here," he said. "I'm very fond of you, baby. I don't suppose there is any way on earth I can jar you off that cushion and this habit you have of sitting on one, making double talk about something when you ought to be up and doing it? You couldn't possibly just take the word of an older hand who happens to have your best interests very much at heart, could you? Because I wasn't joking in the least, you know. Two plane tickets at dawn tomorrow, in spite of anything! Will you do it?"

Her chin lifted, and suddenly her voice was very cool.

"I think I'd rather not talk about this any more, if you don't mind. I don't think I've made myself perfectly clear, Jeremy. Of course I don't mind admitting that there may be risks ahead for Stush and me, but you don't seem to understand that right now there aren't any risks at all. Because I know the way Stush feels about me right now, and the way that I feel about him. Right now everything is quite quite perfect with us, and we both feel the deepest sort of sense of keeping faith with this thing we have together. You really needn't worry about us, Jeremy."

"Oh god!" Jere said. "Young love! Ours be the torch to hold it high! One of the compensations of my advancing age is the certain knowledge I'll never have to be twenty again, with all that to be gone through another time. I apologize. I'm really not laughing at you one little bit. Just you go on keeping the faith. That's my last and single most important piece of advice for the night! I'll see you, lamb."

twenty-six

JERE DINED with Maggie that night, in a restaurant on the beach. The big room was nearly empty because of the weather, the juke box still and dark. Both Jere and Maggie were a little silent and preoccupied as they ate, although neither of them seemed aware of it. When they were done, they lingered over coffee while the fog boiled outside the windows. At last Jere paid the check and they went out into the wet dark night. They groped their way through the empty parking lot to the car, and Jere inched out cautiously onto the highway, to drive the mile or so back to the beach house. They made their way hand in hand down the steep flight of steps and across the sand to where the light shone in blurred yellow patches from the draped windows of Jere's wing.

The room inside was empty, and the fire burning low on the hearth.

"What a night this really is," Jere said as he closed the door. "Now you will have to admit it, Maggie darling, there is weather in California after all."

"I don't have to admit any such thing," she said. "This is the beach, and the beach is different. Besides, where's the seasons, even on the beach? Where's any real winter or fall or spring? There isn't any, and 'life goes on forever like the gnawing of a mouse!' "

"I give up," he said. "I know a lost cause when I'm stuck with one. Would you like a drink? I'd brew you coffee, darling, but I've only got to sort out a couple of books for Joseph and we'll be shoving off again. I think we're fairly late already. We'll get them to brew you up some coffee over at their place, all right?"

"You know what?" Maggie said. "I think I will have a drink. Please."

"Good," he said absently. "I'll have one with you."

Maggie sat down on the divan and pulled up her legs beneath her wide striped skirt. She fidgeted nervously at her hair, her face abstracted, and all at once, she took a deep breath and called out, "Jere? I've got news for you, Tidings. I have just, as of this minute, thrown in the towel, the sponge, and the works. How do you like that!"

"Now what's all this about?" he said amusedly over the clink of glasses at the bar.

Maggie's voice was carefully light and casual, but her face was not at all so.

"I am tired, that's all! I am tired of parties and parties and more parties. I am even a little tired of all those picnics we've taken Jamie, and the zoos and the carnivals. I am also tired of charming people who live in interesting houses and make clever offbeat conversation till all hours of the night over bottles of Scotch whiskey. I'm just tired! It's a wonderful filthy night tonight, and there's nowhere I'd rather be on a foggy night than on the beach. I don't intend to budge an inch from this lovely fire. You just go see this good old Joseph or whatever his name is yourself, why don't you!"

Jere laughed.

"I wouldn't even think of it! Look here, darling. Why didn't you tell me this before, if you were getting fed up with people and parties and things?"

"Oh. Well. Oh, I'm not really," she said. "Your people and your parties are wonderful, and I love it. You can't imagine how exciting it's been for a stay-at-home like me. It's just that I like to spend time with you, too, at least once in a while, you know. Jere, do you realize, I never get to spend any time at all alone with you?"

"Well, bless you, darling," Jere said lightly. "I suppose I really am a restless sort of bloke. I certainly didn't mean for you to feel dragged all hither and yon. I rather thought that people and parties were indicated for you just at this stage in your life, the more of them the better."

"I know," Maggie said. "This really isn't very nice of me, is it, or very grateful. Would you mind if we just stayed here tonight?"

"Now why should I mind, for god sakes," Jere said. "I think it's a very pleasant idea."

He brought the glasses, and then stripped off his raincoat to sit beside her on the divan. She was silent again, her head bent, her face preoccupied. Jere settled himself against the cushions a little wearily, stretching out his legs to the hearth, locking his fingers behind his head.

His eyes strayed away to the fire, and after a moment, he said, mildly, "It just happens, I'm not much in the mood for any good old Josephs tonight myself. Matter of fact, I had a sort of jolt earlier this evening, oh, nothing serious, mostly curious. It's funny, you seal away a part of your life when you're finished with it, and the years go by, and it's so silent from behind the wall that you get used to the idea the animals have gone away. Then one night, you see someone again, and in an instant's time, the wall's breached, and there are the animals, roused up and roaring at you. Oh, it's no great problem or anything, they herd back where they belong fairly easily, the jolt's mainly in discovering that they're still there at all, I suppose. Just the same, I feel a little unsettled tonight, I think I feel the beginnings of a talking jag, and I haven't had one of those in years. Darling, would I bore you if I . . ."

But Maggie was staring grimly into her glass without really even hearing him.

"And another thing," she said all at once, and a little desperately. "Since this seems to be my night for being horridly determined to say what's on my mind, no matter what . . ."

She stopped abruptly, and he turned his head, his attention coming back to her from some far distance.

"Well?" he said amusedly.

Her cheeks were pink as she lifted her glass.

"Never mind."

Jere laughed. He reached out for his own glass and hitched around part way on the divan, so that he sat facing her.

"Don't swallow words with me, my girl! It isn't like you, Maggie. Come on now, let's talk about you, instead, what other thing or two do you have tramping around in that lively mind of yours tonight?"

"No, sir," Maggie said, biting on a bit of ice. "I talk too much, goddamn it, and you encourage me. It isn't fair."

They were silent for a moment, Jere's eyes affectionate as he watched her. The fire on the hearth blazed up and the light and shadow shifted suddenly across his face. He reached out his hand gently to the back of her head beneath her swinging tail of bright hair.

"Maggie," he said quietly. "I know what you wanted to tell me, you know. Would you like me to say it for you?"

"You can always guess what I was going to say," she said. "How can you really know? Besides, it's nothing I wanted to say, anyway —not really, or I'd have said it myself."

"Don't run for cover, darling," he said. "I love you just the way you are, such an honest little goose. Of course I know what you were about to say before you got yourself all overcome with that maidenly modesty of yours and thought better of it. You'd gotten yourself whistled up to tell me, that in case I'm harboring any such foolish notion about it, that you aren't really saving your virtue for Christmas or anything. Now, wasn't that it?"

"Jere!" Maggie sat bolt upright, her cheeks bright red. "Now I think that's damn mean of you!"

Jere was laughing.

"Maggie, you are very wonderful! Well now, the chips are certainly down, aren't they? I think this calls for a long tall drink and another log on the fire, don't you?"

Hours later, when the logs had burned down to embers on the hearth, Jere came out of the bedroom with the dark woolen bathrobe wrapped about him. The room was filled with shadows from the small ruddy glow in the fireplace, but he mixed himself a drink at the bar deftly without light.

He carried it back into the bedroom and sat down on the edge of the bed in the darkness there.

"Darling," he said gently. "Would you like a drink? I'm having one. Though I must say, after this slight fiasco, it is painfully obvious that I need another drink tonight like I need a hole in the head!"

He waited but she did not move or speak, and he leaned over to her on his elbow.

"Darling," he said. "I'm damn sorry about this."

Still she did not speak or turn her head upon the pillow.

"Maggie, what are you thinking?" he said, his voice just audible above the roar of the sea. "You know, this would never occur to me if I didn't know you so well. But I do know you, darling, and that determined fantastic gimmick that you have to be forever selling yourself short. You're not by any mad chance lying there with some wild notion in your head that you were in any way responsible for this something less than satisfactory performance just now, now are you?"

She made a little strangling sound in her throat and dug her head farther into the pillow.

Jere sighed without sound, and reached out his hand to her in the darkness.

"Now you listen to me for a minute, my girl," he said. "You, my darling, are a complete and exciting and very wonderful woman. This happens to have been my fault. Next time we'll get down to this sometime before I've had a fifth or so of Scotch to drink. You know, I'm going to hate myself for this in the morning. It may even horrify me straight onto the wagon where I undoubtedly belong."

He waited again and then he said a little desperately, "Oh god, you're not really crying! Darling, listen to me. Lucy dear, please don't cry!"

She was instantly silent and rigid.

"Who's Lucy?" she said, her voice the merest gulping whisper.

And then it was Jere who was taut and still and unbreathing for a second.

He laughed.

"Oh god!" he said. "This is a love affair that's becoming fairly studded with apologies! Maggie, my darling! Do you believe in Freudian slips? Then this is one that you shouldn't mind at all. Lucy is my wife's name, or I should say my ex-wife's name. She's a woman who once, many many years ago, was very meaningful to me. Maggie, I am sorry. Poor darling!"

"It's all right," Maggie said. "Oh god, it must be dawn, I've got to be getting home. No, don't, Jere. Please. I want to go home."

twenty-seven

THE FOG was gone by the next morning and the day promised to be hot and strangely sultry. Maggie was up early in the house on Juniper Street, whirling about the kitchen, her face tired and drawn, her red hair flying. Pot lids banged to the floor, slender glasses of fruit juice upset in her wake, as she grimly went about preparing the breakfast. After one swift look at her troubled face, Grandpa Kennedy retreated hastily to the table with Jamie, retiring behind the morning paper to read the comic strip captions aloud to the little boy on his knee.

Just as the breakfast preparations were completed, Bud appeared unexpectedly in the kitchen, and Maggie began all over again. He hadn't been able to sleep, he complained, besides who could sleep anyway with all the banging that was going on around there? He slumped down in a chair at the table, resting his head between his hands, his face as weary and miserable as Maggie's own.

At the point when three eggs rolled off the stove to break into a slimy puddle on the floor, Maggie spun around to the table, her face desperately intense. She had just gotten the most wonderful idea, she said. Why didn't they sell this house and go home, all of them, and the hell with California anyway.

Grandpa Kennedy and Bud stared at her silently with such astonished and totally unconvinced faces that Maggie burst into tears.

All right, she said, so they'd all live and die in California, and the hell with that, too. But why couldn't it rain on a muggy day like this, why couldn't it thunder and lightning and blow and clear the air? Just for once, why couldn't it?

Breakfast was a dismal affair, even Jamie was quiet and subdued. Bud and Grandpa fled the house the moment it was over. Maggie barely paused to eat. She packed Jamie off to play in the back yard, and whirled on desperately, giving the kitchen such a cleaning as it had not received in weeks, making beds, vacuuming rugs and doing laundry, all with frantic energy.

Late in the morning she relented and took Jamie on a trip to the grocery store, stopping off to buy him a double-dip ice cream cone. They made their way home again, with Maggie lugging the heavy grocery sacks, desperately slowing her pace to the little

286)

boy's leisurely one as he tagged after her along the hot sidewalk, licking blissfully at the dripping cone.

Once they were home, she was deliberately relaxed and cheerful with him, reading to him from a book until it was time to prepare his bath and lunch. But the moment he was settled in bed for his nap, she went back to her frantic orgy of housecleaning. She did not stop for lunch herself or pause even once for coffee from the big pot on the stove.

While she was on her knees in the dining room, grimly cleaning the dusty floor beneath the buffet, she came upon a worn, faded, covered dictionary shoved into a stack of other books. She hesitated with it in her hands, eyeing it speculatively, and then with her bright hair falling about her face, she spread it open on the floor in front of her. She turned over to the listings under "I," her finger traveling rapidly down the columns along several pages and stopping finally on the word "impotence." She read the brief and totally inapplicable definition carefully, and suddenly hurled the book against the wall with all her strength.

An hour later, while she was balanced precariously on the rickety kitchen stool in the midst of washing the big front window, the telephone began to ring. She leapt down and caught it up quickly, so that Jamie would not be awakened by the sound.

But it was only Tony's teasing, good-natured voice that sounded in her ear. What was the matter, he complained, she never came down to the beach any more? He missed her, didn't she know that? When was she going to give him a break and go out with him some night, anyway? Didn't she know that if she kept turning him down like this he was liable to get discouraged and stop asking her?

That would be too bad, wouldn't it? Maggie said tersely.

Oh, come on, he said, she was much too pretty a girl to be always sitting around by herself, or hanging out with that pansy down at the beach. How about coming down to Tijuana with him tomorrow, they could have a ball in Tijuana.

(287

Maggie's face was grim. She hoped he would not drop dead of shock, she said, she also hoped that he really meant that, because as a matter of fact she would love to go to Tijuana tomorrow. If there was anything she could use just now, it was a change of scene.

They made arrangements for the time of departure the next morning, and Maggie put down the phone. She finished polishing the big window glass soberly, but her need for frantic activity was suddenly gone. She was rather silent all the rest of the day.

When Jamie awakened from his nap she was showered and dressed, and they went off together on a long-promised happy trek through the five-and-ten-cent stores. She went to extra trouble over preparations for dinner for Grandpa and Bud.

At the dinner table, she mentioned her proposed trip to Tijuana, to Grandpa. He assured her pleasedly that she was just to go ahead and have a good time and not to worry a bit about anything. He would see that Jamie was cleaned up and ready for Tom. He would also stay at home with Jamie himself on Saturday night. He and Mrs. Stacy had been threatening for a long time to entertain some friends for cards, and so they would do it. If Maggie was very late getting home, she need not worry at all.

At bedtime, Maggie lingered, with Jamie yawning on her lap. Would he mind if Mrs. Stacy was to put him to bed tomorrow night, she asked him. Because while he was off with Daddy tomorrow she had a chance to take a long auto ride, and she would like very much to do it. After all, he'd be with Daddy having a good time, so he wouldn't mind if she went without him, would he? The only trouble, it was such a long ride that she might be very late getting home and Grandpa and Mrs. Stacy would have to put him to bed. What did he think?

Jamie considered it, sitting erect in his fuzzy blue sleepers. No, he said, he wouldn't mind, but was she going to bring him a surprise though? Oh yes, Maggie said, she was going to visit in a town where they had the most wonderful surprises for little boys.

How would he like jumping beans? Honestly and truly, beans that jumped!

Jamie tumbled giggling on the bed. He was still giggling and tumbling when Maggie put out the light. Mrs. Duck, he said, had been eating jumping beans!

Jere telephoned a little later on that evening, and there was the slightest bit of strain in Maggie's voice. Something had come up, she said, she wouldn't be able to make the Smalls' party tomorrow night after all. She was sorry, and of course she would see him on Sunday certainly. And then she said abruptly that she heard Jamie calling, she'd better run, and put down the telephone.

The weather next day was perfect for an automobile trip, it was not too hot and there was a breeze stirring.

Tony arrived in his unvarying state of broad good humor, and Maggie herself was very gay. They set off merrily, with the top down on the convertible, the sun beating down on them, the radio dinning cheerfully.

They stopped for early lunch and a drink in Laguna, and then sped on, with the sparkling blue sea on one side of the road, and the sere, convoluted brown hills looming on the other. They stopped again briefly for another drink in San Diego, and then traveled the last leg of the journey, winding through the great rolling hills until they reached the border, and the teeming town on the other side. They joined the line of traffic moving out from the town in the direction of Caliente.

They spent a pleasant afternoon at the track, with a great deal of laughter and banter over bets placed and won and lost. Back in town, after the races, they wandered through the tourist shops that lined the wide main street, accumulating sacks and bundles as they went, a bright cotton skirt for Maggie and a silver pin. She refused the perfume Tony wanted to buy for her. Jamie fared even better, a gayly painted, pottery pig bank, a little jointed wooden man astride a jointed wooden horse, a tiny cabinet con-

(289

taining a set of minute pottery dishes, and a whole handful of jumping beans, carefully wrapped in tissue and put away in Maggie's purse.

They ate dinner at the Fronton Palace, and just at the end of the meal, Tony excused himself. There was a man he had to see, he said, if Maggie wouldn't mind waiting. She lingered at the table for a long time, watching the crowd about her with a bright and interested face. On the strength of a bill that Tony had given him, a deferential waiter kept her supplied with hot coffee and numerous bits of advice concerning bets on the games upstairs.

When Tony returned finally, they moved on to a box upstairs for the jai alai games. The loud music boomed and the games went on, one after another, the swift white-clad men racing over the court swinging the great straw *cestas,* and over drinks Maggie and Tony argued endlessly and good-naturedly over possible and probable *quinielas.*

It was really getting awfully late, considering the long drive home, Maggie offered without particular conviction. Well, he still had to see a man about something, Tony said. He was afraid he'd have to leave her again for a few minutes, but this should conclude his business, and after that they would leave for home, if she really wanted to.

While he was gone, leaving the money for bets in her lap, Maggie won twenty-three dollars, and she was ecstatically excited over it when he returned. They saw the games through to the end and had last drinks in the bar.

No, sir, Maggie announced all at once, no more drinks for her. In case he didn't know, she was squiffed, she was actually wobbling.

They waited their turn in the line of cars at the border, and Maggie was saddened when the border guard showed not the slightest interest in all the sacks and bundles of her purchases. But she was giggling again when Tony gravely informed the immigration inspector that he had been born in Keokuk.

Once the border crossing was completed, and they were driving along the winding road through the great dark hills, Tony said there was something that had occurred to him. Since he was a little tight himself for driving safely, why didn't they stop off at a motel he knew of, just the other side of San Ysidro, just for a couple hours until he'd sobered up enough to drive again.

Still in there pitching, Maggie accused him gayly. Why not, he countered with equal gayety, did she really mean to say she couldn't be had. Well, who knew, Maggie said recklessly, after all you really couldn't blame a guy for trying. Anyway, she added hastily, she did think it was a good idea, stopping off and perhaps having some coffee before they attempted the long drive home. After all, they were a little tight, and there was Jamie to think of, she didn't much fancy the idea of getting herself killed on the highway.

They drove in to a placid quiet motel, and Tony made the necessary arrangements with a sleepy and disgruntled man in the office, and then drove the car on back to park it beside a little white stucco cabin. Once they were inside the bare, brightly lighted little room, he said that he had just remembered there were a couple phone calls he had to make. Why didn't she hop into bed and take a nap, he'd be back before very long.

Wonderful idea, Maggie said. A perfectly wonderful idea.

When he was gone, closing the door softly behind him, Maggie steadied herself against the edge of the bed. She bent over and loosened the straps of her sandals and kicked them off, and grabbed at the edge of the bed again for support, smiling ruefully to herself. She stripped off her sleeveless blouse and unfastened her wide full skirt. And then, clad in her brief panties and brassière, she pulled the bed coverings apart and crawled in between them.

The room was very still. She closed her eyes rather cautiously, her hair tumbling over the pillow. There was suddenly a small snapping sound, close by, and Maggie opened her eyes and turned her head quickly. The small sound came again from the direction of the dresser, and Maggie laughed out loud softly, the small and energetic beans jumping audibly within their wrappings inside her purse.

She closed her eyes again, but the naked bulb just over the bed was glaring bright. She got up onto her knees, and after several unsuccessful lunges, caught the string attached to the chain and pulled it, leaving the room in darkness.

She lay down again, pulling the covers over her, and this time she was asleep almost instantly.

When she awakened abruptly, the light was pouring down glaring bright once more from the bulb over the bed. There was a noise and confusion of car motors and voices from outside, and the cabin door stood wide open. There were three soberly well-dressed men inside the small room with her, one of them engaged in methodically going through her purse.

Maggie came bolt upright in the bed, hugging the covers about her, beyond sound or speech, her face dead-white, stunned and terrified.

The man nearest to the bed was examining her blouse and skirt with swift, competent, searching fingers, and Maggie goggled at him, as though she were completely unable to believe what her eyes were seeing.

He was chewing gum slowly and rhythmically as he worked, and he glanced over at her appraisingly for a second.

"Okay, you better get up now," he said quite unemotionally.

He went on to examine her flat sandals carefully, and he said again in the same curiously unemotional voice, "Come on, get up now."

He dropped her sandals onto the floor, and before she realized his intent, he took hold of the bed covers and flung them away from her, all the way down over the foot of the bed.

"You can put your clothes on. Come on now."

Maggie slid off the bed, trembling throughout her body, her

legs rubbery and strange beneath her, her eyes wide with uncomprehending horror.

"Hold it a minute," another of the men said, coming swiftly toward her.

She winced away from him, suddenly wild-eyed, but still incapable of sound or speech. He caught hold of her bare arm, neither roughly nor gently, and twisted it around into the light. He examined her skin critically from shoulder to wrist, and then spun her around and did the same to her other arm, stooping to glance casually over her bare thighs.

"Uh uh," he said, in some brief and knowledgeable communication to his gum-chewing colleague who was now engaged in a thoroughgoing search of the bed and coverings.

"Here, these your clothes?" he said, picking them up from the floor. "We're done with these, you can put them on now."

Maggie took them mutely, her face still stunned. She pulled the blouse over her head and stepped unsteadily into the skirt, but her hands were trembling so badly that she was unable to close the zipper all the way or secure the fastenings at the waist band.

"Naw, nothing here either," the gum chewer said. "I think the room's clean all right."

"Yeah, looks like it," the second man said.

"You ready to go now?" he said to Maggie.

She stared at him dumbly, holding her sandals in her hand.

"What is it?" she whispered at last, forcing the words from between her stiff lips. "Where you taking me?"

The third man strode over, carrying her purse casually in his hand.

"We're police officers, Mrs. Harrison," he said briefly. "This is an arrest."

"Oh, no!" Maggie whispered. "But why?"

Her question was not answered. One of the men took hold of her arm, and propelled her along among them.

Just as they stepped out onto the little doorstep outside the door of the cabin, a man's quick sharp voice called out, "Hold it!"

Maggie jerked her head around, looking toward the compelling voice and directly into the blinding flash of the camera bulbs. The camera clicked with its implacable function and the picture, once it was developed and printed, was clear black and white and rather classic of its kind: Maggie, with her hair undone and tumbling about her face, her look of complete and unbelieving horror with the expressionless burly man beside her holding to her arm, her gaping skirt and the shoes dangling from her hand.

It appeared on the second pages of most of the papers next day under the laconic caption: "Narcotics officers nab pair in motel."

twenty-eight

IT WAS ALMOST nightfall on Sunday, when Maggie arrived home at last.

She came walking along the sidewalk down Juniper Street, beneath the low-hanging, lacy green branches of the old pepper trees, her skirt and blouse soiled and rumpled, her feet dragging wearily. But once she was within sight of the house, she lifted her head and moved more rapidly. By the time she reached the walk she was running, she crossed the doorstep in one bound to burst into the dim shadowy living room.

Grandpa Kennedy came quickly through the archway at the

sound of the slamming screen door, his white hair uncombed and his kindly face harried and lined with worry.

Maggie stood just inside the door, staring at him numbly out of a pale sick face.

"Grandpa!" she said, her voice like a sob. "Oh, Grandpa!"

He opened his arms for her and met her in the middle of the room, holding her tenderly, patting at her back.

"Maggie, now, now! Don't," he said tremulously. "I should of come down there to San Diego myself. I should of come. I wanted to, but that detective fellow that was here said there wasn't any use. He said you'd be coming home and like enough I'd miss you on the way. I should of come though."

"Oh, Grandpa," she said, her voice muffled into his shoulder. "What a stupid stupid mess! Grandpa, I didn't know anything. Even when it was happening, I didn't know what was going on, or anything. I was so scared I was sick."

"I know, honey, I know!" he was saying. "I kept telling that detective fellow you didn't know anything. Now, Maggie, now don't!"

"It was all like a nightmare, all of it," she said desperately. "Waking up in that place with those men there. I didn't know what was happening. I was so scared, I've never been scared like that in my life. It's still like a nightmare to me. I can't wake up!"

"Now, now," he said helplessly and soothingly. "You're home now, honey. It's all over now, honey. It's all over."

She clung to him tightly for a moment or two, and then lifted her head, the tears shining on her face.

"It's all right, Grandpa. For a minute, I thought I was going into a million pieces, but now I'm all right. Ah, Grandpa, look at you! You must have been worried to death. I'm so sorry."

She stopped to wipe her nose on a handkerchief from her purse.

"Grandpa, I feel like such a fool. I just didn't know. I've known Tony from around the beach now for months. He was always just hanging around down there. He was always asking me to go

(295

places with him. I just didn't know anything about him. I should have my head examined. You get used to somebody like that, after a while you forget that you really don't know anything about them."

"Well, now, I'd just forget it," Grandpa said. "You didn't know what kind of fellow he was, honey. Nobody can blame you for that. You didn't know. I'd just forget about it, nor I wouldn't grieve any for him neither."

"Grieve for him?" Maggie said, her face wry. "Ah, Grandpa! The stupid thing is, I didn't even care about him. He was just full of fun, and he made me feel like a woman when I was around him, and that's all. The only reason we stopped at that motel was because we'd had too many drinks to drive for a while. Or that's what I thought we stopped for. Tony had to stop there because that was where he'd arranged to meet the man he sold the drugs to. I was just the cover-up for him. Grandpa, I feel so stupid. I know what you must be thinking. Of course it was stupid of me to stop at a motel with him in the first place. It was stupid of me to go to Tijuana with him in the very beginning. What can I say? Just that sometimes it gets terribly important to you to feel like a woman again. It gets so terribly important to you, and then you do stupid things."

"Well now, it's all right," Grandpa said soothingly. "I'd just try to forget it, honey."

Maggie wiped at her nose again, and suddenly she laughed a little.

"Poor Jamie. He's going to be furious with me, coming home without any surprises. I had surprises, but they impounded Tony's car, or whatever they call it. Anyway, I've got his silly jumping beans. I guess even that real gone narcotics squad could tell that jumping beans aren't heroin."

Grandpa looked at her, his face lined and sunken.

"Where is he?" she said. "Was he awfully upset when he got up this morning and found I wasn't home yet?"

296)

Grandpa cleared his throat, the tears suddenly appearing in his own eyes.

"Maggie," he said helplessly.

He stopped and cleared his throat again.

And then he said, very quickly, "Maggie, Jamie's just fine. Now don't you worry. Tom come over here this afternoon and took him home with him."

"What?" Maggie said, her face perfectly incredulous. "Tom came and did what?"

"Maggie!" Grandpa said. "Now, Maggie!"

She caught her breath, the purse flying from her hands to the floor as she whirled for the telephone.

Grandpa bolted out of the living room and all the way through the house to the back door. He stared out blindly through the screen, his brown work-gnarled hands fiercely clenched together behind his back.

"Grandpa!"

An instant later Maggie erupted into the kitchen, her face livid and furious.

"Oh, Grandpa!" she said, her voice shaking. "I can't believe this, I just can't believe it. Do you know what he said to me? He said he was surprised to hear that I was out of jail! This is Tom! This is the man I was married to for all those years! Oh, Grandpa! He says if I want Jamie back I'll have to have a court order to get him!"

She stared at him with wild distended eyes, and the old man murmured helplessly and soothingly in his throat.

She spun around suddenly and ran again for the telephone in the living room.

The second time it was much longer before she returned to the kitchen, and when she came, she was walking slowly, like a sleepwalker.

She pulled out a chair at the kitchen table and sat down

heavily, dropping her purse and black-covered address book on the table top.

"Grandpa," she said in a dull unbelieving voice. "I've just been talking to Mr. Limmon, my lawyer, you know. Do you know what he said, you won't believe this. He says I'm not to try to get a court order now, because right now I might not even be able to get one. He says I've got to wait, wait the three months till the divorce is final, and then come to court with character witnesses and all of that, and ask for Jamie's custody. He says we ought to keep all this off the court record if we can, and just wait. Grandpa, three months!"

The old man looked away from her tortured face.

Inside her purse on the table, the jumping beans popped and snapped cheerfully, and all at once Maggie screamed.

She leapt up from the table, her body stretched and desperately poised off the tips of her toes.

"Grandpa, three months! I can't! I won't! Because suppose I don't get custody then? Suppose because of this stupid stupid thing, I don't get custody then?"

"Maggie, you will," the old man said. "You will! Maggie, listen to me. I tried to reason with Tom this afternoon, and when I couldn't, I called up Mr. Limmon myself right away. He explained it all to me. He says you're bound to get the custody. You will, Maggie. You've just got to wait. He says you probably would get the court order right now even, but it isn't worth the chance you'd have to take to get it. Because Tom would fight you, and he says it's safer for none of this to come out on the court record. He says let Tom do his dirty work when the divorce comes up, when all this has had a chance to kind of blow over, and you can come into court with witnesses about what a good mother you are and all of that. Maggie, all you got to do is wait!"

"Wait?" she said. "Wait three whole months thinking maybe I won't get Jamie even then, because I was shacked up in a motel with a dope peddler one night. Because that's what they'll say,

Grandpa! And got arrested with him besides! Grandpa, how can you tell me wait!"

"I can tell you wait," the old man said heavily, "Because there isn't nothing else I can tell you, Maggie. There isn't nothing else you can do. Your own lawyer says it, Maggie."

As she began to move, the old man said quickly, "Now you listen to me, Maggie. Don't go raring off and do something foolish. You're awful quick, and right now you're all wrought up. Don't do it. You can't fight this. If you try to fight it now, maybe you'll fix it so you will lose Jamie for good. You got to think of that. You can't go flying off and doing something foolish."

She stared at him for a moment, and then ran frenziedly in the other direction, toward Jamie's room.

When she ran back into the kitchen, she was carrying the battered Mrs. Duck doll, and the tears were streaming down her frantic face.

"Grandpa, hurry!" she said beseechingly. "Tom forgot Mrs. Duck! Jamie sleeps with her. He can't go to sleep without her. He'll cry when he finds she isn't in the bed. Grandpa, we have to drive over there right away!"

The old man's face was stark. He took hold of her shoulders, his hands gentle and helplessly compassionate.

"Now, now, let go, Maggie, and cry. Best thing for you's to cry. Don't fight, honey. Let yourself go. You got to get to bed and try to get some rest. It isn't any use, Maggie. You got to face it, honey, and you got to live with it. Three months, why, three months is just a little short time, what's three months, honey?"

"Grandpa, don't," she said. "I can't rest. I can't go to bed. It's Jamie, Grandpa. He's never been away from me overnight in his whole life. He needs to have me, he's just a baby. How can he understand any of this that's happened? Grandpa, think about Jamie for a minute."

"Maggie, he's with his father," the old man said wearily. "He's not a little boy alone and scared somewhere, he's with his father. You got to remember that."

"What's that got to do with it?" Maggie said wildly. "He's never been away from me in his life. His room is here, and his toys and the things he's used to. This is where he lives, this is where he belongs. Oh, Grandpa!"

She ran again toward the living room, and the old man followed after her as quickly as he was able, the sound of the dialing telephone already in his ears.

When he came into the room, she was saying, "Jere? Oh, Jere! I'm in trouble. I've got to see you, I've got to talk to you right now!"

When Jere arrived there, it was just dark, and Maggie was waiting for him, walking back and forth along the sidewalk frantically. She ran to the car before it was hardly stopped, and as Jere drove off, she began to talk distractedly: of how Jamie was gone, of what Tom had had to say to her, the counsel she had received from her lawyer and from Grandpa Kennedy, and of her need to bring Jamie back to her immediately and her helplessness to know in which way to turn in order to accomplish it.

Jere listened, his face grim in the dim light of the car. She talked unceasingly, the words tumbling out in a sort of desperation, not of release, but rather as though she talked against the time when she knew that she must stop talking and there would be nothing then left for her to do at all.

Jere was silent, throughout the entire drive back to the beach house, and while they descended the steps there and crossed the sand.

But once they were inside, he took her swiftly in his arms and placed his hand gently across her mouth.

"Darling, no more," he said. "You've told me all of it. Now you are only clubbing yourself over the head with it, don't you understand?"

Her body was taut against him.

"Jere, what am I going to do?" she said. "Tell me what I'm going to do?"

"Good girl," he said. "There are several things that you are going to do. First, you're going to wait right here, just for a second. All right?"

He went off swiftly in the direction of the bathroom, and Maggie walked once more, her disheveled hair tumbling about her white agonized face.

When Jere returned, he carried a glass part filled with water and the capsules cupped in his hand.

"Now then," he said. "This is the very first thing you're to do, darling. No, trust me, Maggie, this will help, I guarantee it. Swallow them down, and let me tell you what else you're going to do."

While she gulped the capsules unwillingly, he went swiftly off again in the direction of the bar.

"No, now let me talk, darling," he said. "You're going to sit down now before you literally fall down. You're going to have a drink or two, and although you think you can't, you are going to feel yourself beginning to unwind. You're going to get a little tight and a little drowsy, and either I will phone your grandfather and you'll sleep here, or I'll take you home. And that is the very first thing that you are going to do."

"Jere, I can't," she wailed. "I've got to . . ."

"No, not tonight," he said. "Think about it for a minute. There is absolutely nothing that you can do tonight. Do you want to drive out to Tom's place and make a bloody awful holler and accomplish nothing by it except to frighten poor Jamie out of his wits? No, tonight is only something to be lived through. Do trust me, Maggie. Come, sit down here."

He drew her down onto the divan and placed the glass in her hand.

"There now, see, you can sit down. You can relax, too. What's the good to Jamie if you drive yourself for another five or six hours until you come apart at the seams? There now, let me hold you. Good girl! Let go easily, easily . . ."

Suddenly, she was limp and dead weight against him.

"Oh god," she said. "I was afraid to stop talking or to sit down or anything. I didn't think I could bear it, but maybe I can."

"Of course you can."

"All right," she said. "Maybe the pills will work. I'm so tired. I'm so terribly tired. But that's for tonight. Jere, what am I going to do? What will I do tomorrow?"

"Tomorrow is quite another day," he said calmly. "I shouldn't even think about tomorrow at this point if I were you. Tomorrow you'll be rested, and you'll come to it with a different perspective."

"No, Jere, please," she said quietly. "I'm really not hysterical any more. It's you or your pills or something. Please tell me what you honestly think, Jere? What can I do?"

"Honestly, darling?" he said. "Well, I will certainly call my own lawyer very first thing in the morning. Offhand, though, I'm afraid your lawyer has probably given you very sound advice. No, now listen to me, darling. Of course it is perfectly monstrous for you to be deprived of your child unwillingly for even three hours, let alone three months. But are you really prepared to face up to the genuinely unpleasant business of a court hassle of this sort, and are you prepared to expose Jamie to it? And there's the element of risk involved in it, no matter how slight it actually would be. No, let's say you've simply been the victim of a stroke of preposterously incredible foul luck. But getting right down to it, is three months really such a very great thing for you to invest in something as important to you as the absolute certainty of having Jamie for the next fifteen or twenty years of both your lives? Is it really?"

"But three months," she said despairingly. "Jere, what will I do?"

302)

"Three months is not a very long time," he said. "We'll think of all sorts of things. We'll tick away the days. You'll see."

"Ah, it isn't just the three months," Maggie said. "It's having to live all that time with not being sure what will happen when the three months is over, don't you see? Jere, suppose I don't get custody?"

"Maggie, but of course you will. How can you doubt it? You are an extraordinarily good and devoted mother. There must be dozens of people who would be most happy to say it for you in a courtroom. Darling, a judge really has only to look at you, you know. You haven't the slightest resemblance to the sort of girl who would neglect her child while she spent her time racketing around from motel to motel with nefarious characters."

Maggie was very still against him.

"Oh, Jere," she said softly. "All I've thought of is this thing with Jamie. But what must you be thinking of me? What can I say to you, how am I going to explain this?"

"Maggie, don't," he said. "I feel quite horridly enough responsible for this already, you know. Perhaps you'd like to know that."

"Oh, no!" she said. "How can you say that? Jere, you mustn't feel that . . ."

"Look here," he said. "Apparently I shouldn't have told you that, after all. You've certainly trouble enough just now without thinking for even one minute that you must cope with any of my myriad stray and vagrant guilts. You leave them to me. How do you feel, darling?"

"You know, I'm sort of collapsing," she said a little drowsily. "Must be your funny pills."

"Good," he said.

Her head tipped back, her eyelids slowly closing.

"Jere?" she said after a while, her voice vague and thickening. "Jere, I'm so tired I believe I'm falling apart. I want to cry about Jamie, but I'm so tired I can't. And it's such a complicated wheels

within wheels within wheels to try to explain to you. But I want
to tell you. You mustn't think—no, that's not right. I'm getting
fuzzy. Where was I? Jere? You mustn't feel bad because I went to
a motel with another man. It sounds very silly, but I only did it
because I'm in love with you. I know you're not in love with me,
and that's all right. But I'm in love with you and that's why I went
to Tijuana with Tony in the first place. Isn't that silly? And that's
why I stopped at that motel with him, and I certainly did get
caught at it, didn't I? So silly. But I do love you. You understand
that, Jere?"

His face was very tired.

"Of course, I understand," he said softly. "Go to sleep, darling."

twenty-nine

AFTER SEVERAL DAYS of the lassitude of sheer exhaustion, Maggie
bounced back. And once she did, the sense of Jamie's loss was
overwhelming to her. She could not let it be. Any attempt on the
part of Jere or anyone else to distract her even for a few hours
failed, she lived in a mounting unrelenting frenzy.

She telephoned to Tom by day and by night. At first she pleaded
with him, and finally she lost her temper.

She stormed downtown then for a session with her dry-voiced,
white-haired lawyer, which left him more than ever convinced
of the inadvisability of any immediate court action on her part.

And that was the night, just at bar closing, that she chartered
a taxicab with all the money in her purse, and drove to Tom's

house. It was not a successful venture. Tom, irate in his pajamas, refused to admit her to the house. The ensuing scene was loud, and ill-advised, since at least half of Tom's near neighbors were awakened eventually and on hand to witness it. The kindhearted taxi driver finally collected her from Tom's doorstep in her state of tearful and somewhat alcoholic collapse, and drove her home for free.

Neither Grandpa Kennedy's kindly lecture the next morning nor Jere's offhanded comments concerning the vital necessity for self-control on her part were of much help or comfort to her.

She began to avoid Jere for days at a time after that, as though he might be too closely and painfully identified in her mind with the immediate sequence of events that had led to her loss of Jamie. Instead, she spent more time at the beach in the company of George and Dick Whitfield, who were more indulgingly sympathetic to her, anyway. Whatever hurt feelings Dickie had been nurturing against her apparently had been forgotten at the moment when he first had glimpsed the horrifying photograph of her in the newspapers that Sunday, and he had rallied to her with fierce loyalty.

But as it happened, George and Dickie were not particularly good for her just then. To Dickie, it was quite incomprehensible that Tom, or anyone for that matter, could be capable of such inhumanity regardless of circumstances, and it was at his instigation that many of her more emotional telephone calls to Tom were made. And both George and Dickie were so indignantly sympathetic to her that she began to accumulate a rather unhealthy amount of pity for herself.

She was, of course, deluged with too much well-intentioned advice, and too many clumsy attempts at comfort. Mrs. Martinez, her next-door neighbor on Juniper Street, offered her the philosophic logic, on the one hand, that at least she might console herself with the knowledge that Jamie was alive, however dead to her he might be for the time being. On the other, Mrs. Malott across the street begged her to heed the exhortations of a local evangelist who appeared on television every night and proclaimed that those in sore need had only to place their hands upon the television set to be healed. It did not work for Maggie.

Nothing worked to aid or comfort her, she grieved frantically, without respite or release. Inside herself, she vacillated between a mood of tearful self-pity and one of unsparingly bitter self-castigation for her own stupidities and weaknesses that had brought her to this plight: the senselessly casual involvement with Tony, and even worse, her progressively arrogant, unthinking failure to retain Tom's good will through the months before.

She was not able to forgive herself.

For the first time in her life, she was drinking too much, consistently.

Oddly enough, it was Grandpa Kennedy who often turned to Jere Tidings for advice and comfort those days; they became rather good friends by telephone. Grandpa particularly depended on Jere the times when it became necessary to hunt for her through the local bars, in several of which she was on the way to becoming a tearful fixture.

And no one during those days was able to give her a glimpse into the rather simple heart of the matter: that Jamie himself was well and happy and relatively undisturbed.

Originally, Tom had given Jamie the casual explanation that Maggie had had to leave him for a time in order to search for a job. Jamie accepted that notion readily, in terms of the automobile that Maggie would buy for them once she had found the job, and then he forgot it almost immediately. He spoke sometimes, matter-of-factly, of the long auto ride that Maggie had taken, such a very long one that she still had not been able to return.

Meanwhile, with the easy adaptability and gusto of childhood, he took to the new routines offered him, the kindly neighbor woman in whose charge he was left during the hours that Tom, and Junie, were at work, the frequent novel excursions to carnivals and drive-in restaurants and movies. He slept each night clutching a furry Davy Crockett hat, and after the first night or two never once thought of Mrs. Duck.

But each time he visited a supermarket, he sought silently and determinedly, a wistful small figure trudging between the towering counters, searching faithfully and as best he was able, for jumping beans that honestly and truly jumped.

thirty

STUSH'S FILM TEST at the studio did not turn out to be all that Caro had hoped for. For one thing, Stush arrived there for the appointment that day in a precarious humor somewhere between alcoholic hilarity and glum and surly hang-over. He did not trouble to be very coöperative. But the test was made and even seen reasonably soon by a few particular people that Helen was able to wheedle into viewing it. There was no enthusiasm on any hand, and certainly no talk or offer of contract.

And then, a few days later, a young actor who had been hired for a small part in Harry's current film, already in production, came down with measles. Harry, over an ulcer bromide, and at Helen's apt and artless suggestion, reluctantly hired Stush to replace him.

Caro received the news grimly. She pored over the script the moment a copy of it had been delivered into Stush's hands, and announced tragically that the part really was not suited to him at all. She continued to pore over it, chewing at her fingers in thoughtful desperation. She attempted to discuss earnestly with him the psychological aspects and motivations of the character he was to portray. Stush would have none of it. He was just as rudely disinclined to allow her to coach him with his lines. But he did appear punctually at the studio when he was called.

Several days later, he returned to the house at the beach one night, just after darkness. It was a mild, very clear night, and Jere was outside the door beside the tripod, with his little telescope aimed away into the soft limpid skies above the sea.

Stush came trudging across the sand wearily, his shoulders slumped. He was wearing an old and baggy pair of slacks and a T-shirt, and once he sat down heavily on the step by the door, he tiredly examined a worn and loosening sole on one of his shoes.

Jere glanced at him sympathetically for a moment and then went back to his telescope.

"Hello," he said. "You look beat."

"Boy, I really am, no kidding," Stush said, leaning back against the side of the house. "I got to be out there at six again tomorrow morning, too."

"Tough."

Stush rolled his head an inch or two along the boards, to watch Jere with weary lack of interest.

"Hey, Dad, I wanted to tell you. Last night I was out with that painter girl that lives up the beach here, the one you had over here to the house a week or so ago. That okay with you?"

"Why not?" Jere said. "Up to her, certainly."

"She's quite a girl," Stush said with a feeble grin. "Boy, she's sure one crazy mixed-up kid, all right."

"I take it you got the bit with the mirrors then, too," Jere said, his voice a little absent as he bent down with his eye to the viewing lense of the little telescope.

"I sure did," Stush said. "You, too, huh? Real crazy! Well, just as long as you don't think I'm trying to horn in on your territory or something. Okay, Dad?"

"Perfectly okay so far as I'm concerned," Jere said cheerfully. "Any time I come across something that's special to me, you can be damn sure I'll see to it you don't get a look at her, buster, and vice versa, for that matter."

Stush gave a pleased but weary crow of laughter.

"Have you eaten anything?" Jere said after a moment, still squinting into the telescope.

"Naw," Stush said. "Hell with it. I need a couple drinks worse. Then I'm going to hit the sack."

"Help yourself."

"I will in a minute. Boy, my ass is really dragging tonight. Any phone calls?"

"Caro phoned, she said she'd call later. So what do you think of the motion-picture business, anyway?" Jere asked amusedly.

"Tough racket," Stush said. "Tough in all kinds of ways."

Jere laughed.

"Naw, I mean it," Stush said. "Now you take a guy like Dick Whitfield, you know Dick Whitfield? He works out here, I lived with him for a while when I first come out here. Sweet kid. He's an actor. Big, good-looking kid. Got a real swell voice, you know, knows all the stuff about acting and all that crap. Nice sweet kid. But a guy like him's never going to make it in this racket, you know why? Because it's a tough racket, kid like Dick Whitfield hasn't got the guts for it. It takes guts, all kinds of ways. Boy, those babies out there are tough. Really tough. They're really in the business for themselves."

"You are so right," Jere said. "Do you like it then?

Stush thought about it for a moment, his head leaned tiredly against the side of the house.

"Yeah," he said. "I get a bang out of it, kind of. It's something you do, like anything you do. I figure once you learned the ropes and got really good at it, you'd get a big bang out of it, like driving a car fast, or bringing in a game fish or fighting a guy."

Stush was silent, his face lost and dreaming.

And then he said, "What you think of it, you used to be in the racket? Did you like it? You ever want to get back?"

Jere leaned his elbow on the tripod.

"Well, let's put it this way," he said lightly. "I used to get a bang out of it, yes. But if I had it all to do over again, from the very beginning, I'd rather have been a rocket engineer."

"No kidding?" Stush said a little suspiciously.

"No kidding," Jere said.

Stush got to his feet lithely and stretched, and tucked his fingers into the back pockets of his trousers, turning his face up to the softly lighted sky.

"They ought to get them up there some day," he said. "Takes a lot of dough, huh?"

"I believe so, among other things," Jere said, his eyes wandering upward, too, to the endless patterns of far lights overhead.

"Boy, oh boy!" Stush said softly. "What a bang that would be! Get way up there in one of them things and never stop going!"

Jere looked at him affectionately.

"You know, Stush," he said, "you'd be exactly my candidate to take the first one out, too. Come on, I'll buy you a drink."

Out at the studio, after the second or third batch of rushes, with considerable trepidation and many ulcer bromides, Harry reluctantly arrived at one of his notorious hunch decisions. Stush's part was stretched out a little larger.

Once more, Caro pored intently over the augmented script. And all at once, between her and the studio, Stush suddenly had no time left to himself at all. He was sent off to sessions with a voice coach, and others with a drama coach. He was posed for still photographs. And Caro coaxed and prodded and humored him along to fittings at a tailor's, to certain restaurants and clubs where she wanted him to be seen, to parties where she wanted him to be met.

Stush almost but not quite walked out on it all when he learned that Harry would not allow him to drive Caro's car in road races one week end while they were still shooting with him.

He began to complain, he got drunk at times inconvenient to her plans, he finally took a swing at a man in the bar of one of her fashionable restaurants.

And at last one night they quarreled. But Caro talked him down serenely, and instead of the boxing match that he had wanted to see, they went instead to a party where, she insisted, there would be quantities of people that it was rather important for him to meet just then.

Stush was in a towering bad humor by the time they reached the ornate house set high on a dark hillside in Bel Air. There were people milling and drinks, and just after midnight another group of guests joined the party, laden with floral leis, on their way in from the airport. The mood they brought with them was immediately contagious, there was sudden enthusiastic talk of *huki lau,* and the guests carried their drinks delightedly to sit in a circle on the floor of the huge, softly lighted living room. Guitars and ukeleles were produced, the leis were distributed, the host brought forth a bongo drum, and a starlet, who was already appropriately garbed in a sarong, kicked off her shoes and began to hula. With more drinks, the atmosphere became more thickly and nostalgically insular, it seemed that all the guests had fond memories of time spent in Honolulu. With the exception of Stush, who had never been there at all.

They chanted soft Hawaiian songs, the words to which all of them seemed to know, and with growing enthusiasm they raided the kitchen for cans and pots and pans of various kinds to serve as impromptu drums.

The atmosphere became even more cloyingly, dreamily nostalgic of the Islands, the singing and the hula dancing went on interminably. Stush became more silent and more tense.

And suddenly, right in the middle of a muted and dreamy rendition of some old Hawaiian chant, Stush rose to his feet. With

(*311*

complete and rather magnificent aplomb, he opened his trousers and urinated in one of the cans that served for a drum, and stalked out of the house.

Caro was already waiting for him at the beach house when he arrived there, and Jere was awakened by their voices on his doorstep. He hastily donned robe and slippers and came out into the darkened living room to eavesdrop shamelessly.

"I don't think I've ever seen anything so really embarrassing in all my life," Caro was saying coolly. "I expect you may have thought you were being clever in some sort of way. It wasn't clever of you at all. No matter what you may think of those people, they just happen to be the people that you are going to have to know and get on with and work with, and they certainly didn't think that you were being the least bit clever, either."

"How would you like to shut up and go home?" Stush said. "I'm getting goddamn sick of this."

"I expect you are," she said. "Stush, I don't like for us to quarrel this way any better than you do. And I do see your point of view. I know that parties like that are really very silly. But there is nothing that you can do about it."

"Yeah?" Stush said. "There isn't, huh?"

"Stush, you won't have to do it forever, I promise you," she said. "It's just for now, when you're just starting in, when it's so terribly important for you to make the right contacts. I do so want this to be all absolutely right for you. Then, later on, you won't need these people, don't you see? They will need you. But right now, they don't. They don't need you one little bit."

"They don't, huh?" Stush said. "Boy, that goes double. Now you shut up, because I'm not going to talk about this any more."

"Oh, but we are going to talk of it more," Caro said. "Because you have to understand that you can't afford to do things like this. The most childish sort of behavior, really the most childish!"

"And I'm getting goddamn sick of the way you're acting, too,"

Stush said. "I don't like being picked at and pushed around. I don't take that from nobody."

"Oh, stop it!" Caro said, her voice like ice. "You make such a huge thing of that. You will have to take all sorts of things that you don't like, quite the same as anyone else. You're not really such a special sort of person as all that, you know."

"I'm not, huh?" Stush said very softly.

"No," she said. "You are really not. Where do you come by this absolutely fantastic notion of yourself? And certainly after this performance tonight, which was the silliest, most disgustingly crude and revolting . . ."

"You don't talk to me like that," Stush said. "Who do you think you are, up on that high horse of yours? And what's so special about you? You're a cute little kid with big dark eyes, and that's all you are. What's so special about that? Helen looks just like you, for Christ sakes, and on top of that she's a hell of a lot better woman in bed than you'll ever be in your life!"

The silence was so intensely complete, that Jere peeped out from a fold of the window drape. Under the outside light, Caro stood quietly staring at Stush, her face white to the lips. Suddenly, without a sound, she turned and ran. In seconds' time, there was the flurrying patter of her feet up the steps to the street.

Stush stood tensed and rooted, his legs thrust apart, on the doorstep.

A moment later, there was the angry snarl of her car motor shooting off down the highway, and Stush plunged out across the sand into the darkness.

Inside, Jere mixed himself a drink, slowly and thoughtfully.

After a while, when it was gone, he let himself quietly out of the glass door. He went off noiselessly across the sand in the direction that Stush had taken. On the far side of the big tumble of rocks, he stopped abruptly short.

In the moonlight, Stush lay weeping on the sand. He wrestled with some giant of grief, his hands and toes thrusting down fiercely, his shoulders writhing. The sound of his sobs mixed with the boom of the sea.

Jere stood silently for a moment, and then as silently turned back toward the house.

thirty-one

IN THE DAYS immediately following, Caro did not appear at the beach house again, nor did she telephone. Stush did not so much as even mention her. He appeared to be in quite normally imperturbable high spirits. He worked on at the studio, and frequently it was Helen's long heavy convertible that drove him back to the beach at some hour before dawn. And more often he returned in the company of other women, and now and then that of a handsome boy, a friend of Dickie's, who lived farther up the beach.

About the time that the film was completed, out of his studio earnings Stush bought himself a second- or third-hand sports car of his own. He spent long absorbed hours lovingly tinkering and tuning the motor, and careening about the local highways in it. With the new mobility that it gave him, he was never more at home after nightfall.

One afternoon, just at sunset, Jere lay supine upon his divan, the doors and windows opened to a brisk mild breeze from the sea. There was a drink within reach of his hand, and to the accompaniment of the phonograph, he was lazily blowing a plaintive reedy melody out of a thin wooden recorder.

All at once, Caro appeared in the open doorway, small and slim in the tight dark trousers that she so often wore, and a voluminous wide-necked linen blouse of black and white harlequin pattern.

Jere rolled over quickly onto his feet.

"Caro, darling," he said delightedly. "Come in, lamb. I haven't seen you in positively ages. How are you?"

"I'm very well, thank you, Jeremy," she said. "It's very good to see you. I've missed you terribly, you know."

"I should hope so," Jere said cheerfully. "Wait a second, let me turn off the player."

He crossed the room swiftly to the phonograph and lifted the arm and turned the knob.

"What a very sad song," Caro said. "What's it called, Jeremy?"

" 'Greensleeves,' " he said. "Now, tell me about you. Would you like a drink or anything?"

"No, thank you," she said gravely. "I've just had tea. Are you alone, Jeremy?"

"Absolutely solitary," he said. "If it's Stush you're thinking of, he's off for the night by now. Were you wanting to see him, or not wanting to? Come, sit here."

"No, I'd rather have a cushion," she said serenely.

She helped herself to one, dropping it on the floor in front of the divan, to sit cross-legged upon it, her thin back very erect. Jere settled himself comfortably and began to fill his pipe, his eyes upon her. Her face was as untouchedly cool and remote as always, but he fancied that there were darker shadows around her slanted, heavily made-up eyes.

"Now then," he said at last. "Tell me what you've been doing with yourself, anyway?"

"I expect you're wondering about Stush and me," Caro said. "I don't want to talk about it, Jeremy. It's something that's perfectly finished and done with. Do you mind?"

"My god, no," Jere said cheerfully. "None of my business certainly. Talk about it, or don't talk about it, just as you like."

"Then we'll not," she said. "There's really nothing to talk about, anyway."

Jere shrugged amid a cloud of pipe smoke, his eyes affectionate upon her small grave face.

They were silent for a moment, and suddenly she turned her infinitely poised smooth head.

"Jeremy," she said. "I am going to have to have an abortion."

Jere took a long drink from his glass.

"Oh?" he said, his voice soft and rather casual.

"I don't much like having to trouble you about it," she said. "But I was wondering if you knew about doctors and all of that?"

"I see," he said.

"I expect I know what you're thinking," she said in her clear unhurried voice. "You are wondering why I've come to you with this, aren't you, Jeremy?"

She paused and all at once her huge eyes were filled with pain.

"But you see there's really no one else I can ask about it, except you. I mean, that it wouldn't get back to Helen, practically within the hour. And you must believe me, Jeremy, I'd truly much rather die than have Helen find out about this."

"Yes, I see," he said again softly.

His glass was empty and he got up swiftly, heading toward the bar.

Caro got up from the floor quickly and followed after him.

"I expect I know what else you're thinking, too. Because I couldn't help but think of it myself, and it is terribly ironic. That time, five years ago, when there was all the trouble, because Helen found the temperature chart I was keeping and all of that, trying to get myself pregnant. Of course, looking back, I understand how terribly childish I was being then. I expect you knew why I was doing it though, didn't you, Jeremy? Because it was the one thing that I thought would make Helen really livid! Anyway, it is terribly ironic, isn't it? That I tried so hard to get myself pregnant in those days, and simply couldn't, no matter what I did. And now at a time when it absolutely cannot happen to me, it seems to have come about so very easily."

"Which reminds me, I suppose you are reasonably sure about this?" Jere said.

"Don't be silly," Caro said. "You don't really think I'd be troubling you with this if I weren't perfectly sure, do you, Jeremy? I had the test done over again at another laboratory, just to make absolutely sure."

"Uhmm." Jere made a soft and thoughtful sound in his throat. And then over the hiss of soda into his glass, he said casually, "Had you thought of telling Stush about this, lamb?"

"But of course not!" Her voice was like a whiplash. "What's it to do with him?"

"Oh, come," Jere said. "He's at least halfway involved in this interesting condition of yours, isn't he? Or at least I am assuming he's the one that is."

"But that's exactly the point," she said. "It is only an interesting condition of mine, don't you see, so it becomes absolutely my very own problem."

She hesitated.

"I mean, if it were a question of a baby, it would be something quite different. Of course I understand that, Jeremy."

"Well, it really is, isn't it, darling?" Jere said gently. "After all, babies are the natural outcome of this condition, you know."

"Jeremy, please," she said. "Don't laugh at me. You know quite well that I couldn't possibly have a baby."

Jere slipped his arm about her childishly bony shoulders as they walked back toward the divan.

"Now why couldn't you? Girls have babies every day. Actually, I think Stush would love it. Think of all the marvelously fetching possibilities we have here, too. A huge, serious, blond-haired girl, do you think, with a habit of thinking each thing over a dozen times before she does it? Or, a tiny, happy, dark-haired boy with the vitality of twenty children and . . ."

"Jeremy, stop it, stop it!"

The pain spilled out of her eyes and suddenly twisted her whole small face.

"How can you talk to me like this! You know I couldn't have this child! It's monstrous, I'd rather die!"

"Listen to me," he said sharply. "Why would you? That's what I'm trying to find out."

"Because," she said wildly. "I couldn't have a child that belongs to him. I'd feel unclean, I couldn't bear it. I couldn't touch it. I don't want anything that belongs to him. Nothing, ever ever again."

Jere held her tightly, her face burrowing fiercely into his chest.

"Caro, do you think you possibly could listen to me?" he said urgently. "Because it's fairly important, what you do just now and this way you feel so violently. It's really terribly important to you, darling, for all your life. It's terribly important to Stush, too. And even ultimately to Helen."

She twisted against him.

"Jeremy . . ."

"No, do listen," he said quickly. "Try to get a steady look at yourself. You do care about Stush, more than I'd realized. You care about this child, too. Can't you understand this one thing about yourself? If Stush had slept with any other woman in town, or all of them, you'd have been hurt, I grant you, but not like this. It's because it was Helen that he slept with, that you . . ."

She was suddenly out of his arms and away from him.

"I will not have you talk about it!" she said through her teeth, her eyes enormous. "Are you going to help me with this, Jeremy, or must I do this for myself?"

He stood very still for a long moment, and then his shoulders relaxed.

"All right," he said wearily. "All right, lamb. You know perfectly well I can't allow you to go rushing headlong out of here straight

318)

into probably the worst possible pair of hands somewhere. All right."

"Good," she said fiercely. "Now will you please just tell me the name of a doctor then. Right now, Jeremy."

Jere glanced at his watch, and then walked to the telephone. He dialed rapidly, and in a moment gave an extension number.

After another pause, he said, his voice very gay and light, "Marian, imagine catching you this time of night! How are you, darling? It's Jere, Jere Tidings. Well, I'm fine, darling. No, of course I haven't died or left town, whoever told you such a wicked story? Of course. Well, of course I want to see you very soon."

He waited, sipping from his drink, and then he said, "Marian darling, tell me. I'm calling for a sick friend in Sioux Falls, who's Doctor Smith sending the kids to for abortions these days, anyway?"

He laughed.

"Still? My god, times really haven't changed so much after all. No, darling, of course I haven't changed either, now why should you have thought I had? Thanks a million, sweetie. Yes, I will call you very soon."

He put down the phone gently and turned on the lamp above his desk. He hauled a telephone directory out of one of the drawers and leafed through it for a moment. And then he scribbled on a pad and tore off the sheet. He turned off the light again, and folded the bit of white paper neatly in two.

"Here you are, lamb," he said. "Expensive, but reliable. It's where they send the kids from the studio."

"Thank you," she said.

She unfolded the paper for a second to look, and then slipped it away in her trousers pocket.

"I don't much feel like talking any more tonight," she said gravely. "Do you mind, Jeremy? I think I'd like to go home now."

"Of course," he said lightly.

He walked with her, his arm about her shoulders, and at the

door, he lifted her face, cupping it very gently in his hand for a moment, before he kissed her.

"Must you really do this?" he said.

"Yes, Jeremy." She answered him with her lips scarcely moving at all, her eyes enormous and pleading as she looked up at him.

After a moment, he said, "Take very good care of yourself then, will you, darling?"

"I intend to," she said quietly. "Good night, Jeremy."

After she was gone, he turned on a light or two, tentatively. He picked up his glass and put it down untasted. And suddenly, he caught up a jacket from a chair back and shoved his arms into the sleeves abruptly. Without waiting to close the doors or windows against the evening chill, he plunged out of the doorway and across the sand, tramping rapidly up the beach, his hands thrust hard into his pockets.

thirty-two

LATER ON that evening, Stush returned home very early for him. He walked across the sand with his long lithe stride, whistling softly to himself, his eyes upon a pale half moon like the cut segment of a lemon in the sky. Once he came around the end of the terrace, he saw that there were no lights visible in Jere's wing of the house, and he paused. Just as he turned back, he caught sight of the huddled figure in the darkness on the doorstep.

Stush stood still, his hands shoved into his pockets as he looked. He began to walk away and suddenly he changed his mind and came up the steps in two swift bounds.

"What in hell's the matter with you?" he said impersonally. "You drunk or what?"

Maggie sat forlornly, her head buried on her knees.

"Yes," she said without looking up. "No. What difference does it make anyway?"

"What kind of an answer's that?" he said. "Get up, why don't you?"

"Leave me alone," Maggie said, her voice muffled. "I don't like you. I never did like you. Just go away and leave me alone."

Stush stood and looked at her.

"You know," he said, "it makes me want to puke just to look at you. Why you want to take on like this and let everybody know they're getting at you? Sniveling and crawling around on your belly and taking on! Stand up on your feet for a change."

She did not move or speak again.

Stush looked and a slow thunderous kind of fury began to grow in his face.

"Get up like I told you," he said softly.

"Leave me alone," she said dully. "It doesn't make any difference."

For an instant, Stush lifted his hand as though he meant to strike her, but then instead he grabbed up a length of plastic hose left where Jere had been watering a little twisted cypress tree. He spun the knob on the pipe furiously, and turned the icy blast of water directly upon her.

Maggie came up screaming.

"There," he said as he flung away the hose. "Mother of God!"

Maggie began to cry.

"So go ahead and blubber," Stush said disgustedly. "Anyway, stand on your feet when you do it. Come on, I'll buy you some coffee."

He took hold of her arm, and she went with him passively, crying as she plodded along, in a kind of weary hopeless monotone.

"Boy, oh boy, what a mess you really are," Stush said. "Snivel-

ing and crawling around, coming up here belly-aching to Jere all
the while. You ever stop to think, maybe he's got trouble of his
own?"

He shoved her rather ungently ahead of him onto the seat of
his small black sports car and slammed the door. He swooped off
down the highway, with the motor roaring deep-throatedly.

He did not speak to her again. The little car sped along, swinging in and out of traffic. They drove for a long time, and after a
while Maggie stopped crying, to sit silent and hunched and
miserable beside him.

They drove into an urban area, and finally Stush parked the car
with swift and careless precision. He got out and came around,
pulling her out onto her feet.

"Boy, you sure are a sight," he said critically.

Her skirt and blouse were still dark and damp with water, clinging to her body, and her hair hung in wet bedraggled rattails.
Stush poked her hair back into place behind her ears, impersonally.

"Come on," he said. "This place isn't so fancy as all that."

He led her back up the brightly lighted street, and before they
reached the door, the loud surging music spilled out onto the
sidewalk.

The big room inside was nearly deserted, early on a week night,
and Stush tugged her along brusquely to a booth against the wall
and shoved her down onto the seat.

He waved happily to the Negro musicians on the bandstand,
and then turned to embrace a small curly-haired waitress in a
very low-cut, off-the-shoulder blouse.

Over her giggles, he said cheerfully, "You miss me, doll? Listen,
when you come back, bring my girl friend here a bucket of coffee,
will you? She's already had it."

"Don't do that," the waitress said in a pleased voice, wriggling
as he grabbed into the front of her blouse. "You want the boss to
see you? You're a character, Stushie, that's what you are!"

"Yeah, I sure am," he said.

He gave her bottom a final friendly spank as he walked away. He greeted the musicians cheerfully, and then fell into some discussion with the drum player, amid all the din, his foot braced against the edge of the bandstand.

The waitress returned with a drink and coffee, her eyes upon Maggie curiously.

"Here you are, honey," she said kindly. "This'll make you feel better. You have some coffee and then I'll help you comb up or something, if you want me to."

Maggie looked up at her mutely and gratefully, the tears immediately swimming in her eyes again.

Stush swooped down on the booth.

"Go on, get out of here," he said to the waitress crossly. "What you want to do, get her started in all over again?"

He sat down across the table, groping at the pocket of his shirt.

"Come on, butt me," he said impatiently, snapping his fingers several times.

Maggie moved sluggishly, hunting cigarettes from her purse, and tossing the pack wearily onto the table top.

Stush helped himself, lighting two of them at once, and then he took one from his mouth and stuck it ungently into hers.

"Listen," he said. "You don't like me, that's okay. I'm not so crazy about you, either. But I like that kid of yours a lot. He's a real good little kid. Him and I had a real great time that day down to the beach playing with that hat that the bubbles come out of. What I want to know is, why you taking this so big? Is the kid in trouble or what?"

Maggie looked at him, the tears swimming in her blue eyes.

"Yeah, I know," Stush said. "You fouled up and his old man came and took the kid, I heard about it. What's so bad about that? His old man mean to the kid, is that it? Gets drunk and beats up on him, stuff like that, or what is it?"

Maggie's face was incredulous.

Stush drank from his glass and leaned across his arm, waggling his finger at her for emphasis.

"You know what I think?" he said. "I think maybe the kid's a hell of a lot better off to live with his old man. Boy, looking at you right this minute, I'd be willing to bet on it."

"That's a stupid thing to say," Maggie said, with the beginnings of anger in her voice. "Don't you think I don't know what a mess I am right now? That's got nothing to do with it."

"Now how you figure that?" Stush said. "Listen, what in hell's so bad about the kid staying with his old man for a while? That's what I'm trying to find out. He mean to the kid or what?"

"Of course he isn't," Maggie said stiffly. "It's nothing you'd understand anyway."

"I wouldn't, huh?" Stush said flatly. "You know what I think? I think you're so busy crawling around feeling sorry for yourself you never stop to think about the kid. He's a real nice little kid. Maybe he'd be better off living with his old man for good."

Maggie's chin lifted.

"He would not," she said. "I'm not any prize package either, but there are things you can do to children besides beat up on them, though maybe you wouldn't understand that. It's the kind of person that Tom is himself. I suppose he can't help it because it was the way that he was brought up, but I can't bear to think of him bringing up Jamie the same way."

She stopped, searching for words that Stush would understand.

"Tom lives in a little bit of a world. He isn't interested in anything, he doesn't care about anything. And he's full of hate, he hates everybody that isn't just exactly the same as he is. Just for instance. Take people like the guys playing up there. Tom wouldn't sit down in a seat next to one of those guys on a bus. He's full of things like that. I don't want him to bring up Jamie the same way."

Stush considered it as he drained his glass.

"Okay," he said. "Anyway, he's not mean to the kid, so what's it going to hurt for a couple of months? So you want the kid back, all right. Then why you want to go around fouling yourself up so maybe you lose him for good?"

"Don't rub it in," Maggie said desperately. "It's the waiting! I go around scared to death all the while just thinking about it. I miss him so, and I keep thinking what it would be like if some judge would just happen to give him to Tom. It's the waiting, I can't bear it, I'm no good at waiting! I never have been."

Stush's face was disgusted.

"Boy, it sure took me long enough to find that out, didn't it? So that's what the matter is, why didn't you say so in the first place? It's the way people are built. Some people can sit around on their ass and wait for something, some people can't. If you can't, why the hell don't you go ahead and get the kid back right now?"

"Are you crazy?" Maggie said angrily. "You think I haven't thought of that before? How? Just go out there and take him and have Tom drag me into court right away and that whole stupid story of getting caught in that motel with that character? Any judge is bound to love that. That would be real clever of me, wouldn't it?"

"Yeah, what's so goddamn clever about the way you're doing? Why don't you go on back to your husband then?"

"You really must be crazy," she said. "Besides, he wants the divorce the same as I do. He's got a girl all lined up already that he wants to marry."

"No kidding?" Stush said, his attention caught. "Then what's he care if you're shacked up with a dozen guys in a motel all at once?"

"What's the use of us talking?" Maggie said wearily. "We don't even talk about the same things. Look, he doesn't care what I do, what do you think? He only cares about Jamie. He just used that in order to get Jamie."

"No kidding," Stush said again. "Then he is a bastard. You

know, I think you got something there. That's a real nice little kid you got. You ought to get him the hell out of there."

Maggie laughed a little wildly.

"Oh, lovely! But how? You tell me!"

Stush was already rapidly sorting crumpled bills from his trousers pocket.

"Aaah, there's ways," he said. "Listen, I know a guy. He's a smart cookie. He used to be a lawyer till he got in a jam and they took his license. He's the guy could really tell you. Come on, let's blow out of here."

He went off swiftly to say good night to the musicians, and embraced the waitress once more lingeringly, while Maggie waited at the door.

Then they swooped away in the car, with Maggie slumped and passive on the seat, her head splitting from the liquor she had had earlier, the loud dinning music in the place they had just left, and the relentless rush of the wind, as Stush sent the car careening through the streets.

They drove again for a long time and finally parked on a dark side street.

"Come on," Stush said peremptorily. "We'll find Rollo. Old Rollo, he's a hell of a guy. He'll tell you how to work it."

He set off down the sidewalk rapidly, with Maggie trotting bewilderedly at his heels.

They approached a large auditorium where the last of a fight crowd was slowly dispersing. Inside, the ring lights were turned out, and their feet echoed between the yawning rows of empty seats. Stush led the way into a deserted drafty hallway, and left Maggie there while he disappeared into the dressing rooms below. She waited, her face confused and unbelieving, leaning tiredly against the dirty cement wall of the corridor that reeked of stale tobacco smoke and sweat and rubbing alcohol.

When Stush reappeared, he had in tow a small fat man in a

loud and rather seedy sports jacket, a man with a red, smooth, impassive face, his eyes all but lost in folds of flesh.

Maggie was dragging with weariness by the time they were crowded together in the car, and once more driving swiftly through the quiet streets. This time they came to rest in a dreary down-at-the-heel restaurant that possessed the additional virtue of serving liquor after hours.

Stush settled himself with a drink, while the small, quiet, fat man sat before a great platter of greasy eggs and bacon, and Maggie sipped coffee she no longer had any taste for.

Stush presented her story, and the fat man listened without expression, wheezing softly as he breathed. And finally over mouthfuls of food, he began to talk in a quiet voice, asking questions of Maggie that seemed totally irrelevant to her.

Once he had finished eating and had mopped up the last drippings from the plate with a crust of bread, he shoved back from the table and began leisurely to strip the cellophane wrapping from a squat cigar.

"Here is what you do," he said.

Maggie listened, her eyes slowly widening, shocked and horrified, in her pale face.

"Oh, no!" she said at last. "Oh, no! How could I do it? It wouldn't be fair, it wouldn't be honest! How could I do that?"

And later on, when she and Stush were alone in the car, driving toward Juniper Street, she said it still again, "I just don't see how I could ever do it. That's the one thing that Tom really believes about me, that I'm an honest kind of person. I don't see how it could possibly work anyway, and even if it did, how could I do this to him, even after what he's done to me!"

"All right, don't do it then," Stush said serenely. "You want your kid back, don't you, and you don't want to wait and take a chance. Okay, this is just one way to work it, that's all."

And after a long time, she turned her head to look at Stush wonderingly.

(327

"I don't get this," she said. "Why should you go out of your way to help me? You don't really like me much better than I like you."

Stush laughed.

"But I like your kid though," he said. "Your kid's a friend of mine. What kind of guy lets a friend of his take a pushing around? Let me tell you a little secret. Old Stush is crazy about kids, anyway. Kids are terrific, they're really all right. Boy, I sure wouldn't mind having a couple dozen of them myself!"

thirty-three

THE NEXT DAY, Maggie made necessary arrangements, moving about the house like an automaton. She made telephone calls, she wrote a note to Grandpa Kennedy, she packed a suitcase. Several times she returned to the telephone and once she even began to dial for Jere's number, but, in the end, she only quickly put down the phone again. It seemed to her finally that there was nothing that she could quite bring herself to say to him.

Early in the afternoon, she caught a bus and rode down into town. She hunted the dingy office building from the address written on the slip of paper that Stush's fat man had given her, and made the necessary call there. After that she took another, much longer bus ride.

She walked for several blocks and then down the spick and span suburban street, to Tom's small, neatly painted house. Her timing was exactly right, Tom's car had just arrived there and was standing in the driveway. Once she had started up the walk, Maggie closed her eyes for just one second, saying within herself something a little like a prayer.

And then she walked on, with a smile on her face, and a quick and confident tread, and rang the doorbell.

When Tom opened the door, she dropped her suitcase and flung her arms about his neck.

"Tom, darling," she said. "I've been such a fool! I've called my lawyer and told him I've changed my mind about a divorce. Darling, I've come home to you and Jamie!"

Tom goggled at her speechlessly.

The next moment she had knelt and held out her arms. She held Jamie to her fiercely, tears shining on her face.

"Oh baby, baby!" she said. "Don't worry, I'm never going to leave you again!"

It all came off, actually, very much as Stush's small, wheezing, fat man had predicted that it would. Tom was caught completely off guard, he was badly rattled and thoroughly confused during a period when he might conceivably have taken action. Jamie's presence, and the little boy's blissful delight in having Maggie there, was another complicating factor. Tom did manage a brief and surreptitious telephone call to Junie while Maggie was happily banging away over dinner preparations in the kitchen, with Jamie tagging after her in a transport of joy, his small high voice chattering without ceasing.

Once Jamie was tucked into bed, Maggie was saying brightly that she did adore this house, she really couldn't imagine them living anywhere else, and oh darling, how good it seemed to be home. Tom stared at her unbelievingly, his face puzzled and bewildered. Maggie added that she was so happy that she was honestly worn out with it, she believed she would just go to bed herself.

Since sleeping arrangements were restricted due to lack of furnishings in the house, Tom spent an uncomfortable night in the second twin bed. He lay sleepless for hours, trying to sort out the confusion of his thoughts into some recognizable pattern. He was not able to.

In the morning, Maggie was on hand to prepare breakfast for him, behaving quite as cheerfully and matter-of-factly as though she had been on hand to do so each morning in all the preceding months. She kissed him good-bye lovingly, outside on the doorstep.

By the time Tom arrived home from work that night, she had made friends with neighbors in all directions, confiding to one and all her delight over the reconciliation that she and Tom had affected.

By Saturday, Tom still had not been able to pin Maggie down to the discussion of their affairs that he felt to be necessary and vital, and for the first time, it occurred to him to doubt the genuineness of her motives. He hastily telephoned his lawyer from a booth in the supermarket and learned that so far as the legal aspects of the situation were concerned, he was indeed in the midst of a reconciliation whether or not he was enjoying it.

That night, he tersely announced to Maggie that he was going out for a while. She was sweetly agreeable about it.

The scene that followed between Tom and Junie at her apartment was a stormy one; there were tearful recriminations and desperate explanations. They made it up, eventually, in bed, and just at that point Maggie arrived with her detective.

In the face of Tom's fury, Maggie was rather cheerfully and brightly unperturbed. She didn't really know about a divorce, she said, though certainly it seemed that she now had all the evidence she would ever need for one. If Tom wanted a divorce, of course that was quite a different thing. She would at least be fair enough to discuss it with him. Meanwhile, she and Jamie would certainly continue to live at the house in the Valley.

When faced with that particular point Maggie merely shrugged it away. She didn't know what she'd been thinking

330)

of that first time, no community property indeed! Her lawyer had done his best to tell her even then. This old notion she had had, that Tom's hard-earned and carefully saved down payment for a house should belong exclusively to him, now appeared rather silly to her, on the face of it. Yes, certainly, the house was a factor now to be considered in any discussion of divorce arrangements and settlements. And the car and the refrigerator and the stove and the TV and several other items besides.

Tom got drunk that night for one of the few times in his life.

thirty-four

ALL AT ONCE, the brief California summer turned perceptibly toward fall. There were days of relentless shimmering heat, there were cold misty mornings with a first drizzle of moisture along the beaches. There were winds, sudden chill buffeting blows from the sea, and the vaguely unsettling hot santanas that huffed in through the mountain passes from the desert.

One mid-morning, Jere arose to a gray and misty world at the beach. The light rain hung in the air without ever seeming to fall, a meager vapor of moisture rather than a rain, and the clouds were low on the sides of the great humped foothills.

Jere lighted a fire on the grate, and ate his breakfast beside it, comfortable in robe and slippers with the morning paper propped before him.

The telephone tinkled from across the room, and he went to answer it leisurely, still carrying a segment of the newspaper with him.

His face was momentarily surprised.

"Lucy!" he said. "Darling, how very nice! But of course, come along. I see you seldom enough, come and rummage to your heart's content. As it happens, I hauled out that very box just the other day myself, looking for an envelope of clippings, it's still standing here. See you in a few minutes then."

Once he put down the telephone, he moved swiftly. He cleared away the remains of his breakfast carefully, except for a pot of coffee that he still had not gotten to. He disappeared into the bedroom for a few moments, and when he returned he was combed and very wide-awake, clothed in denims and sneakers and white T-shirt. Last of all he looked at his desk top critically. He quickly removed the top from his typewriter case, blowing at the dust over the keys and scattering a few sheets of paper here and there, and pencils and eraser.

He returned to the fire then, and poured himself a cup of coffee. He was just filling his pipe, when a slender figure in a drab raincoat appeared out of the mist on the step outside.

Jere went to meet her swiftly, sliding open the glass door.

"Lucy dear," he said. "Come in. How very nice to see you."

She turned her face the fraction of a bit away as he bent his, and he straightened immediately without kissing her.

"Let me have your coat, darling," he said cheerfully. "This is quite a dew we have this morning. Come thaw out, why don't you, and have a cup of coffee with me?"

"No, thanks," she said briefly. "I haven't long. I'd like to find those magazines. I'm sorry to disturb you."

"Now why should you be?" he said. "Actually, I got to work early this morning and I was ready for a coffee break, anyway. Sure you won't have a cup?"

"No, thanks," she said again.

She was a slender woman, her slim sharp-featured face and bare arms and legs very suntanned. She wore sandals and blouse and a crinkled cotton skirt trimmed with rows of bright-colored rickrack braid. Her hair, pulled back severely from her face, was red with a little gray in it. She looked rather uncannily like an older Maggie Harrison, but a Maggie who might somehow have lost all her zest, and pleasure in living.

She went down the room rapidly, her thin shoulders very straight, to a large cardboard carton that stood at the end of the desk. Jere walked back to stand beside the fire, picking up his coffee cup again.

"How've you been, Lucy?" he said. "I haven't seen you in ages, you know."

"I'm very well," she said crisply. "Is it this carton here?"

"It might be," he said. "I came across a number of things in there that belong to you. Why don't you take a look. If it isn't there, there's another carton in the closet. How's what's-her-name, Miss Stiles?"

"Alicia is very well too," she said, dropping to her knees on the floor beside the box.

"And the shop?" he said. "How are you doing with it?"

"It's always slow in the summer. It will begin to pick up now in another few weeks. You needn't think you have to make polite conversation with me. I didn't come for that."

Jere was silent for a moment, sipping at his coffee.

"It's not quite all small talk, Lucy," he said mildly. "Can't you imagine that I might be interested? After all, I think it's fairly absurd of us not to be better friends at this far point, don't you? Really?"

"No, I don't," she said definitely, her head lowered inside the box top. "I never subscribed to this theory of friendly divorces. If people were friends, they wouldn't be divorced in the first place, would they?"

Jere laughed.

"How very like you, Lucy dear! Just the same, I'm sorry you feel this way about it."

"How would you really expect me to feel?" she said inside the box. "I've every right to feel this way about it, haven't I?"

Jere put down the cup and saucer gently.

"I don't know, have you, Lucy? But I wish you weren't quite so bitter. It's a damn uncomfortable, unproductive state of mind to live with. It's also one that is never particularly attractive to a woman, either."

She dropped a fat manilla envelope and several books onto the floor beside her with a thud.

"You needn't be superior," she said. "I'm not very interested in whether it's an attractive frame of mind or not. Besides, it seems to be the only one I have. Do you think that my life's turned out so wonderfully well then, or so exactly as I used to think it was going to?"

Jere shrugged.

"Whose ever does? And you think it's altogether my fault, darling?"

"Well, isn't it?" she said baldly.

She dropped a box and a bundle of photographs and several notebooks, and dove back into the carton again energetically.

After a moment, Jere said gayly, "What on earth are you hunting for in that dismal collection of junk, anyway? What sort of magazines, herbs or Unity-by-the-Sea, or what? If you'd tell me perhaps I could help you."

"It's some old *Organic Gardening* magazines," she said. "I saved them years ago because they had all the instructions for making a compost heap. I could use them now."

"Still herb-raising, darling?"

"Yes, I do quite a bit of gardening," she said. "Why do you ask? I always did enjoy gardening, didn't I? You made fun of me for it often enough so I should think you'd remember."

"Lucy, at least be fair," he said lightly. "Now did I ever really laugh at you even once for your little posy plots and things?"

"You made amusing dinner-table conversation out of it, it's the same thing," she said shortly. "Gardening is only a way to fill up your time, the same as any other. Besides, I like living things. I like to see things grow up, I always did."

"Look here," Jere said. "If you're determined to be unfair, at least don't snipe at me with innuendoes. I know you are talking of the baby that you lost, of course, and I was never able to see that that was precisely my fault, no matter what you thought of it. I wonder how many times I suggested to you that we adopt children and you'd have none of it."

"How can you adopt a child with conscience if you haven't a happy home to bring him to?" she said. "Oh, let's not. What's the difference now, anyway? What do you do with yourself these days? I sometimes wonder."

"All sorts of things," he said lightly. "I'm working fairly hard at some television scripts just now."

She lifted her head to look over her shoulder at him through a cloud of flying dust particles.

"Why do you take the trouble to say things like that any more? Don't you think I know you quite well by now, fixing up your desk with papers like a child, and all that talk of coffee breaks? You haven't worked at anything any more involved than a Scotch bottle since you've moved out here, and you know it."

Jere laughed delightedly.

"There's old acquaintance for you! Lucy, I do love you! You're determined never to allow any of us our pretensions, aren't you?"

"I don't see that that's funny," she said, her voice all at once forlorn. "But then you always told me I hadn't any sense of humor and that may be it. There, I've found them. At the very bottom of the box, naturally."

She sat back on her heels, bending her head over the several little magazines.

"Yes, these are the right ones," she said after a moment. "They have the diagrams for the frame and all about it."

She sighed and bundled the magazines together. There was something oddly and pathetically courageous about the way she pulled her slim small body briskly to her feet and started down the room, her chin held high.

"Now I can go make myself a compost heap," she said. "It seems a smelly, unlikely enough kind of business, doesn't it?"

For the first time, his face was moved.

"Lucy, I'm sorry," he said softly and helplessly. "I wish there was something I could do. Please believe me, I am sorry."

"Well, you needn't be," she said as she picked up her coat. "I shouldn't be so waspish either. As you say, it's far past the point for that, for either one of us."

He took the coat from her hands.

"Must you really rush away?"

She turned her head to look at him, and all at once her face had softened, there were tears standing in her blue eyes.

"Jerry, why don't you go away some place?" she said. "Why don't you get some kind of a job, not writing if you don't want to, but any kind of job? Why don't you leave California?"

For an instant he was rigid, and then he laughed.

"My god, what's this?" he said gaily. "Don't tell me you've taken to being concerned about me, darling? Lucy, I do love you! I specially love you when you've found a cause and come off all lugubrious and filled with grim, crusading zeal. In this case, though, I think it might be much more profitable for you to stick to the Navahos, don't you?"

Her face slowly sharpened again as she looked at him.

"I never knew how to do it," she said wonderingly. "You always laughed at me when I tried. You won't share your troubles with anyone, you won't let anyone come close to you ever. All the years that we were married and I never found the way to do it."

"Darling, was I unkind? I didn't mean to be. It only struck me as a little fantastic since I've gone a million or two miles away from what you think of as California, already."

"You mean buying this house so you could hide away here

at the beach?" she said. "I'd heard about that. That's just running away from things instead of trying to solve them. It isn't the same as I had in mind at all. Never mind, I don't want to talk about it any more. It isn't exactly any of my business."

"Darling," he said amusedly. "Do grant me this much. "I'm not necessarily hiding away from anything. I simply live out here because I like it. It's a good and peaceful life. I admit it took a little doing in the beginning, but I've managed to work out a rather delicate set of checks and balances, and now it's a bit like your yoga you were so involved with for a year or two, I float above everything, suspended and calm and free as a gull. Do you think I ought to write a book to explain my method?"

Her face was bitter.

"Coming from you, you can't imagine how fantastic this all sounds," she said. "No, I wouldn't write the book. It only sounds to me that you've pickled yourself in Scotch and somehow managed to put that tremendous ego of yours into suspended animation for a while. If I were you, I'd wait with the book until I saw how long I could make this last."

She went quickly without a backward look, letting herself out the glass door into the rain.

thirty-five

WHILE THE SAME seeping moisture, rain without sound and without form, was wetting the streets and darkening the stucco walls of buildings in the downtown area, Maggie and Tom

Harrison came out of a lawyer's office together, into a drab and dreary second-floor corridor.

Maggie was weeping unashamedly, and there were tears on Tom's face as well. They hesitated outside the door with its crinkled glass panel, and Maggie said, "Jamie, go on, darling, if you want to. Go play on the stairs. Just be careful. We'll be along in a minute."

The little boy ran off, and Tom and Maggie stood together, silent and wretched. A woman in dark slacks and a raincoat, with short hair rather the color of Maggie's own, brushed by them on her way into the lawyer's office, looking at them curiously as she went.

The door closed behind her, the echo booming away in the dim musty corridor.

Maggie said finally, "You'll want him for this week end. Would you like to pick him up at noon on Saturday?"

"Okay, fine," Tom said.

He blew his nose hard into a white handkerchief.

"I guess your mind's made up," he said miserably. "You're not going to stay in California."

"I might come back," Maggie said quickly. "I'm almost sure I will. I'm sorry, Tom, to take him so far away. I just can't help it, I'm homesick. I want to go home."

"Sure," Tom said. "I can understand that. You always wanted to go back home. I guess you got a right to. If you don't come back, I can always come out there in the summer when I have my vacation. Long as I get to see the kid once in a while."

They wept again, both of them.

"Tom, I'm sorry," she said brokenly. "I'm sorry it had to be like this. I'm sorry I had to do it the way I did. I don't feel exactly proud of myself right now."

"It's all right," he said. "I guess I started it. I'm not exactly proud of the way I acted either."

"I don't know how we got into this," she said. "To have to fight each other like we have."

"I know," Tom said. "I sure wish it hadn't had to end up like this for both of us."

Maggie reached out and touched his arm.

"It only ends for us," she said helplessly. "It never ends for Jamie. I understand that now. You're his father, Tom, and I'm his mother. That goes on for always."

"Yeah, I guess," Tom said, his face stricken. "Kids forget pretty quick though. You know that the same as I do."

Maggie fumbled for her own handkerchief.

"I better go," she said. "I . . ."

She left the sentence unfinished and fled weeping for the stairway.

A half-hour later, she was at the telephone, dialing for Jere's number with trembling fingers.

At the first sound of his voice, she wept once more.

"Jere, oh, Jere!" she said. "I had to call you. It's all settled, we've just been at the lawyer's all morning. The divorce thing, I mean. Everything's all right, I've got Jamie, I can take him out of the state or anywhere I want to, it's all settled. Oh, Jere!"

"Maggie, darling," he said. "Look here, my head's spinning. The last I heard of you, my girl, you'd gone home to your husband. I even had to hear that from your grandfather. Now what's this all about?"

"The divorce," she said. "I told you, it's all settled. Jere, I've got Jamie, everything's all right. I'm home at Juniper Street right now. It's all over!"

"Then for a girl who should be dancing in the streets," he said, "you sound remarkably tearful to me. I think you'd better have lunch with me and tell me all about this."

"Ah, I'd love it," Maggie said. "Could we really do that?"

"Of course we will," he said. "I've only been sitting here giving

(339

myself the horrors this morning, waiting for some cheerful thing to happen. Now it seems that it has. This certainly calls for celebration. What about Jamie? Do you have a sitter or will you bring him?"

"Ah, Jamie!" she said. "Jere, you should see him, he's beside himself. All his old toys and all his things! Right now he's over at Martinez' next door. He couldn't wait to see Juan. I know Mrs. Martinez would love to give him lunch, he's too excited to nap today, anyway."

"Right," Jere said. "Can I pick you up in fifteen minutes then?"

They ate lunch in a quiet corner of a hotel dining room on the palisades above the sea, with the gray vapor gathering into drops and rivulets upon the window glass.

Maggie was breathless with excitement, red-eyed and poised continually between laughter and tears. With the coffee, Jere ordered drinks, and then took hold of her hand gently.

"Darling, you'd better have a drink too. You've been flying in all directions, all during lunch."

"I know," she said penitently. "I suppose I'm a little hysterical. But, oh, Jere, to have this over and done, you can't imagine!"

"Look here," he said. "Do you think it would help to talk about this coup d'état of yours, or would you rather start forgetting it right now?"

Maggie closed her eyes and shivered.

"I don't think I could talk about it. I still feel so dirty and ashamed. It's the most completely awful and dishonest thing I've ever done in my life. I pulled it off, and I won, but I lost too, a whole chunk out of my self-respect. Oh, Jere, it was so awful! Not that Jamie isn't worth it, but such a way to have to do it! To go back to Tom that way and pretend that I really meant it, and then to use his very privatest feelings for this girl he wants to marry. And finally to sit down at a table and haggle, with Jamie on one side of the scales and Tom's house in the other, and his automobile and the gadgets, all the things I never honestly wanted or felt entitled to in the first place. Jere, it's horrible, it's like—like . . ."

"Horse trading in each other's weaknesses?" he said gently. "Darling, I doubt if it's any comfort to you, but it is done every day, you know. And these custody things, unless it's open and shut, so often hinge on dragging forth people's behavior at exactly the level where they are most defenseless and least able to help what they do. That's never very pleasant. At any rate, it's over and you have Jamie and I'm very happy for you. Now I'd just forget it, if I were you, as rapidly as I was able."

"I wish I could," Maggie said. "I'll never really forget this. This is something I'm going to have to live with for the rest of my life."

They were silent, and at last Jere said gayly, "You know, this celebration seems to be bogging down on us. We can't have that. Let's be cheerful if it kills us. Tell me your plans. What was all this on the phone about taking Jamie out of the state? You're not really thinking of it, are you?"

Maggie nodded.

"I want to go home. At least for a little while. I'm so damn homesick I can't stand it."

Jere was intent on filling his pipe, and Maggie stole a quick look at him from the corners of her eyes.

"Then you definitely should go," he said. "I often think that home to you is the myth of the happy time and place you knew as a child, which probably no longer exists anywhere in this country any more. But at least you ought to go and see."

"I wouldn't have to stay," Maggie said clearly. "I could come back, you know."

Jere was frowning over his pipe, tamping the tobacco with the edge of a match folder as he drew on it, and the silence at the table became uncomfortable.

Maggie reached out to his arm on the table top.

"Jere," she said. "I'd like to come back."

He took her hand quickly.

"Darling, it's all right," he said. "I understand what you're trying to tell me."

She closed her fingers tight and warm upon his.

"Oh, Jere," she said. "I wish we could just put back the clock. All the way back, to that morning when I started off to Tijuana with Tony. It's been such a nightmare. I've said and done so many things that I wish I hadn't. I hate having you think of me, the way I was behaving those days. I couldn't seem to help myself. I think I was really a little out of my mind. Now it's finally over and I'd give anything in the world if there was a way to just put back the clock for us."

He smoothed at her fingers gently.

"Well, that makes two of us," he said soberly. "But it's a little more difficult than you think. If we're to begin tinkering with clocks, don't you really know we've got to set them back much much farther than that? We'd have to set them back about fifteen years, darling, well, ten at least."

She started to speak, and he said quickly, "No, listen to me for a minute. I think you're at a stage of things just now, where I must be as honest with you as I am able, and I'll try to be. Maggie, how can I really best explain this to you? First of all, you must believe me, this has nothing to do with the way I feel about you, or don't feel about you. And I love Jamie with all my heart, he's exactly the child I've always wanted to have. But it's not quite as simple as that. I think, with your nice country-girl set of mores, that the only deep satisfaction you will ever find is in marriage, and you should marry again. You have every capacity for it. That brings us to the very heart of the trouble. There is a time and a place in everyone's life for everything. And by the sheer mischance of life, it happens that this is not my time nor my place. I'm very bad husband material for anyone, I probably always have been actually. Can you understand that?"

"Since you've brought it up," Maggie said softly, her cheeks pink, "shouldn't I be the one to be the judge of that?"

"No," Jere said. "Because you're a very sweet, fairly inexperienced sort of goose. All right, let's put it another way. I once told you that you remind me of Lucy. Or I should say, you remind me of her as she used to be quite a long time ago. You don't remind me at all of Lucy as she is today, and I hope that you never will. Well, I was married to Lucy, and it's her theory that I'm fairly responsible for some of the more unpleasant changes that came about in her and in her life during that time. Naturally, I have my own opinions about it, but that's not the point at all. The case in point is what Lucy herself believes. Now that's really not a very good recommendation for me, is it?"

"That's very silly," Maggie said. "I am not really Lucy, even if I do remind you of her. Besides, I'd never believe that you could have been responsible for anything bad that happened to her, not ever. And even if you had been, well, you say she's not the same person that she once was, why should you think that you're the same person either?"

"Darling, charity is a quality that it's sometimes fatal to overdo," he said. "I make a very bad husband. Ask Lucy yourself if you like. I am full of bad habits, I don't give of myself very easily, I . . . Look here, in a not so indirect sort of way, I've brought you quite a bit of unhappiness already, haven't I?"

"You have not," Maggie said softly. "Not indirectly or any other way. I got just what I brought upon myself. I won't have you blaming yourself for anything on my account."

"Well, bless you," he said. "That's a switch anyway! There's certainly more than room enough for argument there, but let's just leave it for the time being. It's not quite the point, anyway. Let's get all the way back to the original point, because . . ."

"Now it's my turn to talk," Maggie said. "Please listen to me, Jere. You know, I've changed quite a lot myself these last weeks, all the trouble about Jamie and everything. I've lost a lot of that cockiness I used to have, and I've lost enough of my pride and what you used to call my Indiana maidenly modesty, to be able to talk to you like this, too. I suppose what you're thinking about when you say it's too late for us and all that is . . . I mean, darling, don't you see, it doesn't matter! When you love someone, there are certain things that are much more important than certain other things. You shouldn't feel that . . . I mean, I think that all it is, you've been hurt by something, probably your marriage going wrong for you, and I think I could help you to get over it, and . . ."

For an instant he was taut against the table edge, and then he caught his breath and laughed.

"Maggie, my darling! I do love you, and your funny, warm, impulsive heart! I really think that you've somehow gotten it into your head to be sorry for me, and . . ."

"Oh, Jere, no!" There was consternation on her face. "Of course I'm not! Why should I ever have to be sorry for you? Oh, no! It's just that I don't know how to say things very well, I'm not good with words the way you are. I do think that you need me, but that's not the same thing, I . . ."

"Oh god, my goose is beginning to cook before my very eyes!" he said with comic horror. "Once a woman gets it into her head that you need her, you're in for real trouble. Need, to a woman, indicates a weak spot somewhere, and they'll go for it like tigers. I may have to fight for my life."

"Damn right," Maggie said. "You laugh all you want to. One day you'll stop laughing and begin to listen to me. You'll see. We've plenty of time."

"I'm absolutely horrified," he said. "I'm going to take you straight home, my girl, back to your child where you belong. In another moment, you'll have me right here over the lunch table, bell, book and candle and the works!"

"Oh god, I do have to go home," Maggie said. "We've been here half the day."

And then she reached out quickly, her hand upon his, and the tears suddenly standing in her eyes again.

"Jere," she said. "Leaving all the fun and jokes out of it, I'm not really coming at you like a tiger. I'm just not good at saying things I feel. I guess all of this was just my way of trying to tell you that I love you, and that I could be had very easily, if you should want me."

"Darling," he said very gently. "Don't mind my fun and jokes. Don't you really know me well enough by now to know that I only laugh at things when I don't know what else to do? Maggie, what can I say to you? That I wish with all my heart I'd met you ten years ago? That only sounds very trite, like a number of other profoundly true things. There can't be much satisfaction for you in hearing it either. What am I to say to you then? The simple truth of the matter you won't like to hear, but I'll say it anyway. You don't need me. You used to talk to me of those divorce doldrums you were caught in, remember? Well, do you know what the divorce doldrums really are? Darling, we all tend to see ourselves in someone else's eyes, the eyes of someone whom we love or who loves us. Our whole sense of our own identity gets involved in it. And when a relationship or a marriage ends, ah, we lose far more than the person close to us, we lose ourselves besides. We're left then with the job of finding our own identity again, and it's never easy. Maggie, you won't like my saying this, but you must certainly know it yourself. When you met me, you were grabbing desperately for something. No, not just for a man to go to bed with, more important things. You needed assurance, and you needed terribly to feel that you were a desirable woman again. Darling, don't you know that you were really only searching for yourself? And now you needn't any longer. I expect it's part of the catharsis to what you've been going through these past few weeks. Anyway, seeing you today, I think you're whole again. You needn't grab for any outside assurances any longer. You've found your own identity again within yourself, the very best and most secure place possible to find it. Baby, you're all right now, take my word for it. The next relationship that you make, there won't be any gun point of necessity at your back. You really don't need me any longer."

Maggie looked at him, her face searching and a little bewildered.

"Jere, what can I say to you! Maybe you're right, you're very good with words, I only know what I feel. What can I say, except that I love you, and I think that you need me, too, no matter how you laugh at me for saying it. Jere, I'm not a very clever person. You live in a whole world, after all, that I really don't know very much about. But there's something else I seem to have gotten over, too, that business of always tearing myself down. Right now, I know inside of myself that there are other things I can give you that I do know about, and they are terribly important things, too. I don't mind if I care about you more than you care about me, there's always someone who has to care the most. But I think that you need me, and I think I can make you happy. Almost as happy as you deserve to be."

"Maggie," he said helplessly. "You're a very wonderful girl. It's only obvious that I'm not half the things that you seem to think I am. I hope that one day you'll find that out for yourself, as painlessly as possible."

thirty-six

THE DAY ENDED drearily, with a slow inexorable fading of light, while the rain that was not really rain at all still leaked out of the air to wet the sand and the house and the armload of firewood that Jere carried into the hearth to dry. The sea, too, was gray, the narrow restless strip that was visible before the mist closed in. The looming foothills were only flat, drab, curved cutouts, one superimposed upon another and pasted wet to the colorless sky.

Jere poked up the fire, put a stack of records on the player and mixed himself another drink.

When the telephone rang, he went eagerly to answer it.

"Caro, darling!" he said with genuine pleasure. "You can't think how glad I am to hear you."

"Jeremy, I'd like very much to see you," she said. "Are you alone?"

"Solitary and forlorn," he said lightly. "I've had a terrifying day. Probably the weather. Do come out here right away and say cheerful things to me by the dozens."

"I'm calling from quite near by," she said. "Would you give me tea?"

"I'll even give you high tea," he said. "There's food around and it's too drizzly to go out for dinner, anyway. Let's munch by the fire and tell each other jolly reassuring things, whether we believe a word of what we're saying or not."

She laughed softly into the telephone.

"All right, Jeremy. I'll be there absolutely before you know it!"

Then she was, running lightly up the steps, her smooth head bent against the rain, a long black suede jacket belted snugly over her dark trousers.

Jere met her at the door.

"Darling, I'm so glad you thought of me. You are exactly what I need on a very drear night in the late of my life. How are you, lamb?"

She lifted her damp small face for his kiss.

"I'm very well, Jeremy, thank you."

"Are you sure?" he said. "I've had nothing to go on, you know, except those couple very uninformative phone calls."

"But I am," she said. "Really perfectly all right now. It's amazing how soon you are. It's a bad thing, much worse than ever going to a dentist, but it's not an unbearably bad thing. All the same, I'm very glad it's over with."

"And so am I," Jere said. "I've had quite a number of bad moments, thinking of you."

"I expect it's not very nice to say I'm glad that you did, but I am glad," she said. "I expect it would be absolutely horrible to do it, if you didn't have the feeling that there was someone somewhere who was thinking of you."

He hugged her tightly for a moment, and then said lightly, "Come to the fire. Better have some rum in your tea, you're chill and damp as a little bird. What else have you been doing with yourself, that might be more cheerful?"

"Not really anything," she said, holding out her hands to the blaze. "Except to look a little for an apartment. Do you know, Jeremy, I think I'd like to have a place to live of my very own."

"That sounds like a good idea. You be cozy, and I'll get the tea things."

Beneath her coat she was wearing a rather ornate blouse, with folds of heavy shiny black satin held up by tiny straps over her thin bare shoulders. She settled herself on a cushion by the fire, and Jere carried the tray to the coffee table.

They lingered over tea and sandwiches, and finally Jere carried the tray away again. He settled himself in a corner of the divan, with a drink at his side and his pipe in his hand, his long legs stretched out comfortably to the warmth.

Caro was silent for a long time, seated cross-legged upon her cushion, her eyes pensively fixed upon the flames.

"Penny?" Jere said idly at last.

She turned her head slowly.

"You know, I was just thinking," she said. "I wonder, Jeremy, if you would consider marrying me?"

"I take it this comes under your heading of discussion on the purely academic level," he said amusedly. "So, considering it in theory, I think under certain circumstances I should be delighted to. But I thought you were the one who was dead set against the whole idea of marriage, anyway?"

"I used to be," she said gravely. "I've reconsidered it a great deal since then. I expect I haven't made myself perfectly clear, Jeremy. Would you really think of marrying me? I mean, would you think of actually doing it? Because I would like very much to marry you, Jeremy?"

"Oh my god!" Jere said. "What is this anyway? Twice in one day! What a really hell of a charming guy I must be!"

"Jeremy, you are not to laugh at me," she said. "I am being perfectly serious about this."

"Darling," he said. "I am really very flattered. But isn't this a bit sudden?"

"Is it?" she said.

Jere whacked out his pipe.

"Well, isn't it?"

"No," Caro said serenely. "I don't really think it is at all."

"Well, I'm sure you'll understand," he said lightly, "if I say that we oughtn't to rush into this. I've always been a great one for motives, in my time. Why do you want to marry me?"

"For all the obvious and very ordinary reasons," she said quietly.

"And other ones besides. Because you are strong and good and gentle, and because you understand me better than anyone in the world. Jeremy, this is very silly. There are so many reasons one may have for wanting to marry a person."

"Well, apparently so, in this case," he said. "Look here, my lamb. You are in a doldrums just now and it's quite understandable that you should be. There are probably fairly sound physiological reasons for it, as well as all the psychological ones. You don't want a husband at all. What you really want is a sort of built-in cross between a psychiatric father confessor and a cozy hot-water bottle to warm your bed at night."

"Jeremy, don't patronize me," she said. "Please give me credit for enough intelligence to be able to tell the difference between these passing psycho-physiological symptoms you are referring to and something that is quite separate and very real and lasting to me. I said, first of all, that I wanted to marry you for all the very obvious and ordinary reasons, didn't I? Must we go into the bedroom in order for me to prove that, before we can go on discussing this?"

Jere sat bolt upright on the divan all at once, his face incredulous.

"Look here, you cold-blooded little horror, you," he said softly. "And that's horror with an 'or.' Do you mean to sit over there on that goddamn cushion and tell me that you've really seriously meant any single word of this rigmarole?"

"Jeremy, I think you are being very dense about this," she said calmly. "I thought I'd made myself perfectly clear. I would like to marry you. I was hoping very much that we could fly to Las Vegas tonight."

"Now you listen to me," Jere said, his voice still soft. "There were many times years ago when I was tempted to whale the tar out of you. But there never was a time when I was one-tenth as tempted to do it as I am right now."

"I think you are being terribly overemotional about this," Caro said. "I wouldn't have expected it of you, Jeremy."

350)

"And exactly what did you expect of me, anyway?" he said. "Apparently it's time I dropped the habit and took off the beard. I really do exist, you know, apart from acting as your father confessor, or probably more to the point, as your father to you. For god sakes, what exactly did you really expect me to do about this?"

Her chin was very high.

"If you don't want me, you've only to say so," she said. "I thought we might be able to discuss this like intelligent sort of people. I can't think why you must make this terribly emotional thing out of it."

"You can't, can't you!"

He grabbed up his glass and swooped for the bar.

"You think then that you can just drop yourself like a stray kitten onto people's doorsteps, is that it?"

"I don't think anything of the sort," she began. "I merely thought that . . ."

"You shut up for a minute," Jere said rudely. "You talk altogether too much. You obviously don't think at all."

He stormed back up the room with his glass in his hand.

"Aren't you really able to get out of your in-bound little self far enough, for even one minute, to imagine how I might feel about this? Can't you even conceive that I might have feelings to be considered, too? If you had turned up here with this idiotic proposal several weeks ago, before that extracurricular dental appointment of yours, there might even have been some slight justification for it. But to come to me with it now! This is the sheerest sort of taking advantage of my fondness for you! Do you think that I, or any man for that matter, should be delighted to have himself used solely as bulwark and delaying action against the day when you are terrified that you'll run back to Stush in spite of your pride? Think about that for a minute! You live in a world of flesh and blood and substance, for god sakes, not one of just your own mists and thoughts and vapors!"

She began to cry without a sound, or a muscle moving in her face.

"Jeremy, please listen to me. The two things are quite quite separate. I admit that is true about Stush. I admit that I'm terrified. I'd rather die than go to Stush, I'd truly rather die. But where else do I have to go? What will I do?"

"I assume you'll go back to Stush then, if he'll have you," Jere said. "You will certainly not think of marrying me, against the day, nor anyone else, if you've any wit left about you at all."

"Jeremy, listen, please only listen! If I don't have you, I will go back to Stush because I've nowhere else to go! I know that I will go back to him finally. And I'll loathe myself for doing it, I'll never forgive myself. And that's only half of it. It's the life I'm going to have with him, I'm so terrified. I see it all perfectly plainly, like little bright figures moving in a crystal. I wanted some monstrously simple alive person like Stush, but I can't bear it. I see what my life is going to be like with him, I see what will happen to me! I will be hurt and I will be humiliated each time that he's with a woman until I can't bear it any longer. I'll either dry up and stop feeling altogether, or I'll never stop hurting, and I'll turn into some hateful thing instead of a woman and . . ."

"Raise herbs?" Jere said steadily. "And make compost heaps? Look here, there are many other ways. You are dramatizing yourself to the skies. Do you really think that you're the first woman who's ever had to live with this before? What does love mean to you, for god sakes, as an emotion, as a state of being, as a relationship? Where's your wonderful sense of logic? The very thing you wanted most in Stush is the one thing you are not willing to accept once you have it. And why must you make such a point of oversimplifying, is Stush really such a simple creature then, or actually a very complex one who . . ."

"I am not going to talk to Stush," she said furiously. "I want to talk of you and me, Jeremy. I would like you to listen to me. Will you please listen to me!"

All at once there was a frantic rattling tattoo on the glass door behind them, and at the same instant it slid open and Dick Whitfield catapulted in, a little unsteady upon his feet, his hair hanging down into his wide distended eyes.

The room was suddenly still, except for the murmuring roar of the sea and the crackle of the fire.

"I'm terribly sorry," Dickie said desperately to Jere. "I was at this cocktail party up the beach and I've been wanting to stop and talk to you for a long time. I won't keep you but a minute. I'd like to talk to you alone."

Jere stood rooted, and then with all his strength he hurled the glass in his hand shattering against the wall behind the bar. The shards of glass fell tinkling into the little sink there, and the liquid it had contained began to run down along the wood panels in shining rivulets.

"God in heaven!" he said. "Every witch there is must be on a broom tonight. What kind of public wailing wall have I made of myself? Certainly, talk by all means, why not? You'll never have a better night for it, I'll guarantee you that!"

Caro scrambled to her feet and ran toward the bathroom, her face pale and astonished. Dickie stood uncertainly and almost at the point of tears.

"I'm sorry I bothered you," he said humbly. "This won't take a minute. I don't know just how to begin. I kept going over it in my mind there at the party. I guess I've had too many drinks."

"Do you think another one would help?" Jere said tersely.

"Oh, no, thanks," Dickie said. "This is something I've wanted to tell you for a long time. I've driven by this house, night after night. In the beginning, I used to think about hurting you, what it would be like to get a gun somewhere, and—you know. I guess I'm not the type."

"How very fortunate," Jere said.

"Yes, I think so, too," Dickie said seriously. "Anyway, I don't feel like that any more. I know it isn't really your fault."

"Well, that's comforting. What isn't my fault, if you don't mind my asking?"

"I know what it's like with Stush," Dickie said. "I know you couldn't have been able to help yourself any more than I could."

Jere stared at him.

"I think I've been cursed," he said wonderingly. "I think this night's bewitched. I think the very elements are out of joint!"

And then he said briefly, "Well, it's just as well you didn't shoot me. You'd have made a goddamn fool of yourself. Stush rents a room from me, that happens to be all."

"Never mind," Dickie said with a rather unsteady sweeping gesture of magnanimity. "It's all right if you don't like to talk about it. I know that some people don't. That's not what I came to talk about, anyway."

"Then what did you come to talk about?"

"Well, it's just this," Dickie said, his forehead wrinkling earnestly. "I'm awfully sorry to burst in and disturb you like this, but I wanted you to know. It's terribly important to me. I want you to know that if something should ever go wrong and you didn't want Stush to stay here any more . . . I know how terribly hard he can be to live with . . . Or if Stush ever got sick or in trouble or anything like that, I wanted you to know to be sure to call me. I know Stush doesn't care an awful lot about me, but if he ever needed it, he'd let me take care of him. I'd want to do that. I—care an awful lot about Stush. I understand him now a lot better than I used to. I wouldn't ever want him not to have a place to go or someone to take care of him. You will remember, won't you? I simply couldn't bear to think of him ever without that. You will remember, please?"

Jere's eyes blinked. He was silent, and slowly all the anger and impatience left his face until it was very gentle. He reached out his hand to Dickie's shoulder, and when he spoke, his voice was very gentle also.

"Stush is a very lucky fellow," he said. "So few of us deserve this and almost none of us are ever lucky enough to get it. Of course, I will remember, Dickie. Don't worry about it."

"I guess I'd better go," Dickie said. "I'm really sorry to have disturbed you like this. I know I've had a few drinks and that's probably why I came all right, but I hope you'll understand this is something I've wanted to tell you for a long time. It's terribly important to me."

"Yes, I understand," Jere said at the door.

He stood for a long moment, looking out into the rain and darkness where Dickie had gone, and then he spun around suddenly and clapped his hands sharply together and laughed.

"Now, you dismal little creep!" he said. "Come out of that bathroom where you've been listening to every word of this and tell me what you think. I'm so glad that you were here to hear this for yourself. I wouldn't have had you miss this for anything in the world! You have just had the best possible object lesson in what love is all about. I couldn't have begun to tell you so well. You and your precious screaming little ego! What have you ever given to Stush that could remotely compare to this, for god sakes? You, who are so full of yourself, you hadn't even room enough for his child there! How can you possibly look me in the face now and tell me that you understand anything about love beyond the first a-b-c's of it?"

She came erupting out of the doorway, her face stretched and desperate.

"Jeremy, I don't understand. What was that boy saying to you? Is he saying that Stush is gay? Are you lovers with him yourself, is that it? Is that why you don't want me?"

"Now that does it," Jere said in a deadly voice. "That really does it. You shut your mouth and get back on your cushion and listen to me for a minute. It's the last chance you'll ever have, because, as of tonight, I'm going out of business. No more of this good old Uncle Jere bit, counselor to the lovelorn, consoler to the downhearted. I've had it! I can't think what I've been doing to myself lately to make myself over into this amorphous sort of good-natured slob that gets used as a punching bag for every wounded ego that comes my way. Apparently, it's time I changed my ways, but before I do, there are a couple things I'd like to say to you. How can you ask me if Stush is gay? How can you ask that, for god sakes? What do you mean by it, anyway? This isn't a black and white world that you live in. People are not necessarily this or that, not all of them, not even most of them. Stush is simply what he is, unique as any of the rest of us, neither this nor that nor any category whatsoever. What do you really know of Stush anyway, beyond this simple, exciting male-animal concept that you apparently have of him? You say you love him, then haven't you really taken the trouble to learn anything about him at all? He's a human being, you know, the same as you are. Flesh and blood and bone and all the rest it entails, pride and insecurities, drives, weaknesses, strengths, fears, big dreams and small failures, triumphs, griefs, quite the same as any of the rest of us. Hasn't it ever occurred to you that he might need something more from you than your ambitions? Haven't you ever wondered what it is that Stush is looking for in all these beds he's in and out of, or even if he's looking for anything at all beyond the fun of it? I can't tell you whether Stush will be worth it to you in the long run, you've certainly to decide that for yourself. I can't tell you why Stush behaves as he does, either. I don't know. But this I do know, Stush is simply what he is, and he cannot help himself. Can any of us, for god sakes, do you think that any of us really choose in that part of our lives? Someone once said it better than I can:

> '. . . Love, absolute
> in each chance encounter, blind
> antennae of sex, searching out
> the desperate space for communication.'

Well, think about it for a minute! The perfectly unsought, un-chosen 'blind antennae' and the cruelly 'desperate space.' "

356)

He stopped and began to turn away, and then he said, "As to the rest of that gibberish of yours, no, Stush and I are not lovers. I couldn't say to you, and very few men could, that never once in my life have I ever had anything bordering on a sexual experience with a man. Stush doesn't happen to be one of them. That answers your question, now why don't you go home."

Caro was smiling a little as she came up from the cushion, and for a moment she looked rather oddly like Helen.

"Because I'm not ready to go home quite yet, Jeremy," she said coolly. "Because you haven't answered my real question yet at all. I don't want any more talk of Stush, I want to talk of you and me, Jeremy. I'm relieved to hear you say you've given up your lectures and your homilies, because I've had quite enough of them. I've had quite enough of your theories and your platitudes and your 'blind antennae,' and your 'chance encounters' most certainly! Why should you feel that you have a prerogative to tell me that I don't know what love is all about? Love is a word, it must certainly mean very many different things to different people. I know quite quite well what I feel. I feel a certain thing for Stush. I feel another, separate, very certain thing for you. And why should that surprise you, Jeremy? I'll use the word 'love' if I like, I've certainly as much right to use it as anyone else has. I love you, Jeremy. I've loved you since I was old enough to know what it was about. I love you and I need you now, not tomorrow or the next day or next year, but now. I think you do owe me at least enough to listen to me seriously about this, and believe what I am saying to you. You do owe me at least that much, don't you?"

"My god, my god, what do I owe?" Jere said. "Are you standing there now assuming that I owe you anything in this world because one night years ago I'd had too many drinks and did a pleasant casual thing with a very lovely little girl who was something more than eager for it herself, you will admit!"

"A little girl, ah, yes!" she said. "But I did have feelings quite the same as anyone else, Jeremy. Tonight you've accused me of not considering your feelings, did you ever consider mine then?"

"You had about the feelings of a tarantula right then, I should think," he said. "I was living with Helen at the time, for god sakes, and she's the nearest thing to a mother you've ever known in your life."

"Yes, Helen!" Caro said. "I had to see you with Helen, always and forever with Helen, and I hated her and hated her and I still do. Neither of you would pay attention to me, no matter what I did. I was only a child, some sort of juvenile delinquent, a case, a problem to be solved. Ring up another psychiatrist, pack her off to another boarding school! Well, now it's too late for that, I'm quite grown up. What do you propose to do about me now, Jeremy?"

He was still for a moment, and then he said quietly, "Not let you use me another time to prove still another point between yourself and Helen, at any rate. My god, where did it begin with you, this thing you have about Helen? I don't see the beginning nor I don't see the end, it's like the Chinese boxes, one inside the other. Now I've really had enough of you for one night. Take your Electra complex or whatever term it is that the head shrinkers use for this gruesome state of affairs, and go home and go to bed with it. It's obviously the only thing in this world that's actually alive to you, anyway, or has any reality to you, whatsoever. Does that answer your question!"

She grabbed up her coat and ran.

thirty-seven

WHEN STUSH came home a little later, the record player was turned up high, and Jere was prowling up and down the floor, his hands shoved into his pockets. His light hair was disheveled, his collar loosened and his tie askew, and his oddly green eyes squinted against the smoke of a cigarette hanging from his mouth.

Stush waved through the glass and then slid open the heavy door for himself.

"Hi," he said. "I saw your lights. How you been, Dad? You miss me?"

"Well, I can't say it's been exactly quiet around here without you," Jere said shortly.

Stush came in, moving lithely but tiredly all the same. He stripped off his jacket and slumped down into the corner of the divan, his big body instantly relaxed, his head rolling over as though he were already sleeping.

"Like a nightcap?" Jere said.

"Yeah, nightcap would be real fine. Hey, what's with you? You're all charged up tonight or something."

"Rain," Jere said. "I bloom like the flowers."

Stush yawned.

"Well, the rain's over. Stars are out. There's a big bank of clouds out to sea and it's just starting in to blow."

"Good," Jere said. "Blow the goddamn roof off for all I care. What's with you, buster? You look fairly beat."

"Aw, I been having a hell of a time," Stush said with a reminiscent grin. "Boy, oh boy, what a girl! She was from the West Indies, she said. Jesus, what a skin she had! She wouldn't give me her address, I guess she was married or something. There's one girl I sure wouldn't have minded seeing again sometime."

"Take the word of an old hand," Jere said as he stuck the glass into Stush's limp fingers. "The first time, you're ahead of the game. Go back the second time, your troubles begin."

Stush laughed softly.

"Boy, you can say that again!"

"Look here," Jere said as he wheeled off down the room again. "None of my business certainly, but what about Caro?"

"What about her?"

Stush's eyes flickered behind his stubby pale lashes but he did not move. His body was completely relaxed but strangely hard at rest, as though, even resting, he was actually intensely engaged in soaking in some force of strength and renewal through his very pores.

"I asked you first."

"Nothing about her," Stush said. "She's a sweet little kid. She got too big for those cute little britches she's always wearing, that's all. I don't like nobody trying to push me around. Anytime she wants to come off her high horse she knows where to find me. Then we'll see."

"Good boy," Jere said. "You almost restore my faith in something or other. You keep swinging as long as you can. They'll find ways to get at you soon enough."

"Not old Stush, they won't," Stush said very softly. "No, not old Stush!"

The telephone jangled on the desk, and Jere went impatiently to answer it.

"Jere!" The warm vibrant voice sounded in his ear. "Darling, do sit down in case you're not and listen to this. This is something you are absolutely not going to believe, I just saw it with my own eyes, and I still don't believe it. Is Stush there? No, I don't want to talk to him, I want to talk to you, darling, I'll talk to him later. Jere, you'll never guess where I've been, Pasadena, of all places. Harry sneak-previewed the film out there tonight, I've just gotten in from there. This you will not believe. The film, so so. Poor Harry's having fits and pretending not to. But Stush, and the little bit he had in it, it's incredible. Absolutely two-thirds of the cards mentioned him, one-half of them mentioned him by name. Now what do you think of that? It must simply be a natural phenomenon, no, it's much better than that. You didn't come in for the studio preview, did you? Well, it doesn't matter, it isn't the same until you've actually seen it in a theatre with an audience and everything. Honestly, one of the hardest projections I've seen in years. And no contract. Poor Harry and his ulcer. I really advise you to unplug the phone. It's going to be completely mad the rest of the night. I got away and drove into town like crazy on the Freeway while they were still having drinks and shuffling the cards. I'd really just unplug the phone. I'm coming out, do you mind, darling? I'm very excited."

"I wish you would come, Helen," Jere said. "But tell this to Stush now, will you? This I can't wait to see. Just a second, darling."

Over the lowered telephone, Jere looked at the divan where Stush was sprawled with his eyes closed, like a large and dreaming cat.

"For you, Stush," he said. "Helen has something to tell you."

"Listen, I'm beat, no kidding," Stush said. "Tell her I'll call her tomorrow, huh?"

"Better take it now," Jere said. "This is something you may want to hear."

Stush mumbled, and then heaved himself up to his feet. He stretched, loosening his shoulders, and finally picked up his glass and came.

"Hi," he said into the telephone. "What you been doing, hon? What's with you?"

Jere sat down upon the edge of the desk, his eyes intent upon Stush's face.

Stush listened for a long time, his face unmovedly sleepy and half-scowling. Several times he drank from his glass, and once he yawned widely.

"Yeah, yeah, sure," he said at last impatiently. "Naw, I'm not going to sign nothing, what you think? Hell, no. Sure. Okay, hon, I'll see you, huh? I'll call you. Okay. 'Bye."

He put down the telephone.

"Boy, now there's a girl that really likes to talk on the phone," he said complainingly.

He drained his glass, and then he slowly began to stretch again, limbering and working his shoulders.

"Man, I'm beat," he said. "I better hit the sack. Boy, out there in those islands those girls learn all kinds of things. What a girl! Jesus, I wish you could have seen the skin she had!"

"Oh, my god!" Jere said. "I don't believe it!"

The phone began to ring insistently.

"Well, what about it?" Jere said, gesturing with his hand. "I assume the vultures are already in full flight. You're going to be in for a rugged few days of it, boy. Take my word, I've been there before you. Want to start now?"

"Naw, take it off the hook like she said," Stush said. "Hell with them."

Jere let it ring on to the end, and then lifted it and put it down gently on the desk top.

"Stush, tell me the truth," he said. "Doesn't this seem exciting to you? Aren't you at least surprised?"

For an instant, Stush's pale eyes were open and very direct.

"Surprised?" he said. "Why the hell should I be surprised? I knew it was going to happen, what you think I been hanging around here waiting for? Let me tell you a little secret, Old Stush, he can't miss. It figured to happen, that's all. It just figured to happen."

362)

"And there you are!" Jere said softly.

He shrugged, and struck his hand against the edge of his knee. "Greatest business on earth," he said. "And it gets the characters, like the filings to the magnet. Stush, I love you, baby. Stay just as sweet as you are. Care to do anything riotous, like have a drink, just to celebrate? Beginning of an era, you know."

"What's to celebrate?" Stush said. "This isn't nothing. When the time comes to celebrate, old Stush'll celebrate, don't you worry about that none. Right now, I'm going to hit the sack. Boy, I'm going to really sleep that clock around."

"Okay, baby," Jere said. "May you never have a dream in your life any worse than the ones you'll have tonight."

"Thanks," Stush said, surprisingly. "You don't have to worry about me. You're a good guy, Dad, the best. Keep your pecker up now."

He let himself out the glass door, his magnificent body drooping with fatigue, but moving as always with his superb and self-contained assurance. He was yawning again as he went, and he lifted his hand in a weary casual gesture of farewell before he disappeared into the darkness.

thirty-eight

_____

WHEN HELEN arrived at the beach house, Jere was waiting for her in the darkness beside the highway, the wind whipping at the bottom of his raincoat, and at his hair.

She ran across the road to meet him, teetering a little on her tiny sharp heels.

"Darling, how nice of you," she said, raising her face to be kissed. "It's so good to see you. Must we really go down all those slippery steps again? My god, there must be an easier way. Blast a tunnel, don't you think, or couldn't you rig one of those, what do you call them, bos'uns chairs, that they use for ships?"

"I'll attend to it first thing in the morning," he said. "And especially for you, my darling. Oh god, it's good to see you, Helen. You wouldn't believe what a petrifying day I've had. Ghosts, every ghost you could possibly conceive of, all up and gibbering at me."

"Well, knowing you, darling," she said, "I'm sure that you laid every one of them, too, one by one and end for end. Jere! The way you're talking and the way you kissed me just now! I begin to have the strangest feeling."

Jere laughed as he started down the stairs.

"Tell me more about Stush."

"You tell me about Stush," Helen said. "Was he excited even one little bit when he heard this? Where is he?"

"Well, I doubt if there's a single soul in this whole town who would believe this," Jere said, "but Stush has gone to bed. He was tired. He'd been shacking up with some girl somewhere for a couple days. He was tired, so he went to bed."

Helen laughed delightedly.

"That's absolutely wonderful, and so very exactly like him, isn't it?"

She paused on the bottom step and looked down at her feet ruefully.

"Ah, these shoes!" she said. "Next time, I promise, I'll come in whaling boots."

"Don't be silly," Jere said as he gathered her up and stepped out onto the sand. "My pleasure, darling."

"Jere, now I'm almost certain of it," she said. "You're quite different than you were that other night I saw you. You even feel quite differently as you carry me. I think you're absolutely yourself again!"

364)

"First, tell me more about the preview," he said. "So Stush came off."

"Oh, absolutely and definitely came off. This really is a fabulous business, do you know, Jere? All the years now that I, and you too, darling, have seen them come and seen them go. Just the same, each time there's something exciting and incredible about it when you see it happening. It's so strange, there's never a very good rhyme or reason to it either, really. Not that Stush isn't a little fabulous himself. Is he really a conniver, do you think?"

"My god, how should I know?" Jere said. "Don't tell me that you haven't found that out yet?"

"Do you know that I'm really not sure? I know that he's nothing like as simple as he appears to be, I certainly know that. But it seems so coincidental, don't you think? That he should have just walked into this town, without a dime in his pocket and without knowing literally anyone at all, with nothing on earth really except this rather astonishing commodity of his to peddle. And now he seems to have peddled it with such ease and absolute damn facility. Could it all have been coincidence, do you think, or did he really know exactly what he was about?"

"Coincidence is always an unlikely sort of thing," Jere said as he let her down to her feet on the doorstep. "I doubt if we'll ever find out the answer to this, anyway. Maybe it just figured to happen."

"Well, apparently it did," Helen said. "One thing I can tell you though, he is absolutely one of the finest swordsmen this town has ever seen, present company always excepted of course. I'm not just saying that, incidentally, you're still quite a legend yourself, darling, in a lot of bedrooms in this town, as you undoubtedly know."

Jere laughed.

"Helen, don't you really feel a bit horrid about Stush? After all, Caro did have him rather staked out for herself, didn't she?"

"Jere, how very ridiculous," she said as she slipped out of her pale furs. "What is it that they always say? I haven't had anything from Stush that really belonged to her in any way, or that she is ever likely to miss? Well, it happens to be true and she must certainly know it. My god, she couldn't have had any illusions about Stush, now could she?"

Jere shrugged.

"I'll make drinks, darling."

She hunted her cigarette case and lighted one automatically, with her eyes intent upon him all the while, as he rinsed glasses hurriedly behind the bar.

She got up suddenly and came swiftly down the long room.

"I see you've taken the phone off," she said, her voice totally preoccupied. "Very good idea. Poor Harry, he'll be absolutely going in circles."

She slid up onto the desk top, pushing aside the light on its swivel, and crossing her slender beautiful legs.

"What do you really think, darling? I suppose just a good agent next, don't you, while he's still in a position to have his pick of them."

Jere brought the glasses and sat down in the desk chair opposite her.

"Yes, I think so," he said mechanically. "I was going to suggest that first thing tomorrow morning. Of course Stush may have his own ideas about this. He has a good, tough, practical sort of mind himself, you may have noticed."

Their conversation ran out of momentum and they sat silently, the drinks going untasted and untouched on the desk top, and something between them almost visible in the room, a taut, vibrating, pulled string, stretching tighter and tighter.

Jere looked at her for a long time, the shadow of the desk lamp across his face.

"Just who the hell did you really come out here to see tonight, anyway?" he said softly at last.

Her eyes were steadily upon him, her breathing quick and shallow.

"You, of course," she said.

"Well, good to see you, baby."

"My god, good to see you! Good to really see you, my darling. Last time I came you were like a wax figure of yourself. You frightened me. I couldn't get it out of my mind."

"Well, I'm back," he said. "For better or for worse. I just got in tonight. And now I am back, I can't think of anyone I'd rather see than you."

He reached out rather absently, his fingers moving up the smooth curve of her leg and beneath her knee. And the next moment he had pulled her down into his arms, and they were kissing fiercely and for a long time.

After a while, she was saying softly and breathlessly, "Oh, Jere! Oh, darling! So ridiculous! One of us has to be the first one to say this, and I want it to be me, darling. I wanted to say this the last time I came, but you simply weren't here for me to say it to. Jere, listen to me. We made a stupid stupid botch! We quarreled about all the things that didn't matter and paid no attention at all to the things that did. I've known that for a very long time now, my darling. I want you terribly. I can't bear it."

"I know," he said. "I have to have you, too. I was out of my mind, I thought I didn't. But, Jesus, how I do!"

"Ah, Jere, I'm so glad! So glad, darling. Such a stupid stupid business, whatever made us? All these years we've wasted having to find it out. Jere, never again, darling. I won't have it. This time it will be different. You'll see."

And suddenly he swung her away from him, up onto the desk top again. He leaned forward, his hands hard against the wood on either side of her, the light from the lamp shining bright into his grimly intent face.

"Helen, this one simple thing you must believe," he said. "This time it has to be different! I want you to marry me, Helen. Right now. Right tonight."

(367

For an instant she was rigid, without even breathing, and then she laughed, softly and helplessly.

"Oh, darling," she said. "We're not to quarrel. What kind of start for us is this, if we're quarreling again already? Jere, what difference can a marriage ceremony possibly make to you and me? It's such a pointless, unnecessary thing to quarrel over. It's so ridiculous!"

"Ridiculous?" Jere said. "My god, you call it ridiculous. It's still the money, isn't it, Harry's lovely, filthy, goddamn alimony. You never really intend to give that up so long as you live, do you?"

"Jere, darling, listen to me! What difference could a marriage ceremony possibly make to us? We're not twenty years old any more, either of us, to rush off to Las Vegas with stars in our eyes. What possible difference on earth? Since Patty was born I haven't had a uterus left to make a baby in if I should want to. It's so perfectly ridiculous."

"No, stick to the question," he said. "You'll never marry me, Helen, because you never intend to give up that cushy cushy money from Harry. Now why don't you admit it?"

"All right, I don't mind admitting it," she said. "Why shouldn't I admit it? Harry does awfully well and I like having his money very much. He thought this floozy of his was worth paying a great deal for when he wanted the divorce from me so that he could marry her. Now why shouldn't he pay? I like his money. On top of what I have myself, it makes absolutely the difference to me between living exactly as I like to live, or living some other way entirely. Jere, I do like the kind of life I have, I like it very much. I don't see a single real and valid reason on earth to have to change it. You're being absolutely unreasonable."

"You really believe that, don't you?" Jere said. "God in heaven, you really believe that!"

For an instant her eyes were angry.

"All right. Then what would you be willing to give up for

368)

me, Jere?" she said softly. "If you must insist on us hurling our weaknesses at each other's heads. What would you be willing to give up for me, my darling? The girls, for instance? All those lovely, dewy, young girls, a fresh crop of them every year, every year that I grow older? Would you give that up for me?"

"Coming from you, you can't imagine how ridiculous that sounds, either," Jere said.

"Does it really?" Helen said. "You mean because I'm something of an alley cat myself? Yes, my darling, I am an alley cat. I learned to be from experts. Harry first, and then you, Jere. Oh, Jere, you!"

Her eyes were suddenly bright with tears.

"This is something I'll never begin to understand," she said. "My father came out here from New Jersey right at the beginning, I've lived here all my life, all these years, and I still don't really understand. Sex is the commodity, it's what you all deal in. It's the only commodity that half the so-called talent in this town has to offer. And all the hundreds and hundreds more that come out here every year, and aren't able to make it. Men like you and Harry work with it, get it onto film, can it and sell it by the can like pickles or tomatoes. You work with it every day of your lives. And still you never get enough of it. It's the biggest nickelodeon of all! Blond-haired girls and dark-haired girls and red-haired girls, long girls and short girls, and more of them coming every year, year after year. And your women live with it in all the different ways. They live with it like I do, or they manage to pretend that it doesn't even exist. They go to Palm Springs, or they take to alcohol or yoga or psychiatrists. Or they fight it like Lucy used to, Lucy never gave up fighting it like a brush fire, and that's the worst of all. Except Lucy of course really got the whole ironic works, that finally you could sleep with every woman in this town, but not with her for some unearthly reason, no matter how hard you used to try."

Helen stopped and reached behind her for a Kleenex from a box of them on the desk.

"Now, how ever did I get off onto all this?" she said, patting carefully at the make-up around her eyes. "I'm obviously unstrung tonight. Previews always do unnerve me. Darling, I'm sorry, truly. I don't believe in tears and recriminations, particularly this brand of them, as you very well know. But let's just not quarrel any more about it. There really isn't any point in it, is there?"

After a moment Jere said, "No, no point."

He was leaned back in the chair again, his face once more hidden in the shadow from the lamp, and he was very still.

Helen reached for her drink.

"My god, now I'm quite out of the mood," she said. "Isn't that extraordinary? Here I was absolutely aching to get to bed with you again, and now I only want to go home and have an old-fashioned cry into my pillow. I must be unstrung!"

She sipped at her drink.

"But that's only a passing fancy, I'll have you know. You may be damn sure of that! Jere, don't be dour, darling. We've only to make the best of each other, and it isn't really such a very bad best, now is it?"

She waited but he did not speak, and after a moment, she said, "It's astonishing! Do you know, I'm absolutely buzzing with a million ideas already. You're quite a good director, actually, aren't you, darling? There were those two or three pictures you did, years and years ago, and they grossed very well. I'm just thinking that it might be quite a bit more sensible for you to go back to the studio directing, just at this point, what do you think? After all, darling, you did make your big reputation as a writer outside the studios in the late thirties, didn't you, and a great deal of that sort of writing simply doesn't go these days, anyway. I'll start putting out some feelers here and there right away.

"Or, there is something that just occurs to me," she said. "Jere darling, you could always get hold of Stush, you know, right now, very quickly, before anyone at all's had a chance to get to him. I think Stush likes you, I'm sure you could manage it. Then with Stush safely in your pocket just at this point, you could really walk back into the studio fairly effectively, don't you think?"

"Yes, couldn't I?" Jere said.

She looked at him quickly for a moment, and then put down her glass and slid from the desk.

"Darling, I'm going home," she said. "We've managed to spoil a mood for both of us."

He followed her silently back to the divan and picked up her soft blond furs.

"Jere, you're not angry, are you?" she said.

"No," he said. "Believe me. Not in the least bit angry, my darling."

"Good," she said. "I don't want us ever to be stupid enough to be angry with each other ever again. Oh god, no whaling boots!"

"Blast your tunnel anyway," Jere said lightly. "I like it much better this way."

He carried her across the damp sand, with the bright stars overhead, and the powerful churning roar of the sea, and the wind blowing hard against them.

She snuggled against him contentedly, her hair soft against his chin, and the scent of her perfume strong in his nostrils.

"Jere, I'm really rather glad," she said. "I'm glad we did have this sort of quarrel tonight. I don't think it's in any way a bad omen for us, do you, darling? We've simply cleared the atmosphere now, we've laid the last ghosts for both of us forever. I can't tell you how happy I am. The best kind of happy, the peaceful kind. No sleeping pills tonight. We'll both go to sleep tonight knowing that it's all there again for us, that when we meet tomorrow it will be all new and fresh and wonderful and exciting and fun and good and the absolutely most important thing in the world, for all the years of our lives. Oh, Jere!"

He put her down on her feet on the bottom step and then gathered her back into his arms. They kissed lingeringly and tenderly.

They climbed the steps then, hand in hand.

"Oh god, the perilous ascent!" she said. "Darling, this is a fantastic house, how'd you ever find it? What did you ever buy it for, anyway? And what weather you get out here! Can this be a gale, it feels like a hurricane to me."

Jere laughed.

He walked across the highway with her, and held the door while she got into the car.

"Darling, you're very silent," she said. "You're not really angry, are you? Would you rather I stayed tonight? Would you like me to? Suddenly, I've the strangest feeling that I should stay, Jere."

"No, you're quite right not to," he said. "Not tonight. Darling, believe me, I'm not angry at all, not one small bit. You were quite and absolutely right in everything you said, Helen, and I love you with all my heart. I always have. I always will."

"Good," she said. "Now that's what I wanted to hear you say."

They kissed again through the open window.

"Jere, I'm so happy," she said. "I can't tell you. Really I can't. I'm giddy, I tingle, I'm light-headed, I can't seem to get my breath!"

"Promise you'll drive slowly," he said. "The highway's fairly dark for quite a long stretch through here. Take care, won't you? Good night, my darling."

He watched while she made the U-turn, pulling at the wheel of the long and heavy car. He waved and she honked the horn softly twice, and then the two red taillights shot away up the road.

372)

Jere went down the steps and across the sand.

The room within was very warm and still. He did not take off his raincoat. He poked up the fire automatically, and put a stack of records on the player, and mixed himself a drink. He walked again, rather slowly and absently, sipping from his glass.

And all at once he stopped. He went to the player and lifted the arm, turning the knob on the front of it gently. He pulled the screen across the fire. He went to the desk, swiveling the lamp around again, as he sat down. He took sheets of paper from a drawer and hunted for a pen.

He wrote rapidly upon the top sheet, without pausing once to search for words. It was a holographic will, and, as it turned out, since there was no one who cared to contest it, it was duly probated. He had nothing to leave but the beach house, and he left it to Stush, with the hope, he added, that Stush would never need it.

He folded it into an envelope, and marked it, and propped it against the keyboard of his typewriter.

When he was done, he turned off the lamp.

Last of all, he went into the bedroom for the revolver in the drawer beside his bed, and shoved it into his pocket.

He walked out of the house, closing the glass door softly behind him, and went down to the beach.

About the Author

Since the publication of her first book, WHISTLE STOP, in 1941, Maritta Wolff has written three other novels, NIGHT SHIFT published in 1942, ABOUT LYDDY THOMAS in 1947 and BACK OF TOWN in 1952. In this, her fifth book, she progresses to a different background and a more sophisticated, more complicated set of characters. She truly fulfills the predictions made about her at the time of the publication of WHISTLE STOP, when Sinclair Lewis said, "I suspect that . . . we may salute a young author whom everyone must know." Harry Hansen wrote, "Maritta Wolff is a true novelist"; Lewis Gannett, "You have a sense of an author brimming over with the stuff of many novels. Maritta Wolff will not be a one-book author."

She was born on Christmas Day on a Michigan farm at the home of her grandparents, while her father was still in France during World War I. As an undergraduate in the University of Michigan, she won two minor Hopwood awards for short stories. In 1940 she received her bachelor's degree, was elected to Phi Beta Kappa and won the sole major award that year for her novel WHISTLE STOP. She was twenty-one years old at the time.

She lives with her husband and son in Pacific Palisades, California, in a house overlooking the ocean.